# FINDING BEAUTY

KAT RYAN

FINDING BEAUTY

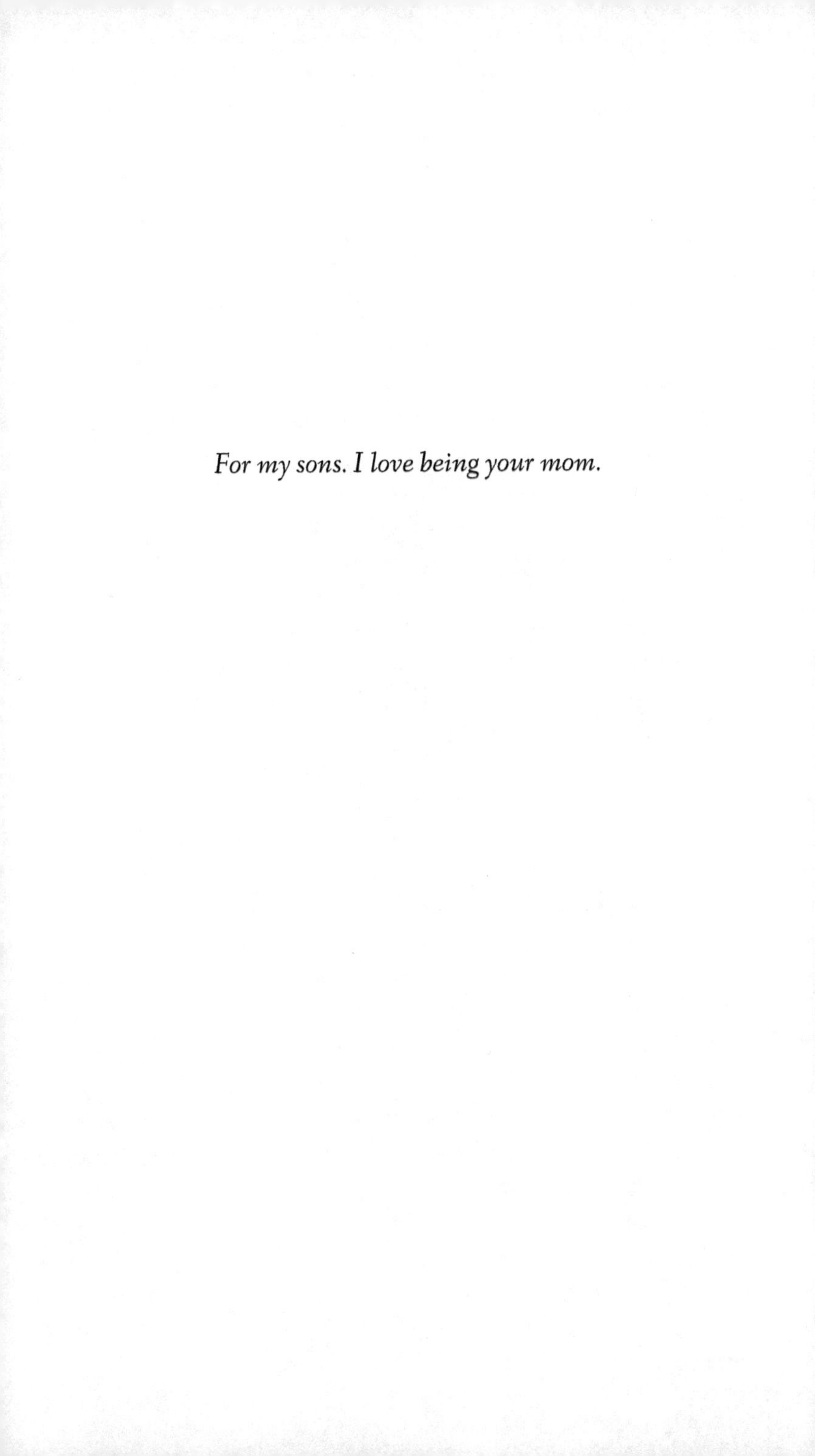

*For my sons. I love being your mom.*

_______________

# SOMETIMES YOU CAN'T GO BACK

**Maggie**

I leaned my head against the window of the truck, fields zooming past.

*Ugh.*

The leather of the bucket seat creaked as I shifted position. Nope. That wasn't any better. Closing my eyes, I worked to clear my mind. Tequila. She was an evil mistress. I was an adult. Why couldn't I stop at one shot? Tonight, if I was being honest, certainly hadn't been one shot. More like several smallish shots followed by a couple of beers. I was a fool. It had been years since I drank that much. What on earth was I thinking?

The noise of a throat being cleared floated across the truck. Glancing over, I looked at Sully's profile. I sighed again and tried to tamp down the feelings of desire that rose up whenever I saw the man. Holy hotness. Dark hair curling over the collar of his flannel. Probably should have gotten it cut a week or so ago, but that was something he wouldn't care about. Brows drawn together as he focused on the road. Just enough scruff at his jawline to hint at a beard, but I'd guess it was only a few days of growth.

I first laid eyes on Cole Sullivan at the age of eight when I headed to my new best friend's house for a playdate after school. Emma Sullivan had been the only girl in my new class that I had any desire to befriend. Her brother Cole, who always went by Sully, was eleven at the time. I could just picture him and his best friend, Maxwell Harp, standing in the kitchen when Emma and I walked in to grab a snack. My little-girl heart waved the white flag; he was it for me. Sully and Max had proceeded to act like eleven-year-old boys do and took turns tormenting us all afternoon as well as for years to come.

That fall day was the beginning of a secret infatuation that would take over my dreams. Sully fantasies lived strictly behind a do-not-cross line for me, never to touch reality. In my heart of hearts, I feared it would never work, so why ruin a great friendship? We were simply too different, too bullheaded, too everything.

Sully's truck bounced through an intersection on the country road, and my stomach flipped, bringing me back to the present. I let out a groan through gritted teeth. Blah. Stomach didn't feel great, but my head was clearing up just a bit. Sully had switched me to water for the past hour at Max and Emma's place. It seemed like we were back in high school once again with the guys trying to watch over Emma and me. Lordy, when they'd come home from college, Emma and I would be lectured nonstop on the evils of overindulging, the danger of being around guys we didn't know well, et cetera, et cetera. I closed my eyes, mortified that I never seemed to be put together or adultlike in front of this man. Damn it.

I saw Sully glance over at me again, lean to the side,

grab something out of his back pocket, and flip it out in my direction. I glanced down at the purple bandanna and met his eyes with some confusion.

Sully gestured toward my face. "You've got a little something..."

I whirled forward, pulled down the visor, and looked in the mirror. Shit, that was just great. Mascara had streaked down my cheeks at some point. Using Sully's handkerchief, I tried to get rid of any traces of the makeup. I thought back on the evening with Max and Emma at Max's farmhouse. They'd only been seeing each other for a week, though she'd been in love with him since kindergarten. I was thrilled for Emma and for Max. Emma and I had been each other's *ride or die* since I moved here in second grade. Neither Max nor I were townies, not having been born in Highland Falls, yet I'd venture to guess that we both considered this small community in Illinois our home. We both had been honorary members of the Sullivan family since we arrived, although if Max and Emma kept on their current path, I had a feeling he'd be part of their family in an official way pretty soon.

That's what tonight had been all about. Emma had been holding back a bit about the seriousness of all that was her and Max. The guys grilled steaks while I chatted with Emma, finding out how everything was really going with her and Mr. Maxwell Harp along with her mindset on all that she was dealing with in general. I was thrilled to hear that things were good, and I mean *really good*. And maybe, just maybe, I might have been a bit overexuberant in my pouring of the shots. You have to understand; I look out for Emma. It's a lifelong mission of sorts. She has the biggest heart of anyone I know, and along the way, that heart has been shattered to pieces.

Tonight Emma showed me that for the first time since forever, she was almost healed. Schoolyard bitches and insecure ex-boyfriends had taken their toll on my girl, and she'd been trying to put herself back together since college. Now, at twenty-nine, I thought she was just about there. I was so damn proud of her tonight that I sang her our song, Christina Aguilera's "Beautiful." It was one I sang to her over the years to remind her to be herself, that she was enough. Tonight I sang it because she now embodied everything the song said. No one was going to bring her down again. As I sang, I might have broken down just a bit. Fine. It was an ugly cry, likely brought on by my liquid nemesis. The type of cry that I didn't want anyone to see but me, maybe Emma. Max and Sully were there, unfortunately, with ringside seats.

Shit.

Our night had brought a lot of feelings up for certain and also important realizations. Emma truly was on her way. She was settled, at a job she loved, and she'd found her guy. That lifelong role of protector wasn't needed anymore. Max had her, and more importantly, Emma had herself.

Maybe it was time I got on with my own plans.

I'd returned to Highland Falls to save up money before moving on, heading for somewhere bigger than our small town. This summer the plan was to travel, checking out this big country that I'd only seen a fraction of before coming back to my job in the middle school in the fall. What if I used this summer to pick my next landing spot? I had quite a bit saved up at this point. I could give my district a year to find my replacement and then move on for good.

My stomach clenched at the thought, but excitement fluttered as well.

Sully cleared his throat again. "Your brain is working so

hard over there smoke might start coming out of your ears soon. Want to talk about it, or are you just planning to sit there in silence?"

I took a breath as my stomach dropped. Was I really going to do this? Was it finally time to move on? I looked out the window into the darkness. A bit of moonlight shone down onto empty fields. Working to pull my shit together, I took a breath and then whispered, "It's fine, Sully. I appreciate the ride."

The quiet rumbling of tires on asphalt settled into the cab of the truck, and I thought he was going to let me go back to my thoughts. And then his strong hand squeezed my thigh, and I yelped. My eyes shot up to meet his.

"Mags, easy. Sweetheart, I just want to know what's going on with you."

*It's Sully, it's Sully, it's Sully. His hand doesn't mean anything. He's just checking on you. You're his little sister's best friend. He's a good guy.* Yep, all the reasonable thoughts in my brain were drowned out by the feel of Sully's hand on my thigh. My nether regions were practically shouting *yippee,* and the devil sitting on my shoulder suggested oh so sweetly that I should move up and let it hit me a bit higher.

Good grief. Down, girl.

I met his whiskey eyes, just like Emma's but smoldering. Damn, I could look into those for some time. "Sully, you're a good guy. Thanks. Nothing was wrong, not really. Promise. The waterworks were thanks to a perfect storm of memories: bitchy teenage girls, being happy for Emma, the evil mistress Tequila, and the beauty that is Christina Aguilera."

Sully looked at me, then back to the road. He nodded his head once. "If you're sure, Mags. You know you can always talk to me, right?"

I leaned back in the seat, looking out the window again

and thinking over the past few weeks or, hell, the past year. Emotions warred just under the surface, threatening to pull me under, telling me that I wasn't as copasetic as I thought I was. "Sull," I whispered.

"Yeah, Mags?"

"Can I stay at your place tonight?" I felt unbelievably lame, but after seeing Emma with Max, I just wanted someone to talk to, someone to be around, even if he was just my friend. The notion of leaving these people I loved in a few weeks for the summer, then moving on in a year? It took my breath away. I felt paralyzed, wanting to move on and wanting to stay where I was comfortable at the same damn time.

Sully's eyes widened. Then he looked back at the road. "Yeah, Mags. Of course you can crash at my place."

I leaned my head against the window once again as the dark Illinois landscape raced past. Emma and I had crashed at Sully's place so many times since coming back to town after college. That wasn't unusual at all. What was unusual would be me staying there on my own. I knew that. I figured Sully knew that. But the idea of being alone tonight? I. Just. Couldn't. Do. It.

Sully squeezed my leg again with the hand that hadn't moved, which was odd, but I wasn't going to read anything into that. A girl could dream and all, but that was a crazy fantasy world. Unfortunately, he let go and then put his hand back on the wheel. "So, do you want to talk about anything in particular?"

"Like what?" I asked as we turned in to the lane to drive up to his farmhouse, the truck rolling up the gravel drive.

"We could debate what concert we should all go to this summer." He pulled to a stop in front of his house. The lights were on in the kitchen off the back door.

"No debate," I said. "Emma and I already talked. Pearl Jam is touring."

Sully groaned. "We've already seen them so many times, Mags. Surely we should add someone else into the rotation."

"Four is not so many times, Cole. And I have zero desire to go to a heavy metal concert, so you and Max might just need to do some kind of guys' weekend for that crap."

Sully chuckled as he turned off the truck. This was a debate we'd had many times over the years. There was no point. We never agreed. Typically, it ended with one group concert, and then Sully and Max might hit another one if the right band was coming anywhere near us. He opened his door and stepped one foot out, then glanced back at me over his shoulder. "You still want to come in, right?"

I looked at him. He was acting a bit odd. "Yeah, if that's still okay. Can I borrow a T-shirt and sweats?"

Sully nodded, and we left the truck, heading in. I admired the way Sully's worn jeans hugged his ass as he moved up the sidewalk toward his house. I mean, it was right in front of me. A girl would have to be blind not to appreciate that beauty. The April night had cooled down significantly, and I hurried after him, ready to get in his house and warm up.

Ranger, Sully's golden retriever, was bouncing up and down as he let out a joyful bark or two. As Sully opened the door, Ranger raced out, jumping up on both of us, laying sloppy kisses where he could.

"Ranger, down," Sully growled. I snorted, like that was going to do anything. Ranger had greeted me the same way for the past five years, and I didn't think that would be changing anytime soon. Sully got his pup around the time he and Jake opened the brewery. Emma and I had been over here often, seeing as we were both big fans of puppies, and damn if Ranger hadn't made me wish over and over that I could get one. Living in a duplex had the advantage of a low monthly rent and the ease of moving at the end of my lease instead of having to find a buyer, but dogs were on the no-go list, so that part was not a win. One day though. Maybe I'd be able to get one whenever I moved? That could be a silver lining at least.

"Grab whatever you want out of my dresser," Sully said with a nod in the direction of his room. "I'm going to take Ranger out and let him run around for a bit. You know where my T-shirts are. Your toothbrush is with Emma's in the same drawer as always. Pick a movie and get comfortable."

I gasped from my spot where I hadn't moved in the doorway. "Are you feeling okay?"

He rolled his eyes at me. "Shut it, Mags."

"Cole Sullivan, you're giving me carte blanche on movie selection? You must really be feeling bad for me right now. I feel the need to milk this for all it's worth."

Sully went over to grab a ball from Ranger's stash of toys, and I couldn't help but check him out as he bent down, looking for something. His flannel stretched across his shoulders, and my hands positively tingled, wanting to run across his back. A thought took me by surprise as I sat with my lust-driven mind: maybe I didn't need to hold back anymore? I mean, I always had because our friendship meant more to me than anything, but the clock was ticking on my time in Highland. If I was planning on traveling this summer and moving in a year, what was the harm? We could have some fun now before the summer hit. Then once I returned in the fall, depending on how we felt, we could pick up where we left off for the school year or just let it go.

I debated for a moment. Was that wise or was that the tequila talking?

Sully stood up with a tennis ball in his hand as Ranger noted it and raced out the open door behind me. Sully came to slide by me to head outside. My heart was pounding, but I worked to call up a smidge of bravery. Sully glanced at me, likely wondering why I hadn't moved. I placed a hand on his forearm as my eyes met his.

"Sully, thanks for letting me stay here tonight."

His whiskey-brown eyes looked down, and then he let go of a grin that reached his eyes. "Mags, you're always welcome here."

He started to move past me through the door, but I squeezed the forearm I was still holding. Whispering, I said, "Seriously, thanks." I went up on tiptoe to place a kiss on his cheek, but he turned to look back at me and stopped as we ended up separated by a breath. Sully's eyes widened. My heart was hammering so hard I was certain he could hear it. Did I move forward? Did I back off?

Fuck.

My hand spasmed on his forearm, and Sully glanced down, then looked back at me. He leaned forward enough to brush his lips over mine before taking a step back. "Think nothing of it, Maggie May." He showed Ranger the ball and threw it into the dark night as the dog tore off the porch toward it. Looking back at me over his shoulder to where I stood frozen, he winked. "Now, go get comfortable before I regret giving you the choice of movie selection."

I blinked before taking a step back and shutting the door, holding back the desire to squeal like a teenage girl. I mean, it wasn't much, but it was a start. Holy shit. Holy shit, holy shit, holy shit.

Now how did I get a whole lot more?

~

**Sully**

Ranger came bounding back from across the yard with the neon-yellow tennis ball in his drooly mouth. Dropping it at my feet, he promptly sat his ass on the ground and waited for me to throw it for him again. After five years of having this guy in my life, I could do our nighttime routine off rote memory alone. And thank God, because tonight my brain was more than a little bit preoccupied.

Hell. Maggie Jameson. My brain, body, and heart were not on the same page here. Maggie was one of my closest friends and had been for years. I mean, before she went to college, she'd firmly been in the little sister category. But in the past few years? Yeah, that had changed. When I looked ahead, I knew what I wanted with her, but I'd waited, wanting to be sure my business was chugging along and moderately successful. I didn't want to move forward unless I was sure we were both ready to build something together.

I was close, so close I could taste it. My brewery partner, Jake Spencer, and I were even getting ready to expand the business into canning. I was at the precipice, ready to begin having a life again after the insane hours I'd worked as we got a small business off the ground over the better part of the past decade.

Ranger pulled me out of my thoughts as he dropped the ball again. I threw it, watching his legs eat up the distance. My lips still tingled from the contact with Maggie's. I thought I might have to convince her to give us a try, but maybe I was wrong? That was a welcome miscalculation on my part. Hoped like hell I was reading her right.

I whistled for Ranger and watched him tear up the yard in my direction from the drive. He passed my truck, a black

1972 Chevrolet C10. It had been my grandpa's. Hell, so had my house. Grandpa had been gone a while now. So had grandma. After they passed, my parents had let me buy the farm from them, and Grandpa's truck came with it. I had damn good memories of driving with Grandpa to town, windows down, hand riding the waves in the air as he drove at the pace of a turtle. He'd look down the rows of the crops coming up, nodding with pride at the land he farmed. I'd had someone in town look the truck over when I got my hands on it, doing what needed to be updated. It was nothing fancy, but it would get me around.

The farmhouse was a different story. My grandparents had lived here for most of their married life. The single best thing about it was the porch that wrapped around the entire place. It wasn't huge, which was perfect for me. Jake and I had done a few updates after I moved in, but honestly, I was outside as much as I could be anyway. Taking the ball from Ranger, I jogged up the steps to the kitchen door, wondering how to play things with Maggie.

Ranger and I got inside, and I turned to close the door, then locked it. My pup stood by his water bowl, looking from it to me, then back to it. "Yeah, yeah, I get your point." I grabbed it to fill it up, listening for Maggie as I did so. There was a low hum of the TV coming from the living room. Since it was an older house, there wasn't much of an open concept to speak of. The kitchen led to the dining room, and the dining room then opened in another direction to the living room. Thinking of the drinks Maggie had, I filled up a glass of water before heading off to find her. Ranger slurped up his water, making a hell of a mess. I glanced around the kitchen, grateful Jake had talked me into spending the cash to update it when I moved in. I tended to be more conservative with money, but the changes we'd made in this place had been well worth it. The white cabinets and dark quartz countertops of the kitchen changed this entire part of the house, making it feel like something of my own rather than a place I was just borrowing. I loved the memories this place and my truck held but also the knowledge that I was making memories of my own. I hoped the signals Maggie was giving me meant we'd be starting something new as well.

I stepped into the living room, and my eyes caught on the TV hanging on the far wall. I held back a laugh. Maggie had picked *The Big Lebowski*. Max and I loved this movie. I could remember when we first had Maggie and Emma watch it. I think they were freshman in college. Damn, it had to be at least a decade old by then. They thought it was absolutely ridiculous—which, to be fair, it was. Then we watched it again a year or so later, and they started to like it a bit more. Max and I could quote it line by line, and much to their dismay, we often did.

Looking down at my leather sectional, I noted that Maggie had not only made herself at home but was out cold. She'd pulled her long hair back into a ponytail, and the strawberry blonde waves were spread out over the toss pillows she and Emma had insisted I needed when I moved in. I noted that she also had pulled out one of the blankets they bought for me. I put the water glass down on the coffee table so she'd see it when she woke up.

My bedroom was just off the living room. I headed in there to find a T-shirt and lounge pants. Once I did, I glanced at my bed. There was no reason to sleep elsewhere, but then I thought of Maggie in the car, how she didn't want to be alone tonight. Our moment at the door played back in my mind. Ranger sat in front of me, his tail slowly sweeping my floor as if he was waiting for me to figure my shit out.

"Fuck it." I grabbed a pillow off my bed, then headed back into the living room. Carefully, I put the pillow near Maggie's head and slid over her to lie between her stretched out body and the back of the couch. It was a tight squeeze, but also exactly where I wanted to be. Maggie immediately rolled into me, her head tucking into my neck and resting on my arm. I let out a breath, willing my body to calm down. Did I want more, hell yes? But she needed sleep. It would be better to begin that conversation tomorrow anyway.

I glanced up at the TV. The Dude and Lebowski were discussing the issue of his rug. I smiled as Maggie's hand slipped around my waist as she moved closer to me. Leaning down, I brushed a kiss over her forehead. Yeah, our conversation could wait. We were swimming in time.

~

## *Maggie*

The bass drum in my head woke me up, reminding me that all bad choices have consequences. Damn it all. Before I could even crack my eyes open, my heart began to race. Unless I was mistaken, there was an arm around my waist. And my pillow was certainly not my pillow but felt more like a biceps. Keeping my eyes closed, I slowly revisited the night before. I had flashes of the ride home and a conversation with Sully. Heat flooded my cheeks when I recalled asking him if I could spend the night. Loneliness welled up once again as I thought of Max and Emma, of leaving Highland. I snuggled closer to the heat at my back even while cursing myself for needing it.

Scanning my memories, I recalled starting the movie while Sully took Ranger out, but that was it. My heart skipped a beat as I remembered my decision to get my groove on and not only plan my move for next year but actually hit on Sully. Jesus. That had been a bit impulsive. I guess it wasn't shocking that I'd fallen asleep. It had been a long week, capped off by more than a few beverages. But that didn't explain the arm or man at my back. No fucking way. Was I really squeezed onto this couch with a sleeping Cole Sullivan? I slowly opened my eyes, then tipped my head back to look up. The morning light from the living room windows lit a pair of gorgeous brown eyes looking back down at me with more than a bit of amusement. Well, damn. That's that.

"Morning," he whispered.

I brushed my hair back from my face as I stared up at him. Shit, this was going to be a hard one to explain to Emma. "Um, morning, Sully. Sorry. I guess I missed the movie?"

He smiled down at me. "Yeah, and that was a kick-ass choice too, Mags. I watched it, then just crashed out here with you. Didn't seem like you were too keen to be alone."

Embarrassment at being needy fought with the joy of lying against Cole Sullivan. Joy won. "That's nice," I whispered, "but did you need to sleep on the same part of the couch as me?"

"Well, it wasn't all about being nice. Part of me was being greedy..." He trailed off, a corner of his mouth rising up.

Now I was confused, and I rolled over to face him, careful not to off onto the floor. "Why? What are you being greedy about?"

Sully looked at me, his eyes seeming to darken as one of his fingers lightly traced my lips before gently sliding under my chin, tipping it up toward him. "This." He pressed his lips down on mine, his open and his tongue gently probing my lips until I parted them. Our tongues met while my brain short-circuited.

Seriously, I didn't know a kiss could feel this good, so I leaned into it and took whatever I could get from him. If I was dreaming, I was going to be seriously pissed. My entire body felt like it was on fire. Tingles raced down from my head to my happiness wonderland where my legs met. Could I just throw all my clothes off and climb on top of him? Too much? Probably. *Easy, Maggie.*

Sully pulled back as I groaned over losing him. We panted, staring at each other. "Sorry, Maggie. That got hot fast. I didn't mean we have to...," he started.

Good Lord, stupid man. Like hell this was stopping now. I grabbed his head and pulled it to mine, kissing him for all I was worth. While I was drowning in all that was wonderful with Sully's mouth, I let my hands run up his abs to his chest over his T-shirt. A rumble came from his chest that told me he was fully on board with these moves. Remembering the view last night in those worn jeans, I slowly ran my hands back down and around to squeeze his ass. Well, that felt better than imagined. Sully's hips thrust up to meet me, his erection leaving no doubt how he was feeling. I let one hand leave his fabulous ass and slide over his length, which was obvious in his sweatpants. That should answer any questions he might have about where I wanted to take this. Sully moved to kiss my neck, stopping at the crook and kissing his way across my collarbone.

"Mags, need to make sure. You good with this?" He whispered against my skin.

"Hell yes. If anything, we're wearing far too many clothes."

Sully pulled back to look at me, nodded, and then it was almost a race to see who could be naked first as we both hopped up and started shedding clothes. Modesty? Hell, it must have flown out the window. Or maybe my sleep-addled brain just hadn't caught up. Who knows? My God, I'd never acted like a hormone-crazed teenager, even when I was a teenager, but that was how I felt now.

"Here or the bed?" Sully asked, glancing to his room, then back at the couch.

I looked at his door. That was several steps we'd have to take. Looking back at Sully, our mouths met before I could answer him. His hands slid around my naked body, stopping right under my butt. I got with the program and jumped up, wrapping my legs around his waist as he moved us to his room, then came to a stop by the side of the bed.

Sully lowered me so that my feet were on the ground. I got my first look at all of him as I sat back on his bed. He placed a hand on either side of my hips and kissed my nose as he pushed gently. I slid back and lowered down onto the bed with him following. Holy shit. God must be really happy with me, because he was a thing of beauty. I sent up a quick prayer of thanks.

Coming to a stop with my head near the headboard, I looked down the length of his body, then back to his face. "Can I get my cell phone and just snap a few photos of you? Because I can't dream up anything this good, and I don't want to forget it," I said, grinning up at him.

This was happening. This was finally happening. I thought for a minute about how this could change things and decided that I could have that conversation with myself at another time.

"No phones, babe. But, just to say, you are a fucking vision yourself." He pressed a kiss to my lips. "So"—another kiss to my right breast—"much"—and a kiss to my left breast —"beauty." Sully lowered his body to my side as his mouth came back to hit mine. His hand wandered south, parting me as he slid a finger in. I gasped into his breath, our eyes locking as warmth and tightness started spiraling through me, taking me higher and higher. In what felt like seconds, I was panting and ready to lose my mind. I arched into him. Ahh.

"Ready," I breathed out, more than ready for him to get moving here.

Sully chuckled. "Hell no, Mags. We've been building to this for a while. I have lots of fantasies built up about you."

"Fantasies?" I panted.

Sully lowered his lips to my breast, tugging a nipple into his mouth. "Oh yeah." Worshipping one breast, he moved across the swell to the other one. His tongue traced my nipple as he watched me, his fingers still sliding in and out as well. I couldn't focus. Sensations washed over me, and I was overcome with feelings. I watched his gaze sharpen as his hands picked up speed and he leaned down to tug on a nipple with his mouth. That did it.

"Sully," I breathed out as my entire body arched up and my climax hit faster than any had before.

Sully gentled his kisses, and his fingers slid out after my climax. His hands traced over my hips, then around to my butt, back to my stomach, and over my breasts, dancing constantly over my skin. I felt like I was lit up from within. Finally I opened my eyes to see his gaze positively devouring me. Catching me watching him, he leaned in to press a kiss to my mouth.

"That was fucking hot," he growled.

I raised a brow. "Yeah?"

His nose nudged under my jawline as his tongue trailed down my neck. "You get a flush from your neck over your breasts when you orgasm." He sucked my neck a little, then pulled back to meet my eyes. "Hot."

"So we're done here?" I asked, biting back a grin.

His eyes darkened. "I've waited years, Maggie. We're nowhere close to done." He slid his fingers back to my core, circling my sensitive clit and sliding in. His mouth landed on my neck again. "So damn sexy, babe."

My eyes closed as I dropped my head to his as he began to slowly build something inside me once again, faster than I ever thought possible after I already climaxed. Within seconds I was panting and ready to lose my mind once again. The man was a magician.

"Sully, come on," I begged, working to get my breath. "Please."

"Protection?" he growled, pulling away from me.

"I'm on the pill," I whispered, trying like hell to pull him back to me.

"Condoms too, drawer." His head jerked toward the side table. I rolled over to check it out. Pulling open a drawer, I saw the box inside. I pushed away the thought of how often he might need one here with someone else and grabbed one off the strip before handing him the foil packet. He tore it open with his teeth, then rolled it on. Positioning himself between my legs, our eyes locked. He dipped his head, kissing the swells of my breasts, then coming back up to meet my mouth. "It's been a while, Mags, I'm not going to last long."

"We don't have to be one and done, right?" I asked, thinking I might lose my mind if we didn't get moving here.

"I like the way you think, Maggie Jameson," Sully whispered.

"Well, thanks, Cole Sullivan. Now let's stop screwing around and make this happen," I panted.

He grabbed a pillow, which he slid under my ass, then gently lined up and gave me everything I'd been wanting for far too many years.

Holy hell. Stars. I mean, I was no virgin, but sweet Jesus. That's not to say I've had a parade of guys through my bedroom, but there have been a few over the years. And I enjoyed sex before, I really did. But this? Damn. We'd barely started before Sully switched angles and I gasped. I'd heard stories of that fabled location called a G-spot, but I'm pretty sure no one ever found mine before. I could only assume that was what was happening, but before I knew it, I came completely apart. I was vaguely aware of Sully following me over that cliff as he slowed down and then collapsed on top of me as we both panted. I took a breath, then another, trying to tamp down the swell of emotion that threatened to spill out.

**Sully**

I took a deep breath and worked to get my racing heart under control. How had the very thing I dreamed about for so long become my reality? Mind-blowing. I'd always guessed Maggie and I would be amazing together. Good to see I wasn't wrong there. Shifting above Maggie, I worked to turn the two of us to our side while remaining connected. It was ridiculous, probably, but I didn't want to lose her yet. Maggie's eyes were closed, and I couldn't read her expression. I pressed a light kiss to one eye, then the other. Slowly, her eyes opened and her warm gaze met mine.

"You good?" I whispered.

"Beyond good," she whispered back. "Not sure if I can move."

I laughed. "We good?" I asked, my heart threatening to skip a beat. Hard to explain how much her answer here meant to me.

Maggie gave me a wide smile. "Well, not sure if I should speak for both of us, but I'm very good with where we are right now." She leaned over to press an openmouthed kiss to my chest, then peered up at me. "As a matter of fact, if you don't have any plans for this morning, I'm fine spending some more time proving that to you, Cole Sullivan."

I chuckled. "Cole, is it?"

She wrinkled her nose. "I feel like this might be a Cole, not Sully, kind of moment."

I took a second to let out a small cheer inside. This boded good things, right? But it was a conversation we needed to continue once I ditched the condom. I started to pull out though I felt like I could stay joined to her forever.

"Stay," she whispered.

"Let me get rid of this condom, then I'll be right back." I moved, kissing her neck as I went. Pulling out completely, my gut clenched when I glanced down. "Shit, Mags..." I froze, unsure what to do.

Her eyes shot to mine. "What?"

I looked down at all that was Maggie, and everything I wanted for my future, lying before me on my bed. "God-damn condom broke," I growled. Anxiety spiraling, my mind played back the past half hour as I worked to bite back the panic. Meeting her wide eyes again, I remembered her saying she was on the pill. "Okay. It's okay, Mags. Right? I swear I'm clean. You've got nothing to worry about." I leaned down and kissed her nose, then headed toward the bathroom.

After closing the door to the bathroom, I leaned against it and worked to calm my racing heart. I hoped Maggie couldn't tell how freaked I was. I didn't want her to think I was regretting anything. I just needed to get control of this feeling of impending doom. It was an overreaction, sure. Damn, after having sex for over fifteen years, I guess it wasn't shocking that a condom would break at some point. But I couldn't explain the terror that shot through me when I looked down and realized it had. But we were fine here.

Damn if the broken condom hadn't had the unfortunate consequence of Dad's voice popping in my head. Talk about inopportune time to think of your father. I fought a grin at that, thinking of how often he lectured Max and me about safe sex over the years, the importance of double protection, always. At least until you were in a committed relationship and were okay with having a kid.

Kids. My heart lurched a little, thinking about that concept as I cleaned up, disposing of the POS condom before washing my hands. We were covered there, thankfully, since Maggie was on birth control. But what if we hadn't been? I wasn't ready to be a dad, not yet. I needed more money in the bank, more equity built up in our brewery, to pay off more of this house. That's what this new canning venture was all about. Getting me set up so that I could be a solid provider for a family one day. Because hell yeah, I wanted that. I wanted it all. But after watching my parents struggle through some lean years farming, I knew the financial shape I needed to be in before that happened.

Shaking my head, I looked up in the mirror as I dried my hands. I looked like I'd seen a ghost. *Get your shit together, Sullivan,* I told myself. I needed to take care of this and get out to Maggie. Fuck, I hope she believed me that she had nothing to worry about in terms of STDs. Now I just needed to thank God for birth control pills and get us back on track with our morning.

Taking a deep breath, I opened the door to walk back into the bedroom. My gaze first hit the bed, which was empty. What the fuck. Turning my head, I saw Maggie struggling into her clothes by my dresser.

"Maggie?"

A tearful face turned toward me as my heart clenched. She looked tortured. What in the world?

"I need to go home," she said in a broken voice.

I blinked, shaking my head to try to make sense of my current reality. "What? Maggie, talk to me."

She took a deep breath, closed her eyes, and then another one. She turned her head to look out the windows, away from me. She whispered, "I'm sorry, Sully. We can talk later. I really need to go home right now."

My gut clenched. I thought we'd been on the same page. Had I somehow pressured her? Had she not wanted this? Fuck. Nausea welled up as I croaked, moving to place myself in front of her. "Maggie, was this—I mean, I though you wanted this too. Did I pressure you?" I closed my eyes, not even sure I could look at her as she answered.

Her hand came up to tilt my chin down, and I looked at her. Tears were now streaming from her eyes, but her gaze was soft. She leaned up and kissed my nose. "Cole, you could never pressure anyone. I'm a mess, and I'm sorry. This wasn't a good idea, but not because of you, because of me. And I really need to get home right now." With that, she slid away from me and walked to the bathroom, shutting the door behind her.

I moved to my bed and sat down on the edge. I'd wait right here so I could see her the moment she came out. Damn if I didn't feel like I had just had my heart torn out. I could still smell the flower scent of her perfume in the air of the room. The bed was still a mess from sleep and sex. An hour ago my life had seemed like it was pretty perfect. How did everything go from perfection to disaster in the matter of a few minutes?

~

## *Maggie*

I stood on the other side of the bathroom door from Cole, panic threatening to take me down in a heartbeat. A broken condom. Didn't see that one coming. Normally, that wouldn't be the end of the world. God knows I was clean. I never had sex without a condom, and got checked out every year at my annual just in case. And it wasn't like I'd been with that many guys anyway. And knowing the Sullivans for all these years, I'd had plenty of *safe sex* talks from their mom, Anna, to Emma and me during our teen years. I had no idea if my dad knew that Anna had taken me on for those conversations or if he'd asked her to, but from middle school on, Anna had preached to us about sex to the point that Emma and I joked she'd written her own handbook. She told us often that consent was everything, and it went both ways. That sex was amazing as long as it was with someone you felt comfortable and confident with. And double protection was the rule, always—or until we were old and gray. Bless.

And now look where I was. Even when Sully tried, we failed. Because what he didn't know, and I didn't remember until just a few minutes ago, is that we went from thinking we had double protection to none. Fuck. Fuck, fuck, fuck. When he said those fateful words, *the condom broke,* my brain flashed back to my stomach flu just a few days ago when everything came up, violently, for a bit over twenty-four hours, including, I'd assume, two days' worth of pills. At the time, I'd thought nothing of it. But now...

I stepped to the sink and looked at myself in the mirror. It was fine, right? What the hell would the chances be of me being pregnant after one time? One time when we thought we'd done everything right. One time when I'd been stupid enough to think that I could finally have the guy of my dreams, even if it was only for a little while.

I shook my head at the naive girl looking back at me in the mirror. *Should have known, Maggie. Should have known more than to reach for the stars.* Disgusted with myself, I tugged the ponytail holder out, then smoothed back my hair and pulled it up once more. Walk out, tell Sully we needed to leave, get in his truck, head home. Then I could have the breakdown I deserved in peace. I just needed to get home. I could do this. I could.

Deep breaths, I opened the door and took one look at Cole sitting on the bed, facing the bathroom. His legs were spread, elbows on his knees, hands clasped together, head hanging down. Hearing the door, he lifted his head to look at me, a tortured expression on his face. I closed my eyes and let my head drop. I couldn't say anything to him right now. I fucked this all up. If I hadn't tried to reach for just a bit more, we'd still be friends, arguing about the best movie or band as he took me home this morning.

"Hey, hey," I heard him say, feeling him coming closer to me. "It's okay, Maggie. I swear it is." He pulled me into a hug, and I let him because I didn't know if I could handle much more this morning.

I stood there, still, for a moment before speaking into his chest. "Cole, please take me home." I felt his body stiffen, and I knew we'd never be the same.

**Sully**

The truck bumped over the last intersection in the country before we hit the city limits of Highland Falls as I headed on autopilot to Maggie's duplex. She hadn't spoken for the entire ten-minute ride into town. At one point I'd even put on some Pantera, knowing that typically she'd give me shit for listening to what she called screaming metal, but there'd been no reaction.

Fuck.

I hated leaving her like this. But maybe she just needed some breathing room. I knew Maggie. She wasn't afraid of anything. She worked things through in her own time, processed her options, and moved on. She hated being pressured into conversations or making choices before she needed to. I just had to trust our friendship, trust our foundation, and let her process our morning.

I just couldn't figure out why she was so freaked. As I drove down the streets bringing us closer and closer to her place, I went over the morning again. She said she knew we'd been safe. She was on the pill. She'd wanted the same thing, so what happened? Unless maybe she'd decided she didn't want more with me? But we'd lit the bed on fire. That wasn't it, right?

I braked to a stop in her driveway and turned off the truck. Reaching for the door handle, As Maggie reached for the door handle, her voice cut through the silence. "Sully, you don't need to walk me up."

I looked over at her. "What? Of course I do."

Her tearful face looked determined. Inwardly, I groaned. I knew that determination well, and it meant I was truly fucked right now. Maggie would be listening to Maggie and no one else.

She took a deep breath. "Sully, thanks for looking out for me last night. And this morning was, well, amazing. But I think we're better off as friends. I appreciate the ride home." She turned to open her door.

"Are you out of your damn mind?" I growled. Her face registered her shock as she turned back toward me. Not my finest moment, but no. We weren't doing this.

"Maggie, I have no idea what's going through your brain right now because, I will note, you won't tell me. But we didn't just meet. I know you. I've known you since you were eight years old. I know you won't hear a damn thing I say right now, but hear this. I won't stop you from leaving me out here even though it's the last thing I want. I know you need to go think through whatever is spinning in that gorgeous brain of yours. But after a little bit of time, we're talking this through because before that damn piece of plastic decided to fuck with our morning, we were right where I've wanted us to be *for years*, and I'll be damned if I'm letting that go for much longer, babe." Well, I guess I was just laying it all out there this morning. I looked over her face as her eyes narrowed.

"Cole Sullivan," she practically growled. "I am no longer that eight-year-old girl who did whatever you said. If I say we're going to go back to being friends, then that's what happening, *babe*. So you're just going to have to deal with it." And with that, she slid out of the truck and slammed the door. I watched her vibrating with energy as she marched up the walk to her back door. Unlocking the door, she went in without a backward glance, and I could hear the door slam from there in the truck. Groaning, I let my head drop to the steering wheel. Why had I thought anything with Maggie would be simple? I thought ahead to the bike trip Jake and I were taking in three weeks to check out some Midwest breweries and their canning operations. Maybe it would be better for all of us if I moved it up to give her a little space.

What a fucking mess.

## 2

## WHEN THE SHIT HITS THE FAN

***Five weeks later***

**Maggie**

My head throbbed as I leaned against the cool tile of the staff bathroom wall. Jesus take the wheel. I glanced up, ensuring I'd locked the door and wouldn't be interrupted. Privacy was required for this potential meltdown.

It had been a long day—middle school, during the last weeks of May, and only five days left of the school year all came together for a special brand of crazy. *Deep breaths*, I told myself. My heart raced as I looked in the mirror. The relaxation breathing that Emma and I had practiced in yoga came back.

*Breathe in, two, three, four; out, two, three, four.*

Closing my eyes, I tried to gather some courage. I had this. I was fine. In just a week I would have a summer stretching before me and my biggest concern would be where I wanted to travel first. My lease expired on my duplex in the fall, but I had arranged for a sublet starting at the beginning of summer and couldn't get in my new place until August first. My road trip across the country was keeping me going right now. Stopping when I wanted to rest, read, relax, or experience someplace new. Breathing deep, I daydreamed of mountains and/or oceans. I had this. I just needed to get the hell out of Highland Falls.

Opening my eyes, I glanced down at the pregnancy test on the edge of the sink. Blinking once, I tried to focus my eyes and blinked again.

Holy fucking shit.

Quickly, I grabbed the box and looked at the back once again, telling myself that two lines surely meant you were clear, not pregnant. Right? I mean, it was once. Who gets pregnant due to one accident?

*Get a grip, Maggie*, I told myself. Apparently, you can get pregnant the one time you had unprotected sex. This was, after all, the textbook definition of what happens when you have an accident. They might as well as plaster my face into the Sex Ed PowerPoints about safe sex. That would be a lesson for the kids, their former middle school teacher knocked up.

My heart started pounding, and I could feel the panic building. I began feeling clammy, and a glance in the mirror showed my skin was a bit paler than was typical. Terrific. I didn't need my first act as a cognizant mother to be passing out and whacking my head on the ground.

Not giving the first shit about the fact that I was in the staff bathroom, I slid to the floor, putting my head between my knees, and worked on breathing some more. Saying a quick word of thanks for our amazing janitor, Larry, the pride he took in our school, and floors that were blessedly clean, I worked on breathing in through my nose, out through my mouth. *Get yourself together, Jameson.*

One of my strengths was being able to quickly assess a situation and develop a plan of action. This came in tremendously handy as a teacher to adolescents who were going through puberty. It was also a great trait to have while sitting on the floor of a bathroom, pregnant and not married. Hell, not married didn't even touch it. Not in a relationship would be more accurate. Jesus, Mary, and Joseph.

*Well, the church did warn against premarital sex,* the stupid voice in my head sang.

"Fuck off," I muttered. Not the time.

The broken condom had been a wake-up call, fate splashing a bucket of water on my simple fantasies of a life that was not meant for me. I should have known better, of course. A relationship with Sully was a dream, and I'd learned long ago that those dreams were not for people like me.

Sully and I couldn't be together. My plan had always been to come back to Highland Falls, teach for several years, and save money so I could leave. Move on to a city like Chicago or New York. Somewhere big where everyone didn't know my whole story. Where they didn't pity the girl whose mom had passed away far too young. The girl with a dad who switched jobs like most people changed coats. Highland Falls meant Emma and the Sullivans, but it also meant small towns where everyone knew who you were, for better or for worse. Anything with Sully would keep me in this cage, I was ready to move on, and already decided to start my trip in a few weeks.

Since that moment with Sully, things were tense, to say the least. We didn't see each other daily, of course, but with Max and Emma getting together and with my best friend being his sister, with our friendship over the years, we were thrown together many times over the course of a week. Since our moment five weeks ago, he'd texted, called, and I'd been a bitch and ignored it all. Could. Not. Go. There.

I'd been so panicked that we'd end up exactly where I currently was I'd chosen to freeze him out. Surely if I became the world's biggest bitch, that would mean we wouldn't have any unintended consequences from failed contraception. Well, beyond a friendship I treasured being destroyed. I lightly banged my head back against the tile. Ignoring him didn't change this. What in the hell was I going to do?

Max and Emma both noticed the tension, but I managed to avoid Sully for the most part. Luckily, the past two weeks had been blessedly drama-free. He'd gone on a road trip on his bike with Jake, co-owner of The Homestead. They'd left the brewery in the hands of their new manager and headed off to visit other small breweries around the Midwest. Emma kept me informed of their whereabouts, which meant that I knew their stop last night in Festus, Missouri, was their last. They should be heading home in the next day or so. I didn't know if Emma had guessed what had happened or why she'd decided to share about his travels, but I soaked up anything she told me like a woman in the desert dying of thirst.

Sudden light knocks on the bathroom door brought me back to reality. Shaking my head, I called that I was coming and gathered my stuff. I had my giant leather purse today, which was just as well. I stuffed the test as well as the trash from it inside the box it came from and buried it at the bottom of my purse. No way was I leaving that for anyone to find in here.

Taking a deep breath, I opened the door. My eyes looked down into the worried eyes of Bridget Masters, my principal and dear friend. Bridget had been in our building as long as I had but was younger than most administrators I knew. She and her wife, Sam, had two amazing kids—Aggie and Gus. Between her experience as a parent and an educator, our staff respected her immensely, and she treated us all like family. She'd been a godsend over the years.

"Maggie, what gives? You've been in here for a while," she whispered as she tugged me out and guided me down the small hall of the main office to her office.

I glanced around and realized the office was empty. Everyone had already taken off for the weekend. Four in the afternoon on a Friday meant this place closely resembled a ghost town. Any other day of the work week would find teachers here for hours after the bell, getting caught up on grading, socializing with colleagues, giving students some extra time. Fridays, forget about it. The parking lot was filled with taillights as my colleagues got their weekend started as soon as the kids left the building.

Even with the building being deserted, Bridget shut the door for privacy as I moved to my favorite spot, her couch. Her office was decent-sized. She had a small spot for her desk area, but the majority was taken up with a couch, armchair, and some large bean bags.

Sinking into the corner of the couch, I let my purse hit the floor and tucked a leg under my body as I turned to face Bridget getting into the same position in the other corner. If I were in a better mood, I'd laugh. She was positively swallowed up by this furniture. While I knew she was somewhere in her late thirties, she could easily pass for a decade younger. Her hair was a rich red that spilled over her shoulders, making my strawberry blonde look more blond than strawberry. I didn't consider myself tall, but at five foot eight I had easily seven inches on Bridget. That being said, this diminutive person in front of me could run this school like no one I'd ever seen. Kids towered over her, but they loved her completely, and she gave that right back. Whatever you were doing, you wanted Ms. Masters on your side. And right now I needed her.

Looking down at my hands, I debated where to begin. My mind raced. Could I be fired for being an unwed mother? Surely not anymore. Yet this town, this county, was pretty conservative. What the hell would I tell the kids? Questions raced through my mind as I felt my heart rate kick into gear.

Bridget cleared her throat, and I looked up. "While I am a big believer in wait time, it's Friday afternoon. Maybe I can help you along?" She looked at me with a kind smile, the kind that reached your eyes. "How can I help?"

Boom. Waterworks. Tears slid out, flowing over my cheeks with no possibility of holding them back. I gulped, looked down at my bag, and reached in, pulling out the positive test, and held it up as I looked at Bridget with watery eyes.

Her eyes grew wide as she glanced from the test in my hand to my still-flat stomach, back to my eyes. "Shit," she whispered.

"Yep, that about covers it," I mumbled.

Then she did what makes her a great administrator. She closed her eyes, took a breath, and switched into problem-solving mode. "Well, okay, let's start with the most obvious question first. Do you want to keep it?"

I physically felt like I had a punch to the gut. "Yes!" I gasped.

Bridget's hands immediately came up in defense. "I'm sorry. I know you're Catholic. I meant did you want to consider adoption..." Her voice trailed off.

*Deep breaths, Maggie,* I told myself. "I'm sorry. I'm a bit of a hot mess right now. I mean, yes, I'm Catholic, but our church is also against premarital sex, so I'm not exactly a poster child for my religion right now. And while I also believe in a woman's right to choose, that's not a choice for me. No judgment on others though." Bridget nodded at me, so I continued. "As for adoption, I think that is a wonderful gift to give a couple who cannot conceive. If I was younger, maybe that would be something to explore. As it is, though..." I closed my eyes and put my hand on my stomach.

"It's just not the right choice for you." She finished for me softly.

I looked up and nodded. "It's crazy, but I want this baby. I don't know how to explain it. I had an inkling I might be pregnant for the past two weeks or so. My periods can be really light, so I was just hoping I had missed it. But one test telling me I am, and boom, everything is different. I'm on the pill, but I had the stomach flu a while back. Shit..."

Bridget inclined her head, smiling at me. "No need to try to explain everything to me. I get it, including the sudden attachment that can come with this. Sam carried Gus, I carried Aggie. Everything changes in an instant and will never be the same again. As unexpected as I'm guessing this is for you, it can also be one of the best things that has ever happened, bar none."

Bridget got up and brought me some Kleenex, then crossed to a mini-fridge she had in the corner and pulled two water bottles out, handed me one, and sat back down. "So, let's address the elephant in the room. Unless you had an immaculate conception, there's something you're holding back. Hmm?"

I guzzled some of the water, trying to decide how to begin. "Shit, Bridget, this is hard to say." I took a breath, gathering courage. "There's a guy I've had a thing for pretty much forever. We obviously got together one night, but I panicked and nothing happened after. Honestly, I've been avoiding him ever since."

Her brows were drawn together, and I felt like you could almost see her mind working. "Why the hell would you panic? Was it bad? And that's not like you to avoid a situation. You usually face everything head-on. It's one of the traits I love about you. You're fearless."

Her words made me warm and cold at the same time. "I know. That's why it shook me so. I don't run from a challenge. But being with him, just for that one time, I began to dream big and fast. Those dreams flew in the face of the plans I'd already decided for myself. Then he said the condom broke, and all self-doubt bubbled up, and that bitch of a voice in my head came in telling me *of course* nothing could work with him, so I ran." God, even saying it pissed me off.

Bridget smiled at me. "Well, I guess you're going to have to get over that now so you can tell him." Her eyes widened in alarm as she studied my face. "Maggie, you *have* to tell him."

I pulled up my knees to rest my head on. "I know, I know. But I'm going to need a few days to get there. I just need to get used to this before I share it with him." I took another breath, let it out, then whispered, "I just don't want him to be pissed or feel like I trapped him."

"Good grief. Of course you didn't trap him. It isn't your fault the condom broke. Hell, it isn't his fault either, for that matter." Bridget looked a bit irritated. "But Maggie, this is his baby too. He has a right to decide how involved he wants to be, go to appointments with you if he wants, etc. You can't cut him out of that. You don't have to be involved in a romantic relationship if you don't want to be, but you're now part of a relationship with this baby from this point forward. He needs to have that too if he wants it."

My heart squeezed. I'm not sure what would be worse, if I gave Sully the chance to be in a relationship with me and he rejected me, or if I told him about the baby and he rejected both of us. It was stupid, but I hated even having to give him the chance.

"So, Ms. Jameson, want to share who was this one-shot wonder that you're now forever linked to? Is he gorgeous? It's not my catnip, but was he any good? I mean, I hope you at least enjoyed yourself because that memory might need to last you a while." Bridget grinned at me. "And, most importantly, when do you think this precious bundle will be arriving? Because I'm going to need to be thinking about what sub we want for your leave. Thankfully, I've got the summer months ahead of me to ponder that choice."

"Always focused on work, aren't you, Bridget?" I asked, laughing because that was far from the truth. My heart sank as I realized that after I got through this crisis, I still needed to talk to Bridget about leaving after next year. Shit. Now that would be leaving with a baby. Tears threatened, so I pushed that down. "Doing some fast math, I'd guess I'd be due around the first of the year. So, if all goes well, I'd have to take off most of the third quarter." I paused, then continued, "As for who it is, I'm not sure I'm ready to share that." I looked at her hesitatingly. It wasn't that I didn't trust her, but how do you even talk about this?

Bridget met my look and then leaned forward as she placed a hand on my knee, whispering, "Just guessing here, but I'd say Cole Sullivan has some news coming his way."

I gasped, my eyes widening. What the fuck. Was she a witch?

"Maggie, you aren't as hard to read as you think.

Remember, I've been to The Homestead with you too many times to count. When Emma is around, you give her crap about her older brother constantly. It seems like it's all in good fun. But when you're not spouting off about him, and you don't think anyone is watching, your eyes follow him around with lust and longing mixed in with equal measure." She squeezed my knee. "You've known the Sullivans forever, so if I were a betting woman, I'd say Cole needs some cigars. How'd I do?" She sat back, looking pretty pleased with herself.

"You're a bitch," I muttered, to which she grinned back at me. "And yep, Sully and I did the deed. Now what am I going to do?"

Bridget slid across the couch, resting right next to me and wrapping her arm around my shoulders. "You're going to suck it up and tell him. Then you're going to do a deep dive into your crazy brain and figure out what on earth would make you run from that beautiful man. And, while you're at it, you're also going to figure out how to tell your best friend that her brother knocked you up, ideally *after* you tell him he's going to be a daddy. That's what you're going to do."

"Uhhhhhhhhhhhh. Bridget, you make it sound so simple. But it is anything but simple. How the hell do I do this?" I whispered. I just wanted to go home and become an ostrich. I wondered if there was a way for me to teach via Zoom for the next nine months. I mean no one had to know I was pregnant. Maybe I could tell Sully later. When the baby was born and I'd moved far, far away.

Bridget smiled at me. "My friend, you have got this. You know you do. And you're going to do it like anything else that's hard, one step at a time."

I dropped my head on the back of the couch and looked

at the ceiling. She was right, but that didn't make any of this easier. My vibrating phone brought me back to reality, and I looked down to a text from Emma.

**Emma:** *Max and I are cooking out. Want to come over? I'll provide the tequila. It will just be the two of us and the pup. I want to see you!*

I grimaced. Bridget was right, Sully needed to know first. But he was out of town, and I couldn't hide forever. Grabbing my phone, I quickly replied.

**Me:** *Wrapping stuff up at school now. I can be there in an hour. No tequila for me. My stomach isn't thrilled with booze right now. What do you want me to bring?*

**Emma:** *YAY! Cookies please! See you in a bit.*

I looked back at Bridget. "Thanks for being here, for talking me off the ledge." Shaking my head, I glanced out the window. "I bought the test at lunch today and figured I'd take it when I got home. But when the kids left, I knew I couldn't wait another minute."

Bridget grabbed my hand and squeezed.

I whispered, "I'm so glad I was here, I'm so glad you found me. I have a feeling I'm in a much better place as a result than I would have been."

Bridget stood up, pulling me up with her, and gave me one of her famous hugs. "Sam and I will both be here for you no matter what. If you need advice, a sounding board, or just someone to commiserate with on the joys and pitfalls of pregnancy, please lean on us. And keep me posted on how it all goes."

"Thanks, Bridget. You're the best." I gave her one last squeeze and headed to grab my stuff from my classroom. I needed to head home, change, and grab some cookie dough from my freezer. I could bake them at Max and Emma's place. All the while, I needed to figure out how to make sure my best friend couldn't read my face and tell that something had just rocked my world.

This should be an interesting evening.

~

### Sully

Jake headed back toward me at the high-top I'd taken over in the corner of the bar. A few women sitting at the bar turned to watch him move away, which was nothing new. Jake and I had met in college. Well, I was in college. He worked in construction. His second job was at the brewery where I also worked for extra cash. Jake had always gotten a lot of attention from women. He was just a few inches shorter than my six-foot-four frame, but he was leaner, having been a runner since he was a kid. His dark hair was shorter than mine, and like myself, he was rarely ever clean-shaven.

I soaked in the atmosphere of this place, Main & Mill brewery in Festus, Missouri. This was the final stop on Jake and my two-week brewery road trip. We'd hit breweries all over the Midwest, talking to owners about their canning operations and just brewing beer in general. Owning a brewery was like belonging to a small club. I doubted seriously that The Homestead would have made it through the past five years without advice from other owners. They'd helped pave the way for our success. The past two weeks had been a fact-finding trip, sure, but it had also been a celebration for the two of us. We'd survived the start of our business and now were getting ready to grow some more.

I couldn't wait.

Jake pulled out a stool at the table before dropping a

basket of fried pickles in front of me. "Placed an order for our late lunch. We can eat and hit the road."

Nodding, I grabbed a pickle before dipping it in the sauce. Popping it into my mouth, there was a burst of flavor. I glanced at the sauce once again. It looked like a pinkish ranch. "Sriracha?" I asked Jake.

He nodded before grabbing his own. "Sriracha ranch. We should add something like this to our menu." Jake looked around, taking in the brick walls and U-shaped bar in the warm glow of old-looking light bulbs. The scent of beer and some type of grilled meat filled the air. There was a decent crowd considering we were a bit early for their happy hour. Lunch had passed. Dinner wouldn't begin picking up for several hours. We were grabbing a bit of food here before hopping on our bikes and heading back home. I figured we'd get in just a bit before seven.

Grabbing another pickle, Jake nodded to my open laptop. "Running the numbers?" he asked with a smirk. It was common knowledge that I was the finance guy in this partnership. We were equal partners, sure, but we both had different strengths. From our time in the brewery during my college years, we knew how the overall operations worked and the brewing process. Both of us were more than passable in the kitchen and had a heavy hand in developing our menu. Jake had headed up all the construction as I helped out with whatever he told me to do. He also was far better than me in dealing with our staff, scheduling, and hiring. I was the numbers man. Give me a spreadsheet, and I was at home. I loved watching those numbers for our loans go down, the income go up. It was a beautiful thing.

And yet we were preparing to take out another loan. I should be freaking out, but it was such a great opportunity. There was a Main Street program that our town had used over the years to revitalize the downtown. We'd gotten small loans and applied for grants through them when we were just getting started. Each year they awarded some low-interest loans out to businesses that had completed their business boot camp program. Considering we'd not only gone through the program, but given back by sharing our story to other local businesses and mentoring a few, we'd decided to apply for a larger loan and dive into canning. A month back we'd found out we qualified. All that was left was finalizing our business plan for this arm of the brewery and signing the loan papers when we got back to Highland.

I shook my head at him. "You know I am. Need to keep us solvent. You and your big dreams make that difficult at times." Jake was clearly the big picture person in our brewery. I kept us grounded.

"Speaking of, did you see that outdoor dining area they have here? We could look into something like that. Maybe the lot next door? Imagine some bands in the summer, would do good business..." Jake trailed off. Clearly his mind was filled with visions of what we could be.

Me, however? His dream inspired dollar signs. How much would that cost? We had an option on the vacant lot, but that was not budgeted right now. I needed to keep our bottom line in the black. Hell, having grown up in a farm family, I knew how quickly your finances could be impacted by unseen forces. For my parents, it had been weather. Mother Nature can be a bitch. Several years of less-than-ideal conditions along with the need to purchase new equipment had almost caused Mom and Dad to lose the farm. I'd promised myself to never feel the pinch like they'd had. It was damn scary to have everything you'd dreamed of and almost lose it all.

"Sullivan, you there?"

I looked up to see Jake watching me with a concerned gaze. "Sorry, man. You started talking, and my vision filled up with bills. Can we maybe tackle one expansion of the business at a time?"

He laughed as the waitress came over to drop off our food. I slid my laptop into the bag before glancing at our order.

Jake nodded at my plate. "I got you the Red Bird, which is some spicy-ass chicken. My burger is known as the Ghost."

"Ghost pepper?" I asked. Damn, that would be hot. In college we used to try to top each other, eating spicy shit whenever we could. Back then we were always experimenting in the kitchen. Jake's creation known as the Atomic Burger was fire on a plate. But damn if I was that young anymore. Now I just wanted some good food.

"In the cheese. Your sandwich has some too."

I glanced at my water to make sure we were topped up. Why did I have a feeling we'd regret this? Picking up the sandwich, I took a bite. Holy hell. Spicy, but awesome. Flavors were pinging all over my mouth. "Shit," I said, wiping off my mouth on a napkin. "That's damn good."

Jake nodded with a mouthful of food and raised up a finger for me to hold on. I took another bite, then tried a fry. Also unreal. We were both picky as hell about fries. Double frying them at our brewery had made the difference between a passable side dish and one that people came to get specifically.

Jake cleared his throat. "One, I win. No way is your chicken spicier than this burger."

I raised an eyebrow glancing at his burger. Looked like there was a shit ton of peppers there. Shrugging, I replied,

"Well, I'd say that you ordered, but also, it's your colon, man. Not sure if I'd call that one winning anymore."

"Fucking awesome burger. Still winning."

The waitress came back to check in, and Jake ordered some cans packed up to go since we weren't going to drink and hop on our bikes to go home. We'd been out here last night as well, so I didn't feel like we were missing anything necessarily.

"Two"—Jake called my attention back to him—"you doing okay with this whole loan situation?"

The man knew me, after all. Years of business together had proven my caution time and time again, but that caution had also helped lead to our success. "Thanks for asking, Spencer, but I'm actually doing okay. Well, that is if you don't try to convince me to add in outdoor seating this year. That's pushing too far."

He laughed at my expression. "Not trying to give you a stroke, Sully. I got you, one thing at a time." He paused, downing some water and wiping his forehead. Not sure if he was trying to exaggerate the heat of the meal or not. Could go either way with him. Looking more serious, he asked, "Does your pops know the impact of lean years of farming on your business sense?"

I shrugged and took another bite and thought about growing up on a farm. Swallowing, I debated how to answer that question. "Maybe? I mean, my parents never sat us down and told us everything was hitting the fan, but I wasn't stupid. Emma was young, maybe three or four, so I'm not sure if she noticed or if she even remembers. I was six or seven. I couldn't help but notice that they were stressed. I heard some conversations late at night and put it together. Mom crying one night was the final straw for my dad. I think I was eight then, right before Max moved to Highland. I remember seeing my dad holding my mom, promising her it would be okay. She got up, went to the bathroom."

I stopped talking, thinking about my dad's face when my mom had gotten up off their bed and left the room. He'd walked to the windows of the bedroom, looking outside. I could only see him in profile from my spot hiding at the door, but it was enough. His face was ravaged, and before I left, I had watched his shoulders begin to shake as his head dropped, tears coursing down. Looking back to Jake, my voice was lower, and he needed to lean in to hear me. "He was destroyed. It can happen even when you're doing everything right."

Jake's eyes were locked on mine. "Fuck, Sully. That's heavy. I'm sorry, man. I know I give you shit that you always have this plan, but you know I'm screwing with you, right? Your plan hasn't steered us wrong yet."

I threw my napkin on my plate and pushed it away. Damn, sitting on a bike for the next three hours was going to be tough. That was no light meal, which might have been a better choice for the ride home. Realizing Jake was waiting for me, I blew out a breath. "I know you are."

"Change of topic." Jake pushed his food back too. The waitress reappeared to place our bill folder on the table along with our cans to go and then took our plates. "How goes your other plan?"

My brows drew together as I considered his comment. "What?"

Jake shook his head at me. "Man, I've talked to Max, and I have eyes. One spitfire of a strawberry blonde has been markedly absent from our brewery for over a month. Hell, even Daryl noticed. He bartends every yoga night, you know. He said Emma and Maggie haven't been coming in on the regular for their yoga-night special for over six weeks. Spill."

I dropped my head to my hands, considering the table. I hadn't said anything to Max, other than I didn't want to talk about it, because I didn't want to put him in a weird spot with him and Emma finally figuring their shit out. But maybe putting this out there would give me some new perspective. Hell, it couldn't hurt. I couldn't get Maggie to talk to me.

Looking back to Jake, I laid it out there. "So, I've had a thing for Maggie for a while."

"No shit."

I jerked back in surprise. "How the fuck do you know that?"

Jake laughed. "I hope to hell you don't think you've been subtle about that. The two of you have had enough smoldering chemistry for the past few years that it's a damn miracle the brewery didn't burn down around you."

I nodded. Interesting. I hadn't figured anyone else would have picked up on my feelings. But Jake said *we* had chemistry. So maybe Maggie had been feeling more than a one-night desire to see what came of us. Who knew since the woman was radio silent. "Anyway, almost a month and a half ago, Maggie drank too much when we were at Max's. I took her home, but she asked to stay at my place." Jake's head tilted at that. "I didn't act on anything that night. She'd had far too much to drink. But the next morning, we both jumped off the ledge we've been on."

"Kaboom?"

I laughed. "Yep. Shit-hot chemistry. Best I've ever had."

"Then why is she a ghost?"

I shrugged. "Fuck if I know." I decided to keep the broken condom and tears to myself. Not sure how much

Maggie wanted shared of our morning together. Hell, the answer was probably none of it.

Jake nodded, looking over the bar, then back to me. "So, where does she fit in your plan?"

"What plan?"

"Don't fuck with me, man. You have a plan for everything, and I'm guessing Maggie Jameson features pretty heavily into it."

I sighed. "I don't know, Jake. In an ideal world? Maggie and I'd get together, date for a while, and spend the next fifty years or so making each other crazy."

"Kids?"

"Fuck yeah. Just not yet."

Jake shrugged. "Who knows, Sullivan? Man plans, but God laughs. Maybe Maggie just needs you to relax."

"I'd be glad to if the woman would just talk to me. Beyond all the rest of this, she's a good friend. I hate that we might have fucked that up. I've worked out more this month, put in more hours at the brewery, because I'm trying to honor her unspoken request for space." I ran my hand through my hair, wanting to tug it out in a fit of frustration.

"So why didn't you just appear on her doorstep?" Jake asked, watching me with interest. I knew damn well that in our over ten years of friendship, he'd never seen me torn up over a woman. Asshole was probably enjoying this.

"Maggie doesn't like to be cornered. She's always said she's leaving Highland Falls one day." I shrugged, trying to ignore the clench in my stomach when I thought of that. "Didn't want to give her reason to speed up that move."

"How does this move fit in with your future plans for fifty years making each other crazy?"

Tipping my head back to look at the ceiling, I let out a sigh. Looking back to Jake, I uttered two words, "It doesn't."

3

## COOKIES AND PEARL JAM

***Maggie***

Emma was dancing around Max's kitchen singing into a wooden spoon. I couldn't help but grin at my friend. Her brown hair was curled in soft waves, and she tossed it from shoulder to shoulder as she belted out lyrics to "Shallow" from the *Star is Born* soundtrack. Originally, we were doing it as a duet. However, since she was on the third time through with the same song, I'd moved on to baking cookies, and Max fled the kitchen to man the grill.

Emma's voice rang out as she began the song again. God, I loved Em, but she was no Gaga. Tonight should be fun. It would keep my mind off my own issues, that was for certain.

I placed the chocolate chip dough balls on the parchment paper, then slid the trays into the oven. Emma piped up from over my shoulder, "Mags, thanks for the cookies. Yours are the best!" She grinned and spun around, hair flying like a cape.

This was a conversation we had often. Emma was a hell of a cook, but she couldn't figure out baking for some reason,

47

which puzzled me. Shaking my head, I smiled and held up the yellow Nestlé's bag. "It's all right here on the back of the bag, my friend. That Ruth Graves Wakefield knew what she was doing."

Emma shook her head at me. "Nope, your recipe is different."

"No seriously, it's not that different. You just need to commit these two secrets to memory: cream the hell out of the butter with the sugar *and* refrigerate the dough in balls for at least three hours before cooking. That's it. You'll get kick-ass cookies too, my sweets." I leaned over, setting the timer on Max's oven, then grabbed my sparkling water as I hopped up on the counter and considered Emma. "So, when are you moving in here?"

Emma slid my purse to the side and hopped up on the island in front of me. She kicked her legs out, tapping my feet, then let them fall back. I glanced from her feet, bare with bright pink nails, and looked back up at her. Emma looked out the back door to Max—he'd left the grill to throw a small tennis ball around the yard with Poppy—then her eyes came back to me. "Well, I'm essentially in now." She grinned.

"Yeah, yeah, but when is it going to be official, you know? Like when will all your possessions be contained in this household?"

Emma rolled her eyes and grabbed her wine. "I only listed my house a few days ago. Several showings are scheduled this weekend. I don't see any point in moving in officially until it's sold." She tipped her head back, considering Max's ceiling, before looking at me again. "God, I hate packing. Frankly, I'm just putting it off as long as possible."

"I respect that. I hate it too." I leaned forward to high five her in a show of solidarity.

"Does that mean you can give up the idea of moving away from here as soon as you make your first fortune?" Emma put her palms together in a pleading gesture as she gave me a hopeful expression.

"Nope, nope." I shook my finger at her as my stomach clenched. Six weeks ago I'd decided that move was happening sooner than she thought. Now I had a positive pregnancy test in my purse. I couldn't think about all this right now. "No pleading-cat-from-Shrek eyes, Emma Sullivan. You know that isn't allowed."

Emma laughed, dropping her hands, and grabbing her wineglass instead. Her eyes twinkled with amusement as she considered me. "Sorry, but I will always try to keep you here, Maggie. I can't imagine you moving away." She looked sad for a moment, then glanced back at the bottle of wine. "You sure you don't want any?"

I shook my head and murmured something about my fabulous students sharing their various viruses with me. A lie, but a necessary one. That seemed to appease her, and she hopped down as she danced over to the bottle, refilling her own glass herself. I watched, thinking about our decade long debate about where I would end up, a topic on which we never found agreement. While Emma and I had separated to go to college, we always knew we were going to try to come back to the area afterward, and we did.

Emma wanted to come back to Highland to stay. I'd always said I was coming back for just a bit. Emma, ever the optimist, tried to ignore that last part. The past few years I'd seen Emma settle back into Highland Falls and could tell she was home for good. Even before Max's return, she'd begun to come into her own here. I'd always heard that as you aged, you started to give less of a fuck what others thought of you. That you became more at peace with who you were. That was evident with Emma.

Outwardly, most people probably thought I'd always been like that too. A person who had zero fucks to give about what other people thought of her. However, that wasn't completely true. Growing up without a mom, with a dad who was amazingly kind but couldn't provide for us, I'd cared what others thought, likely too much. Being in this tiny town, I'd felt suffocated by the judgment of others. I'd hoped that feeling might go away when I was older. Unfortunately, from what I could tell, it had intensified. I didn't allow the opinions of others to change my mind on what I did. It's just that it took up my brain space. I thought of what other people would think before I did something. And that pissed me off. I just wanted to live somewhere I was one of many, not one of a few. I wanted to get away from a place where everyone already thought they knew my story.

"I'm not moving away tomorrow, Emma." I decided to put out a feeler. "Not for at least a year." I smiled at my friend while she looked on, a bit teary.

"I'm going to ignore that time frame, Maggie May. But I will note that I feel like this summer road trip you're gearing up for is the first step." Emma asked as she leaned back against the counter across from me, considering me over the rim of her glass.

My heart sank as the reality of my planned gypsy summer hit me. I didn't know much about babies or pregnancy, but I knew I'd need to have doctor appointments over the summer. Thinking back about Bridget and some other teachers in my building, they seemed to go at least once a month at the beginning. Maybe the trip was still viable? Ugh, I'd have to look into it. Glancing up at Emma, I saw she was a bit tipsy, or more like a bit emotional. Oh boy.

To cheer her up, I grabbed a wooden spoon out of the utensil holder on Max's kitchen counter. "Pearl Jam?"

Emma's arms shot up in a *V* as she shouted, "Eddie!!!!"

We both jumped down, leaning over her phone to pick a song. A pang hit me as she scrolled. Would I really be able to move away from her? She'd been part of me since we met in second grade. Sucking down the waves of emotion, I pushed it aside. *Think about that later*, I told myself. I had time. Part of me knew that the pile of crap that I need to face, to deal with, was growing larger and larger, but I just couldn't do it now. Briefly I thought of telling her about this life growing inside me, but Bridget was right, Sully should know first.

Just the thought made my heart race as the first notes from one of the greatest songs ever filled the room. Pearl Jam's "Black" flowed out from Max's speakers, and I let the music fill me as I lifted my wooden spoon. "Heyyyyyy...."

Nope, not stressing out now. Now was time to sing.

### *Sully*

I glanced over at the gas station where Jake had ducked in to grab a quick drink before we hit the final leg of this two-week road trip. We'd driven a little over half the way from Festus to home, and I was exhausted. It had been amazing to visit breweries all over the Midwest, and I was glad to have the knowledge of how to get our canning process started, but my ass was tired and I was ready for my bed. Noting the text from Max asking if I wanted to stop by for steaks, I pulled out my phone and placed the call.

"Yo."

"Harp." I smiled at what I assumed was Emma's dog

Poppy yapping in the background. "I'll be back in town in a little under an hour, but I'm passing on the steaks. I'm dead tired from riding today, not to mention for the past two weeks. Need to head home."

"Where are you guys?" Max asked as I heard what was likely his grill closing. My mouth watered a bit.

"Gas station just past some giant-ass cross on the side of the highway," I laughed. We'd used it as a landmark on the way home, knowing it meant we were pretty close, thank God. "Jake wants to get back and hit the brewery tonight, check in with Finn. I'm leaving him to that since I'm on tomorrow and crashing in my own bed. I fucking cannot wait."

"Understood," Max said. "Pulling the steaks off now and they're looking damn good. You're missing out, Sullivan." He chuckled as I heard him moving around.

I glanced back to the gas station to see if Jake was headed back. Nope. The sounds of Pearl Jam floated through my phone. Emma was likely in charge of the music selection tonight, though we were all fans.

"Jesus." Max let out a quiet laugh.

"What?" I asked.

"Maggie and Emma are dancing around the kitchen, singing like they did when they were in high school," he said.

I laughed. "Those two always did like to let it fly when they were having a few."

"Only Emma tonight, Maggie said she's feeling off," Max said. "Shit, Emma just shoved Maggie's purse over to make room for her stage on the island. I might need help wrangling her tonight."

"Your problem now, bud." I'd struggled at first with my

best friend dating my sister, but now it seemed like a great solution. Emma and Maggie together were a dynamic team. I bet Emma would be feeling this tomorrow. I heard a bit of commotion from Max's end while also catching Jake's eye as he headed out of the station and across the parking lot toward me.

"Good Lord, what the fuck is happening there, Harp?" I asked.

"Hell if I know. Emma knocked Maggie's purse off the counter so she could have a stage. Now she's grabbing all the shit that fell out. Why do women carry so much around with them anyway? Damn, that would be heavy after a while. Holy..." Max's voice stopped.

"Harp? I asked.

"..."

"Max?" A nervous feeling washed over me. I could hear the girls in the background, but couldn't make out what was going on. Jake came to a stop in front of me.

"Holy fuck," Max whispered.

"Max, yo, Max!" I called, putting up a hand to stop Jake from saying anything. "What the fuck is going on? Jake and I are heading back on the road in just a minute."

"Man, I need you to get home. I'm going to need some testosterone around here," Max murmured. "I think our Maggie might be pregnant."

A sound like I'd never heard came out of me. What in the literal hell had he just said? My voice creaked out a quiet, "What?"

Max quietly spoke. "Well, from what I can tell, Emma picked up a pregnancy test that fell out of Maggie's bag. Now, Maggie's sobbing in Emma's arms. You draw your own conclusions. I've drawn mine."

I cleared my throat. It was a damn miracle that I hadn't

had a heart attack. "Text me if Maggie goes anywhere. I'm on my fucking way." With that, I hung up.

Holy hell.

Jake stood in front of me, looking me over with what I could only assume was apprehension. "How much of that did you hear?" I asked him.

"Enough to suspect that our conversation from earlier just got a whole lot more interesting."

I ignored his shit-eating grin. "I'm headed straight home, no stops."

"Understood."

I swung onto my bike, pulled my helmet on, and pointed it in the direction of home. Maggie. Pregnant. My God. She might have ignored me for the past five weeks, but clearly the time for games was over.

Fuck.

The next sixty miles sped by without much thought. Jake had pulled ahead of me leaving the gas station, likely to give me something to focus on. I followed his bike with the word *pregnant* dancing through my mind. What the hell did it mean? Clearly I could propose to Maggie tonight, but that would likely result with my head on a platter. Not the way to go.

I thought back to two months ago, when we were actually talking. Maggie had shared the summer road trip she had planned. Would she still do that? My gut clenched, thinking ahead. She planned on moving too. Did that mean I'd only see my kid on holidays?

Deep breaths. I was getting ahead of myself. I needed to talk to the woman. How long had she known? Did she plan to tell me? I needed to know what her mindset was before we talked. Knowing Maggie, she could spook and decide she was moving tomorrow. Just the thought made me want to wrap her up and never let her go.

Jake's signal popped on to take us on the two-lane highway to Highland. Following him, my thoughts drifted to the brewery. Fuck. Canning. My stomach rolled. With a kid coming, what were my expenses going to look like now? Maggie had health insurance, right? So no big expenses for the next few months at least. I racked my brain, trying to think through what kind of financial plan I'd need for this. College savings accounts? Whose insurance would cover our baby? What did babies cost once they were born? They didn't eat food for a while, right? Diapers were likely as expensive as fuck.

I felt like I was breaking out in a cold sweat under my flannel. Jake eased on down the road, and I knew then that our friendship was going to take a hit. We were supposed to sign the loan for the canning operation on Monday. I'd wait to hear from Maggie, but I think that was going to have to be put on hold. Damn.

The turn off the highway for Max's farm was about a mile before town. As Jake passed the turn, he raised his arm up in the air in acknowledgment. I'd deal with his disappointment tomorrow once I figured out what in the hell was going on in my life. The miles to Max's were eaten up quickly as I scanned the flat prairie for Maggie's car, wondering if she'd stayed at Max's or had already headed to her place. The sun was getting closer to the horizon, and farms dotted the fields here and there. Heading down the road, Max's farm was to the left, and I turned in, coming up the drive.

I pulled my bike to a stop and looked to the back porch. Max was sitting in an Adirondack chair, feet up on the rail, appearing to be waiting for me. His eyes followed me as I moved up the sidewalk and sank down in the chair next to him as if my legs couldn't keep me up for one more minute.

Without commentary, Max passed me a beer. I glanced at the label, Zombie Dust, a beer Max had introduced me to a month or so ago. Staring at the label, I said, "Jake and I stopped at this place on our trip."

Max looked over, then back to the prairie. "3 Floyds?"

I nodded.

"You really want to talk about breweries right now?" he asked.

I closed my eyes, tipping my head back. "She still here?"

"Nope. Sent you a text about a half hour ago. She took off after that scene in the kitchen."

Fuck.

"Told her to text me when she gets home. Hasn't yet."

I nodded, lost in thought. Maggie loved driving in the country when she was stressed. She'd done it in high school with Emma. Hell, I'd driven her around more than once over the years. Her senior year she'd been at my parents' place a lot. I'd driven her around while she'd worked through college decisions. My guess right now was that she was driving over country roads, windows down, music blaring, hair flying. I just hoped she was okay emotionally. And I wished like hell I was with her.

I stood suddenly. I couldn't be with her wherever she was, but I needed to be waiting when she got home. Handing my untouched bottle to Max, I said, "I've gotta go."

Max looked up at me. "Not going to pry, man, but know Emma and I are here for whatever you need."

"Means a lot." I headed down the walk to my bike.

Minutes later I was on the road and headed for Maggie's, praying I'd get there before her. There were so many emotions warring inside me. Nervousness about being able to provide for Maggie and the baby, fear that Maggie would just up and leave, but what was coming through more and more was excitement. A baby. Maggie and I made a baby. Somehow, without having even seen her, I knew it was my baby. Maggie didn't date a lot, and there was always a chance, but the feeling in my gut was that it was mine.

Wasn't it just a few hours back that I told Jake I wasn't ready for kids? I guess that plan got shot to shit.

The fact that my plans were down the toilet made me think of Maggie once again. She was just as much of a planner as I was. How was she feeling about all this? Had she had anyone to talk to, to help calm her down?

Pulling into her drive, I parked back by her place and glanced around. Her car wasn't here. Just in case, I jogged up her walk to the back door and knocked. Nothing. Peering into her duplex, it was dark. I knocked again, just in case. Nothing.

I turned to sink down onto her porch. Leaning my back against her place, I stretched out my legs to wait. Hopefully she'd be home soon. We had a lot to talk about.

## 4

## YOU NEED ME

**Maggie**

The interaction of two country roads flowed under my car, giving my belly a floaty feeling. Emotions rolled through me like waves as I worked to center myself. Some of that yoga stuff would sure come in handy right now. Emma had recently introduced me to a new band, Nathaniel Rateliff and the Night Sweats. They were amazing, but his solo album was speaking to me. Currently it was blaring from my stereo and out my open windows to the rapidly darkening sky. Wind in my hair, I sang out Rateliff, praying that it was actually still all right as he suggested.

Thinking back over the past hour, I shuddered as I remembered the pregnancy test flying out of my bag like some bad joke in a rom-com. Emma had been working her way up to the counter so that she could sing to her adoring fans when the shit hit the fan, as it was. She'd hopped down immediately to help me pick up, and we'd both seen it. My heart had thudded, thinking maybe if I threw it in my bag quickly, she wouldn't be sure what she saw, but no dice.

*Emma looked from the test in her hand to me and back to*

the test. In her eyes I saw what I'm sure was mirrored in my own: confusion, hope, fear, excitement, circling back to confusion. "Mags, by any chance do you happen to have someone else's pregnancy test in your purse that you're holding on to for safekeeping?"

I looked at her with what I was certain was a look of incredulity. "What in the hell would I keep someone else's pee stick for?"

Meeting my eyes, she whispered, "Just trying not to jump to conclusions about my best friend being pregnant."

With that, I promptly burst into tears. Since we were already on the floor, Emma tossed the test to the side and slid to encircle me with her arms and legs. I curled into her and cried, cried, cried. I paused for a minute, certain that there could be no more tears left, and then they came again. Emma didn't say a word beyond murmurs to comfort as she smoothed her hand up and down my back as we rocked back and forth.

My brain was pinging from thought to thought without focusing on any one thing too much. If I let myself focus, I'd have to acknowledge I was up the proverbial creek. Finally the tears subsided, and Emma pulled back to smooth down my hair and wipe the tears from my face.

"Sweetheart," she whispered, "what do you need? Where do I need to bury the body?" She glanced over my shoulder at the back deck. Shit. Max was out there. He hadn't come in, so I was guessing he'd seen the meltdown and stayed far away. Smart man. She appeared to make eye contact with him, then looked back to me. "Max is good for a lot of things, and he will absolutely help us if we need to smack someone down. Just say the word."

A feeling of dread washed over me. Would she say that if she knew who had knocked me up? And Sully didn't deserve *a smackdown. If anything, I did. I'd ghosted him when he'd been perfectly wonderful. My gut clenched as I realized that was a conversation I did not want to have.*

*Looking back at Emma, I whispered, "Time. I just need some time."*

*Emma kissed my forehead and whispered back, "You have that, my friend. I'm here, we're here, whatever you need. Anytime, day or night." And then she simply hugged me tight and let me stand.*

*Tears still swimming in my eyes, I pulled her up. "Right now what I need is to go home. I'm so sorry." I could tell she wanted to ask me to stay, but I needed quiet. I also needed to sort my shit so I could really talk to her about this.*

*"Can I give you some food to take home? I bet the steaks are done," she asked, squeezing my hand.*

*"No, I'm good. Rain check?"*

*"Of course. Babe, you know…" Her voice trailed off.*

*I closed my eyes as I pulled her close. "I know, I know. I love you."*

*"And I love you. Always and forever," she whispered.*

*Grabbing my purse, I quickly made my way out the door before being stopped by a wall in the form of one Maxwell Harp. His huge hand tilted my chin back to meet his green eyes. "You okay, Mags?"*

*I cleared my throat and quietly said, "I will be, Max."*

*His lips grazed my forehead as he squeezed me tight. "We're here, babe."*

*My chest filled with emotion, fear of the future, love for these friends who were more family than anything else I had. "I know, Max. I need to get home."*

*"Text Emma when you get there, okay?" he asked, pulling back to look at me and wipe away some of my tears.*

*"You bet, Dad-o."*

*With that he pushed me away, laughing. I moved away to my car and looked back, seeing Max pull out his phone as he grabbed the steaks with his other hand and whistle for Poppy to follow him into the house.*

I shook my head as I drove down another country road and realized with a start that I'd driven myself to the road that Sully and Emma's parents lived on. Rateliff sang on as I sang with him. The lyrics for "You Need Me" filled my car. I laughed at the irony of the song. Yeah, I might need more than a few people in the near future. That wasn't going to be easy for me.

I passed the Sullivans' place and looked to see if Lee or Anna was outside, but neither were there. Glancing at the clock in the car, I figured they'd likely be cleaning up after dinner or even settling in for a relaxing night. Lee was likely watching a ball game. Anna would be reading or knitting. I'd spent so much of my childhood there it felt as close to home as my own house, maybe more. Not my dad's fault he wasn't around a lot. As a single parent he'd done what he could to make sure we had what we needed. It just hadn't always worked out.

My phone lit up in the phone holder on my dash. I glanced at the navigation screen of the car and saw "Dad calling." Speak of the devil.

Tapping the screen, I answered the call. "Hey, Dad." Turning away from Lee and Anna's, I began to drive toward town. The rolling fields of the bison farm were on one side of the car, a preserve on the other. Without the music filling the night air, I could hear an owl in the distance and the crunch of gravel under my tires.

"Princess." My dad's gravelly voice greeted me, making my eyes water once again. Damn.

"How did I get so lucky to warrant a call today?" I

asked. As a long-haul trucker, Dad and I tried to schedule our calls so that we could do them on an afternoon he wasn't driving, preferably over Zoom so I could see his face. We weren't scheduled for another call for another week.

"Pulled in to Kansas City early and thought I'd call my girl and see how she was. Meeting another driver for dinner in a few, so I don't have long, but for whatever reason, really wanted to say hi today," he replied.

I smiled. My dad had tried his best once my mom was gone. It had just been the two of us, and thank God. It was hard enough to make ends meet with just us. Getting his CDL license my senior year had really been a godsend for him. He loved the lifestyle and had even been able to save up some money in the past ten years.

"You following our rules, Dad?"

Dad laughed, I'm sure recalling our long-ago conversations about the rules he had to follow if he was going to be a long-haul truck driver. In my seventeen-year-old mind, it was important that he walked for at least thirty minutes around a rest stop, or wherever he was, when he was done with the hours for the day. Truck drivers sat so much of the day. He needed to work in some activity. He also had to stock up on fruits and vegetables he could eat in the cab to keep his heart healthy. And, most importantly, he had to be a safe driver.

"You know it, sweet girl. Tonight I'm even going to have a vegetable."

I gasped in shock. "You're familiar with those?"

His easy laughter made my heart lighter. "It's those little green things, right? Circular in shape?"

I shook my head and rolled my eyes, though I know he couldn't see me. "Peas, Dad. And yes, that would be great for you. Maybe go wild and have a salad?" I drove through town and around the courthouse square.

Highland Falls had been settled in the mid-1800s. The town was a mixture of older buildings dripping of history to newer spaces. I doubted it would ever grow too big. The town limits were within an area that measured around ten square miles with a population right around ten thousand.

Everywhere I drove, I saw memories. Coming around the square, I could see the bench that Emma and I had eaten ice cream at all summer long when we were preteens, trying hard not to crush on the boys in our class doing skateboard tricks across the way. I passed the new bookstore, Pages, as well as a few other restaurants.

It was a Friday night, and people were out strolling the sidewalks that were lit with older lampposts that had been part of the Main Street revitalization grant the city got a few years back to fix up the downtown area. It helped. I think now more folks saw the downtown area as a destination for eating and socializing than they used to. Small restaurants were opening and doing well. I'm sure the success of The Homestead helped them see they could make a go of it too. There were some tables outside restaurants on the sidewalks, folks scattered here and there under strings of white lights. I settled.

"You there, princess?" my dad called to me.

Oops. Got lost in thought there for a bit. "Yeah, Dad. So everything is good?" Turning left, I headed away from the downtown and toward my duplex.

"Yep. The routes have been great lately."

"You still listening to audiobooks on your rides? Need suggestions?" My dad spent hours in the cab of his truck. I'd introduced him to some amazing podcasts, but a few months back he'd asked if he could read something I was reading and we could talk about it. Since he likely didn't want to dive into the romance books I read, I recommended a popular young adult book my seventh graders were reading, and he'd devoured it. Since then I'd set up a page for my students to leave recommendations for him and reviews. He would check it when he could and leave his thoughts on what he read back to them. It was a way for him to be connected with my life that I hadn't realized he'd wanted.

"Nah, I just finished Connor's suggestion of Barry Lyga's *I Hunt Killers*. I think I might check out the sequel. I'll leave him a note on my review sometime this weekend."

I heard a voice in the background of the call before my dad came back. "Gotta go, honey. We're heading in to eat."

"Salad, Dad. Get a salad."

He chuckled. "Not sure. My body might revolt at that much green."

"Dad..." I pulled into the drive of my duplex and came to a stop. I turned the car off and laid my head on my steering wheel, listening to my dad and wishing he was here.

"Kidding, baby. I eat healthy, and you know it. Made that promise to you years ago."

I closed my eyes and took a deep breath. "Have fun tonight, Dad. Drive safe. Love you."

"Love you more, babe. Always." And then he was gone. I soaked in his voice from my car and wished that I could lean into him for a hug, wished I could sit with him for a meal. Watching Emma with her mom over the years, I'd been so damn jealous that I didn't have my own mom. Now, with Dad's job, I felt like I'd lost out on him too. I loved that he'd found a job that was perfect for him, but damn if I didn't miss him.

I pulled my forehead from the steering wheel and came

back to the present. After driving around for almost an hour, I was no closer to any answers than I had been before, but even the short time talking to my dad had made me feel more settled. House, pajamas, hot chocolate, and a book. Comfort. I needed that so badly right now.

Making my way to the back door, I pulled out my keys, flipping through them to find the one for my place. Stepping onto the porch, my breath caught in my throat. Sully was sitting against the door, his eyes meeting mine. His hair was wild, windblown and tousled in every direction. His jeans were well worn and had a tear in one knee as he sat with one leg out, one bent with his forearm resting on it. His thermal long-sleeve T-shirt was fitted, stretching across his chest and making me think about what it covered which, momentarily, distracted me from the fear that was making my heart race once again.

"Hey, Mags. Something you wanted to tell me?" he asked, his voice low and thick with emotion.

"Hi, Sully," I said, my heart in my throat. The settled feeling had disappeared in a breath. Tears blurring my vision, I moved toward him.

5

# HARD CONVERSATIONS

**_Sully_**

I had been waiting on the deck for ten or so minutes, trying to wrap my brain around the notion that it looked like parenthood was closer than I'd ever realized. I'd worried about Maggie, my friend, for the past few hours. Maggie didn't have a lot of family in her life beyond her dad and the family she had created for herself in mine. I was certain she was likely terrified, and knowing Mags, that would mean she would put up walls to protect herself. I had a feeling I'd better be prepared to work my ass off to break down those walls if I wanted in, and I sure as hell did.

Finally I heard Maggie's car in the drive. Glancing from my spot on the porch, I watched as she moved up the back walk. She didn't notice me at first as she flipped through something in her hand, but when she looked at me, she took my breath away. Normally Maggie wore expressions of amusement or one that was full of orneriness. Lately, since our night together, her expression had morphed to one of longing or sadness. I'd tried to talk to her since then, but she'd kept her distance. It'd been such an exercise in frustra-

66

tion. I couldn't understand why what seemed to be the start of something beautiful had, instead, seemed to have been the end of one of the strongest friendships I'd ever had with a woman. At least that was what I'd feared. Tonight, however, her expression was not filled with amusement, orneriness, longing, or sadness, but complete bewilderment and confusion. Maggie looked like a kid who had lost her beloved dog and needed to be rescued. Her eyes met mine, and I saw they were swimming with tears.

"Hey, babe. Something you wanted to tell me?" I asked, working to keep the desire to wrap her in my arms and tell her it would all be fine at bay.

"Hi, Sully," she whispered.

Before I knew it, she crashed into my chest, and I wrapped my arms around her. Maggie's shoulders shook with racking sobs, and I found myself saying, "Shhh..." I rubbed up and down her back, smoothing out her hair, trying to get her together.

"Maggie, give me your key. Let's get you in your place."

I felt her nod her head against my chest and hand over her keys. Keeping one arm wrapped tightly around her waist, I pulled Maggie toward the door and let us into her home.

Flipping on the lights, I glanced around. I'd been here several times in the past few years with Emma. You entered the duplex in the living room, and it spilled over into a small kitchen. There was a second bedroom and bathroom off that. To the left there was a staircase that ran against the wall in the living room, heading up to her master loft. It was on the small side but worked well for Maggie. The wall under the stairs had quite a pile of boxes stacked up below it. Glancing from them to Maggie, I raised my brow. Was she already packed for her trip? What was with the boxes?

Maggie looked from my face to the boxes and back to me. "I'm supposed to go on a road trip this summer and am putting my stuff in storage while I'm gone."

My stomach felt like it had a solid punch to the gut. I knew about the trip, but the boxes seemed like something more, though it made a shit ton of sense for her to rent this place out if she was gone for months. Looking over her face still swimming with tears, I told myself it wasn't the time to have this conversation. I simply wanted to help her, comfort her, get her back to the Maggie I knew.

Tugging her hand, I led Maggie to her couch, and she sank down into the corner. I grabbed one of her chunky cable throws from the basket at the side of the couch. Passing her the blanket to curl up with, I took her purse from her trembling hand and dropped her keys inside while I glanced to her kitchen, then back. Typically I'd grab her a beer, wine, or something stronger. Looks like that was out. Clearing my throat, I caught her eyes. "Water?"

"Please," she said, drawing her knees up and resting her head on them.

Placing her purse on the counter, I then moved toward the cabinet and nabbed two mason jar glasses. I filled them up with some ice and water as I watched Maggie. Her gaze was out the windows, lost. Returning to the couch, I gave Maggie a glass before sinking down next to her and placing my glass on the trunk that she used as a coffee table. I willed myself to stay calm and let her share whatever she needed to, but I also knew I'd have to get us started. I looked up to see Maggie's watery eyes staring back at me.

"Um, so I think we have two conversations we need to have..."

"Two?" she whispered. Her brown eyes looked enormous on her pale skin.

"Well, yeah. We could talk about why you ghosted me after we hooked up last month, or we could address what I hear is the repercussion of that hookup. Where do you want to start?" I gently placed my hand on her knee, letting her know I was here but holding myself back. What I really wanted to do was pull her over to me, place her on my lap, wrap my arms around her waist, and bury my face in her hair. But there was too much shit going down. We needed to clear the air, and I needed to know what the fuck was going on. *Take it slow*, I cautioned myself.

Maggie looked at me and about broke my heart. Her eyes were filled with such misery I didn't know if I could handle it. Was she so sad because she was pregnant? Or was it that we'd crossed that barrier between friends and more? Maybe she hadn't been where I'd thought she was, hadn't wanted to explore more between us, though it had sure as hell seemed like it. Shit.

"Well"—she took a fortifying breath—"let's start with last month and my lack of communication..."

"That's one way to put it." I smirked, attempting to lighten the mood.

Maggie smiled, seemingly relieved at the slight joke. "That's my fuckup, and I'm sorry."

"What happened? Did I push you?" I asked, nerves filling my stomach.

Maggie's eyes seemed to roam all over her living room, looking anywhere but at me. I leaned forward and lightly nabbed her chin, pulling her to me. "Mags, I'm not mad. I'm confused, worried, a bit freaked out, but not mad. Please talk to me."

"Shit, Cole. How can you be so nice right now? I feel like a flighty bitch." Tears again began to run rivets down her face. "Of course you didn't push me. You were wonderful."

I brushed them off her cheeks and leaned forward, kissing each cheek in turn. "Okay, one, good. Two, regarding being a bitch, how about you let me make that call? Because I think you're just fine. Tell me what happened."

Maggie leaned back, but snagged my hand and squeezed it. That seemed to give her comfort, so I left my hand there on her knee, and she began. I listened as she talked about how the broken condom freaked her out, bringing her back to the present, making her question everything we'd just done, how I really felt about her, and how that might impact her plan to leave Highland in a few years.

I listened to Maggie try to explain her actions and thought about the girl I knew. She'd had casual boyfriends over the years, but no one who lasted more than a few weeks. Her last one had lasted all of a month or more before moving out West. She hadn't even seemed to consider keeping that relationship going but just let him leave without any show of sadness or wishing things could be different. Before, I'd wondered about that. Now I had a feeling that was by design. Don't let anyone get too close, don't let anyone break your heart.

Maggie and I'd been close for years, but only because it was a friendship. In shifting that relationship, she was worried that she'd lose one part of the small little circle she considered her family. Well, this I could deal with. One thing was for certain. Slow was going to be the name of the game. Maggie needed to know she could rely on me no matter what we were to each other. Especially now.

As Maggie trailed off, I gave her a slow smile before saying, "So, did you have Harp or Emma in your business like I did for the past four weeks? They both seemed awfully curious as to what was going on between us."

Maggie laughed, looking far more relaxed. "Hell, yes. Your sister is unrelenting!"

The tiny duplex seemed to breathe easier for both of us. I debated but then went for it, pulling Maggie over to my lap while keeping it as friendly and unromantic as possible. I squeezed my arms around her, thinking she might need support for this next conversation. Hell, I knew I did. "Babe, you want to tell me the rest?"

Maggie closed her eyes, took a deciding breath, and opened back up to look at me. I wanted to cheer at the sight, thinking *that's my girl!* I could see her grit and determination returning.

"Sully, I'm pregnant. And I hope it goes without saying, it's yours."

My heart broke a bit because as much as I could see her strength returning, I could also tell she was bracing for bad news. I wanted to say *what the fuck? You know the kind of man I am.* But I'd never been in her shoes. Who knew how this might fuck with your head? Instead, I looked at her, brushed her crazy gorgeous hair away from her face, and said, "Okay, where do we go from here?"

"How did you know?" she whispered.

"I was on the phone with Harp who had a front-row seat when Emma found the test. He told me what he was seeing, not having the first clue how that might tie to me."

"Oh, I didn't think about that." She took a deep breath. "I'm glad he told you, but I swear I was going to. And I didn't tell Emma it was yours."

"Why not?" I asked, confused. Unless she didn't want to keep the baby, didn't want anyone to know. I began to sweat.

She looked at me, confusion in her eyes. "You deserved to know first—although Bridget does, but that couldn't be helped."

Relief flooded me, along with some confusion. "Bridget? Wait. That's your principal, right?" She nodded. "Maybe we need to back up. When did you find out? Have you been to the doctor? What do I need to do to support you both? How are you feeling?" The questions that filled my mind threatened to spill out all at once.

Maggie watched me with something like astonishment on her face. She sat quietly for a moment, not answering me. I squeezed her waist, trying to reassure her anyway I could.

"Cole," she whispered.

"Cole?" I asked, raising an eyebrow.

She gave me a small smile. "Somehow this feels like a Cole, not Sully, kind of conversation."

I laughed. "We've been down this road before."

She smiled as she shook her head. "I truly am sorry about all this. I'm on the pill, but I'd had the stomach flu the week before and apparently should have been more prepared—"

I interrupted by leaning forward and lightly kissing her forehead. "Let me stop you right there, Maggie. I don't blame you. There were two of us in that bedroom, remember? And I had the broken condom, right? While not planned in any way, I don't regret what we did, baby or no baby. And let me just say, I'd never regret having a baby with you. So move past that right now, okay?"

Maggie kept her eyes on me as she took a deep calming breath. "Thanks. And I can quickly answer the questions you just ran through. Yep, Bridget is my principal. I'm three weeks late today, roughly, which equates to somewhere around seven weeks when looking at a pregnancy term. Today I bought a test on my lunch break. I took it after school because I couldn't wait anymore, and she happened to find me as I was having a mini meltdown. And I have no idea what I need beyond to stop crying so easily. I think I've cried more today than I have in the past ten years combined." She paused for a moment before continuing, seeming to gather some strength. "Strike that. I do need something."

It was ridiculous the joy I got at the idea of helping her. "What? Anything."

"I'm starving." She gave me big brown eyes.

I smiled at her. "This I can handle. Do you have any food in this place, or is it a barren wasteland like the last time Emma and I were here?"

I laughed as she gave me a small eye roll. "It wasn't a wasteland. I just only go shopping once a week."

"Condiments, Maggie. You didn't even have condiments." I popped up off the couch to check out what she really had to work with. I opened her refrigerator, happy to see that she had more food in here than last time.

"Well, mayo makes me squeamish ever since I got sick on tuna salad one summer. And I have no idea why I didn't have anything else other than I prefer to eat at the brewery," she said to my back as I moved to the kitchen. Looking over my shoulder at her, she grabbed the throw to wrap around her shoulders and followed me over to the kitchen.

"Do you have pasta or Arborio rice?" I scanned what she had available.

Looking in one of her cabinets, she pulled out a box of mini rigatoni. "Does this work for what you're thinking?"

"Yep." I grabbed it and placed it on the counter,

dumping some chopped pancetta, mushrooms, half an onion, cream, and parmesan on the counter.

"My mouth is watering already. What are you thinking?" she asked. "And how quickly will we be eating?"

"Well, I usually make risotto with this stuff, but I think it would work with pasta too." I nodded my head to the counter, grabbing a skillet.

"Want me to make a salad?" Maggie asked.

I gave her what I hoped was a firm look. "Mags, I'm taking care of you tonight. You've had a shit day, and knowing you, you've been wondering if you were pregnant for three weeks, convincing yourself you weren't and freaking a bit the whole time. Sit your ass on that stool and chill. Want some tea?"

Maggie closed her eyes and blew out a sigh. "Well, you aren't wrong. It was a shit day. That being said, it's looking up. And peppermint please."

I immediately looked over to her. "Are you feeling sick?"

"Good Lord, this is going to be a long nine months if you're going to stress over everything," she grumbled. "No, I just like peppermint."

I shook my head at her and headed over to where she stored her tea. Maggie grabbed her phone out of her purse and hooked us up with some music. The next hour passed easily. I let the conversation move away from the pregnancy and the two of us, sensing Maggie needed some normalcy, at least for an hour or so.

As we were cleaning up the dishes after dinner, the topic once again returned to the one I'd let drop. "Did you get a chance to schedule a doctor appointment today with all the craziness?"

"I sent a request through the hospital's website. I haven't checked my email to see if they replied before they closed for the night," she explained. "I'm hoping the folks in scheduling saw my note about getting the appointment either in my doc's early-morning slot before school or after four. I can't take off during the day for the next week. There's just too much to do to wrap up the school year."

"Want to check now? If it's okay with you, I'd really like to go with you to the appointments," I asked quietly, not wanting to alarm her at my desire to be involved. In some ways she reminded me of an easily spooked horse my grandfather had worked on rehabilitating when I was a kid.

Her eyebrows went up.

"What?" I asked.

Maggie's cheeks colored. "Um, it's just a gynecologist appointment isn't something I thought I'd be experiencing with you. They're a bit, well, exposing."

I nodded. I'd never been to one, clearly, but I knew a little about them. "I understand, and if you don't want me there, I'll respect that. But if I can go, even to a few, I'd like to."

Maggie watched me for a moment. "Sure," she said, moving toward her phone. "Let me check my email."

She sat for a few minutes, scrolling through what I assumed were her emails. "They said I have a slot after school on Monday." She looked up at me. "Does that work for you?" She held her phone out for me to look at the email.

I scanned it as well, then grabbed my phone. I opened the calendar app and added the appointment to my calendar before handing Maggie back her phone. I slid my phone in my pocket and leaned back against the counter.

"Sully?"

I snorted. "Sully again, not Cole?"

A laugh burst out before she could help it. "Cole is for serious conversations, or if I'm pissed, and then I'd need to break out the 'Cole Patrick Sullivan.' I was just going to ask what you were thinking about."

Before I could stop myself, I grabbed her hand and kissed it, placing it back on the counter after I realized what I did. Space, Sullivan, give the woman space. "I just wondered what you were doing tomorrow night? Want to come to The Homestead for dinner? I'm on, but I could break away to eat with you if you wanted."

She looked worried for a minute. What was that about? Maggie looked down before finally meeting my eyes. "Um, Sully, I'm down for eating at the brewery anytime. But I want to make sure I'm clear. Just because I'm pregnant does not mean we've automatically become a couple, okay?"

A flash of irritation welled up in me before I could tamp it down. "What the hell, Mags. Why not? We already established we're attracted to each other. We've found out that there is some hot-as-fuck chemistry between us. And now we're having a baby together. Why wouldn't we explore becoming a couple?"

It sounded like Maggie growled. Interesting.

"Sully, we aren't going to screw this up. This baby needs a mom and dad that are on good terms, not two people who jumped into a relationship out of a sense of obligation and then had the relationship implode on them. I'm not willing to chance that friendship."

"You were four weeks ago," I pointed out.

"Momentary insanity," she growled again.

I pushed away from the counter and walked toward her living room. I needed a breath. Running my hands through my hair, I fought to get a grip on my emotions. After I counted to ten, and then again, I turned to see Maggie fighting a smile. "What?"

She clearly tried not to laugh. "It's not funny. I mean, I

know it isn't. It's just you had the same posture on a regular basis when Emma and I were going through high school and you were trying to keep us out of trouble."

I shook my head at her. "That's because you were always convincing her to break out of her mold." I took a breath. "Okay, we're just going to table this relationship conversation for a bit because I can't rationalize with you when you're being you. Never could."

"Hey!"

"Moving on, we'll proceed for the moment as what we've always been, friends. And FYI, this friend is spending the night tonight."

"Fine," she bit out, throwing her arm out toward the couch. "You know where everything is."

"Nope, friend. We have a kid growing inside you right now. I'm not saying this is what has to happen every night, but tonight I really want to be in your bed, next to the two of you." Glancing at her expression, I raised up my hands in reply, "No, no, nothing is happening. We're just sleeping. I just want to be there." I paused, looking down at her worn carpet, then meeting her eyes again. "Please, Mags?"

Maggie's expression softened. "Sure, Sully. You can stay, but clothes on, your side of the bed."

I gave her a big smile. "Yes, drillmaster."

A few hours later, I lay on my side facing Maggie who was sprawled out on her back. She'd growled at me when I climbed into bed in my boxer briefs but hadn't fought when I pointed out how uncomfortable sleeping in my jeans and shirt would be. I hadn't missed the heat that flared in her eyes but figured we could tackle that issue later, maybe literally. It had only taken her a little bit to fall asleep, but I couldn't drift off. There were far too many things on my mind.

Sliding closer to Maggie, I looked at her tiny pajama shorts and tiny tank. Good Lord, she was amazing. My body begged to do more than sleep, but I ignored it. Maggie's curves were on full display in all their glory, although her stomach didn't give any indication of the enormous transition that was underway. Well, at least not yet.

Moving ever so gently, I slid up her tank so her stomach was bare and laid my hand over it. I slid down and gently kissed her belly before lifting my head up an inch or two to whisper to our unborn child. "Hey, kid. I'm your dad." I glanced up, making sure Maggie was still out. "You have no idea how lucky you are. You have the best mom in the world. We can't wait to meet you, but make sure you're easy on her, you hear?"

I lightly kissed her stomach again before settling back in the bed. I glanced up at the ceiling, wondering how quickly sleep would find me. I grabbed a spare pillow to pull over my face with my arm draped across it, soaking in the feeling of being here with Maggie.

## 6

## LOOKING UP

**Maggie**

I rolled up my yoga mat, nerves threatening to overwhelm me. Moving as slowly as I thought I could get away with, I slid the mat away and took a fortifying breath. It was now or never, but I suddenly had a strong desire to live in the unknown. Goose bumps popped out on my arms, and I could sense her hovering. Chancing it, I glanced up and found that I was right. Emma stood there, watching me with eyes just like her brother's. Damn. We'd known each other for over twenty years, so I could read the expression on her face at a glance. She was concerned and trying hard not to pepper me with questions or take over with some problem solving. I could make her wait, but why prolong the inevitable?

"Want to get some coffee? Looks like Allyson is getting ready to open," I asked, hiding my inner amusement at the impatience rolling off her in waves.

I wandered over to the counter where Allyson was getting the machines ready to make coffee for anyone lingering after yoga. Glancing over my shoulder, I watched as Emma seemed to have a conversation with herself before deciding to follow me. I briefly wondered how long I could prolong the conversation she was dying to have. Not only was it a bit amusing to see her trying to figure out how to bring this up, I really wasn't sure how to share this news.

Leaning against the counter, I glanced around the space. Emma's neighbor, Lou, had opened the Sanctuary coffee shop in the town's original Catholic church when the congregation had outgrown the space and they built a new one decades ago. The coffee shop was small, cozy, with high ceilings. Lou had run this place for years, and we liked to joke that her attempts of world, or at least town, domination had been headquartered at this very counter.

A year or so ago, however, Lou had hung up her apron when Verdell, her husband, made his own move toward retirement from the county's sheriff department so the two of them could travel more and visit their kids. Allyson had moved to town and purchased this place and, before she was even a year in, opened a satellite location at the local park outside town, Highland Woods.

Emma and I tried to attend the Saturday-morning yoga class that rotated between the two locations. There was also a class that met on Mondays and Wednesdays at the community building. Kristine ran the classes at a variety of locations because she didn't want to be tied to a studio just yet. The nomadic feel of the classes worked for me on a variety of levels.

When Emma had originally mentioned yoga to me, I thought she was nuts. But after a solid year of classes, I couldn't imagine life without it. Teaching can be stressful, and yoga had helped me to find some peace to let go of things that would have bothered me in the past. That being said, yoga was amazing, but nothing was going to eliminate the stress that was currently devouring me.

I ran my hands over the old wood of the counter, gathering my courage. Sully and I had agreed that this didn't need to be a secret. He was headed to tell his parents this morning and agreed I could share the news with Emma, but the knot of fear that she'd somehow be angry filled my stomach and took hold of my heart. This fear had no basis in reality. Emma was one of the kindest souls I'd ever met, but the worry about how she'd react to this news was eating me alive.

"How about I start?" Emma asked me quietly, placing her hand over mine. I met her eyes, raising a brow. Her brown eyes were filled with warmth. "Max told me after you left last night he had a gut feeling that the new journey you have suddenly found yourself on might be tied to my brother."

I widened my eyes in surprise, and they filled with not a small number of tears. Damn, Max was far more perceptive than I gave him credit for. "How..." Where did I start?

I could see emotion dance across Emma's face as she locked her gaze on mine. "Max wasn't certain, but putting two and two together when you both were off for the past month added to Sully's mindset when he swung by last night looking for you, well, is he right?"

I braced, unsure as to what on earth I should even begin to tell her. Did I tell her about a crush that began when we were kids, but I'd hid behind jokes all this time? Did I tell her about a hot night in the sack with her big bro? That seemed to be in poor taste. How do you tell someone you've had the hots for their sibling for years? Hmm. Maybe we could take a pause so I could go give Max a call. Surely he'd have some advice on how I needed to proceed. Sully hadn't punched him when Max and Emma had hooked up a few weeks ago, so there was that.

"Maggie. Earth to Maggie..." I glanced back at Emma as she squeezed my hand. "So it's true, you and Sully?" Her eyes looked a little moist too if I wasn't mistaken.

I gave a small nod.

"When? For how long? Why didn't you tell me?" At that I noticed that while she was trying to hide it, there was a little wounded expression hiding in there. Fucking fabulous. On top of everything else, I'd potentially hurt my closest friend.

Taking a fortifying breath, I glanced around, ensuring we were truly cocooned in our own little world over here. While Highland Falls wasn't huge, it did excel at the speed at which gossip could travel. Make that gossip that one of the town's middle school teachers was knocked up by the local brewery owner, and we might approach warp speeds. I didn't need that yet. Even though we were in the clear, to be safe I tugged Emma down the bar to where it met the corner of the café. I closed my eyes, gathered some courage, and decided to take life by the balls, as it were.

"I've had a crush on your brother since I met him." Pause, keep going Mags. I could do this. Emma's incredulous look threatened to make me laugh as she sputtered, trying to talk.

I held up my hands to hold her off. "I'm sorry I didn't tell you. We could do a year-long psych study on why I didn't, but I think I'd be ashamed as to what that said about myself, so moving on." I noticed Emma had fallen silent now, her mouth was hanging open a bit. Well, balls out, finish up. "I swear, Em, I never thought anything would happen. We aren't a happily ever after, don't worry. I'm not going to get hurt when this crashes and burns, and neither is Sully. A few weeks back, about five to be exact, you and I drank a shit ton of tequila. Sully drove me home. Now we're here."

I knew Emma's pissed-off expression when I saw it. Man, she was going to be a great mom to teens. I worked hard to school my own expression and waited it out. It really was her turn. "My brother slept with you when you were drunk? I am so going to kick his ass, but I might have to get in line behind my mom—"

"No, no. Please don't kick his ass. Your bro was, as always, a total gentleman. He brought me to his house to sleep it off, and then in the morning, I got a little excitable and he joined in. I'm not getting into the details with you—"

"Thanks. I haven't eaten yet, and my stomach is weak..." Her words were drowned out by the whir and crunch of a coffee grinder thankfully saving us from the awkward moment.

"Whatever, but we were doubly protected. Or we thought we were. But life is filled with cosmic jokes, and this happened to be one of them."

"And so I'm going to be an aunt?"

"You're going to be an aunt."

Emma whispered, pulling me in for a hug. "And you're going to be a mom?"

My head dropped to her shoulder as I tightened my arms around her.

"Yes." My heart raced with that thought. What did I know about being a mom?

"And Sully is going to be a dad?"

I closed my eyes. "Yep," I managed to get out.

"Holy shit."

I nodded from my spot wrapped in Emma's arms, my own circling her waist as she rocked me slowly. Holy shit indeed.

We stood there for a few minutes. I wasn't sure what Emma was doing, but I was taking a moment to get myself in order. I needed to catch my breath and stop the tears that threatened to spill out anytime I had a hit of emotion. It was ridiculous.

Finally Emma pulled back. She glanced down the counter at Allyson. "Aly, two vanilla lattes please." Allyson nodded at her and Emma swiveled to look at me. "Shit, I didn't think. Is that okay? I have no idea what you can and can't have when pregnant."

I shrugged. "I'm thinking coffee is okay, as long as I'm not mainlining it all day long. If I can't have it, we're in for a world of hurt over the next thirty-some weeks."

Emma sank down onto a bar stool as she scanned my face, then down to my toes before meeting my eyes. "Mags," she whispered, "you're pregnant."

I pulled out a stool and sat next to her. "I know," I whispered.

Allyson walked down and sat the drinks in front of us. Clearly reading our body language, she gave us space and headed back to the counter. Bless.

"So five weeks ago was when both you and Sully were acting like moody teens. This was why?"

I nodded and dropped my chin to my hands. The murmur of the café surrounded me, and I stared at the raised area where the altar would have been housed when this was a church. I could use a little guidance here. Maybe I should send up a prayer? Couldn't hurt. Closing my eyes, I thought over the past month. Honestly, I'd behaved like a bitch. Sully had reached out time and time again, and I'd refused to talk. I'd known him as long as I'd known Emma. He was one of the closest friends I'd had in my life, much less my closest male friend. What had I been thinking?

The answer was easy. I was scared to death.

A slamming door and a warm summer breeze pulled me out of the downward spiral. When I looked up at Emma, I found that she was watching me.

"Did you say something?" I asked.

"Nope. Waiting for you to work this out in your head," she said with a smile. Damn if she didn't know me well.

Okay. Time to spill. "Let's do the Spark Notes version of what happened. Sound good?"

"Perfect. Go."

"Well, you were there for the tequila night," I began.

"Not doing that again anytime soon. I still feel the headache."

"Clearly." I gestured to my belly. "At any rate, you know Sully drove me home that night. Before we got there, I asked to go back to his place."

Emma looked confused. "Why?"

I shrugged, not really wanting to explain to her the lonely feeling that had overwhelmed me. "Not sure. At any rate, in the morning things happened. It was awesome"—Emma wrinkled her nose—"and the condom broke. At that point I realized I'd had the stomach flu just a week or so before and puked up everything including my pills for two days and..."

"You freaked." Emma looked at me knowingly.

"Yeah. I had Sully take me home immediately. Emma, I have to make sure you know he was great. He tried to talk to me then and later, but I was in my head and panicking. I couldn't talk to him then." Guilt hit me so hard it threatened to take my breath away. Why had I acted so horribly to him? Damn, I prided myself on being far more mature than I'd shown for the past month.

"So when did you begin to suspect you were with child?" The corner of Emma's mouth tipped up.

"*With child?* What is this, the Dark Ages?"

"Answer the question, my friend."

I paused to take a long drink of coffee. Damn, Allyson made it hard to want my coffee at home. This was just so much better. Looking over at Emma, I figured I'd get this all out quickly so we could get on with our day. "I immediately jumped to worrying that I was pregnant when the condom broke because that just felt like something that would be my luck. Then I went and behaved horribly to your brother. Last week I was beyond late, so I started thinking it wasn't all in my head. It could be reality. I went out and bought a test Friday and took it after school."

"By yourself? I'm so sorry, Mags. That must have been horrible." Emma's hand squeezed mine.

I took a moment to look around. The Sanctuary now more closely resembled a coffee shop versus a yoga studio. Tables with mismatched chairs had been put back into their spots. Armchairs were taken up by yoga attendees as well as folks just out for an early Saturday morning. The aroma of coffee was surrounding me like a blanket as was the quiet hum of conversations. While I was anxious about what was ahead for me, I also felt content, at peace. That realization was surprising.

Looking back to Emma, I gave her a reassuring smile. "I wasn't alone for long. Bridget found me, and we talked it out."

Emma nodded. "I'm so glad, Mags, but I hope you know I would have been happy to be there. Anytime, anywhere."

I squeezed her hand. "Well, Sully is telling your parents this morning, so I might need your support more soon if that doesn't go well."

Emma dropped her head back and let loose a head-turning laugh, which was a welcome sound. Wiping away tears, she looked at me. "Are you for real? You've met my mom, Mags, more than a few times. Anna Sullivan is going to be over the moon. You might need help holding her back, if anything."

"Truth."

"And your summer road trip? Is that still on?" Emma watched me, nibbling on her lower lip.

"I'm guessing it is." I knew she wasn't thrilled about this idea, which her current expression just highlighted. I had a headache just thinking about trying to juggle doctor appointments with my travels, but a large part of me felt like if I didn't leave this summer, I never would. Like I was running out of time, which didn't make any damn sense. Looking back to Emma, I realized I'd have to share at some point that this trip was now having the dual role of allowing me to travel and pick somewhere to move for next year. Damn, she was going to be pissed.

Emma watched me for a moment and arched her brow, her sign indicating she knew I had more on my mind, but she wasn't pushing me. Yet. She turned to face the counter and took a swig of her coffee. Sighing, she looked at me over her shoulder. "What's today on a scale?"

We'd used a scale of the day since middle school. I thought about it for a moment. Still needed to think about my summer trip, my move. Still needed to share that news with Emma. Still pregnant. Still no idea what to think about that. But I was here. The sun was shining. "Hmm, the day is looking up. I'd say we've hit a solid eight."

Emma gave me a smile as she turned back to the counter. I sat, shoulder to shoulder with her, and relaxed for the first time in weeks. Yep, things were looking up for sure. We'd get to the rest of it later.

## 7

## HOLDING ON TO DREAMS

***Sully***

Glancing at my parents sitting across the kitchen island with their coffee, pancakes stacked up in front of them, I was suddenly grateful that they were as active as they were. If not, this truth bomb I just dropped might have resulted in twin heart attacks. As it was, it seemed that they had just both fallen into silent shock together.

Lee and Anna Sullivan were, I thought most of the time, the best parents a kid could have asked for. Tough but stubborn. Fair but swift to dispense justice as they saw fit. Dad farmed, and Mom stayed home when we were kids. She was a substitute teacher in the local schools after that. Now, in their late fifties, they both worked part-time. Dad farmed as additional help when needed, but at this point he'd turned over a good deal of the work on our land. I occasionally did some work helping at the fields when my schedule allowed, but Dad mainly hired Richard as needed. Richard was a young farmer a few fields over that also farmed for Max. My parents had enough set aside for retirement but still liked to keep busy. Mom subbed if she felt like it that month or if she liked the grade level. They both loved to travel and did that much of the winter, only returning when there was no snow on the ground and planting season was imminent.

"Mom, Dad?" We might as well get on with it. "Guys?"

Dad blinked a few times, then grabbed Mom's hand, locking eyes with her before turning back to me. He cleared his throat, and I braced. I absolutely hated disappointing them, always had. "Well, Cole. I'm not sure we know what to say. So Maggie is pregnant? Our Maggie?"

I had to smile. God, I loved them. They'd pulled Max and Maggie into their family years ago, and I could've predicted that this was going to go down with ensuring that she was okay first. That's all right. That's how they had raised us too.

"Yep, our Maggie is pregnant." My gut clenched, waiting for their reaction while my mind was also miles away at the brewery, where I was heading next to meet with Jake and talk about moving ahead with the canning business.

Or not.

Mom looked back at my dad, then back to me. "And you're the father?"

At this point I looked down at the counter. It was hard to look at your mom and acknowledge that you'd had sex, though she was aware I hadn't been a virgin for quite some time considering she found my stash of condoms back in high school. Staring at the butcher-block countertops, I let it out a quiet reply. "Yep, I am the father."

"Oh my God. I'm going to be a grandmother!" I was unprepared for her squeal of delight and looked up as she threw her arms up in the air and raced around the island.

Reaching my side, she quickly squeezed any air I'd had in my lungs right out. Holy shit.

"Easy, Anna," Dad said, moving over to where we stood. Mom looked back, and I felt like I had the wind knocked out of me just looking at the happy tears she had spilling over her lower lids.

Dad laid one of his huge hands on my shoulder. "Cole, it's none of our business, but where do you and Maggie stand? I think I can speak for your mom and myself in that we had no idea you two were together."

"Total shock!" Mom interjected.

God, that was so like her. She was all in, filled with joy, and only seeing the positive. Not the shit that was swirling around me. "Dad, Mom, you two are going to have to slow way down. Maggie is feeling rather uneasy about all this, and whether I'd like to pursue a relationship or not, that isn't where she's at right now. And you both know that while what's going on with your first grandchild is totally your business because Mom would never stand for anything else—"

"You're damn right I wouldn't. So you're saying I shouldn't call Maggie up and offer to let her wear my wedding gown?" Mom had a familiar mischievous glint in her eyes.

Hell.

"No, Mom. No calling her. Don't pester her. Don't hover around her. Don't freak her out. This is Maggie—as you said, *our Maggie*. Any excessive attention and she is going to burrow in and keep us all out." I felt a bit like my heart was racing. My mom was the sweetest and kindest person I knew, but damn if she didn't like to insert herself in any spot she felt needed. If she descended on Maggie now,

Maggie would think I set it up, and then any progress I'd made last night would be gone in a flash.

Mom wrapped one arm around Dad, leaning her head on his shoulder, and looked back at me as my dad watched me with a calculated look. "Cole, I'm teasing. Of course I won't bombard Maggie with maternal love. That isn't something she grew up with, and as much as I've tried to teach her over the years, it isn't something she feels like she deserves. We're still working on that. But I will let her know we're here. This is going to be a scary time for her. Maggie is going to be facing stuff she'd rather ignore. And," she reached out, grabbing my chin and tilting it to face her just like she did years ago, "I hope you are aware we will be here for you." I tried to tug my chin away, but she held firm. "I realize this isn't the journey you saw yourself on yet, but it is the one that is meant for you. You are going to be a father and a damn fine one at that."

At that, my dad was done waiting to speak. "Talk to us, son. Where's your mind at?"

I moved away from my parents, and my gaze drifted to look out the windows. I heard my reply of being fine without even realizing I'd said anything.

"Cole," my dad said, moving to my side and allowing an arm to lie across my shoulders. "It's natural to be thrown, son. This wasn't in the cards, at least, not yet."

I shook my head, clearing out all thoughts of business. I'd deal with that soon enough. I slowly stood, wrapping one arm around my dad's waist, and used my other arm to tug my mom to us. They, in turn, wrapped their arms around me. When I spoke, it was into my dad's shoulder. "God, I love you two."

Dad clasped the back of my head, "And we you, Cole Patrick Sullivan. This isn't planned, but you are in for the ride of your life. Buckle up, kid. It's going to be an adventure."

My heart thudded in my chest. No, this was absolutely not the journey I saw myself on yet. I'd been ready to start something with Maggie, yes. The brewery finally didn't require all my attention, but parenthood? In a few years, absolutely. Right now? Scary for sure. I wanted kids, always had, but trying to be there like my dad had been for us, I didn't even remotely know how to do it, but I was going to figure it out. And to start, I had to make some business decisions, even if they weren't what I wanted.

I looked back to my dad who was watching me with his hawklike stare. It was the same one from when I was a kid and certain that he could read my mind. Apparently, that skill was still with him, because he squeezed my shoulder. "You don't need all the answers now, son. You know that, right?"

I gave him a small nod, trying to reassure him. He returned the greeting, if somewhat uncertain. "Right. Anna, Cole, these pancakes can't go to waste, They're too damn good."

We all moved back to our plates and dug in. I took a bite and looked outside, wondering how the conversation with Emma and Maggie was going. Looking back to my mom and dad, I saw them both watching me with worried expressions. I wasn't sure how to reassure them. I'd need to reassure myself first.

After pancakes and helping my parents with some chores on the farm, I steered my bike back to town and the brewery, the pancakes sitting in my stomach like a rock. Jake was pouring beer when I walked in and headed toward the bar area. I glanced around at the light afternoon crowd and felt the feelings of gratitude that I always did when entering the brewery that we'd created.

It had been eleven years since Jake and I met back in college at the brewery near my university. Our friendship's foundation was formed over late nights at work, blowing off steam about my college courses for my business degree, and Jake's long days working in construction. The brewmaster had taken us under his wing and shown us the ropes. We began working on our own beers in those first years after college, screwing with recipes until we began finding a few that we thought showed promise. The past decade found us getting some recognition for our beer at competitions while establishing our brewery in my hometown.

Originally, I'd never dreamed we'd open here in Highland Falls. My hometown wasn't large, and I wasn't sure if it could support what we'd envisioned. When Jake and I'd first began this dream, I was certain we'd open at one of the nearby college towns in downstate Illinois where the restaurant business was more stable. However, when the old barn near the downtown area of Highland became available, the two of us couldn't ignore how amazing the space could be. With Jake's experience in construction, we were able to do a lot of the work ourselves using other licensed contractors Jake had known from his job.

Years ago when the town had been settled, the barn sat as an outbuilding for one of the original founders. Over the years the town had built up around it until the quirky property had stood just outside the business district of Highland. The barn had been foreclosed on, and I was certain that the bank had assumed someone would buy it and tear it down for the land, but Jake and I'd seen possibility.

Over the course of two long years, we'd turned an old barn into a cozy brewpub with a space for the brewery equipment, a kitchen, a dining room that had a combination of tables and sitting nooks. In the nooks there were couches, armchairs, and low tables. Winding through that you came to the bar area, backed with barn wood and warm lighting.

As I took in the crowd, I simply felt gratitude and more than a sense of relief. It'd been just over four and a half years since we opened, and we were operating comfortably, finally. Both sets of our parents had helped finance the place with the two of us, a small loan from the Main Street program, and a loan from the bank. It took the first three years to feel secure in the notion that we'd be able to make a go of it *and* pay them all back, but we were finally there. Monday we were supposed to sign the papers for our larger loan from Main Street. That's what our road trip had been about, stepping into canning and local distribution of our beers instead of only selling in growlers. Before the news from Maggie, I'd been confident we should go forward and do it. Now I had reservations. I was concerned that maybe we needed to play it conservatively for a while. Whatever we did, I needed to talk to Jake.

"Yo, Sully, Black Hole Sun?" Jake grabbed a pint glass and headed toward the tap for my favorite beer we brewed, a kick-ass IPA.

"Thanks, Jake." I gratefully took the beer from Jake with a chin lift. "Jake, can you have Daryl take over for a bit? Need to have a word." I nodded over to a high-top in the corner of the bar area before the dining room.

"Sure." Jake moved to talk to Daryl before heading to the table.

As he pulled out a stool to sit next to me, he gave me a once-over before taking a drink of his own beer. Then he glanced back at the bar and proceeded to hunch down a bit in his stool.

Interesting.

I looked over at the bar to see a woman who'd just taken a seat. Looking back at Jake, who looked like he'd like to disappear into the ground, then back to the bar, I grinned. "She yours?" I asked.

"Shut it," Jake muttered. "Not mine."

The woman was totally eyeing up Jake, but she didn't seem to be his type. For one, she was tall and had killer curves. From what I could tell, Jake didn't like a lot of height in the women he dated. Though I'd say Jake and I were around the same height at six foot four, so it wouldn't have been a problem. However, it was the neediness vibe that I was getting from her that made me certain that this was not the girl for Jake. "You know her?" I asked.

"Met her at one of the bars in Bloomington a few weeks back, and we talked for a bit. Let's just say she wants more than I do, but she hasn't gotten the message. Now, moving on, as much as I love this little chat, I'm assuming you had something you wanted over here. What's up?" Jake asked.

I debated for a moment how to proceed, then just thought, *fuck it. Get on with it.* "Well, I don't think there is much of a way to ease into this one. Maggie is pregnant with my kid." I registered Jake's head nod and figured he was either supremely relaxed or he'd overheard some of my conversation with Max when we'd driven back and had started to put some things together. I continued, "I don't know much about this shit, but I know she's early. We're telling my family and you for now, so I'd appreciate if you could keep this between us for a bit. And no, we're not together."

Jake watched me carefully. "Well, fuck. Are we toasting this news?" he asked. "Hell yeah, let's toast." We toasted our glasses together as his smile grew. "You're going to be a dad. Shit, man. That's wild."

My phone vibrated. Pulling it out, I glanced to see a text from Emma.

**Emma:** *Congrats, big bro.*

I looked up to Jake. "Need to text Emma real quick."

Jake glanced over at Daryl. "No worries. Need to get behind the bar for a sec. Be back in a few."

I looked back at my phone and debated how to talk to my sister about the fact that I was going to be a dad. I shook my head. Still mind-blowing. Looking around, I soaked in the hum of the people scattered around this place. I saw familiar faces and folks that must be visiting town. This was good. This place was good. I began to feel more reassured. Jake wanted to expand the business, but we'd built something amazing here. Canning could wait. We needed to rely on our foundation before reaching for more.

**Me:** *Hope it was okay that Maggie told you instead of me.*

**Emma:** *Yeah, she said you were talking to the parental units. Go okay?*

**Me:** *About how you'd expect.*

**Emma:** *Shock, acceptance, and Mom wants to plan a wedding?*

I chuckled. Yep, she had Mom pegged.

**Me:** *Well, she talked about Maggie wearing her dress, so yeah, about like that.*

**Emma:** *Hell, no. They got married in the late 70s. Just, no.*

I raised an eyebrow while considering my sister's text. Unless she knew something I didn't, the fact that my mom's dress was beyond dated would have been the least of reasons that Maggie wouldn't want it, much less want me.

Jake reappeared and collapsed into his stool. "Needed to change out a keg. Thinking our new brew will be able to go soon?"

I nodded, thinking of where we were in the process. "A week or so."

Jake ran a hand through his short hair. "Okay, man. I have a ton to check off before the dinner crowd tonight. Several parties are descending on us. Thrilled about the kid. Anything else?"

I stalled, taking a drink of my beer. Fuck, this was going to hurt. But it was like a Band-Aid, right? Better to just rip it off. Meeting his eyes, I said the words I dreaded, "We need to hold off on the loan."

Jake was mid drink and froze, his eyes finding mine, then narrowing. Slowly, he put his glass down. "Repeat that?"

I dropped my head, my eyes not even focusing on the old wood tabletops. It was too hard to meet his eyes. "I don't want to sign off on the loan on Monday."

Silence. Laughter came from the table to our right. Daryl called out to our hostess to our left. Music filled the background, but I couldn't even focus on the song or band. I hated disappointing people, and letting down the ones I was closest too was even worse, but this was the right call.

Gathering some courage, I lifted my head. Jake's expression was a mixture of anger and hurt. "I'm sorry, Jake. We thought this was the next logical step, but I think we need to get a bit more in savings, have some time where we're comfortable and not stretched so thin, then we can go ahead."

Jake stood, not breaking eye contact, and leaned in so I

could hear his low voice over the growing noise around us. "Bullshit, Sullivan. You and I both know what this is. You're afraid. Maggie Jameson has thrown you for a loop, and you're pulling back, playing it safe. And that would be fine, if we weren't already doing great. This is the smart step, the next step for us, and until twenty-four hours ago, you knew that too." He took a deep breath and looked up at the ceiling, trying to gather some patience before meeting my gaze again. "This is a huge mistake, a great loan and a damn amazing opportunity for us." He shook his head and pushed back from the table before leaving with a parting shot, "But fine. Make all the decisions for us. I'm just not going to sit here and listen to you spin these crap excuses into gold. I have better things to do." With that, he stalked off toward the tanks.

Damn. That could have gone better.

## 8

## SECRETS UNCOVERED

**Maggie**

Running the trails at Highland Woods was exactly what I needed this morning. Last night Emma and I had stopped by the brewery for a while. Sully, Jake, and Max had been there. It was like one more in-your-face moment proving that my life was heading for a dramatic change. First, things with Sully were awkward for all involved. We weren't together romantically but were having a baby. How do you address that? He and Jake had been off too, which was strange. Then the kicker... no beer, no tequila, no wine? I mean, I wasn't a huge drinker, but that was a tough one. On top of that, after I drank my coffee at the Sanctuary on Saturday, which had been delicious, my stomach began to roll at the smell. Surely coffee and I wouldn't be on the outs for the rest of the pregnancy. That would just be cruel.

Sully had asked if I wanted to leave and find someplace to talk more last night, but I had begged off. What else there was to really say right now. It wasn't like he could do anything. The deed had already been done, so to say. He'd settled for pulling me aside before I left, asking how I was doing and checking on our appointment time for today. When we'd talked, even for the moment, I'd gotten emotional.

*Sully tipped my chin up to meet his eyes. "Hey, hey. What's going on? I'm sorry, Mags. I didn't mean to make you cry."*

*I let my forehead drop to his chest, hating the feelings of weakness that I had right then. "I was just really looking forward to my trip this summer."*

*"I have no idea if your trip is a big deal or not. Talk to the doctor tomorrow? I honestly don't know what is involved at this early stage. Maybe it's no big deal." He rubbed my back, trying to soothe me.*

*I mumbled from my spot pressed into his chest. "But it's not fair to you if I stay away all summer, right?"*

*Sully rubbed my shoulders, which felt amazing. "Mags, sometimes you need to put yourself first. We're not worried about me right now. Let's just table this until the doctor appointment tomorrow. Then we'll know better what we're doing, okay?"*

*I nodded. We stood there in silence. Then a thought popped into my head. "Oh shit!"*

*"What?" He asked.*

*"I sublet my duplex anyway for the summer, and my next lease doesn't start until August. I have to move out next week." I thunked my head against his chest multiple times. "What am I going to do?"*

*Sully cleared his throat. I looked up, and he smiled. "Babe, you've got my baby in you. You're not going to be homeless. If you end up staying in town, you can stay with me."*

*"With you?" my voice creaked. "Are you just trying to get me back in your bed?"*

*Sully put a finger under my chin as he tipped it up to meet his eyes. "Babe, I'm just saying I have an extra room. It is yours anytime you need it. Understood?"*

*I studied his expression for a moment, then whispered, "Understood." Leaning forward, I brushed my lips across his, then wrapped my arms around his waist and settled in for a tight hug.*

*Sully returned my hug before whispering in my ear, "Mags, not that I'm complaining, but what was that for?"*

*My heart felt full, so I waited a minute before responding. "For being one of the good guys, Cole Sullivan. And the world needs more of the good guys."*

I'd waved off a ride home from anyone last night and walked, needing to sort out my own head, but it hadn't worked. By the time I got to my place, all I'd wanted to do was crawl into bed and sleep, exhaustion and stress getting the better of me. Typically, I got about six to seven hours a night and was good to go. Apparently, growing this little bean meant that my mattress and I were going to become closely acquainted. Gracious.

This morning I'd driven out to Highland Woods for a run before school. My head was just not in the right place, and with five days of school left, I needed to get in the game. Turning onto the yellow trail, which was a two-mile loop out to the river and some small falls, my mind was filled with questions. This was one of my favorite trails, flat and peaceful with great scenery, exactly what I needed today.

The trails out here were fabulous, but you had to be on the lookout for uneven ground or the roots that would jut out unexpectedly. The air smelled fresh, what I associated in my brain with the smells of spring. The blue sky was cloudless. It was a gorgeous morning, if a bit warmer than

I'd expected. I ran, the quiet of my footfalls on the needle-covered trails giving me unexpected reassurance.

My appointment was in about nine hours. Nine hours and I'd know officially that I was having a baby. Sully's baby. Nine hours and I might have some answers as to how I'd be spending my summer. Nine hours.

I ran on.

The trail opened up, leading me toward the river. Glancing at my watch, I saw that I'd made it about a mile in. The trees were a little closer here, blocking out more of the sunlight. I worked on my breathing, trying to bring in more air, exhale my frustration.

I turned off the trail and moved down the side path that led to the falls. The sound of the water reached me before the sight did. The space opened up, and there were large rocks encircling a pond with water cascading over the farthest one. The sun was softly filtering through the trees, and the space brought a feeling of tranquility to me that I hadn't realized how badly I craved.

Breathless, I moved over to a flat rock that jutted out over the water, and I flopped down on my back on its surface, soaking in the warmth of the rocks as I drew my knees to my chest and rested my chin on them, stretching on my hamstrings. I looked up at the trees, letting them blur as my mind wandered.

Sully had asked me to move in with him. What did I do with that? I rocked back and forth, allowing my back to stretch a bit in what Kristine called happy baby pose. Pulling my legs to my chest again in a ball, I thought about my options. One, I could still go on my trip if my doc gave it the okay. Two, I could move in with Emma and Max. I was sure she'd offer it up. Three, I bet I could move in with Lee and Anna. Four, I could find another place to sublet. Five, Sully.

I looked off into the pond and watched the water for a moment. None of these options were ideal. Well, going on my trip was, right? I thought of the map I'd created in an old atlas of the places I wanted to go in the Midwest. I thought of my drive up to the northern part of Michigan that I'd mapped out to start with, camping out by the lake, away from the whispers of small towns and people who thought they knew your story. Was that all gone now?

More importantly, why didn't it sound as appealing as it had before?

As for the other options, living with a brand-new couple sounded like torture. Lee and Anna were amazing, but I had no desire to go back to living with parental figures. Finding a place to rent at this late notice would seriously dip into my nest egg. And then there was Sully.

Shaking my head, I slid off the rock. I didn't have a ton of time before I had to get to school. I ran back, eating up the distance to my car, my brain in a whirl. As I sorted through my thoughts, I wondered briefly if I should have gone with Sully last night. Those feelings of loneliness were back with a vengeance. I shook my head and let my legs pound my frustration into the ground. I still had a full day ahead of me and kids to teach.

Hours later, the knock at my door brought me back to the present and out of my daydream that was really more like a late afternoon, early evening nap. I rolled off the couch, tossing the cream throw over the arm, and stumbled toward the sound. Though the window I could see that Emma stood waiting for me.

Throwing the door open, I mumbled my hello as I trudged back to the couch.

"You look like hell," she said, closing the door behind her and moving to the kitchen.

Plopping back down on my couch, I tucked my legs under me and wrapped back up in my throw. "Sorry, babe. I'm just beat. Give me a minute, and I'll wake up fully and be present. While I do that, mind telling me why you're here?"

She glanced over at me, then down at the bags she was unloading on the counter. "Well…"

I looked over at her, then focused on the bags. "Umm, are those from The Homestead?"

The corner of her mouth turned up in a smirk. "Will my answer impact whether you actually eat the food?"

"Fuck, no. I'm starving. I just want to know who is being the hovering mother in tonight's scenario, you or your brother." I stood, wrapping the throw around me like a shawl, and made my way across the living room to my tiny kitchen.

"Oh, my big bro is totally the hovering mother here. Please tell him that when I can see his expression." Emma smiled, pulling down a few plates.

I glanced at the counter. Cheeseburgers, fries, and salad. "Shit!" I exclaimed, slamming a hand to my head. "Our yoga-night special, I completely forgot about class tonight."

"No worries, babe. It looks like you needed that nap far more than a bit of stretching. I swung by the brewery after class, and Sully mentioned you guys had gone to the doctor and you were exhausted. I told him I'd bring you food and take mine to go since he couldn't leave," she said as she loaded up her plate. "So, want to tell me how the appointment went?"

I loaded up my own plate, and we moved over to my

couch, taking opposite corners. I forked up a large bite of salad, letting out a groan. I mean, where had I ever had salad that made me moan? That was how good it was. Pausing for a moment, I looked at Emma. "Sully didn't just tell you everything already?"

Emma rolled her eyes, waving a fry at me. "Don't be bitchy. He told me I could talk to you but that everything was good." She regarded me as she took a bite of her burger. Not even bothering to get all her food down, she mumbled, "You should know that's all I care about."

"Good Lord, woman, chew." I shook my head at her, moving on to my cheeseburger. Taking a bite, I gave a happy sigh. The bean might be pissed about coffee, but this burger and salad was making me all kinds of happy. Hopefully the fries would find the same reception. "And of course you care about me and this little bean."

Emma leaned over, taking a swig of water, then continued. "I just meant I'm not here to get the skinny on you and my bro. I just wanted to know that all was well, that *you* were well."

I looked around my room, taking a moment to think as I munched on a fry. Yep, glorious. Emma loved me completely, but I wasn't sure how to have this conversation. While Emma had always been completely supportive of me, we didn't see the world through the same lens. It was impossible to get Emma to understand exactly where I was coming from no matter how much she wanted to be there for me.

"How about I start?" Emma interrupted my thoughts. She placed her plate on my trunk and stood up, stretching a bit before glancing around my living room. Her yoga pants were topped by a baggy T-shirt proclaiming her love of romance books, stating HEA ALL DAY. I shook my head as she headed over to my wall of boxes.

"So," she began, gesturing to the boxes. "Where are you heading first?"

Before I could even begin to think about stopping myself, the damn burst and tears flowed down my cheeks in rivers.

I felt Emma hurry back to the couch. She slid next to me, wrapping her arms tightly around my shoulders. "Mags, Mags. What is it?"

I growled, frustrated beyond comprehension. "Damn it all. I never cry, and now I'm becoming some type of tear factory. What the hell?" I asked, wiping my face off on my long sleeve. Poor Nathaniel Rateliff. He and the Night Sweats didn't deserve my snot and tears on their T-shirt.

"Just going out on a limb here, but I'd guess that might have something to do with hormones."

I sprang up from the couch, throwing my arms up. "How? How? Dr. Graham said that right now he isn't even the size of a bean. He's the size of a blueberry. A blueberry!" I paced back and forth in front of my couch. "How can something the size of a blueberry be making me cry, be making me so damn tired, be making me want to puke when I smell the nectar of the gods. I mean, how is that even possible?" With a loud growl of frustration, I fell back into the couch and crossed my arms over my chest.

Emma looked at me, an incredulous expression on her gorgeous face. "Well, are you done? One, I'm betting Dr. Graham told you that all this is normal. Two, do you want to tell me what you're really pissed about?"

"What the hell? You don't think I'm allowed to be pissed that my entire life is upended after one stupid night?"

Emma's hands went up in a defensive gesture. "Okay, babe, easy. Absolutely you get to be pissed. Confused even. You can be as emotional as you want. It's just, knowing you as I do, I don't think we've gotten to everything you're mad about yet."

I tipped my head back on the arm of the couch and gave Emma's words some thought. Thinking about it, I had a feeling she was right. "I think I'm upset that my plans have changed."

"I'd say that is valid. Keep going." She rubbed my leg, giving reassurance and telling me to spill.

"I'm mad that I probably should stick closer to home this summer. Maybe only do short trips, especially while this nausea is with me." My heart thumped with nervousness.

"Also valid. I might be a bit exhausted traveling for the next few weeks too if I was you. What else?"

My heart sped up as I got down to it. "I think I'm upset because I don't know if traveling is even what I want anymore." Tears came flooding down again. "I'm upset because I don't know what I want."

Emma slid over, wrapping her arms around me and laying her head on my shoulder. "And that is totally valid, Maggie. Your life just took a curve you weren't expecting. Be kind to yourself. Maybe take some time to think about it. Don't make any rash decisions. Summer is just beginning. You are swimming in time."

I let out a deep sigh. Even though I was still an emotional wreck, I needed to get this out. "I'm not swimming in it. Not really." Big breath. "I made the decision that this year will be my last one at the middle school. I'll finally make my move next summer."

Emma looked at me in shock, waiting.

What did I say? Emma had always supported me, but she didn't understand my desire to move. I closed my eyes, trying to summon some strength. Looking at her again, I whispered gently, "Em, it's time."

"But you'll have a baby," she whispered back to me.

Damn, that was a pang to my heart. "I know."

A tear snaked down Emma's cheeks. Sadness poured off her in waves. "I just, I mean, I want you to be happy, Mags. I know this is what you want. But will my niece or nephew know me?" Her eyes widened a bit on a gasp. "Will they know Sully?"

Apparently, my tears had no end. They kept flowing as I reached over to wrap my arms around Emma, and she did the same in return. "Of course they'll know you. And Sully. I'd never keep the baby from him." I pushed Emma's long brown ponytail away from my mouth as we rocked back and forth together.

For a few beats, we sat there in silence.

Finally Emma spoke. "But you think you might stick around this summer?"

I pulled back a smidge to look at her, giving her a look that said I *would* be moving on eventually.

Emma gave me a watery smile. "Not saying you're not leaving next summer, but I'll be glad to keep you as long as we can."

I squeezed her one more time before sliding back to give us room. "Maybe... but my duplex, the sublet..."

Emma ran her hand down my ponytail and onto my back. "I know Sully said you could stay at his place. You can stay with Max and me or my parents. Hell, I'd let you stay at my old place, but I accepted a bid today. It looks like I'll be officially moving out."

I smiled, happy for her. "You sold it? Congratulations!"

Emma smiled, wiping away my tears. "Thanks, babe. But how about you? What do you think you want to do?"

I looked over at the boxes, then back to Emma. "I love your parents, but my days of living with guardians are over. And you and Max have my heart, but I'm not staying with the two of you where I can hear sex noises coming from your room every night."

"Hey!"

"Come on, babe. You know it's true."

"Whatever. So, Sully's?" Emma said, looking over at my stack of boxes.

"I guess Sully's."

"Mags, he's not going to pressure you. He just wants to help."

I knew that. God how I knew that. The thing was, I wasn't sure if that was what I wanted. Living in the same house was going to throw that back in my face. Every. Single. Day.

I looked at Emma. "So you and Max. Officially living together?"

Emma smiled at me, squeezing my hand. "Yep." She took a breath, "And you and Sully. Having a baby."

"Yep." My waterworks started back up as I squeezed her hand back. "Things certainly have changed," I whispered.

"But maybe the changes are good changes," Emma whispered back, pulling me in for a hug.

I closed my eyes, chin to her shoulder, as I said a quick prayer. *God, I hope so.*

9

_______________

# OUT OF MY COMFORT ZONE

**_Sully_**

Home from work, I changed out of my clothes that smelled of brewed beer and went out into the yard with my pup. I stood in the yard, zoned out as I threw the ball for Ranger for so long I felt like my arm might fall off. After a while Ranger decided he was done, looking at me like I'd clearly lost my mind as he dropped the ball by my feet and laid down by it.

"You done, boy?" I asked.

His tail beat quickly, but he didn't move, so I guess that was his answer. Giving up, I sat on the steps of the porch that led to the kitchen as Ranger moved over to drop his head to my knee.

"I know, bud." I stroked his head.

He looked at me like he knew I clearly didn't know what I was doing. I wasn't sure what it said about me that my dog knew I was a hot damn mess. At least he'd still be loyal to me no matter what.

The rumble of a bike brought me out of my downward spiral of emotions. I glanced down to the country road and

111

saw Max turn off it to pull up the drive. Coming to a stop, gravel shot from under the tires. Max swung off as Ranger barked happily in greeting.

Max dropped his helmet on the seat and called out, "Yo." As he headed in our direction, I tried to gauge his mood.

"Harp," I said, trying to remember if we had any plans.

"Sully," he said, coming to sit next to me on the porch.

I waited a few minutes, but he didn't say anything. Finally I broke the silence. "Did I forget that we had plans?"

Max whistled for Ranger, who was glad to find someone else who wanted to pet him. "Nah. Maggie called Emma. Said you guys had an appointment yesterday. Em said Mags was pretty emotional. Figured I'd check in."

My heart thudded when he said Maggie was emotional. Maybe I shouldn't have left her last night. But I had work and Emma had swung by, so I figured that was for the best.

Looking at Max, I raised an eyebrow. "And you didn't text before heading this way because..."

Max gave me an incredulous look back. "Because you'd be full of shit and say you're fine. Like you aren't a man who has had a bomb dropped in his lap."

I stared down the yard to the road and the fields beyond. Planting season was underway, and farmers were out checking the moisture in the soil, hoping for consistent days so that the seeds could germinate. I saw Richard, the guy who farms the land around my house for my parents, drive by and wave. I waved back, then looked over at Max who was watching me with narrowed eyes. His hair wasn't pulled back in a bun like he typically had it. I guessed that the helmet for his bike was the reason behind that.

"Hair's getting long, Harp."

His brows rose up. "Are we fucking talking about our

hair right now? I could point out you could use a cut," he said as he leaned down and grabbed the ball Ranger had brought him. Apparently the pup had his second wind. Max let the ball fly, then bit out, "So, you good?"

I sighed, leaning back on my elbows on the porch behind me. "I'm good, swear. It's just been a lot. Sorry I didn't tell you in person."

"Not about to heap any guilt on you, man. The text was fine. And you had to know Emma would share." Max nodded, taking the ball from Ranger and throwing it again. Ranger barked happily and charged after the slobbery ball. "So, thoughts on being a dad?"

A bunch of starlings took flight from a tree on the edge of the property, flying in their swooping patterns over the field to the north, their black shape stark against the brilliant blue sky. I watched, lost in thought for a moment before Max's voice pulled me back. "Cole..."

Shaking my head, I whistled to Ranger who had dropped the ball and was investigating a smell at the edge of a field. He glanced over and took off at a sprint to come our way. He ran up the few steps to be by my side, and I gave his head a good rub before looking over to Max. "Being a dad is both the best thing I can think of at the same time as it is the most terrifying prospect I can imagine."

Max nodded and leaned back against a post on the porch. "Makes sense."

Ranger left my side to get a good drink of water from the bowl that was always on the porch for him. I leaned back again on my elbows, watching the flight of the birds. "Not the timeline I'd planned on, but that doesn't make me want this baby any less. Couldn't ever be disappointed in a child, you know?"

"Yeah, but that doesn't mean you can't be upset that your plans have been upended, Sully."

I sat with that for a minute. There was truth there, but it also didn't feel right. "Not sure I have the words to explain my thoughts, Max. Part of me is excited to meet this person I've helped to create, to watch them grow. Part is worried about Maggie and how she's feeling, what this has done to her. Then there is the concern that this means the canning project at the brewery needs to hit pause. I need to make sure I'm ready to be a dad financially. That I can support a family."

I looked over to see Max watching me closely. "Bullshit."

I gave him a look. What the hell? "Thanks for your support."

He looked irritated. "It's not that I don't support you, but I'm calling bullshit on you needing to pause your business to be a dad. What you're feeling is the fear I'd assume most sane people would feel when they find out they're going to be stepping up to care for another human being. That's a lot, Sully, and it's okay to be a bit overwhelmed by it. But as for needing some mythical amount of money in the bank, bullshit."

I let Max's words soak in. They brought me some comfort, but also conflict. Jake and I had talked only in short conversations since Saturday. Yesterday we should have signed the loan and begun to invest in the canning operation, but because of my conflicted feelings, we didn't. Jake was pissed and had every right to be. By not signing, we'd lost the chance, and Jake seemed to take my lack of trust that this opportunity could be successful as a personal criticism.

"While you're chewing on whatever is swirling in that

brain of yours, you want to share what's up with you and Mags?" Max asked. "I mean, I assume that the reason you two were moody as hell last month had to do with you and Ms. Jameson."

Ranger had been patrolling the porch but came to stretch out next to Max. He dropped his head on Max's legs with a sigh. Max absentmindedly stroked his head as he watched me.

"Yeah," I said, looking down at my hands. Meeting Max's eyes, I asked, "How much did Emma tell you? Not sure what Maggie shared."

"Well, clearly I know you two had sex. Emma said it was the night we grilled and had tequila. Then something about protection failing and Maggie melting down..." He trailed off.

I nodded, "That about sums it up. Nothing happened that night because she was on the path to too much alcohol. The next day things got heated. Afterward, I saw that the damn condom broke. Maggie's walls went up immediately. I took her home because that was what she wanted. Then she barely spoke to me until I came back on Friday when you told me she was pregnant. And now"—I held out my arms—"here we are."

Max looked at Ranger as he pet the dog's silky ears, running them through his fingers. "That would fuck with you, Sully. Especially if Maggie was someone you'd been seeing as more than a friend." He looked up at me, tilting his head in a silent question.

No point in denying anything here. Max would just figure it out anyway. "Yeah, Max, I've wanted things with Maggie to be more than friendly for a while, but I was waiting until I was ready, until the brewery was in a good place."

"I feel like this is the spot where I point out that I about lost Emma for trying to control when I decided we were ready to move from friends to more..."

"Yeah, there might be some parallels there," I noted. "At any rate, things are upended, and I need to take my lead from Maggie."

"And what does Maggie say?" Max asked, his hand dropping from Ranger's head when the dog saw a squirrel that dared to come down from a tree and about lost his mind chasing it over the grass.

I snorted. "Maggie doesn't seem to know what she wants. Friday night she said she wants to be friends, that there is a lot going on and she needs to process. However, we've texted on and off, went to the doctor appointment yesterday together."

Max tipped his head back and stayed silent for a moment before meeting my eyes. "Is she still planning on traveling this summer?"

"Not sure. I think she's pretty conflicted on that front. The doc said she could, but she's nervous." I looked down at my work boots, scuffed to shit, dirty as hell. "I did offer to let her move in here. She's already got someone moving into her duplex, so she doesn't have anywhere else to go."

Max's grin turned into a smirk. "You're trying to get her to be roommates when she doesn't know what she wants in regard to a relationship with you?"

"Screw off, Harp. It's Maggie. She's been a friend far longer than I've wanted something else with her. I'm not leaving her without a place to sleep, especially when she's having my baby."

Max's grin widened. "Not saying you should, man. Just pointing out how you're using this situation to your advantage."

I sighed and stood up, whistling Ranger back to the house. Looking at Max over my shoulder, I asked, "Ride?"

Max rose to standing. "Just screwing with you, Sullivan. I know you're not taking advantage of Maggie."

I walked up the stairs to let Ranger into the house and grabbed my helmet from the bench by the door. Pulling the door shut behind me, I followed Max onto the porch. "It's just, I'm out of my comfort zone here. I want to do right by her, by my kid. I'm just not sure what the right thing even is at this point."

Max walked over to his bike and leaned down, grabbing his helmet, and looked my way with a shit-eating grin. "It will work out, Sully. And I can't wait to watch the two of you navigate this possible platonic friendship while living in your place. Being roommates with the woman you're interested in? Should be fun to watch."

Helmet on, I swung my leg over my bike and raised a one-finger salute back to Max as I started it up and pulled out onto the road into the quiet spring evening. I said a silent prayer that this ride would clear my head because my conversation with Max certainly hadn't done the trick.

## 10

## ROOMMATES

**Maggie**

After a full day with kids, all I really wanted to do right now was curl up on my couch and watch TV. Today we'd headed on a walking field trip to the library in all my classes. It was maybe a five-minute walk from the middle school, but good Lord. Five minutes of walking each way with around twenty-four kids per class, three days left of the school year? It was exhausting.

I reminded them that we didn't need any signs of affection as we walked to the library, that it wasn't time to take selfies for social media, and that we should stay on the sidewalk and didn't traipse through people's yards, et cetera. It was a miracle we all survived. Sometimes I thought corralling cats must be easier that teaching middle school.

Emma and the folks at the library had been amazing, as usual. Emma had Tim, one of the guys that she worked with, book talk some of the new releases in young adult literature, specifically highlighting the authors who would be visiting next year. Tim often hung out with us at The Homestead, along with his partner, Eric. To say he was like a one-man comedy routine would be an understatement. He had the perfect level of snark that made the seventh graders howl with laughter but also pay close attention to everything he said.

Emma had gone through the summer reading program the library was hosting for teens. The kids seemed a bit disengaged until she explained it was all about reading minutes, not a prescribed list of required texts. And they were pumped when they heard that if they hit sixteen hundred minutes of reading over the course of the summer, they'd get a small gift card to the new bookstore. Many of my students were voracious readers, so just the idea of a new bookstore was enough to excite them, much less some free cash to spend. The kids scribbled down a list of books to read from the stack Tim had shared and took the flyers Emma handed out that listed the website they could sign up on and track their reading. It looked like she might have a lot of interest.

They were all on my mind as my Jeep made the final turn into Sully's drive. Glancing at the clock on my dash, I knew I'd likely beat him here. He'd been working at the brewery, but he'd invited me over for dinner to talk through our plans. He'd said the back door would be open, and I'd need to let Ranger out. I was happy to do it. Ranger was one of the most chill dogs ever. I'd always wanted a pup. I guess if I actually moved in with Sully for the summer, I'd get my wish.

Ranger greeted me just inside the door, jumping up to greet me. Sully would order him down, but I loved the greeting. He wasn't aggressive at all but almost leaned in to hug me. I ran my hands along his sides, giving him a good rubdown.

"Hey, pup. You lonely?"

Ranger panted back at me, seeming to be overcome with happiness. After allowing another lick, I leaned over to open the door. Ranger took off into the yard, and I turned back to the kitchen.

Sully had told me to make myself at home. I thought about starting dinner, but I wasn't sure if he already had something planned. Looking around, I admired the space. Sully's place wasn't huge, but it was a gorgeous old farmhouse.

Looking around the kitchen, I took in the clean lines. It was lined with white cabinets on the lower half of the walls, open shelves with a live edge on the wood. There was a massive island in the middle with a butcher-block top. Over the sink were huge windows looking out to his driveway and a small barn to the side that he used as a garage.

As I moved through the house, I came to the living room. There he had more open space where he used one half of the room for a dining room table, the other half for his leather couch and flat screen. There were tons of windows in there too, along with the door to the front of the house and the porch. Upstairs he had two guest rooms, one bath. I figured either room would work for me for a few months, though I hadn't really looked closely at them before.

A noise brought me back to the kitchen. Ranger stood on his hind legs in the doorway with a tennis ball in his mouth. Well, I guess Ranger had other ideas as to how I'd spend the time until Sully arrived.

After about twenty minutes of throwing the ball for the pup, I was grateful to see Sully pull into the drive. Apparently, yoga hadn't built my upper arm muscles sufficiently. I'd be feeling that tomorrow for certain. Sully's bike came to a stop, and he pulled off his helmet as I admired him from a distance. He headed my way, leaning down to pick up the ball Ranger dropped and throwing it long for him.

"How long has he had you at it?" he asked, reaching my side.

"Only about twenty minutes."

That earned me a grin as he took the returned ball from Ranger and threw it once again, the dog bounding off with joy radiating with every bounce. "I bet you'll be a bit sore tomorrow."

"Bite me." I shot back.

He chuckled in response and moved us up the steps and in the back door. Ranger decided that he'd rather be inside with us than outside with all the smells. I wondered how long that would last. The pup entered the kitchen and slurped up enough water that I figured a return trip outside would be sooner versus later. Then he collapsed on the floor in an exhausted heap, his mouth practically grinning as he lay there, panting at us. I smiled and caught Sully's eye. He just shook his head at the dog and headed toward the fridge.

"Are you in the mood for anything in particular?" he asked, scanning the contents of the refrigerator.

"What? You mean you hadn't planned an elaborate meal?" I replied.

Glancing over at me he shook his head. "I have lots of options, just wasn't sure if the little guy was messing with anything you typically liked to eat."

Damn. So thoughtful. Again. I wondered if this was our new norm or if we'd return to the teasing and bantering part of our friendship that I was used to. "I'm starving, and as long as it isn't coffee, I think I'm good right now."

"Sorry about the coffee thing, babe. That must be tough for you. But, regarding dinner. How do you feel about nachos?"

"My feelings regarding nachos depends on the type of meat we're having with it and if you have avocados for fresh guac." My stomach gave a growl telling me it really didn't give a damn, but just wanted to be fed.

"Those are some strong feelings, Maggie May. You will be happy to hear that we absolutely have the shit needed for the guac. And regarding meat, no one has ever been disappointed in the meat I provide." His eyes twinkled as they watched for my reaction.

He wasn't disappointed as I hooted with laughter and slapped at his shoulder in response. "You have an awfully high opinion of your meat, Cole Sullivan."

"Well, you are a connoisseur of my meat, to be fair." He raised his eyebrows up and down as he spoke. "I guess you would know of which you speak. Did you need a repeat sample to make a final decision?"

Okay, I needed to calm this conversation down or I was going to take it in a direction I was not comfortable with. "Sweet Jesus, I just wondered if we were going with browned hamburger on the nachos or something more interesting."

Sully noticed my attempt to bring us back to some lightness because he immediately returned to looking in the fridge and replied, "We have hamburger, sure. But I also have leftover chicken or steak we could use."

Steak. I immediately had an immense craving for steak. "Yes, steak."

Looking over at me, he grinned wickedly. "Choice meat, babe."

"Sully!"

He raised up his hands in defense. "Sorry, I'll stop. I promise." He pointed at me. "You're on guac duty."

I nodded, grabbing a few avocados out of the bowl he

gestured toward on the counter. Turning, I found some lemons in the other bowl. "Cilantro or no?" I asked, grabbing a knife and cutting board.

"I love it and have some in the fridge, but if you don't we can skip it."

"Nope, I love it too. I just know some people think it tastes soapy." Moving over to the fridge I found some of the controversial herb in a drawer and headed back to the island and began to assemble the guacamole.

"So, we going to talk about it?" he asked as he preheated the oven, then turned to chop up the steak.

Part of me really wanted to reply with *talk about what*; however, seeing as I was going to be a mother, it seemed wise to grow up a bit. Besides, I had initiated tonight's conversation. "Is there anything specific you wanted to talk about, or did you want me to go first?"

Sully glanced over from his spot as he began to line up all the ingredients on the counter to assemble the nachos on a cookie sheet. "Well, I have two main things on my mind right now."

I mashed avocados in a bowl, a bit of dread filling me up as I wondered where this conversation could go. "Hit me."

"How are you feeling today?" He grabbed an onion and held it up before I could answer. "I was going to sauté some onions to go with the steak. Maybe some beans as well?"

"Sure." I nodded, squeezing some lemon juice into the mashed avocados. Then I added some seasoning before dumping the cilantro in. "And to answer your question, I'm feeling fine. Thanks." I dipped my finger in the guac and tried it. Not bad, but it needed a bit more salt. As I added that, I prodded him to continue. "What was the second thing on your mind?"

Standing at the stove, he turned to me briefly. "Have you given any thought to this summer?"

"I have lots of thoughts about summer. Mostly good thoughts."

"Maggie, you know what I mean." Sully returned to stirring the onions before they burned. "Stop deflecting."

My stomach began to growl in earnest. "Sorry. I do know what you mean. And that's what I wanted to talk about too. I've given it a lot of thought, and I think, for at least a few weeks for certain, I need to stay in Highland Falls." Sully stopped stirring and turned away from the stove, leaning against the counter and looking at me across the island. "If the invitation to stay here is still open, I think I'd like to take it."

Sully's eyes were soft as he considered me and nodded. "Move in here."

"If it's still okay."

"Roommates?"

"Roommates."

"With benefits?"

"Dammit, Sully." I could feel my eyes roll without meaning to.

"I mean"—he gestured back at the skillet—"my meat is hard to resist."

"Cole Sullivan, if this is how it's going to be, maybe I will just stay with Emma and Max." I growled, turning my attention back to the guacamole. I could feel my heart racing. Damn infuriating man.

"Mags." Sully moved around the island to my side. "You don't want to stay with Max and Emma. They're going to be at each other like rabbits."

"Ugh, I know." I continued looking at the counter.

*Don't look him in the eye, I thought.* I could resist him as long as there was no eye contact.

"I'm sorry, Maggie. I want you to be comfortable here." Long pause, then he went on. "You've made it pretty clear you want to remain friends and only friends."

What the hell? *I've* made that clear?

"I'm trying hard to respect your wishes." He continued as he moved right in front of me. His finger came under my chin as he tipped my face up to look in his eyes. "And that is so hard."

Christ, that wasn't the only thing that was hard right now, I thought as he brushed up against me. Oh my God, where was this going? I needed to be able to pause this scene for a moment and try to psychoanalyze everything, then get back to him. Was that possible? No? Why the hell not?

"Sully," I whispered breathlessly.

Sully brushed a kiss on my forehead as he pressed me against the island, then gently kissed my lips before pulling back. "Roommates it is, Maggie. You need to move in by Saturday, right?"

With that, he walked back to the stove, and I stared at his back. Holy shit. I actually thought I could live with him and nothing would happen? I wondered if fool was written all over my face.

Roommates indeed.

## 11

## NEVER DULL

***Sully***

By the time I hit the brewery, the servers were getting ready for the lunch crowd to come in an hour or so. Every time I stepped into this place, I couldn't help feeling a sense of pride.

The front doors opened up to the hostess stand with the main room of the brewery just beyond it. There were tables and nooks for people to sit throughout the large open area of the original barn. That space was flanked on either side by the bar on the far wall, the tank room in the opposite direction. The tank room had several beer tanks along with a handful of high-top tables for when folks came back for tastings and we explained the beer-making process. The interior wall of the tank room was filled with large windows allowing you to look back into the dining area of the brewery. The kitchen and restrooms were right off the hallway that took you to the tanks.

Moving toward the tanks, I could hear Jake's music flooding the restaurant at a level far louder than it would be during the times we were open.

Speaking of Jake, he had a beer in hand and was headed to the table glancing at his phone when he caught sight of me moving toward him.

"Hey man, I was just going to message you," Jake said in a voice that was still far from his normal tone. "You ready to try A Trip to Grandma's?" he asked, sliding over a second beer that was on the table.

Accepting it, I muttered, "Hell yeah." We tapped glasses, then took a small drink, each letting it settle and thinking through the flavors of the beer.

Jake spoke first. "What do you think?"

"Fucking perfect," I replied.

"My thoughts exactly," Jake said with a tense smile. He tapped the barn wood table for a moment before meeting my eyes. "Originally, I had thought this would be perfect beer to begin our canning process with, along with Black Hole Sun."

My stomach dropped with the feelings of anxiety as I prepared to have this conversation with Jake. For the past week we'd danced around this topic but hadn't really gotten into it since last Saturday when I made the decision for us. I felt like a dick and it wasn't fair, but all my focus had been on being a provider for my family, not going into more debt.

Jake broke the silence since I couldn't figure out what in the hell to say. "Just be honest with me, man. Not this bull-shit about how we need more money in the bank because that doesn't fly. We'd had the same in savings the week before, and you were right there beside me, pushing to move ahead." He ran a hand through his hair while he looked out at the brewery through the windows. Glancing back my way, he dropped his voice. "It's Maggie, right? The pregnancy?"

I met his eyes. I didn't want to get into it because I still couldn't figure out the feelings swirling in my own damn head, but I owed him this. Hell, I owed him so much more. "I can't fucking explain it. It's like I heard I was going to be a dad and immediately panicked about money. All that I could think was that it was the wrong time to take any chances with our business." Remorse filled me up as I thought of how I'd just dropped the bomb that we weren't moving forward without any thought to what Jake thought. We were in this, equal partners. What the hell would I have done if he'd pulled something like that?

Looking at Jake, I could tell he was trying to calm down, that he didn't want to rail against me here. I appreciated it, but it was more than I deserved. "You've got it wrong, Sully. Now is the perfect time to invest. You want to grow this business, not stay stagnant. Expanding this way makes perfect sense. We've already done all the groundwork and were ready for the next step, and then you just decided we were done."

I was an asshole. Period. End of story. "Jake, I can't tell you how fucking sorry I am that I just made that call for the two of us. My mind was filled Maggie and a baby. Everything else just felt like noise, and I needed to focus." I took in a deep breath and was grateful for the peace of this place right now. Thankfully it was just our employees getting ready and the music. I wasn't sure if I could hand much else yet. Meeting Jake's gaze, I asked the impossible. "How can I make this up to you?"

Jake sank onto a barstool at the high-tops we were leaning against. Looking up at me, he seemed conflicted. I'd put money on that conflict having something to do with empathy for my position and a general pissed-off attitude that I'd changed our plan. "You're looking at this wrong, Sully. Once you get your head out of your ass, you'll see that an investment in your business makes smart business sense. We've proven that we can make money. Canning just allows us to increase that income. Which is good for you. Also, once that gorgeous redhead calms down, she'll recognize that a relationship with you would be the stuff romance novels are made of."

"What do you know about romance novels?" I asked, curious.

"Got a sister who reads a shit ton of them," he replied.

I took another sip of our beer, letting the flavors burst in my mouth. Damn, it was good. Looking back to Jake, I said, "Ah, thought you might be reading them, and was going to give you some shit."

He looked personally insulted, "Not my usual type of book, but I've read plenty and they're terrific. Nothing wrong with a happy ending." Giving me a shit-eating grin, he continued, "Maybe if you read a few you'd realize how fucked up you are and get your head on straight."

Well, he wasn't wrong. But I couldn't let him have the last word, even if I was happy that he seemed to be somewhat letting go of his completely justified anger at me. "And no comments on Maggie's looks."

At that, he laughed. "I'm not blind, Sully. And when she gets that pregnant belly going, along with the breasts that come with it. I mean, good luck, man. I won't be the only one who notices."

I took another swig of beer. It was better than what I wanted to do. Now he was just being an ass to prove a point. "You really want me to take a swing at you, asshole."

"Not going there. Just reminding you what you have."

"I don't have anyone. And a woman isn't a possession, Jake. Maybe this is why you're single."

Jake stood, stretching up as Laurie walked into the tank

room. Laurie was younger than either of us, midtwenties, and had the huge misfortune to have married an asshole right out of high school. Two kids later, she found herself blessedly divorced but needed a job that understood that kids get sick and sometimes you can't plan that shit. In the past year I'd seen her confidence built back up as we gave her more and more responsibilities when she'd shown she could handle them. Now she managed the front of the house for us and did a damn find job. I guessed her arrival meant the conversation with Jake would have to be tabled for now.

"Hey guys, giving you a heads-up that we have a crew for lunch today. The local business owners are holding their Rotary meeting here because their normal location has an issue with catering today," she said, looking at the iPad in her hand. "There will be about thirty people."

My mind quickly thought through the tables in the dining room, nodding as I considered table locations. "Do we need to send a message out on social media that we're closed for lunch to accommodate that group?"

Laurie dragged some things around on her iPad, furrowing her brow as she did so. "Nope, should be fine. We'll still have some tables available, along with the high-tops. The group chose to come in at eleven to help us out and avoid the lunch rush. I think we'll be fine. Just letting you two know because..."

"We'll need to have all hands on deck, right?" Jake finished for her.

Laurie looked up again, considering us both for the first time. "I'm sorry. Did I interrupt something?"

Jake shook his head. "Nope, just saving me from having to beat some sense into this big lug. That's all."

Laurie laughed, then turned and headed back to the brewpub.

I stood up, grabbing both my glass and Jake's, and headed for the sink. As I sanitized them, I realized Jake hadn't followed Laurie. Placing the glasses on the counter, I turned back to Jake as he spoke.

"Sully, I get where you're coming from with the loan, but I think you're dead wrong."

"I get that, but—"

"Hold on, man. I'm just saying let's table this conversation for a bit. We've already lost the opportunity to have the Main Street loan though that doesn't mean the idea of canning is dead completely. There are other options, and I want to explore some of them. You need to get used to the idea of having a kid, which I'd like to remind you won't be happening for months and months. Let's talk more in a week or so. Take some time. I'm talking with the guys over at Knobs Brewery on their canning process next week. They're local, so I'll have a bit more intel for you on what their first year looked like. I wonder if you'd feel better to have some more numbers to run."

"Fine, we'll talk then." I was conflicted. I'd been so certain giving up the loan had been the right call, but something was nagging at me after talking to Jake. The missed opportunity, the chance to expand, the notion of what I needed to feel secure. I itched to hop on my bike and ride out of town. Turning to Jake, I had to make sure that we, at least, were okay. "So, we're good?" I asked.

"We're good, man. No matter what. That being said, I'm absolutely going to convince you that we need to move ahead. However, in the meantime, Harp said something about you getting a roommate..." Jake grinned as we turned to walk back into the brewpub. "Did you think you were going to be able to keep that bit of knowledge to yourself?"

"You guys are fucking gossips, you know that? Miss Lou has nothing on either of you." I looked around the dining room. The tables were ready for lunch, the tables for the group pulled together into two long rows on one side of the room.

"When is this all going down?" Jake said as we moved toward the bar where Daryl was wiping the wood surface until it gleamed.

"Needs to move in by Saturday. I figured I'd grab Max and get that done while she was at school tomorrow. She doesn't need to be lifting anything," I said, pulling my phone out and texting Harp to ask if that would work. There was so much I couldn't do for Maggie, that I couldn't fix. But by God, I could take care of her. "And I've known Maggie since she became a teacher. The last day tends to weigh on her. I'm guessing that will be even harder when she's dealing with pregnancy hormones."

"Oh, this is going to be excellent," Jake said with a chuckle. "Are you planning to be overprotective the entire pregnancy, or just at the beginning?"

"What? I mean, she has to teach tomorrow, and she's exhausted all the time already. I just figured..."

"Sully, just giving you shit, man. And if you need any help, let me know."

I glanced down as my phone vibrated and saw Max's reply. "Good to hear, Jake. Feel like moving some boxes around ten a.m. tomorrow? And keep it quiet if Mags comes in tonight. I want to surprise her."

"Good God, man. You are so whipped, and you're not even together yet. These next few months should be fun."

"You in or you out, Spencer?"

"Oh, I'm totally in. I wouldn't miss this show for the world."

I felt Jake slap my back before he headed back to talk to Daryl. I quickly sent Harp a text setting up a time to meet at Maggie's tomorrow. One more day and she'd be living at my house for at least a few weeks, maybe the entire summer. If I was honest with myself, I both looked forward to it and dreaded the time. Seeing her every day and keeping my hands off her was going to be torture.

Glancing back at my phone, I saw a reply from Harp.

**Max:** *I give you two, three days, then you two will be back in bed together.*

Three days. I closed my eyes, a vision of Maggie naked in my bed appeared. Three days might be too long.

## 12

### MOVING IN

***Maggie***

I dragged myself up the walkway to my place, drained from the last day of school. Hell, it had even been an early dismissal today, and I was still wiped. This wasn't pregnancy, though, but the end-of-the-year shitstorm of exhaustion and emotion that hit me every time. After seven years in teaching, I'd come to expect it. My students and I became a family, and now I missed them already. It took me a few days of summer vacation to shed my melancholy mood as those kids had taken a piece of me with them when they left.

Stepping through my front door, I stopped and looked around in confusion. My house was empty. To be certain, the furniture was there, but I'd rented the place furnished. The mountain of boxes in my living room was gone. All personal effects had been removed. I'd say I was robbed, but the person who robbed me also stuck around to vacuum the carpets and wipe the kitchen down, which would be odd. Glancing at the kitchen, I saw a note on the counter along with a large drink and paper bag. Curious.

My mind still reeling, I reached the counter and grabbed the drink. Sadly, it wasn't coffee because this little bean was not about that, so obviously my thief knew that bit of intel. Taking a sip, I recognized the citrus mint tea with honey from the Sanctuary. I sent up some gratitude to the heavens and peeked into the bag. Score! Two chocolate muffins that Allyson made that were to die for. I'd be glad to marry this thief and have his babies. Glancing down, I opened the paper folded in half and laughed. Seeing that my thief was Sully, the baby part was already done and marriage was not on the table.

*M-*

*Moved your shit to my place. Left a key and a snack. See you after I get off work.*

*S-*

I briefly considered being pissed that he had invaded my personal space and moved stuff I hadn't even packed but quickly got over that. Unpacking would be enough work and would likely take me a week or more. I moved through the duplex and double-checked that he had gotten everything. Not only was everything moved, but the place was cleaner than when I moved in. My landlord had told me to leave the keys in the mailbox, so I grabbed Sully's keys along with my treat and headed out the door. I locked up, then dropped the keys in the box and headed to my Jeep. As I pulled out, I noted there was no emotion welling up, making me sad to move on. I truly felt more saying goodbye to my students an hour ago than I had walking away from the place I'd lived for seven years. I hoped that meant I was making the right decision. Time would tell.

After driving straight to Sully's place, I walked in to have Ranger greet me like a long-lost friend. I gave him a good rubdown, took him out to do his business, then headed for the stairs as he followed me. I had a bit of energy left in me after the day. Might as well find my leggings and T-shirts, get a few items put away, and grab a shower before having some dinner. I had a feeling I'd crash as soon as I did all that.

I was grateful Sully was working late at the brewery tonight. My body hummed with nerves at this entire roommate situation. The fact that he wasn't here as I moved in helped a lot. Ranger, I could handle. A gorgeous guy that made my hormones sing? I wasn't sure if I'd ever have enough willpower to resist him. How on earth did I think this was going to work? Maybe I'd just plan on staying out of his house if he was home. Ships passing in the night. That might work.

The lies we tell ourselves.

I glanced in the first room on the top of the stairs, but there were no boxes, so I moved on. The door to the other spare room was closed. Grabbing the knob, I swung it open and stopped so suddenly that Ranger ran into my legs from behind. This was certainly the room I was staying in, but there weren't any boxes. What the literal hell?

Sully's master bedroom downstairs was large, but this room was almost as big. It had a wall of windows that over-looked the back of the farm, fields stretching out to meet the horizon, dotted here and there with neighboring farms. There was a queen-sized bed to the left, with a beautiful old wedding-ring quilt that lay over a fluffy duvet. There was a riot of pillows on the bed.

On the dresser and bookshelves, I saw many of my frames arranged as well as books and mementos. I pulled open the closest dresser drawer and shook my head at my clothes that were carefully tucked away in the drawer. Moving across from the bed, I opened the closet and saw my clothes hanging up, shoes lined across the bottom. Emotions welled, and I choked back more than a few tears.

I turned back to the room and took in my throw on the armchair by the window, my current book sitting on the small table right by the side instead of the nightstand I'd left it on. Holy shit.

I headed to the bathroom and, at this point, was no longer surprised to see my makeup and lotions neatly arranged in the medicine cabinet and on the vanity. I was taken aback to see another note on the marble counter. Picking it up, I saw Sully's writing once again. I shook my head as I read.

M-

*Emma, Max, Jake, and I got your stuff unpacked. No worries, Emma took care of anything we thought you wouldn't want us to see.*

Well, trust my friend to make sure the guys didn't lay their eyes on my vibrator. At least there was that.

*Anything we didn't think you'd need right now we put in the closet of the spare room. That's all still in boxes and labeled if you need it. Dinner is in the fridge. Just needs to be warmed up. Take a bath and crash. I'll see you tomorrow.*

S-

I padded across the hall and swung open the closet in there to find boxes neatly stacked and labeled. Tears pricked my eyes. I quickly moved back in my room and grabbed some leggings out of one drawer, a tank out of another.

Entering the bathroom, I glanced over at the claw-foot tub. I hadn't appreciated it enough on my first trip in here, my brain clouded with the overwhelming nature of everything around me. I glanced at Ranger, who was still following me around like I had a treat in my pocket.

"Holy shit, pup. Your dad did good."

Ranger wagged his tail back and forth, apparently in agreement.

I started the bath and grabbed my phone. My first text was to Emma.

**Me:** *Shit, lady, thanks a million.*

Then, I texted Sully.

**Me:** *At your house. Thank you.*

I looked over the five words and felt like they might be inadequate, but what else could I say? I went ahead and hit the arrow to send it.

Immediately, my phone buzzed. I glanced down with a little excitement, but saw that it was Emma. Still, I opened the text and laughed out loud.

**Emma:** *We got your back, Mags. And no worries, I packed and unpacked the vibrator and all the romance books. Best friend at your service. You settled? Cried out over the last day yet?*

I quickly typed out a reply.

**Me:** *You know me well. Getting ready to take a bath and crash. Your bro left me dinner.*

She sent me back a message in seconds.

**Emma:** *And how are you feeling about said bro?*

I thought about it for a moment as another text arrived. Glancing down, I saw that it was from Sully. My heart rate accelerated as I opened it.

**Sully:** *No problem. And just a FYI, it's now your house too. Rest up.*

Damn, that man. I decided not to text him back because right now I just wanted to send him a message that said I'd be in his bed waiting for him. Not the way to begin the first night as roommates. Well, I suppose it was one way to begin it, but not the way I planned on. Instead, I texted Emma back.

**Me:** *Feelings regarding your bro = conflicted. I'll say this, he's pretty awesome and I wish we could be more.*

Heart thumping in my chest, I sent it and turned off the bath. Stripping down, I sighed. I couldn't remember when someone had thought of me the way my friends had. This was exactly what I needed. I slid into the warm water and looked to my left. Ranger stood there, staring at me, his nose to my nose.

"I hope you don't plan on jumping in here, pup. I mean, I'm all for loving you, but my bath is a solitary experience."

Ranger whined at me but slid to the floor with a thump, lying right where I'd need to step out in a minute. Hmm, maybe dogs understood us more than I knew?

I laid my head back on the edge and looked up at the ceiling. Closing my eyes, I thought over the ten weeks that stretched ahead until school would resume. I could laze around, I could still find time to travel, or I supposed I could do both. However, it seemed I'd be upchucking on average of one to two times a day for the foreseeable future, and the end of the first trimester was weeks away.

Thinking more about it, staying closer to home sounded good. Resolve filled me up as I soaked surrounded by the peace of the country. I could absolutely do this. I could stay home this summer, take care of the little bean as he grew, and be friends with Sully. Surely as my belly got bigger, I would be uninterested in sex anyway. It would be easy. And goodness knows, he wouldn't be attracted to me anyway, much less when I was sporting a bowling ball on my front. I nodded a few times and then looked over at Ranger.

"I've totally got this, Ranger. No sex, just friends, and you and I can hang out all summer. No sweat."

Ranger glanced up with a quizzical look, then laid his head back down on his paws. He didn't seem to have any faith in me.

I put my head back on the edge and closed my eyes. Well, whether the dog believed me or not, I had this. Just friends. No problem.

~

### Sully

By the time I finally got home, it was after midnight. I cracked the door and whistled softly. After a moment, Ranger came barreling through the room as he raced to meet me. Opening the door wide, I let the dog out into the night to do his business. Maggie had never owned a dog, and I wasn't sure if it would have occurred to her to let him out, much less feed him. I knew what the end of the year was like for Maggie, and if I hadn't, Emma had called to remind me. I hoped she went to bed early because I was certain that growing a baby wasn't going to help this scenario out.

Watching my dog race around the backyard, I stared up at the night sky. The stars were out in full force and made me feel insignificant for a moment. We really were just a speck in this world. A breeze blew out of the west and brought a chill to the air. In a month or so the crops would be much taller and would cocoon the farm from any outside noise.

Ranger raced up to greet me, business complete. I gave him a good rubdown, and we moved back into the house, locking the door and turning off the lights as we went. Hitting the kitchen, I saw the note that Maggie had left on the island for me.

*Dinner was amazing. Leftovers in the fridge if you're hungry. Thanks again.*

M-

I looked over the note. There was only friendship there, which was fair. My notes to her were similar. I briefly wished for more, but didn't want to rush her. Maybe when she was comfortable. Maybe after a few weeks when she felt more secure.

Ranger whined from over by the couch. Glancing in his direction, I saw the top of Maggie's head sunk down into a cushion. Moving over, I came around to the front and took her in. Her strawberry blonde hair spilled over the pillows in waves. She was curled up on her side, with a wide band of skin at her belly exposed. Just taking in all that she was made my dick jump to attention. She was wearing leggings in some kind of headache-inducing print, but they left little to my imagination. And her tank top had tiny little straps, one of which was sliding down her shoulder. Good God, resisting her like this should earn me some type of award.

Placing a hand on her shoulder, I whispered her name. "Maggie. Mags."

She rolled from her left side to her right, now facing the back of the couch and nestling into the pillows a bit more.

I thought briefly about leaving her here on the couch but she'd rest better in bed. Resignedly, I leaned down and scooped her up in my arms and headed for the stairs. Before I reached them, however, I made an abrupt turn for my room. One, taking her upstairs meant I had several chances to whack her head on the banister and the wall. Two, I really didn't want to take her upstairs; let's be honest here.

Entering my own room, I moved to the bed and laid her down, scooping the quilt out from under her and then covering her with it. Moving over to my closet, I quickly shed my jeans and T-shirt, leaving them in a heap on the floor. If I'd been alone, my boxer briefs would have joined the pile. Tonight, I figured, that might be pushing my luck.

Moving back to the bed, I slid in across from Maggie, Ranger settling on the foot of the bed on Maggie's side. I rolled to my side for a moment, watching Maggie in the moonlight. Just over a month ago I'd brought her home to this very bed. Our actions the next morning had changed the course of both our lives. And now she was back here with me.

Rolling to my back, I looked up at the ceiling and took a deep breath. While I wasn't a very spiritual guy, I still took a moment to say a prayer of gratitude right then and there. The odds that had been against this baby even being conceived were ridiculous. But this little bean, as Maggie had taken to calling it, had brought us together. And even though it was under the guise of friendship, Maggie was here. We were going to be roommates. I was damn grateful to her. Everything wasn't where I wanted yet, but I felt like we were slowly taking some steps toward our future. I just had to make sure I was ready for it.

Closing my eyes, I tried to make sure to give her space. I'd love to have Maggie in my bed every night, wake up with her every day. But that wasn't where she wanted us. She hadn't flipped out when we'd slept together at her house that first night after we'd found out about the baby, but if she woke up and I had a raging hard-on pressed into her back, she might be a bit offended. It could truly be one of those two-steps-forward-one-step-back scenarios. And I didn't want any more steps back.

Glancing to my right one more time, I lightly ran my hand through her hair, brushing it back from her face, and simply whispered, "Thank you," before closing my eyes and falling asleep.

~

## *Maggie*

I woke with a start. It was dark, darker than I ever remembered in my room, with a sliver of moonlight providing light instead of the annoying street light I was used to. It took a minute before I remembered I was at Sully's, not my place. My momentary confusion grew when I remembered I'd fallen asleep on his couch. I'd been reading a great romance book on my phone and thought I'd take a quick nap before he came home. I thought I'd wait up for him, see if he wanted me to warm him up some food or just to talk after work. Emma and I'd occasionally crashed at his place over the years after cookouts or family parties, and hanging out in the late-night hours was always a blast. I'd hoped that reminder of what we'd been would keep me remembering that the two of us belonged in the friend zone.

Coming back to my current reality, I could feel Ranger down by my feet. That meant I could be in only one spot, Sully's bed. Well, I guess it wouldn't be the first time. I rolled over to face him and was grateful he was out cold because I definitely sucked in a breath at the sight of him. The quilt was low at his waist. It was dark, but his chest and arms were visible in the low light. His dark hair was tousled on the pillow and the stubble on his chin looked like it had been at least three days since he last shaved. Part of me wanted to run for the hills. Part of me wanted to snake a hand below the covers and really wake him up. All of me wanted to lean over and kiss him, just to see what would happen.

*Get a grip,* I told myself.

My body acted without waiting for my mind to catch up. I slid across the bed and curled against his side. It had been a long day. One week ago I'd found out that the last time I was with this man I'd left with a bigger reminder than just some memories. Yes, I wanted Sully. More than I cared to admit. But more than that, I just wanted the comfort of him, the feeling that I wasn't alone. His warmth flooded my body.

I stretched one arm across his stomach and laid my head in the crook of his arms. My top leg draped across his, and I felt his arm curl around my back, pulling me into him in his sleep. My entire body relaxed as I sank into him and drifted off, feeling calmer than I'd felt in a long time. Maybe we could be roommates that were just friends after all.

～

### Sully

I swung off my bike and headed up the walkway to my parents' place. Waking up next to Maggie this morning had been unreal. It was like a dream. Before I got two steps from my bike, I felt the vibrations from my phone in my pocket. Pausing to tug it out, I saw a text from Jake.

**Jake:** *You sure it's cool for me to take off today to head over to Knobs Brewery? You were here late last night too.*

I thought for a minute about what to say.

**Me:** *Not keeping score, man. You're going there for work too.*

**Jake:** *Okay. Planned on hitting their space next week, but they had something going tonight that they wanted me to see.*

I paused, not sure what to say to Jake anymore, which I fucking hated. We'd been close for so long, but now I felt like I'd let him down. Worse, I was second-guessing myself all over the damn place. Should we have gone ahead with canning? I was beginning to think so. But I'd been worried and hesitated. Now we'd lost out on that loan.

**Me:** *Have fun and let me know what you learn.*

There. That was a subtle way to let him know I was still interested in learning more, right? Maybe? Damn if I didn't feel like an indecisive kid right now. I shook my head and headed into my parents' place.

"Mom, Dad?" I called out as I entered the farm kitchen.

"Out in a second," I heard my dad call from the direction of their bedroom. I grabbed one of my mom's chocolate chip scones off the counter and took a bite. I closed my eyes to really savor it since I hadn't had one for a while. It was a good thing I didn't live at home anymore. I'd easily weigh ten more pounds, minimum.

I headed down the hall to the family room, thinking I'd meet up with Dad. Halfway there, I slowed, my eyes catching on one of the photos Mom had framed on the wall. Mom often joked that her decoration style was photos. She didn't like them to be posed but candid shots where she got to see people as they really were, or so she said. As a result, there was a shit ton of photos of someone taking a bite of food at various family gatherings over the year. I asked her about that, and she said she was always trying to capture the blissed look on someone's face when they had a bite of food that they really loved.

The photo that caught my eye, however, was after some Little League game. I was still in my uniform standing with my dad and facing the tall corn, grain elevator in the distance. The sun was going down, bathing the whole sky in gorgeous colors. I was guessing my mom was behind the camera, and she had captured the shot that had my dad resting his arm on my shoulder as we watched the sunset. I'd put money on some Dairy Queen ice cream in my hand, since that was the tradition after most games.

Emotion flooded me as I stood there. From my spot in the hall I could see many pictures in either direction with my dad giving Emma or myself his quiet support. Hell, even Max and Emma began to show up in these pictures at some point, and he did the same for them. How did he know how to be what we needed? I went frame to frame, seeing Dad cheering us on at a football game, pitching the ball to me in the yard, encouraging Emma in a cross-country meet, dancing with Emma in the kitchen when she was small.

I came back to the picture of us at sunset. I was about eight, which was at the tail end of what I considered the lean years here. Years where I remember seeing my dad at the dining room table late into the night, trying to figure out how to make ends meet. I'd put money on Emma having no memories of those times. Hell, I bet my parents would hate like hell that I even knew about them, but they'd impacted me, clearly.

Looking at that photo, though, I didn't see that stress reflected in him. I saw my dad standing by my side after watching my game. A dad that somehow scraped enough together to pay for my fee to be on the team, my uniform, my ice cream treat after the game, even though it probably hurt. Did I appreciate that enough then? I dropped my head and put a hand on the back of my neck as I considered the wood floors. Do I now?

This morning I'd woken up with Maggie curled around my body as I lay on my back. Opening my eyes, I'd looked down to see her strawberry blonde hair spread out over my chest, and I'd wondered briefly how in the hell I could get this to be a regular thing. Before I got to enjoy it too much, she'd woken up and teased me mercilessly over the fact that I'd put her in my bed instead of hers. She seemed to have moved me firmly back into the friend zone, and while I treasured her friendship, it might kill me.

A throat cleared, and I looked up to see my dad at the end of the hall watching me. "You good, son?" he asked, moving down the hall to my side.

I felt myself relax just being near my dad. Just being with him made me feel like a little kid, safe in the knowledge that he had me, even when things were tight. Though I was certainly worried then that we might have to move, that he would have to find another job, I always knew we'd be together. Looking at him now, I smiled. He'd clearly been finishing a chapter in his latest book. He was wearing his reading glasses with a book in hand. "Yeah, Dad. What did you want to meet about today?" I asked.

"You working tonight?" he asked, ignoring the question. Looking at the picture I was standing in front of, he snorted. "Shocking that your mother would have a photo of a sunset up here."

"She does love them," I agreed. Then I answered his question, even though he'd ignored mine. "And yeah, I'm working. Jake's down to Knobs Brewery to check out their canning process."

He nodded. "That's right. When are you two kicking off your first batch?"

My heart sank. I didn't want to have this conversation today. Searching for another topic, I seized on the one I didn't think we'd ever talk about. I tapped the sunset picture. "I think I was eight here."

He nodded.

Gathering some courage, I continued. "I remember those were some lean years for the farm..."

Dad turned to face me. "You do?"

I still faced the picture, it was easier than looking at him for this. "Yeah. Heard you and Mom talking some back then."

Dad must have decided looking at the picture was easier too because he turned back to it. "Shit, Cole. Wish I'd known."

We stood in silence for a bit. I wondered briefly where Mom was. I'd put money on her being out back, gardening. The silence of the house felt like a spell that I didn't want to break. Eventually, I did. "Why didn't you talk to us about it?"

Dad let out a big sigh before placing an arm over my shoulder just like he had in the picture. Turning me, we headed back toward the kitchen. He dropped his book on the counter and let go of my shoulder. "Want a scone?" he asked.

"Had one," I replied.

He grabbed one for himself and took a bite, letting out a quiet moan. "I swear, your mom is trying to kill me with her baking. I mean, how is a person to resist these?"

"Dad..." I hopped up to sit on the counter and watched him.

Leaning against the other counter, he regarded me. Mom and Dad were in their late fifties, but both were still extremely active. I figured if their genetics worked out for me, I was looking at a mirror image of myself in a bit over twenty years.

"Didn't want to burden you, son," he quietly said. "Man is any kind of man, he makes life easier for those he loves, doesn't weigh them down. Your mom and I examined the cards we were dealt by Mother Nature and worked like hell to get us to a good place." He looked over my shoulder out the window, lost in thought. After a minute or so, he looked back to me. "I hope like hell that you didn't dwell on it."

"Oh no," I blatantly lied.

Dad snorted. "Bullshit." He shook his head at me. "So I guess I now know why you are so damn tight with money. You certainly don't get that from your mom. As long as the farm is doing well, she's happy to boost the local economy anyway she can."

I laughed at that. He wasn't wrong. "Has she met the new bookstore owner yet? I bet that's a place that will have her loyalty."

"Not sure. You met her?" he asked.

"Yeah, few weeks back, Ivy. Came into the brewery. She just moved to the area this spring. Said she used to have family here and wanted to open a store in a place like this. Said she's calling it Pages. Sounds cool, though she was a trip."

"A trip, how so?" he asked.

"Nothing big, seems nice. Her style was just interesting. Name is Ivy. Ivy Abrams, I think. She would have fit right in during the seventies."

"The seventies? Your mom will love that. She a hippy?"

"No idea. Emma said something about boho, but I have no idea what that means." I smiled at the memory of Ivy coming in to talk to Jake the other day. It was one of the moments of the week where I had hope that we'd get back to normal soon. "She had on some long flowy dress with a shit ton of hair. She talked to Jake for almost an hour about crystals, moon water, and astrology, then recommended some books." I snorted thinking of Jake's confused expression.

My dad leaned back, letting out a hoot of laughter. "So, what sign is he?"

"No idea." I laughed with him. "I think Jake escaped to the kitchen at that point." I looked up to see my dad watching me.

"Asked if you wanted to swing by this morning because I needed to get my eyes on you, to see if you were really okay," he said, his voice dropping to his don't-bullshit-me tone I remembered well.

I raised an eyebrow at him. "Why wouldn't I be?"

He crossed his arms, widening his stance as he watched me with a measuring gaze that I knew I'd see reflected back at me in a mirror. "Your life has taken quite a turn. From what Emma says, you now have a roommate." His gaze dropped as he looked over the top of his glasses at me.

Well, maybe I should have let them know about Maggie's new living arrangements. In all fairness, we'd had a lot going on. "Yeah, Dad, Maggie moved in. But we're operating as friends here. Everything is good."

Dad watched me for a beat or two. Part of me wanted to pull up a spot at the kitchen table and spill all my insecurities out, about the business, about Maggie, about how I was fucking all this up already. A larger part of me knew I wasn't going to do this. I needed to be strong like he'd been. I needed to get my shit together and stop making impulsive decisions based on fear. Jake was right, which he would be delighted to hear. Not sure if that meant that we needed to be canning quite yet—it still might be early—but he was right that I shouldn't have made the decision impulsively. Hell.

I realized I'd been lost in thought, so I looked back to my dad to see that he was still watching me. "I'm good, Dad. Swear. Just working through stuff."

He nodded twice, then stood up. "All right. I'm just going to trust that you are old enough to know that your mom and I are here if you need anything. Now," he tapped the book he'd placed on the counter, "have you read this Reacher? Damn good book."

I jumped back down to take the book that my dad was handing to me and read the back. I appreciated that he was giving me the space to figure out what I needed to without letting me feel alone in doing so. One more way he was showing me what it looked like to be a good dad. How would I ever live up to the path he'd blazed for me?

## 13

## FINDING A NEW NORMAL

**Maggie**

It had been a week, but living at Sully's had already begun to feel normal. Well, I should say it had become a new normal. Other than that first night, we kept our distance for the most part. With every day, with every action, he showed me that our friendship was as solid as it ever was. Hopefully it was strong enough to take on the new role of parenting. There were times I longed for more than a friendship, but that feeling had been present for so many years I felt like I could ignore it.

Maybe.

The knowledge of what we could be, what it was like to be with him as something more, made it so much harder. But this was what we were. I wouldn't be sticking around Highland Falls for good, and this was Sully's home. We couldn't be more, but for the baby's sake, having a strong friendship to raise a child—especially when we didn't live in the same town, was important.

I told myself this on a daily basis. My nagging inner voice told me I was an idiot.

Whatever.

After a week of lounging around his house, building up some arm strength throwing the ball around for Ranger, and coming down from the emotional roller coaster that was the end of a school year, I realized: I needed a job. While a summer stretching out unscheduled in front of me was delicious in many ways, days filled with nothing gave my mind time to wander.

My mind wandered when I saw Sully throwing the ball with Ranger, shirt off, sweat over his chest as it glistened in the sun after his morning run. It wandered when I watched him humming to himself in the kitchen as he moved around the island. Standing there in lounge pants, snug T-shirt, kitchen towel thrown over his shoulder, he was a damn vision. Add to that the notion that he was cooking dinner for me on nights off from the brewery or making breakfast for me each day, and it was hard not to jump him.

My mind wandered to when he came in the bathroom after me on one of my many visits to the porcelain throne to throw up all the contents of my stomach. He didn't ask permission, he didn't tell me it would be okay. He simply slid behind me, holding my hair back in one hand as the other stroked my back. When I was done he would stand up, grab a washcloth that he'd soak under the faucet, and hand it to me, moving out of the room quickly to let me have my space. We didn't talk about it, but often when I came out I'd find some snack on the counter—saltines, toast, or peppermint tea were the most common.

He was taking care of me without making a big thing about it, and each day I told myself not to get used to this. Cole Sullivan was a good guy, the best kind of guy. To him, I was a responsibility. He cared about me, for sure, but I needed someone who loved me for me, not out of an obligation or sense of duty. Someone who wouldn't be tied to the town I needed to leave. Someone who hadn't known me since I was young, who didn't pity me. That was not Sully, no matter how much he made my entire body tingle whenever he touched me. The fact that he turned me on was not in question here. It was just one more reminder that I needed to get out of this house, this town, ASAP.

Our little bean had really thrown a wrench in my plans.

Today I was on a mission to find something else to occupy my wandering mind beyond the gloriousness that was Cole Sullivan. Because the end of the school year had been insane, I hadn't had a chance to get to the new bookstore on the square. Sully and Jake had mentioned the place and the owner, Ivy. Emma had met her too and thought she was someone we should get to know. Emma said she gave off a relaxed vibe, one of being super empowered, super feminist.

Ivy had actually worked with Emma and me on Emma's author series project for the next school year, but our communication had all been via email and I hadn't met her yet. I was actually surprised Emma hadn't immediately conned her into attending yoga with us, though I'd missed the last few classes, so who knew, maybe she had.

Emma was always looking for new women in town to connect with. She was such a nurturer and always wanted to ensure no one was ever left out. It was one of the reasons we'd become friends when I moved here. Well, that and the fact that I kicked Chance Miller's ass the first day we met in second grade because he was a prick to Emma. My temper flared just thinking of that second grade bully.

I parked just outside the bookstore and considered their storefront, forest green with black awnings. The name of the store, Pages, was spelled out in the windows in giant typewriter keys. It was a small storefront but absolutely adorable. I moved toward the bright yellow front door.

Inside I felt like I was in my own version of heaven. Maybe Ivy and I would become friends, and I could just live here? Walls of books surrounded the small room with gleaming hardwood floors and tables of books taking up the center. Moving around one long shelf, I came upon two women that were about my dad's age. They were browsing, but upon seeing me, one turned to the other with a whisper and glance in my direction. Yep. Joy of small towns. Could be anything from the fact that I was a teacher to the intel that I was knocked up to some pity story. Whatever. Moving on.

There were a few nooks where you could curl up with a book, and the register was toward the back on the left at a small counter. It was there a woman stood, humming to herself, eyes closed, as she danced in the small space. She was a bit shorter than I was, probably around five foot five. Her blond-brown hair tumbled in waves over her shoulders and down her back. She wore a tank and flowy skirt, lots of bracelets and a few chain necklaces. I noticed the wireless headphones tucked into her ears. This must be Ivy.

Not wanting to scare her, I tried clearing my throat. Nope, she was still humming and dancing, clearly in her own world. Crap. I moved closer, standing across the counter from this dancing whirl, and reached out to tap her arm that she had raised out to the side as she moved. Her eyes sprang open, and a huge smile spread out on her face that seemed completely natural and gorgeous without any trace of makeup.

"Hey!" Ivy said. She tossed her headphones on the counter. "I'm so sorry. I shouldn't wear these when I'm in here. The bookstore melts away, and I'm compelled to move."

I grinned. Anyone who could dance with abandon in a public setting when she wasn't drinking was my kind of person. I stuck out a hand. "Hey, I'm Maggie."

"Emma's Maggie?"

I laughed. "She's taking ownership of me now? Fabulous."

Ivy's eyes twinkled when she laughed. "We meet in person, awesome! So, school's out? How are you feeling?"

I took a breath. Might as well get used to this. "Well, pregnant."

Ivy's glanced dropped to my stomach, then back to my face. "No way! Congratulations! How far along are you?"

"Eight weeks. So not out of the first trimester, but far enough along to be having some morning sickness."

"Wow." Ivy came around the counter and hugged me, placing her hand on my stomach. "Sorry, I guess I should ask you first. And you aren't even showing or anything. I just love pregnancies. How cool is it we get to grow a human? I mean really!" She hugged me again, then took a step back to lean against the counter. "Emma didn't mention anything about a baby last time we talked, but this is new, right?"

"Yep. Apparently, it's my new intro for the next thirty-plus weeks."

Ivy held my hand and squeezed it before letting go. Giving me a look filled with curiosity, she asked, "Now were you planning on traveling this summer, because I feel like that is something she mentioned."

Placing my hand on my stomach, I shook my head. "I'd planned on it, but this threw a bit of wrench into the works."

I noticed that when Ivy talked to you she listened. Not like someone waiting to get her turn to speak, but like she really cared about what you were going to say.

"Momma?" A soft voice floated from the back of the store.

"Right here, Addie," Ivy called out. Glancing at me, she whispered, "My daughter."

I was taken aback. I don't think anyone mentioned Ivy had a daughter. Minutes later a sleepy-eyed girl appeared clutching a picture book. She looked to be around three or four and was a miniature Ivy. Long wavy light blond-brown hair, vivid blue-green eyes. She was adorable.

"Hey Addie," I said by the way of greeting. "I'm Maggie."

"Maggie is a teacher to big kids," Ivy said pulling her daughter up to sit on her hip. She quickly leaned in, giving her a loud kiss on the cheek, then pulled back and looked at me. "Hey, I just had a brilliant idea."

"What's that?"

"This place is new so I haven't hired anyone to work here besides me. However, if there is a chance you would want to work some place a few hours a day, I could absolutely use someone to open in the mornings, ten a.m. to twelve p.m. Monday to Friday. Then this sleepyhead wouldn't need to get up so early." She tousled Addie's hair, and my heart gave a small pang. Not unusual—my mom had been gone for so long—but sometimes it just hit. "You'd need to come around nine-thirty a.m. so you could be ready for opening, but it would be a really low-key job, that is if you were thinking of something like that. Sorry, I often just jump to conclusions, and with you not traveling, I thought... Never mind. You might be completely done in after the end of the school year and all." Ivy grinned at me. When she smiled, she beamed.

"Are you the sleepyhead, Miss Addie?" I asked Ivy's daughter. Pangs to the heart or not, this kid was beyond adorable. She nodded sleepily at me. So sweet. Looking over at Ivy, I met her grin with one in return. "I'd love to work here. Books are absolutely my thing. It is just one of the many things Emma and I have in common. And I was just thinking today that I needed to find something since I planned on being around this summer."

"Cool! Want to start Monday?"

"Sure." I looked around the little store. I could absolutely see myself spending time here this summer. The bell over the door rang out while the gossiping ladies called out goodbyes to Ivy and she to them.

I glanced around at the shelves again and smiled. I wondered if I'd end up spending more money than I made. Spying the young adult section, I had an idea. "Want me to write up some recommendations? I always have a list on my whiteboard in my classroom for the kids to know what books are hot or highly recommended. I could easily do that here."

Ivy started bouncing with Addie in her arms, which made the little girl laugh. "I *love* that idea! I have a template for shelf talkers on my computer. You're welcome to write your recommendations and print them off, sticking them by certain books. And you absolutely should put your name on the recommendation so the kids who come in will know it is from you. This is fabulous!"

Addie squirmed a bit, and Ivy quickly let her down. She immediately headed around the corner toward the rear of the shop.

Ivy watched her go, then looked back at me. "There's a

room in the back that I have set up for book clubs. It also has some bean bags where she loves to sit. That being said, you're a huge help. She loves to sleep and have lazy starts to her day."

"Forgive me if this is too personal, but is her dad around? Can't he help?"

Ivy shook her head, but didn't lose her light. "Nothing is too personal. I'm an open book. And no, he's not in the picture much. It's just been Addie and me for the most part since she was born." She looked over her shoulder at where Addie had disappeared. Then glanced at and took in my face. "No, no. No pity, Maggie. That's the way I wanted it. Addie was the product of a happy relationship, but it wasn't a serious one. Her dad knows about her, but that wasn't his plan for his life. While I'd love it if he wanted to see her more often, that's not where he's at right now. Addie has never known any different, so she's pretty well adjusted for a four-year-old."

She glanced at my belly, then back up. "So, did you want to share about your partner in this new adventure? Or are you doing a solo gig too?"

I shrugged, glancing around the shop and confirming that we were truly alone. "Well, it's not exactly secret, but it's also not public knowledge."

A serious look overcame Ivy as she quickly crossed her heart. "I am a vault."

I laughed out loud. "Okay, vault. Emma's brother, Cole Sullivan, is the father."

Ivy's eyes widened. "Well, holy shit, that's fun. I'm assuming he's aware? What was his reaction? Are you two a thing? Emma was holding out!"

I considered how to shorthand the entire history of my crush on Sully, the one crazy night, and our new normal.

"Yes, he's aware. And no, we're not a thing beyond childhood friends."

Narrowing her eyes, Ivy seemed to consider my reaction before proceeding. "And is that what you want?"

I could feel heat flood up my body, which mean that my neck and face were going to be flushed. What I wanted was not what could be, but just thinking of what I wanted made tingles race up and down my body and my heart rate increase. Damn that man. He could even get to me in my thoughts. Insanity.

"What I want is truly irrelevant. I don't plan on staying here for good, and Sully does. So we're working on a strong foundation of friendship to raise this baby." Good, I told myself. I actually sounded like I meant it. "I'm even staying at his place this summer since I had already sublet mine so I could travel."

Ivy considered me carefully before throwing her head back with a riot of laughter.

"What?" I asked.

Wiping tears from her eyes, she met my questioning gaze. "Soooo you are living as *just friends* with this man who, by the way, I've seen..." She waggled her eyebrows. "And just reading between the lines here, you're pretty sweet on him. Am I warm?"

I nodded reluctantly, but my flush probably gave me away anyway. She set her hands on her hips and narrowed her eyes at me. "But you think you'll be strong enough to be around that gorgeous man day in and day out *and* resist any horizontal action?"

Rolling my eyes, I muttered, "Is that all?"

Ivy leaned in and hugged me before letting go to continue dispensing her wisdom. "I'm just so glad you'll be working here."

Skeptically, I asked, "You are?"

"Hell yes! Now I get a front-row seat to this real-life love story. Woo-hoo!" She raised her arms above her head and spun around laughing.

I shook my head, debating trying to explain how wrong she was, but decided it wasn't worth it. Instead I laughed and watched her continue to spin and reflected how grateful I was to have found a new friend, even if she was a bit nuts. Getting a part-time job in the process was just gravy on top.

## 14

## UNWELCOME DINNER GUESTS

**Sully**

As I entered the kitchen that night I was nervous with anticipation. Maggie had texted that afternoon asking if I was working the late shift or if Jake could cover. She had news she wanted to share. I immediately replied, asking if everything was okay with the baby. She'd promised that all was well but wouldn't give anything else away. My mind had been on overdrive for the past five hours. Did she want to find her own place? Had she decided to hit the road after all this summer? I coached myself to be supportive no matter what.

Before heading off to find where Maggie was in the house, I was stopped short. The kitchen smelled amazing. Moving over to the oven, I opened it to see rows of meatballs baking, a golden-brown color on each. My mouth immediately watered. "Maggie!" I shouted. "Are these meatballs done?"

"Impatient much?" she said, wandering in. Grinning, she hip checked me away from the oven and looked inside. "Yep, they should be good."

"They look and smell fucking amazing. Where did you get the recipe?"

"Where all amazing recipes come from, of course. The one, the only, Ina Garten."

I looked into the oven, resting my chin on her shoulder. I reached around to poke at one meatball, testing it. "Who the hell is Ina Garten?"

"Um, only the most brilliant cook ever. She's also known as the Barefoot Contessa." She smacked my hand to keep me from snatching a meatball right off the tray and eating it immediately. They looked that good.

I reluctantly backed away. Apparently, there was no sampling the meal. Well, at least not yet. Racking my brain, the name Barefoot Contessa sounded familiar. "Does she make cookbooks?" I asked, thinking of the cookbooks that lined a shelf in my mom's kitchen. Heck, I was pretty sure Emma had several too.

"Yes, and every recipe she has is actually fabulous when you make it, which is so rare."

I nodded, heading to the fridge. Many of the recipes we used at The Homestead were based on family recipes from Jake's or my own. Our head chef, Pete, also brought his own batch of recipes in. But trying to replicate what someone else did could be tough. I just hoped these meatballs were half as delicious as they smelled.

Pulling out a beer from the fridge, I glanced at Maggie. "Do you want anything?"

"Nope, I'm good." She added some meatballs to a pot with sauce.

I debated how to begin our conversation. In some ways Maggie could be as skittish as a cat. I felt an intense desire to help her to relax, unwind, and feel at home. She'd done that a bit in the past week, but I felt that she wasn't all the way there. Yet. I couldn't decide if she didn't trust herself or me. I was betting it was likely a little of both. "So, you said you had some news," I prompted.

"Yes!" Maggie spun away from the oven to face me, and all my blood rushed south. Her eyes were sparkling with light. I could see it from across the island. Her hair flew around her, waves of strawberry blonde tumbling over her shoulders. Her light skin was tinged a bit with color, like she'd been outside for an extended period of time today. But what was killing me was her short pajama shorts with a tiny tank and a loose cardigan. I could absolutely picture a day a few months from now where those shorts would have to ride under her belly and the tank would be stretched to the limits by her stomach.

Who knew I'd find pregnant women so sexy?

"I got a job!" Maggie exclaimed, oblivious to the situation going on in my pants.

"What?" Confusion warred with the efforts to get my other brain under control. "You have a job."

Maggie rolled her eyes as she moved my way. I worked to keep the counter between us without being obvious as I moved around the side.

"I don't mean my teaching job. I mean I went to the bookstore today and talked to Ivy. She needs someone to work there a few hours each morning, Monday through Friday. I thought that would be fun."

"Ahh, you met Bookstore Ivy? What did you think?" I asked as I continued around the side, moving farther away as she came closer again. Good Lord. I was trying not to be obvious, but the closer she came, the more I could see through that tank, which just made the tent situation I had going on in my pants even worse. Damn.

"Ivy is awesome. I'm not working full-time or anything,

just for a few hours every morning Monday through Friday to give her daughter a chance to sleep in a bit."

"And you are good with that? You don't think you'll need to rest up or anything?" I scanned her face, seeing if there was any tension there, but found none.

Maggie laughed. "Sully, women have been having babies since the beginning of time. I don't think most of them get to sit around and just watch their belly grow. I'll be fine working ten hours a week. I might spend everything I make on romance books and books for my classroom, but that's a chance I'm willing to take," Maggie replied before tilting her head and considering me from across the island where I'd moved to make sure we weren't on the same side. "Umm, Sully, what are you doing?"

I took a swig from my beer, attempting a casual look, before looking back at her. "What do you mean?"

Maggie took a step toward the corner of the island. I took a step to the opposite corner. "Do I smell?"

"I don't know what you're talking about," I said, even as I prepared to move again if she did.

"That's it!" Raising her finger to point at me. "Stay right there, Cole Patrick Sullivan." She quickly moved around the island.

I stayed in one place with my hips leaning against the island, praying she wouldn't notice anything. I felt like a damn teenager, which was the last time I had this little control over myself. Good Lord, this might send Maggie running for her life. Instead of calming down, her fiery eyes had stirred me up even more.

Maggie reached my side and quietly asked, "Sully, what's going on?"

"Nothing, I swear." I looked down at my beer.

"Did I do something?"

Shit. Her voice was soft, unlike her typical larger-than-life personality. I couldn't have her thinking that. I lowered my beer and placed it on the counter. Then I turned toward Maggie and pulled her body flush against mine until we were against each other, my issue becoming obvious to all.

Maggie's eyes widened. "Ohh."

My mouth quirked. "Yep, ohh about covers it."

"Umm, how did that happen?" Maggie whispered.

"You happened," I replied with a shrug loosening my grip on her, but noting that she didn't move back.

Maggie's voice squeaked out as a blush spread across her cheeks, making her freckles stand out even more. "Me?"

"You, your pajamas, your curls." I looked at her, then let my hands drift down, my fingers running over the sides of her breasts. "Your lack of a bra."

"Bras are made by the devil," she whispered.

"I'm a fan of the no-bra look," I whispered back, my eyes locked on hers. "Feel free to get rid of every last one. You can burn them out back if you want."

Rolling her eyes, she muttered, "I'm sure you'd like that."

"What can I say. I'm a giver." My eyes locked on hers. I saw a hell of a lot of heat there.

"Sully, what are you...?"

That was all she got out before my mouth claimed hers.

I briefly wondered if I was alone in this out-of-control feeling, but Maggie's body immediately told me I wasn't. Her mouth opened, allowing my tongue to slide in, hers finding my own. Her hands raced up my back, to my hair, then back down to tug my T-shirt from my jeans, coming around to the front to lightly trace over my stomach muscles as they dove down, driving me closer to the edge.

I gripped her ass as I pulled her to me, then up, placing

her on the edge of the island. Maggie let her legs fall to the side so I could step into the open space, pressing myself right to her sweet spot. She moaned in pleasure, and I pulled her in even tighter. Damn, this woman drove me crazy.

My hand roamed under her tank, teasing her nipple, as her hand slid into my jeans. Right as I let out a moan of pleasure, everything came to a crashing halt when I heard the door slam open and a chortle of laughter reached us.

We ricocheted apart, panting as we made eye contact, and looked over at the door to see Emma standing there, hand over her mouth as she tried to hold more laughter back. Max simply stood in the door, leaning against the frame, with a wide grin peeking out of his beard. Ranger's head popped around Max's legs, apparently ready to come back in and join the party.

"So," Emma said as her laughter threatened to bubble over. "Want to go over again how you two are just friends?"

Maggie let her forehead drop to my shoulder as I encircled her back with one arm, using my free hand to flip off my best friend and sister. What did I do to deserve this kind of timing?

Maggie whispered in my ear. "Umm, one small thing I forgot to tell you? I invited them to dinner."

"Out," I growled.

"Fuck that. I smell meatballs," Max said, moving into the kitchen. "Staying."

"And I need to borrow Maggie," Emma said, shoving me as she grabbed Maggie's hand and tugged her out of the room. Maggie looked over her shoulder at me and shrugged, mouthing, *I'm sorry.*

I looked at her, then over at Max who was cracking

open a beer as he stood across the island from me. "Asshole," I growled at him.

Max took one look at my face, down at my crotch, and roared with laughter.

Damn it all to hell.

## 15

## NO BULLSHIT

***Maggie***

Emma's eyes were positively dancing as she sat across from me on Sully's bed. My curiosity got the better than me as I glanced around his room. I hadn't been in here often, but even I had to admit his room was pretty sweet. Leaning back against his pillows, I pulled my knees to my chest and glanced back at Emma, waiting.

I didn't have to wait very long.

"So, it looks like you and my brother are going to forget this idiotic 'just friends' idea and go for it. Thank God!"

"Emma, I think you have the wrong idea..." I started to try to explain to no avail.

As she continued, I could tell her emotions were running high. Her hands were waving around as she gestured and practically danced with glee from her seat. "I mean you are both two of the best people I know. And you're having a baby. Together! You deserve all the happiness in the world, Maggie May."

It was upon those words, delivered straight to my heart,

that I promptly burst into tears. Well hell, this was the hormone roller coaster that never came to an end.

"Maggie, what is going on?" Emma pulled me forward, wrapping her arms around my shoulders as I sobbed into my best friend. I didn't have a sister, but in Emma I had found one so many years ago. I knew she wouldn't judge, and I hadn't realized how much I was holding back. I tried catching my breath, but the tears kept coming.

Thundering footsteps headed toward the two of us. Wonderful.

"Christ, Emma. What did you say?" I heard Sully's hushed voice over my shoulder at the door, but the dam had burst and there was simply no going back. Trying to catch my breath just caused the stuttering sound that made me sound like a lunatic. In seconds an additional set of arms wrapped around me from behind. Sully.

"Sully, I've got this," Emma said from my front. "Get your ass out of here."

"Got this? You caused it!" Sully hissed at his sister over my shoulder. "You go."

Christ. God save me from these two and their good intentions. I just wanted to pull it together. Stop. Fucking. Crying. What the hell? Maybe I was pregnant with a girl after all? Could the female hormones needed to grow a girl make me more emotional? Was that even a thing? Mental note to add that to the gargantuan list to ask Doc Graham next time.

Another stuttering breath slipped out. Damn it.

Max's voice floated in from somewhere by the door. "Well, isn't this a pretty picture? Want me to snap a shot for this year's Christmas card? Or maybe this can be the photo for a baby shower invite?" His amusement was palpable and only served to piss me off, which in turn helped begin to slow the tears.

I caught my breath. "Go to hell, Max."

"Aww, there's the Maggie I know," he replied with a soft smile.

"I'm fine. Really." I tried to reassure them all. The sobbing had subsided at least. Silver linings and all.

Sully ran his hand through my hair and down my back. Damn, it felt so good. My body just wanted to curl up with him, pull the covers over both of us, and sleep for days. Well, let's be honest. Sleep would not be the only activity that came to mind. *Don't wiggle back against him. Don't do it, Maggie.*

I took another fortifying breath and thought about relaxation breathing. My heart rate slowed down. The tears stopped. Sully's hand slipped lightly over the back of my shirt. His light touch moved up and down my back again, ending at my waistband as he traced it from one side to another.

"Breathe, Maggie," he whispered.

Gradually, the tears stopped.

Emma pulled my chin away from my chest, and I met her eyes. "You're good?"

"I will be," I whispered.

She looked into my eyes for a minute, then in a no-nonsense voice that would fill any teacher or mother with pride said, "Anyone who has a penis, out. Girl-talk time, and you two are not invited."

I felt Sully stiffen behind me, but then Max said, "Yo, Sullivan. Let's give them a few. Maybe get a drink and head outside?"

At the word *outside*, Ranger perked up and took off to the kitchen and back door, barking the entire way.

Sully sighed, letting his arms loosen around my waist, and he began to pull away. Before he left me, his mouth found my ear and he whispered, "I'm not far. If you want me to kick these two out on their asses, I'm on it."

A laugh escaped and my chest loosened. So he was a mind reader. That could work against me and my good intentions. "I'm good. I swear. Pregnancy hormones are running amuck."

Max leaned over and squeezed my shoulder, then headed back toward the kitchen. He really was great, even if he treated me like a little sister. Sully gave me a glance, then followed him. I sat, staring down the hall after them, contemplating what God put those two amazing male specimens in my life.

"All right, chickie, spill. What the fuck was that?" Emma's eyes were dancing once again. "Or more to the point, what the hell did we walk in on?"

I fell back into the pillows, looking up at the ceiling. "I have no idea." I said, more confused than ever.

The thing about being friends with someone since the age of eight is that there isn't really any hiding from the truth.

Emma spoke up. "I want zero details about my brother in the sack because eww." She shuddered. "But you say the word if he doesn't know his way around the clit, Maggie May. I'm not a librarian for nothing. I'll be glad to point him in the directions of a few resources."

That did it. I threw back my head with a laugh while I wiped happy tears from my eyes. "Please"—I worked to catch my breath—"let me be there when you offer that service up."

"I got you, babe." Emma grinned.

I debated if I wanted to say anything else to her. While I

typically didn't shy away from sharing about my sex life, this felt different. Not just that we hadn't had sex since that first time, but also, this was Sully. It didn't seem to be something I was comfortable discussing, which was interesting. Maybe it was the uncertain nature of our relationship.

"It's crazy, Emma. I feel like Sully and I are in some type of relationship purgatory. Since I've moved here, I've had you. Through you, I've had Max and Sully. You are my pillars, you all, your parents, along with my dad are what has kept me stable for the past twenty years or so." I started tearing up again. Damn it. This bean had to be a girl, and I'd been so certain it was a boy. "I don't know what to do with this."

Emma sat there, watching me. I could tell she was weighing what she wanted to say carefully. "Mags, no matter what, you are stuck with the three of us for life. Pregnant or not, relationships between Max and me or whatever is going on with you and Sully, we will always have each other's backs."

"I know, but..."

"No, hold on. Let me finish." She leaned forward and wiped the tears from my cheeks. "Babe, we are all here for you. Always. But if you are going to sit there and tell me that what happened with you and Cole was an accident, I'm calling bullshit on that."

My face flamed up. "Emma—"

"Nope. Still my turn. *Shush.* I've watched you drool after him since we were in middle school. I've watched you devour him with your eyes since high school, even when you tried to make jokes about it. And in the past few years, I've watched him do the same to you."

"Wait, what?"

"Shut it. I don't know what it is that you two have. I

don't know what it could be. What I do know is that what Max and I walked in on in the kitchen was hot, if I can remove the fact that it was my brother from the equation. Watching you both over the past few years, I thought you might be good together if it ever happened and you didn't immediately drive each other crazy. Walking in on that in the kitchen, and whatever that tension was just a bit ago when we were all *sitting on the same bed*—I mean come on, Mags—I know there is potential between you guys. My question is, whose ass do I need to kick to get you both to act on it?" She looked pointedly at my still-flat stomach, then back at my face. "Well, act on it again, I mean."

My mind wandered to every interaction with Sully from the moment on this bed just over a month ago to his actions since he found out about the baby to stolen kisses to sleeping—just sleeping—with him to him taking care of me to him throwing the ball with Ranger. To, to, to. I wish I could just dive in, trust that he could learn to love me. That I wouldn't be a charity case. Sully would love me, he'd always love me, but I wanted him to be *in love* with me. Not in a relationship because he was the best guy and felt like he should give his child a family. Add to that the fact that Sully had known me as long as Emma. He *knew* me. He'd known me as a kid and knew my story.

"Emma, I need to leave here." I paused.

Her eyebrows came together and creased. "Sully's house or Highland Falls."

"Both." I thought about that for a second, then continued, "But I'm leaving Highland in a year."

She watched me for a few beats. Emma would be a great teacher, excellent use of wait time, I noted. "You've said this for years, but you've never explained to me *why* you feel the need to leave. Do you just feel that Highland is too small?"

I guess we hadn't really talked about it. But Emma wasn't going to understand. How do you explain what it feels like to be someone who is pitied when you are from a family everyone respects? I stood up, feeling the need to pace. I walked back and forth between the bed and the windows looking out over the moonlit fields, a country road a ribbon in the distance.

"I'm not sure I can explain it to you," I muttered, running my hands through my hair, twisting it up on top of my head in a knot that I secured with the ponytail holder on my wrist.

"Try me. No bullshit, remember?"

I let a rueful laugh out at our teenage friendship motto. It had served us a well over the years. The only way out was through, and all. "Emma, the thing is, here I'm always going to be the little girl who lost her mom in a car accident when she was young. The girl who had a dad that took lots of jobs to make money for his family but always came up a bit short. The girl who was constantly given charity in the form of food, gifts, and more. The girl who couldn't stand on her own. Don't you get it? I *have* to leave. I need to be some-where that people won't pity me for the rest of my life. I need to be away from the gossip of small towns." I looked down at my stomach and laughed. "Guess I screwed that up even more. Regardless, I need to start over, and Sully's life is here. Even if he didn't look at me that way, he couldn't leave, and I can't stay." Tears were streaming down again. Maybe I'd just give up mascara and any form of makeup until this pregnancy was over.

I finally stopped pacing in front of the windows to look at Emma. She had been stretched out on the bed but had pulled herself up to a seated position so she could look at me like I had sprouted two heads.

"I'm trying to be super respectful, Maggie, because I think you believe all that bullshit you just spouted, but are you serious? You think the town pities you? That my family does? That I do? What the hell?" Her eyes were flashing.

"Emma, you do not get to tell me how to feel. You cannot sit there and tell me that you didn't feel bad for me growing up because I know you did. You said as much when we were kids."

Now she joined me in my pacing, her arms flying. "Of course I felt bad for you. You lost your mom! But I never pitied you, at least not how I think you mean. And while this place runs on gossip at times, the town is all about helping when it is needed. We're like a big family. And in a family, if you see a member who needs something and you can do something about it, you step in and do it. If the world worked that way, it would be a better place. And you do it too."

That caught me off guard. "What the hell are you talking about?"

"Bridget told me how you anonymously adopted a family this year. Your student Matt, was it?"

"I don't know what you're talking about."

"Bullshit. She said the family called the school because gift cards to the grocery store began anonymously showing up at their apartment. Someone went on their behalf to the organization who helps pay electricity bills when people are short. The mom had said Matt confessed he talked to you about being hungry, that he told you they were struggling." Emma raised her eyebrows, indicating she felt that she had won the argument.

I disagreed. "Not sure what this proves."

"So do you look down on Matt in your class compared to the rest of your students?"

"What? No, of course not."

"Do you pity him? Do you blame him for his problems?"

I walked to the window again, staring out and not seeing anything at the same time. "I see what you're saying, but I can't explain how it felt to know that we needed so much from all of you growing up. How it felt to watch my dad work himself to the point of exhaustion but still not have enough. I felt empty, lacking. Sometimes I still feel that way." I took a breath, and the rest came out in a whisper. "I just wonder if that feeling would go away if I wasn't in this town anymore."

I felt Emma come up next to me. She slipped her arm around my waist and leaned her head on my shoulder. I put my head on top of hers.

"Maggie, you're right, and I'm sorry I flipped. I don't know what it was like for you. But what I want to be sure you do understand is that the town, my family, we were happy to help. No one looked down on you or your dad. My mom and dad were as proud as anyone else when he got his CDL license. And while it isn't great that you don't get to see him as much now, he seems to be happy, right?" She squeezed my waist.

"He loves trucking," I said, my voice soft as I looked out the window. I hadn't called him to tell him about the baby yet. I wanted to do it in person, but with long-haul trucking, that was sometimes tricky.

In the darkness, the window was practically a mirror. I looked into her eyes as she met mine.

"Babe," she said. "I need you to remember we love you. When you love someone, you help them out if needed. No one blamed you for being poor, just like no one blamed your dad. My dad constantly said that your father was the hardest-working man he knew."

My eyes widened. "Really?" It was something I had always felt, but didn't know if others saw. My parents had both had high school educations but couldn't afford to go to college right away. Their families hadn't had much either, and their plan had been to take turns going back to school. My mom had been in college to become a teacher when her car was hit, ending her dream and my dad's.

Their love story broke my heart. No happily ever after there.

"Really." Emma met my eyes. "Maggie, I think you might want to give this some thought," she suggested gently.

Now I was confused. "What?"

"Why you really feel this way. If you truly felt the town looked down on you, or if maybe you did."

I started to protest the ludicrousness of that statement, but then she leaned over and kissed my cheek, whispering, "No bullshit, remember?"

I met her eyes and looked away. "Let's go check on the guys."

16

———————

## ASSCLOWNS

**_Sully_**

Standing on the back deck with Max, a beer, my dog, and a moonlit sky was good for the soul. I took a swig of beer and glanced up at the stars that were visible, counting my blessings once again that my parents had let me buy my grandparents' house from them. There was nowhere I'd rather be tonight.

My mind flashed back to Maggie on the counter before our quiet night was interrupted or Maggie on the bed in my room, her body straining *not* to collapse back into mine. Well, I guessed there was *somewhere* I'd rather be. More to the point, there were two people that I could do without right now.

"What's the deal with you two?" Max interrupted my thoughts.

"She's skittish," I replied, trying to decide how much I wanted to share, how much I wanted to keep to myself.

"Looks like my bet on being in bed in a matter of days didn't pan out," Max said with a grin before tipping back his beer.

"Well, same bed, yes. Any action in said bed, nope."

Max let out a huge laugh, filling the night with the sound.

Asshole.

Ranger glanced up from his spot lying on the deck with a hopeful look, but dropped his head when he saw that no one had a ball.

"What's so funny, man?"

"I'm wondering how many showers a day you're taking with her walking around your place in short shorts, tanks, and pregnant with your kid."

"Fucker, you don't need to notice what she's wearing."

"Man, I'd never do anything against your sister. I'm just not oblivious. And I know you. How's it going?"

Looking from Max back to the fields, I muttered. "Skin is drying out. Might need lotion after all these showers."

Max nodded as he sank down into one of the Adiron-dacks I had on the porch looking into the yard. I relaxed into the chair next to him. We sat for a few minutes in complete silence. Typically, we always had music playing, but I hadn't thought to grab my phone and play anything through the speakers. While I was tempted to get up and fix that problem, the quiet of the night was also calming.

"How goes the journey into parenthood?" Max asked as he looked off into the night.

I glanced over at his profile, but he didn't seem to be screwing with me. I let out some air. "Not sure how to answer that one, Harp. It's going, and I have no idea what I'm doing?"

I could see him nodding from the corner of my eyes. "Seems about right."

Leaning forward, I let my elbows rest on my knees as I held a bottle in my hands. I picked at the label of Alpha

King from 3 Floyds brewery. Damn if they weren't doing everything I wanted to be doing at The Homestead.

The distant rumble of a motorcycle drew my eyes to the road. I watched as Jake pulled into our drive, coming to a stop by the sidewalk. Placing his helmet on the seat of the bike, he turned and moved up the walk toward us.

"You guys have another one?" he asked.

Max and I stood to greet him as I watched Jake's expression, wondering what brought him out this way. Max leaned over to the beers we had out here in a small cooler and passed one to Jake. Our friendship seemed to be hovering on a tentative truce for the moment. Jake was too good of a guy to hold a grudge for long, but I could feel that we weren't where we typically were, and I wasn't sure how to get us back there. Maybe spending more time together was the answer, just face the music. But he'd been doing small trips to local breweries, still gathering information. I worried what would happen if, ultimately, I still felt like we couldn't go ahead. Would he accept it? Was I really even considering it? I'd never been this indecisive in business, and I hated it.

"Maggie call you and invite you to dinner like this assclown?" I asked, nodding to Max.

"Assclown." Jake chuckled as he grabbed a bottle opener off the arm of a chair. "Nice." Opening his beer, he took a long drink, then glanced at the label. "Good shit."

"You know, assclown isn't used enough. What a great descriptive, though it doesn't fit me." Max mused, rubbing his damn beard in thought like he was wise or something.

"Need I remind you about what you interrupted earlier. Fits." I growled.

Jake shook his head at us. "Anyway, I apparently didn't rate for the dinner invite. Figured I'd swing by before work tonight. Wanted to see if you'd looked over the numbers from Knobs Brewery that I got last week."

My stomach bottomed out. Damn, I felt like I was letting people down over and over. "Sorry, man. I hadn't got to the report yet. It was on my list to do tomorrow during the day."

Jake leaned over and tapped the neck of my bottle with his own. "Not a worry. I was out for a ride before work and was in the area. Wanted to swing by and check, but we can talk more about it later."

Dusk was falling with a few birds calling out to each other. We sat in silence for a moment, me wondering why I'd put off looking at the numbers Jake had gotten. Was I worried that he'd resent me if I changed my mind and we decided to give it a go after all? I lost the opportunity for us to grab that loan. Damn. I wouldn't blame him if he did.

Max cleared his throat, wanting to break the quiet. "You guys starting soon? I'm ready to stock up on some beer."

Jake gave me a questioning look, realizing I hadn't shared my decision with Max. Yeah, yeah. Closing my eyes, I sighed. Best just lay it down. "Not sure we will be canning this year after all," I gritted out.

Max's expression was one of surprise. I'd told him I'd been unsure, but not that I'd acted on anything. "Why the fuck not?"

"Not sure it's the time to add on additional expenses or take risks, Harp. I have other priorities now, man." I worked to sound like I believed it myself. "Jake is looking at some other options for us, but we passed on the loan from Main Street."

"Are you kidding me?" I turned to the sound of a pissed-off voice that I knew well coming from the kitchen door. There I saw Maggie. Hands on her hips, strawberry blonde hair trying valiantly to escape the pile on top of her head. The light from the kitchen framed her in a silhouette, making her hair appear even more red than usual. Her tank and pajama shorts hugged every curve. "I'm just going to echo Max's wise words," she said. "Why the fuck not? And if little bean here or myself have anything to do with these priorities, please be prepared for me to kick your ass, Cole Sullivan."

I watched her, body strung tight, eyes flashing. I looked at Emma, who shrugged, standing in the doorframe behind Maggie. Glancing over at Max and Jake, I noticed that my best friend had a grin on his face and was leaning against the deck's railing, like he was ready to watch a show. Jake was covering his mouth, clearly fighting a laugh. Apparently, I wasn't getting any support here.

Maggie's narrowed eyes watched me, then she looked at Jake. "Jake, you're welcome to join us for dinner. You can have Sully's portion if we don't have enough. I'd consult him to see what he thought, but apparently that's not something we do." With that, she turned and headed back into the house.

Great, just great.

## 17

## AUCTION SURPRISES

**Maggie**

Sully had earned the cold shoulder from me for the past thirty-six hours. After overhearing his conversation with Max and Jake, I had known immediately that he was holding back on the canning business because of me.

Unacceptable.

Sully had talked to Emma and myself for the past year about the cool designs they'd found for labels. He had worked out the logistics in canning. They'd been preparing to begin right around the end of the school year. I should have asked him about it in the past week, but clearly I'd been a bit preoccupied. He and Jake had gone on more than one trip to breweries in the Midwest to learn all they could, the last one just a few weeks ago. So he could deny it all he wanted, but I knew, *I knew*, that the only thing that had changed since he got back from that last trip was the little bean that was growing inside me.

Nope.

The stubborn ass had tried to give me some song and dance about how he and Jake were putting the brakes on canning for the next year, that there were more expenses than they'd anticipated. Bullshit piled upon more bullshit. I wasn't having it. Because if Sully was holding back on this brewery because of some sense of obligation to the little bean and me, I was going to be pissed. If he was lying about it, I was going to be livid. And make no mistake about it, he was lying. Cole Sullivan was a crappy liar. It just wasn't in his nature. He and Max had gotten into a ton of trouble over the years, not because they got caught in the act, but because Sully couldn't tell a lie to save his ass, or Max's, it seemed.

So one might ask why, if I was still angry, why on earth I was cruising toward a shed on the edge of Floyds Knobs today with him? Simple story, really. I would do anything for Lou and Verdell Williams, that's why.

Lou and Verdell, Emma's former neighbors and honorary grandparents to many of us, had been traveling a lot in retirement, but recently Verdell had taken up a new job. It seems that years ago he had gotten his auctioneer license. The town of Floyds Knobs, twenty minutes from Highland Falls, had an auction every Sunday, and Verdell was the new auctioneer on the first Sunday of each month.

Lou had sent out a request to all the girls. Could any of us help out at the auction today? All that was needed was to bring up items from the tables to the front display where Verdell would start the bidding. It didn't seem like a hard skill, but they were shorthanded. None of the girls were available, so Sully took Emma's spot, and we were headed in. Hopefully this didn't require any speaking on my part, because I really only wanted to talk to him if I could tell him off. I figured he had at least six more hours on my shit list unless he wanted to stop with the lies and actually have a conversation like a grown adult.

I wasn't holding my breath.

Pulling up, I was shocked to see the cars lining the lot and the road. This place was hopping. Emma and I had always talked about trying to come out on a Sunday, but sleep seemed to win out each week. Lou said there were great deals if you were willing to dig through some real crap. I had a feeling Emma would be sorry she missed out.

Sully pulled to a stop and jumped down from the truck while I tossed my phone in my purse. Before I could move to open my door and get out myself, he was there to help me. I seethed inwardly. It would be a lot easier to be pissed at him if he wasn't such a nice guy.

Matching my strides, he fell into step next to me. "So, just wondering, is this silent treatment going to be shorter or longer than the one where I strapped your bikini to the dog and then it got torn in that fence? I mean, in my defense, I thought the suit was Emma's and could never have anticipated that old dog could run that fast."

I glared at him. That suit had been the perfect turquoise color, and when you are thirteen and don't have a job, it is hard to get nice things.

"I know, I know. You and Emma had looked for *ages* for the suit. I had offered to replace it, if you remember. Mom said something about the good suits being gone, which seemed insane. It had been just a few weeks into summer. You always had to be so stubborn and refuse any help." He glanced at me and muttered, "Apparently things don't change."

I felt my spine stiffen. Oh no. I wasn't being the idiot here. That was all him. Whatever. We reached the building, and he opened the door for me. Entering the shed, I immediately wished Emma was here. This place was a trip.

A huge shed barn was stretched in front of me. To the

right there was a counter to check in and get a number to bid with. Ahead on the right was where people could sit. There were armchairs, kitchen chairs, folding chairs, and a few lawn chairs. In front of them were rows of tables piled high with what can only be described as loads of crap. People milled around, checking out the tables, and the scent of freshly popped popcorn settled over it all.

Each table had a number on it. I assumed that helped you know when the items on those tables would be bid on. Then past the tables facing the seats was a raised platform with a table and a microphone. Verdell was up there, cowboy hat perched on his head, talking to some people standing below him.

Sully and I were easily the youngest people here by thirty years.

"Hot damn, we've got workers!" Lou shouted as she headed our way, her silver hair weaving through the crowd of other silver-haired people. She reached us and gave me a squeeze while her gaze raked over Sully with an appreciative nod.

"Lou, behave!" I admonished.

"Child, I knew his grandmother. I'm not going to bite him, but I'm absolutely going to appreciate him. You take it where you can get it, if you catch my drift." Her eyes twinkled, and I wondered, not for the first time, what she was like in her younger years. Hmm. I wondered how she and Verdell met. Maybe she'd been locked up in the county jail? Wouldn't have surprised me one bit.

"Hey Miss Lou," Sully said, leaning down and kissing her cheek.

He was immediately swarmed by a group of blue hairs, each squeezing his cheeks, and yes, I think a few squeezed the lower set. These women were shameless. Sully wasn't fazed, though. It seemed that he knew many of them. To the ones he knew, he greeted them with a hug or a kiss, asked after their family. To the new ladies, he was polite and unfailingly kind.

All sorts of my body parts tingled. Lordy, I wanted to be pissed at him, but I also wanted to jump him. Luckily, a bunch of seventy- and eighty-year-old women were currently blocking my way.

Lou appeared at my elbow. "So, how pissed are you at the boy? My girls will distract him for a bit, but when you think he's had enough, say the word."

I glanced over at her wicked grin. "Lou! How did you know I was pissed?"

"Girl, you know better than to try to keep secrets from me. Emma told me Mr. Sullivan over there was in the dog house for being a stubborn man. I figured we'd give him a little penance in the form of these old biddies. Some of them haven't pressed up against a fine young specimen for many years. They won't get too handsy, but maybe he will appreciate you a bit more when we're done." Lou glanced over at the ladies surrounding Sully, then pointed out one whose hair leaned more toward blue than silver. "That's Mabel. Watch her hands. She's always trying to cop a feel, even with Verdell."

"Umm, Lou, these 'old biddies' aren't a lot older than you," I pointed out.

"Pul-ease. They have at least six years on me, if not more."

I closed my eyes, shaking my head and wondering what world I had been dropped into. Opening my eyes back up, they locked on Sully's, where his grin widened as he met my gaze. He shook his head slowly from side to side as if to say, *What the hell has Lou done now?* There was really no way to answer that, so I glanced down at Lou and smiled.

"I feel like Sully needs to spend some more time with your friends. Maybe he will have thought some more about how to apologize after we go spend some time with Verdell, hmm?" I linked my arm with hers.

"Maggie, I like the way you think." Lou cackled, tugging my arm to head over to Verdell's platform.

I glanced over my shoulder and caught Sully's expression as he realized I was leaving him to the ladies. Reading his lips, he said, *You will pay.* The tingles in my body intensified, and a flush began marching up my cheeks. I turned away and headed with Lou to Verdell and safety.

Several hours later, I was exhausted. We had worked pulling items from the long tables to the center spot where Verdell would have people bid on them. Other than Sully and myself, the median age for one of the workers must have been seventy-eight. I did not understand how they all were still going. I wanted a snack and a nap, and I didn't care in what order I got those things as long as both were in my future.

The frustrating part of this gig was that I couldn't predict what items people were interested in. I'd put up some item I thought was nice and zip, zilch, no bids. Verdell would have to have me grab another item to go with it, and then presto, bids. Then one of the older workers would put some piece of crap up for a bid, and there'd be a ton of interest. It made no sense.

We were finally down to the very end. While some folks hadn't stuck it out until now, the stalwarts were left. Sully grabbed a concrete dog and placed it on the block at the front, glancing back to Verdell to make sure we were good to go.

Verdell began, scanning the room as he went. "Last item of the day, folks. It's a dog, a mean ol' dog. Woof! And we're going to start it at twenty. Do I have a twenty?" And he was off.

Sully's eyes met mine as he silently asked me, *Woof?* and I lost it. Leaning over at my waist, I couldn't hold back the laughter. The morning had been crazy. Sully had been accosted by a bunch of blue hairs. The items for sale had ranged from some beautiful antiques to some household items to complete crap to a ton of romance books that I would have bid on myself if they hadn't gone so high. One of Lou's friends had taken that haul. Lou told me they had a group that passed around the books, and the steamier, the better.

Not sure I had needed that intel.

Now we had a mean ol' dog. *Woof.* What on earth?

"Sold! Bidder 242 for sixty-five dollars. Thanks for coming, everyone. Make sure you settle up with the cashier," Verdell called out.

Done. We were done. I jerked my head to Sully and the door as I sped toward the grassy parking lot. I figured the faster we got out of the building, the faster we'd get away from all the people who would want to talk to us.

As I perfected my speed walk while waiting for Sully to catch up, my mind immediately wandered to his house and how I still had the majority of the day left to laze away. I briefly pondered what romance book I wanted to start once we got home and I found some joggers. Or a nap.

A kiss on my neck quickly brought me back to reality, and I came to a stop right before Sully's truck. He pressed his body flush to my back as he whispered in my ear, "It's a mean ol' dog. Woof."

The sensation of his breath on my neck broke down any

lasting anger I had. Silent treatment be damned, I needed this guy. If only as a friend who liked to flirt with me, I'd take it. Or maybe if I was lucky, something more, at least for today.

I laughed quietly. "You should have bought it. That could have been a no-maintenance friend for Ranger."

"We need to talk about you leaving me with those women, Maggie May. I have bruises in places I shouldn't have bruises," he said as he ran his fingers down my side, tracing my ribs.

My nipples perked to attention, screaming a silent *notice me* to Sully's hands. *Shush, girls.*

"You're a big boy, I figured you could handle yourself," I whispered.

Sully pressed into me tighter from behind. Oh yeah, he was a big boy. Holy hell. It had been weeks, but that didn't mean that one night didn't star in all my fantasies. Gracious. He had ruined me for anyone else.

Sully growled, "I can handle myself, but I'd prefer you to handle me, Maggie." He spun me, my back to the truck as he pulled me up and my legs wrapped automatically around his hips.

A groan escaped before I could help it. At least I think that was me. Maybe it was Sully. My entire body was alight with sensations that made me dizzy.

Sully pushed my hair back from my face and nipped at my lower lip. "What do you want, Maggie? Tell me, baby. I'll make it happen." He rocked up into me and I groaned again.

Holy freaking hell. Yeah, I was done with the cold shoulder, at least for now. I reserved the right to revisit it at a later time.

His eyes were warm, the whiskey brown more of a

chocolate brown as he stared back into my own. I leaned forward and nipped his lip back before touching my mouth to his as I whispered, "You, I want you."

Our mouths crashed together as soon as the words came out. I wasn't sure if I was the aggressor or if he was, but I was certain that I didn't care. Sully ran his tongue along the seam of my lips. They parted and his tongue entered, wiping away any reservations as my heart asked for more, more, more.

"Yoo-hoo? You two need anything?" We pulled back at the call, and I looked over to see Lou standing a row or so away, staring right at us with a bunch of her friends. Her phone was up like she had been capturing our moment. I might kill her. Yep, that likely needed to happen. Sully growled, and I amended that thought. He might kill her first.

Lou waved her phone at us. "I'll just send this over to Emma. She'll be delighted you two are speaking again." She walked off, chuckling with her little group.

My eyes met Sully's once again. "Your house. Now. Please."

Sully grinned as he leaned down and kissed my neck up to my chin, then my lips. "Your wish is my command, princess. Just don't change your mind before we get there."

"How fast can you get us there?"

"Twenty minutes. Fifteen if you want to shed some of these clothes along the way."

I crinkled my brows together in confusion. "Why would that make you drive faster?"

Sully lowered me to the ground. Once my feet were under me, he grabbed my hand and put it on his cock. It twitched under my hand.

Yum.

"Because, princess, this is where I'm at already. I need to get to my house just as much as you do." Sully leaned over my shoulder and opened the passenger door of his truck, helping me up to the seat. My heart pounding, we were tearing out of the lot and en route to his place within minutes.

Locking gazes with me for a moment before he turned back to the road, Sully grabbed my hand. "No overthinking. No internal debate. Fifteen minutes and we are picking up where we just left off, Maggie. I don't care if we drop into the grass and give Ranger a show or we make it to my bed. I just want you."

I squeezed his hand in agreement as we drove over the country roads. The nagging voice in my head reminded me that he probably just wanted me for now. I was convenient. I told that bitch in my head to shut it. For today, I simply didn't care. I needed him as much as he needed me. The rest would sort itself out later.

I hoped.

## 18

## PARENTAL ADVICE

***Sully***

The drive to my place took no time at all but also an eternity. Maggie's hands were roaming everywhere she could reach. At one point she unfastened her seat belt, trying to slide over closer to me.

Glancing in her direction, I growled, "Seat belt." I wanted her more than anything, but I also wanted her and our little bean safe. She gave me a half an eye roll. I gave zero fucks. One, she was speaking to me again, and the silence of the last day was a thing of the past. Two, we'd be at my place in five minutes—no, three—and we were finally going to be back where I wanted us to be. Trying to be around Maggie for the past week or so and let her take the lead had been pure hell. The cold shoulder from her because I was a damn fool and hadn't shared what was going on in my life had been another form of torture. And then she'd come out of the house this morning in short denim shorts with her long legs, a blue band T-shirt, some kimono-type thing, and her strawberry blonde hair spilling over her shoulders. Fuck me. Wave the white flag, I was done.

Whatever.

By the time we reached my driveway, my body was thrumming. I felt wound so tight, I was certain I would burst. I had been joking about sex in the yard, but I might combust before we ever reached the house.

Turning down the lane, I tugged her hand to my lips. "Mags, it has been far too many weeks. You and I have some catching up to do." Her head dropped back against the headrest as I pressed a kiss on her arm, still keeping my eyes on the road.

As a groan slipped past Maggie's lips, my focus slipped from the beautiful woman in my passenger seat to the truck parked ahead of us in my drive.

"What the fuck?" I grumbled.

Maggie's eyes opened, and she looked from me to the truck. "Is that...?"

"My parents." The words escaped my mouth even while I tried to deny the reality in front of me.

"Well, that sucks," Maggie whispered, but I could swear it sounded like she was trying to hold back a laugh.

I parked behind them, then looked over at Mags. She bit her lower lip and looked at me, her eyes twinkling. "Something amusing you, princess?"

Glancing at the house, she murmured, "So, they have a key."

"Yes," I said, hardly masking my irritation. I mean, I loved my parents, but right now I was not thrilled. "Anything else you want to say before we head to see what the fuck they're doing here?"

Maggie glanced down at her phone which I could see was lit up with a text. Laughing, she held it up so I could see

Emma's message asking if Maggie was getting any. Looks like Lou had sent a message after all.

Maggie's fingers began flying. "What are you texting my sister?"

"Nothing much. Just that we've been cock blocked by your parents."

"Maggie..."

"Sully..."

I glared at her, trying to express my displeasure.

Her grin widened. "What? I love your parents, but you can't deny that's what's happening here."

I slid out of the truck and went around to Maggie's side to help her down. We made it a few steps before I had to stop, pulling her against me, and my mouth crashed to hers. Heaven. I soaked in the feeling of Maggie wrapping herself around me, wondering how long I'd dreamed about being about to do exactly this.

Before we could take this any further, a bark pulled me back to reality as Ranger bounded off the deck and jumped up to greet us. Glancing up, I saw my mom waving from the kitchen door where she'd clearly let Ranger out.

Maggie giggled, "See, cock blocked by your mom," as she waved to her and looked up at me.

Glancing down at Maggie, I leaned forward and brushed my lips across her forehead, muttering, "Not for long," before heading up the walk to the house.

Anna and Lee Sullivan were two of the best parents a kid could ask for. That didn't take away from the fact that I wanted to send them packing with no explanation right now. Entering the kitchen, I looked over and saw my dad leaning against the counter, enjoying a beer as he stood back and took in Maggie and me together.

Dad tilted his head to the side, tipped it toward Maggie, a silent question of *is all good?*

I gave him a chin lift, sending back the message of *would have been better had you not been here.*

His smile widened.

"Your mother and I stopped by to make sure you knew about the cookout at Max's in a few hours," he said.

"Max and Emma's now, Lee," Mom said, beaming.

I gave a half smile. Even being pissed at the change in plans for the afternoon didn't take away how happy I was for my sister, for Max. The two of them had been essentially moved in together since they got serious last month, but for the past week she had packed up anything remaining at her little house in town and moved it all to Max's place. Their place. She'd closed on the sale on her house just a few days ago. I'd completely forgotten about dinner at their place tonight. A *welcome home* of sorts, also a *welcome to the family* party for their new dog together, Winnie.

"Yeah, I know about it," I said. Glancing at Maggie, I tilted my head in a silent ask of whether she planned on going. With the silent treatment she had given me, we hadn't talked about our plans for the weekend, beyond her roping me in to help out at the auction. She gave a small nod, and I turned back to my parents, "We'll be there."

Looking from my mom to my dad, I figured we'd might as well just dive in. "Was that all that brought you guys over?"

Dad gave a pointed look at Mom, who had the decency to look remorseful.

I waited a beat. "Mom?"

Mom typically never looked unsure, but she certainly gave off that vibe now.

Maggie stepped forward, grabbing her hand. "What is it, Anna?" Worry was etched on Maggie's face.

I worked on not laughing as I watched my mom lose any grip she had on trying to keep her emotions down. She began speaking at a rapid speed.

"It's just, I'm just, I'm so excited for you two. And I wanted to come over a million times in the past few weeks and talk to you both. But Maggie, you were so busy with the end of the school year, I didn't want to bother you. Then we had to have that trip this week." She looked like she might burst. "And then I saw pictures of you at the auction this morning and realized I hadn't seen you, talked to you, and *you are carrying our grandchild.*"

I was pretty sure there was no Italian in our ancestry, but the way my mother's hands were flying, you'd never know. Glancing at Maggie, I was relieved to see a smile stretched across her face, but noting the tears in her eyes, I cautiously moved behind her. Maggie knew my mom well, but if her pregnancy hormones were going to kick in, I'd absolutely be there for her.

"Pictures of me at the auction?" Maggie asked, cocking her head to the side. Interesting that she was apparently choosing to focus on that part of Mom's impassioned speech.

Mom pulled out her phone. "Of course. Lou added them to the auction's social media page." She held up her phone, and there were several that she flipped through. "And then, of course, she sent me a few right after we got here." Mom's face flamed up at that comment.

Good freaking Lord. Lou was sending Mom the picture she took in the parking lot?

"You should just be grateful Lou didn't post that one online," Dad said, indicating he could still read my mind.

"Though I did try to get your mother to head back home after she got that one."

"Thanks, Dad," I said, giving my mom a pointed look.

"I couldn't!" Mom said before moving in and throwing her arms around Maggie. I watched as Maggie waited a beat before wrapping her arms around her. Rocking back and forth, Mom continued, "I just couldn't wait another day before telling you how happy we were."

"You've sent me text messages," Maggie whispered. "I knew."

"Pshaw. Text messages. My dear girl, we adore you. That requires a visit in person, and this evening was just not going to be soon enough." Mom pulled back, holding Maggie out to get a look at her. Scanning her up and down, she took in her long legs in her cutoff denim shorts with her Jason Isbell and the 400 Unit T-shirt. Her favorite cowboy boots were in place, and her hair hung down long and loose. Freckles were dotting over her skin, but she had a bit of a light tan from being outside for the past week, though no matter how often she was outside in the summer, she was never what would be considered tan. Mom gave her one more look before pulling her in for a tight squeeze.

"No baby bump yet, Anna," Maggie said, laughing.

"Of course, my beautiful girl. It's too soon. How are you feeling? Cole mentioned morning sickness." She ran her hand over Maggie's hair down to her chin, tilting it up to assess her gaze.

Maggie's nose wrinkled up in a way that took me back. I remembered her face when she was younger, wrinkling her nose when she didn't like something Max or I'd bring home, like frogs and snakes. The way she'd look at the two of us after football practice in sweaty clothes. Or the way the nose wrinkle would mesh with an eye roll during one of the many times we'd disagree after we all moved back to Highland after college.

My feet knew where I was heading before my mind caught on. Tugging Maggie from Mom's grip, I spun her toward me, catching her against my chest.

"What...," Maggie started to get out.

"Shh," I whispered as I leaned down and kissed her nose, lightly. "You crinkle your nose a lot. Always have. Drives me crazy, baby," I said before letting her go.

My parents moved to stand side by side against the counter, watching Maggie and me together. I could see pure love shining in my mom's eyes as she mouthed *baby* to my dad. Here's hoping she could stay on an even keel and not freak out.

Maggie pushed back, then looked over at my parents warily. "Anna, Lee, I can't tell you how much it means that you both are here. I love you all to pieces..."

"And we love you," Mom said.

I watched Maggie, trying to decide where she was going with this. I could almost see the steel reinforcing her spine as she stood tall, then continued. "But I don't want to give you the wrong idea from this," she gestured to where I stood, still holding on to her hip.

"Or from the driveway," I finished for her.

"Or the auction," Dad chimed in, raising his eyebrows at me. I grinned back.

"Sully," Maggie hissed.

I gave her a bit of shrug, then let go to head to the fridge, snagging a beer and joining my dad leaning against the kitchen counter. Tapping my can to his in solidarity, I leaned back to watch the show.

Mom swooped in, hugging Maggie, then leaned back before breaking out in a huge grin. "Maggie Jameson, are you telling me that Lee and I shouldn't reserve the golf course for the wedding reception just yet?"

I soaked in the look on Maggie's face. Emotions flitted past, and unless I was mistaken, there was excitement mixed with fear and a little heat in her cheeks. That was something to look into. Later.

"What? No. One, I don't want my reception at the golf course," she began.

"Legion Hall?" I muttered.

Maggie swung her gaze toward mine as she narrowed her eyes, "Shut it, you. Not. Helping."

"Watch it, son. She's feeling feisty," my dad murmured.

"Pregnancy hormones," I said, under my breath.

"Death wish," my dad replied.

"I'm right here," Maggie gritted out.

"Ignore those two assholes," my mom said. "Two peas in a pod."

Maggie took a deep breath. "Okay, contrary to the messages that your son is sending out," she glared over, and I raised my beer in a salute, "we are just friends."

"For now," I muttered.

"Cole Patrick Sullivan, knock it off." Maggie's voice was her firm teacher voice. I figured it must work wonders on the kids in her classes, but it made me want to throw her over my shoulder and head to my room. For all I cared, she could order me around all night.

"Babe, just saying, we are having a baby together."

"Careful, son," Dad murmured.

"Relationships aren't built just because the other person is convenient. At least mine won't be. I deserve more than that," Maggie's voice trailed off.

Shit. I saw a few unshed tears building up in her eyes.

Was that really how she thought I saw her? Like this was only an option because we were both in the same place?

"Mags," I began.

"Nope!" Her hand was up as her finger wagged back and forth. Maggie avoided my eyes, looking up at the ceiling, and continued her tirade. "Not now, mister. I'm soaking in your big-ass tub before we go over to Max and Emma's just because I can. Ranger is welcome to follow me. Beyond that, I need some privacy." She took a deep breath and looked over at my parents. "Lee, Anna, love you both more than I could ever say. But if you'll excuse me, I need a soak. I'll see you in a bit." With that, she kissed them each on the cheek before heading out of the room toward the bathroom, kimono flying.

I noticed I didn't merit a kiss. Interesting. I briefly debated the idea of following her to the bathroom, but then I caught my dad's eye.

"Son, you're getting a bit old for advice, but if I was a betting man, I'd say that following your Maggie right now would be a colossal mistake."

I hopped up, sliding back on the counter, and rested my elbows on my knees, considering my beer and how I'd gotten to this place in my life.

"Cole," my mom began, leaning on the counter to my side. "You're going to have to tread lightly here."

"I know, Mom."

"Honey, I'm not sure that you do. I've watched that girl grow up in front of my eyes. The Maggie she lets everyone see is not all that there is. It isn't even the tip of the iceberg. That girl is precious to me, and she deserves the world. She just needs to believe that a bit more too."

"What the hell, Mom? Emma was the one who struggled with self-confidence. I wouldn't ever say the same about Maggie."

Mom gave me a look that told me she thought I was an idiot. "We all have our own insecurities. You will need to learn what Maggie's are. But honey, that girl needs to know she is valued, loved, adored, and not just because she happens to be carrying your child. That's the job you have cut out for you."

Dad spoke up. "Anna, want to meet me out in the car in a second?"

I glanced over at my dad, who was nodding as he tossed his can in the recycling.

Mom nodded, gave me a kiss, and slipped out the door.

"Private conversation?" I asked.

"Of a sort," he grinned. "Just can't let your mother know all my secrets."

I shook my head, watching my mom standing in the middle of the yard, face thrown back to the sun, light brown hair floating down her back. It looked like she was soaking in the sun, the world. She was in her late fifties, but she looked like she was at least a decade younger, thanks—in part—to her regular trips to the hair salon or, like she called it, the fountain of youth.

Shaking my head, I looked back at my dad. He was also staring out the window at Mom with, what I was uncomfortable to realize, was not just a little heat in his eyes.

"Dad?"

He shook his head. "Your mother has a joy in her that amazes me a bit more every day that I am lucky enough to wake up by her side. It's been that way for thirty-five years, and I hope like hell that we get at least that many more together."

I considered how I'd won the parent lottery, they were a

shiny beacon of what a marriage could be. I knew I took them for granted, but I also knew how incredibly blessed I was.

"So is that why you wanted Mom to leave? So you could gush about your wife without her knowing? That might have been the wrong call, Dad. I bet she would have loved to hear that."

Dad leveled me with a look. "Nope, I wanted to make sure you had your head in the right place with the girl soaking in your tub right now. This is Maggie we're talking about, son. You need to not go there again unless you're ready to go the distance."

I suddenly felt like I was being lectured, and part of it pissed me off, part of it embarrassed me. "Dad..."

"Nope, listen. You and I have had many talks about women over the years starting with the importance of consent in everything you do, moving along to safe sex, and a whole lot more. I told you those conversations weren't a one-and-done kind of thing, and we're picking it up now. I've said it all along, and God knows I've tried to model it, but please remember that when you decide you've found the one, your work is just beginning." He paused, glancing out the window at Mom once again.

"Dad, I'm working to make sure I can support Maggie and this baby in every way."

He looked sharply at me. "Emma said you are thinking of waiting to package the beer. Does that have something to do with this?"

I groaned inwardly. Maggie and I hadn't even begun that conversation, but it needed to happen. I wasn't over-joyed about diving into it with my dad either. "Dad, it just doesn't make sense to do a huge investment into the business when I'm going to have additional expenses coming up."

"I see where you are going with that, Sully. But I also think you need to be thinking of your future, your family's future. And from what Emma said, Maggie was pissed that you hadn't shared this. She doesn't want to be thought of as a burden. If you want to be together, you two need to figure out how to communicate. Making decisions without talking to her, shutting her out, gives her the opposite message that you want to be sending."

Damn if he didn't bring up exactly what I'd been mulling over since she got pissed on Friday night. "I screwed that up, and I know it now, but that's too late. And I'd never think of her or my kid as a burden. But it's hard to figure out where to go here. She doesn't think we're in a relationship, so what's the line? What do I share without coming on too strong?"

Dad shook his head, smiling at me. "You two will figure it out. My thought would be treat this as you want it to be moving forward. She can tell you she doesn't need to know information about your business if she doesn't want to, but this is Maggie. I'd think she would be happy you talked to her. Beyond everything else, she's a friend. If you want her to have faith in you, you have to do the same. And son, your job is to figure out what it is she wants and support her in this life so that she can get it."

I felt a bolt to my heart. "Even if that means encouraging her to go? What if she doesn't want to stay in Highland Falls? She's always said she is going to leave." I slid off the counter, turning and facing out the window to look beyond our vehicles, out at the vast line of prairie.

Dad stood, throwing an arm across my shoulders. "Yep. Even if. And Sully, just remember, if she needs to leave, you could always go with her. Your mom would cry, and I can't say it wouldn't suck not being able to see you as often as we do, but you go where you need to go. And if your girl needs to leave, give her the strength to do that."

Shit, he was right. Jake and I could figure out something with the brewery if I needed to, but I'd always envisioned growing old in this town, in this house. But if I had to pick between this town and Maggie, there was no contest.

"But son, just a suggestion. You might want to help her figure out what it is she's running from. Why is she so certain she needs to leave the place surrounded by people who love her, especially now that she has a baby on the way? Help her figure out what she wants, what she needs, and then fight the world to ensure she gets it. Just make sure you're doing it by her side."

He slapped me on the back a few times, then went outside, joining my mom in the yard. She threw her arms around his shoulders, kissing him square on the lips before grabbing his hand, and headed for their truck. My gut tugged, praying that Maggie and I would have that thirty-five years from now. Could I be half the husband, father, that my dad was?

I shook my head and whistled for Ranger to take him outside. Dad had given me some stuff to think about. Now just to figure out how to open up time for a conversation with Maggie when I simply wanted to get her horizontal every time she was in my presence.

Talk first, action later. I could wait. Maybe.

## 19

## QUICK EXITS

**_Maggie_**

The night had been magical. I was a big fan of parties: loud music, good food, letting go with some friends. Emma and Max's cookout was just that and more. Really, it was a housewarming, of sorts. While all fun adult beverages were off-limits to me right now, it was kind of enjoyable to sit back and watch everyone else. Emma was beaming as she talked to some friends from work. As the music got louder, I listed another good thing about living in the country was not having neighbors close enough to worry about.

Emma and her colleague, Tim, had moved out to an open space in the grass, a type of makeshift dance floor. I felt my smile stretch across my face as I saw Tim whirl Emma around and around. Emma was in her element, joy radiating out of her like a halo.

As I swayed by myself, the song changed to one from The White Buffalo. Emma and Tim slowed from their frantic twirls to end in a hug before Max claimed Emma for a dance. Eric, Tim's partner, did the same. The couples dancing fell into a slow rhythm, moving around in the grass, lost to the music.

A pang of longing hit me square in the chest. Watching the two couples, I wanted that. I wanted that person to watch me make an ass out of myself as I danced with abandon under the stars, then grab me for a slow dance where we could be pressed up against each other, nothing between us. I wanted the person that would bring me some pain reliever in the morning when I had been a fool and overindulged before making me a greasy breakfast so that I could recover.

Pulling my eyes away from the swaying bodies, my eyes found Sully's where he stood, leaning against the back porch where another group was gathered. He arched his brow at me in a silent question.

I shook my head, trying to indicate that everything was fine, and moved toward Max's barn. Tears filled my eyes, and I was pissed with myself. I wanted to stay in the moment, enjoy a night with my friends. But my emotions, it seemed, were no longer my own. I felt like pregnancy was one giant hormonal roller coaster, and it pissed me off that I couldn't control it.

"Dammit," I muttered in frustration as I reached the back of the barn and looked at the fields.

I absentmindedly kicked some lumber Max had stacked and heard a chuckle over my shoulder. Glancing back, I saw Sully was closing in on me.

"Maggie May, what did those logs do to you?" He came to a stop in front of me, near enough to hear him, but far enough away that I couldn't just fall on his lips.

Not that I was thinking about that. Much.

"What are you doing back here, Sully?"

"Wanted to check in on you."

"Why?"

Sully took a few steps toward me, pausing to brush some hair back that had fallen out of my ponytail behind my ears. "Was curious why you went from looking like you were having a good time to looking like someone had just kicked your puppy."

Looking at Sully was dangerous. It was like he could see deep into me to see what secrets I was hiding. I wanted so badly to keep a layer of protection between the two of us. I needed that wall, however thin it was. Because I knew what this was, what we were. His friendship was one I treasured. Sex with him was amazing, and I was not opposed to a repeat of that performance. But for whatever reason, I still needed that separation. This wasn't a long-haul thing for him or for me. For Pete's sake, I wasn't even supposed to be here this summer. And then in a year I'd be gone anyway.

Though now that would also include a baby. Adjusted plans. It was fine. Everything was fine.

So why was it I wanted to wrap myself in this man, bury my face in the nape of his neck, and pray he never let go?

Damn it all.

"It's nothing, Sully. Pregnancy hormones and all."

Sully put his hands on my hips, tugging me to him, and looked long. "Hmm, there it is."

I'm sure a look of confusion crossed my face. What in the world was he talking about now? "There what is?"

"You're protecting yourself once again. Holding back."

"What the hell are you talking about?" I asked. I sounded pissed, and I knew it was irrational. But how did this man know me so well? It was infuriating. He was infuriating.

"Babe."

"Seriously, Sully. Babe? Is that supposed to be an

answer?"

"I'm just trying to decide what answer will get me in the least amount of shit right now," he muttered, trying and failing to suppress a grin.

"Sully...," I growled.

"Maggie...," he parroted back.

We stood there, staring at each other for a beat. Music from the party was floating around us along with sounds of the country. Darkness cocooned us out here, making it feel like we were in our own world even though everyone was just on the other side of the barn. Sully's hands on my hips tightened, gently adding a bit of pressure to pull me toward him. He was wearing a worn T-shirt from the brewery, and it stretched over his chest. I rested my hands on him there, the thin material between us.

Mmmm, that chest.

"Maggie," he whispered this time.

I licked my lips without thinking, debating whether pulling him into the grass was something to do when you were stone-cold sober. Technically, the two of us were going to be parents soon, or maybe we already were? How does that work? Do parents have wild sex at parties when they're within a hundred yards or so of their friends? Certainly they didn't have sex at a party when the guy's family was nearby, right? And most importantly, why the hell could I be pissed off at this man and want to scream from the rooftops one minute and want to get busy in the grass the next?

Shit. I really did want to jump him.

"Babe, where did you just go?" Sully was watching me.

I hesitated. I might be nearing certifiable. "Promise not to judge me?"

Sully grinned. "This should be good."

I rolled my eyes. "Well, I had many thoughts beginning with wondering if I should shove you down in this grass, moving on to if that was what parents did, jumping to whether we were already considered parents, ending with whether it was cool to have sex this close to a party."

I glanced at his incredulous expression. "Well, you asked," I pointed out. "Oh, and I wondered how I could be angry with you and want to get busy at the same time. It's like you're magical."

Sully pulled me closer, front to front, before saying anything. "One, I fucking love the way your mind works. Two, yes, I consider us parents already. And three, babe, we could drop down in the grass and go for it, but I'd really like to spend all night worshipping your body, and I don't want to pause to drive home. Besides, mosquito bites are a bitch."

"Are mosquitoes even out yet?"

"Seriously Maggie? That's what you're focusing on in all that I said?"

I laughed. "Well, I do like that you enjoy my mind. I supposed I should have acknowledged that as well," I glanced up at him. Mmmm. His eyes looked pretty turned on, from what I could tell from the moonlight and the lights from the drive and the house. Maybe it was just wishful thinking that I wasn't alone here.

Sully lowered his mouth until his lips were at my ear. "Margaret Jameson, I love your quick mind and your hilarious sense of humor. I love your gorgeous hair that reminds me of a sunset in summer. Those eyes remind me of pools of chocolate. But right now, baby, I really just want to get you home because at the top of my list, I truly love when your body isn't wearing anything, and if that doesn't happen in the next five minutes, we *will* be dropping to the grass, party and mosquitoes be damned."

His lips found the sensitive skin right below my ear and pressed soft kisses there while I tried to get my brain to slow down.

*He loved, he loved?* Surely that was just his other brain talking, right? Actually, let's be honest here. Who cares at this point?

"Sully?"

"Yeah, babe."

"Take me home."

He pulled back, looked in my eyes and, apparently seeing what he wanted there, turned and headed directly for his truck parked in the grass, taking us away from the barn and the party both.

Laughing, I whispered, "Sully, aren't we going to say goodbye to everyone?"

His long strides ate up the distance to his truck. "Hell no."

I jogged to catch up with him. "Why not? We're being rude. And I left my Tupperware from the cookies over there."

"We can get it later," Sully said, moving even faster, like we were in danger of being called back at any moment. Which, considering our track record of late, I understood. I was grateful I'd left my purse in the truck when we arrived. One less thing to worry about.

Sully opened the passenger door and helped me up before heading to his side. As he slid in the truck, slamming the door behind him, he leaned over and placed his hand under my chin, tilting it up so that my lips could meet his for a light kiss. "Because if we went back it would be an hour before we could actually get out of there. Remember, I've seen you and my sister saying goodbye at parties before."

"But..."

"And babe, just saying, I want to get you home before you change your mind."

I pulled back. "I am *not* changing my mind."

"Great. Let's go." He pulled out, luckily not spraying any gravel once he reached the drive.

We drove in silence for a bit. The feeling in the cab confused me. There was the pent-up energy that, hopefully, would finally be released when we got to his house. But there was also an awkwardness, a feeling that I had done something wrong. I tried to put my finger on what it was.

Sully glanced over at me, then snaked his hand out to grab mine as he drove. "Want to tell me what's on your mind?"

"I'm not sure."

I watched the smile break out on his profile as he kept his eyes on the country road and his hand squeezed mine. "You're not sure what's on your mind or you're not sure you want to tell me?"

Rolling my eyes, I leaned back in the seat. "I'm not sure what's on my mind. I feel like I'm about to get in trouble."

"Mags, that's because we just left a party, and everyone saw my truck pull out, and they all know you are in it with me. You're probably freaking inside that beautiful brain of yours that everyone knows where we're going and why."

My eyes rolled so hard I wondered if they might pop out. Apparently, I had decided to channel my teenage self. "Sully, that is so not true."

Sully turned in to his drive and came to a stop near his house. "Which part isn't true? The part about what's bothering you or the part about everyone knowing we're minutes away from a horizontal type of dancing? Because knowing you for as long as I have, I'd argue both are completely true."

"Sully...," I began but then felt my phone vibrate. I glanced down to see a text from Emma.

**Emma:** *You and Sully certainly made a quick exit. I don't need too many details because, eww, but I'm cheering for you both from here.*

My stomach danced with nervousness. I looked from my text, back to Sully. "Shit, you're right. They know."

Before I could completely freak out with the realization that he was right and that he knew my brain better than I apparently did, Sully was at my door, tugging me from the truck. He pocketed my phone and pulled me against him.

"Hey, my phone..."

"Babe, nope. No phones, no people coming to interrupt. None of it. I've waited for weeks to be back here with you. To have you in my bed. To see that gorgeous body of yours below me." He ran his lips down my neck, then back up near my ear. "To taste you." His lips found mine. "I'm going to get it through your stubborn brain, Maggie. You. Are. Mine." With that, his lips opened over mine and took my breath with them.

I melted into his kiss, opening my lips and letting his tongue inside. I wrapped my arms around his torso, pulling him closer. I was both turned on and felt completely safe at the same time. It was too much, and I could feel my knees begin to buckle.

Before I could just slide down his body to the ground, he reached down below my ass and pulled me up. My legs wound around his waist, and he began walking toward the house. My inner voice tried to come up for air, reminding me that this was just to release some pent-up energy, that we were still just friends, but friends that got to have sex. That was perfectly acceptable, right?

# 20

## AS YOU WISH

***Sully***

Time seemed to melt away as Maggie's mouth caressed mine. Picking her up, she wrapped her legs around my waist, pressing against me. I walked to my house and somehow got us through the door while I proceeded to kiss every inch of skin I could find.

Ranger went out to do his thing while my mouth devoured hers. I couldn't think, couldn't breathe. All my focus was on Maggie and the hums of pleasure coming from her.

With Ranger outside, I lowered Maggie to the butcher-block counter in the kitchen and pressed more kisses to her temple, over her face, down her neck to that sensitive spot at her nape. Her fingers ranked through my hair as she said my name in a throaty voice.

Pulling back, I met her eyes. "You still with me?"

"Fuck yes," she said, her eyes hazy.

Ranger came back to the door, pawing it to show he was ready to be let in. "Give me a minute," I whispered, tucking a strand of hair behind her ear.

Her eyes narrowed. "No longer, Sullivan."

Smiling at her, I asked, "Impatient much?"

"Just not feeling certain that someone we love won't appear in your kitchen doorway any moment," she said.

Well, you couldn't argue with that. There was a history.

Letting Ranger in, I passed over a large bone to keep him happily occupied for the foreseeable future and moved back to the counter where Maggie sat watching. Walking straight into her legs that were spread, I wrapped my arms around her, supporting her ass as I pulled her to me. She immediately moved to wrap her legs around my waist again, and I took us to my room.

Her mouth moved over my neck as she murmured, "Just saying, I do have the ability to walk."

I pulled her closer. "But then I couldn't have you kissing me as I got us back here. I'm thinking this was the way to go."

"I like this logic," she whispered, her tongue tracing my jaw.

After what seemed like years but was just minutes, we crossed the threshold into my room. Lowering Maggie until she was able to stand, I first tugged off her kimono. Then her T-shirt met it in the pile. She kept her eyes on mine as she kicked off her boots and pushed down her shorts. My brain felt near overload as I ran my hands up her arms, to her shoulders, then back down. Holy shit, she was fucking gorgeous. Her bra and underwear were a dark blue lace where I could just get the hint of what lay beneath, and it drove me mad.

"You seem to be overdressed," she murmured, pushing my shirt over my head while I toed off my shoes and pushed my jeans down to join the rest on the floor. I was at once both impatient to be naked with her and wanting to slow down and soak in every minute.

Down to our underwear, we stared at each other, waiting to see who was going to move first. Maggie's warm brown eyes darted down to my hard cock, barely contained by my boxer briefs. Looking back at me, her grin stretched into a smirk, and we were drawn together as if by a magnet.

As our lips met, any thoughts beyond kissing her senseless completely evaporated from my mind. My hands were everywhere all at once. I traced over her curves at her hips, back to squeeze her ass, then skated them over her stomach to her breasts. While that felt amazing, her bra was clearly standing in the way. I slid my hands around her back to unhooked it. A strap slipped down, and Maggie looked up at me with a raised brow, daring me to get moving. My mouth followed the strap down her arms until I slid it off and tossed it to the side.

Maggie impatiently slid her underwear off while I kicked mine down until we were completely naked and pressed against each other. Our hands roamed like we couldn't decide where they should go next. I felt like a teenager and wondered how I could gain some control or this would be over far too soon.

Taking a breath and thinking of my to-do list at the brewery to try to calm down, I backed Maggie up until the backs of her legs were pressed against my bed and lowered her down. Nope. Still feeling like I was going to blow. Glancing at Mags as she settled on the bed, her hair cascaded in ripples over the pillow as the lamp on my dresser lit the room in a soft glow. Yep. Needed control. Should I count? Think of grandmas? Deep breaths?

"What?" she asked.

I shook my head a bit, feeling like I was coming out of a

trance. "Just love the sight of you on this bed. Your hair spread out on the sheets. Shit, Maggie, you're like my fantasy come to life, and I'm a bit worried that I won't be able to last long enough here, like that scene from *Mystery, Alaska*."

"Sully! One, I absolutely remember that scene, and that's not happening here. You've already grabbed my boob, and no one has gotten off yet."

I groaned. Just kill me. Not helping. "Don't speak too soon."

Maggie's expression softened as she got up and moved to where I stood by the bed. Kneeling with her upper body pressed against mine, she traced my hairline, wrapped a hand around my neck, and pressed her lips to mine. Pulling back, she looked at me with a softened expression. "It's not like this is the first time I've been in this bed. It's not even the first time we've done this."

Her lips brushed mine again. "And Sully, while the last time did end in a way that was somewhat stressful, I couldn't help but notice that it was pretty damn amazing."

Tension unknotted from my neck. "Yeah? Why do you think that is?" I lowered my mouth to her neck, pulsing small kisses there as she wrapped both hands around my back and pulled me closer.

Her breath stuttered as my tongue dipped into the hollow of her throat.

"Mmmm," she answered.

I pulled back, finding her eyes closed, but they fluttered open to meet mine. "Why did you stop?"

Kissing the tip of her nose, I whispered, "Wanted to hear your answer."

"Oh." She looked surprised for a moment, then her face relaxed. "Well, I don't think I've ever been with someone who knows me as well as you do. That has to make a difference, right?"

This woman. Her brown eyes were warm, trusting. I didn't think she had any idea how revealing her expressions were. Her uncertainty hovered just a bit under the surface, but there was also love there. Could be the kind of love between friends, but that could be a hell of a foundation to build on.

"Babe," I whispered, overcome with my feelings for Maggie, for our little bean. I placed a knee into by her, helping to lower her down to the bed while I lay by her side. Slowly, without much thought, one of my hands came to rest on her stomach, and my gaze met hers. Keeping our eyes locked together, I leaned over and brought my mouth to her belly, kissing it with all the emotion swirling inside me. Looking up at her, I said, "It helps, Mags. And I feel it too." Pressing another kiss to her stomach, I ran my fingers lower, teasing her inner thigh, skating over her mound, then back up. "You still feeling okay?" I ran my hands over her belly.

Maggie's eyes focused as she looked at me. Clearing her throat, she spoke in a deeper voice than typical for her. "Yeah, Sully. Feeling pretty good today."

I kept my eyes on hers as I placed several openmouthed kisses on her stomach. "Mags, I can't wait to watch your belly grow."

She blinked a few times, and I noticed moisture gathering there. Feeling concerned, I asked, "What's wrong?"

She shook her head like she was getting rid of whatever was bothering her. I could practically see the internal conversation she was having.

"Mags," I prompted again.

Finally she looked back at me. "I was just thinking..." Her voice trailed off.

"About?" I waited a minute or so as I stretched out next to her, letting my hands trail lightly over her body, watching goose bumps pop out in their wake.

She was watching me. "How did you know I was upset?"

I smiled, thinking of all the times over the years I'd watched her debate something in her head. Placing a finger under her jaw, I tipped her face up to be inches from mine. "Mags, we keep coming back to the same thing. I *know* you. I've watched you reason with yourself on a variety of topics over the years. You get this pensive look on your face, your lips purse, and your eyes dart back and forth like you're watching a tennis match. You did it when you were trying to decide if you should go out with that tool, Greg, in middle school. Poor choice, by the way."

"Hey!"

"And you did it when you were trying to decide between going away to college on the east coast and staying in state." I went on.

"Well, to be fair, the scholarship money did end up making that decision."

"I'm just saying, how about you spit out whatever you're debating about here because I have some other things I want to get to." I waggled my eyebrows up and down suggestively, trying to get her to smile.

Her smile was tentative, but she also looked crazy nervous. "Maybe we should just get to those other things?" she asked in a small voice.

I ran a hand through her hair. "Nope, Maggie May. I want you to be able to experience the second time we make love totally present, not stressing out about whatever is hiding behind those eyes. Spit it out."

She flinched a little when I said *make love,* but I chose to ignore that for the moment.

"I just got a bit emotional when you talked about watching my belly grow..."

I looked at her in surprise. "Are you freaked out about gaining weight?"

"Hell, no! I mean, I suppose I can be vain, but not that vain. The idea that I might not see my feet in a few months is a bit off-putting, but it's for a good cause." She rolled against me, tucking her face into my neck. "I guess I just got sad because I remembered I am only living with you until August, and you won't be around to see this belly get bigger by the day. I mean, clearly you'll still be here, but not like this." She gestured between the two of us. "It just made me sad, that's all, but it's ridiculous. I'll still see you."

Arrow to the heart. Fuck. I had no desire for her to move out. But I had a feeling if I asked her to move in permanently, her walls would spring up automatically. I blocked those thoughts away with everything else I didn't want to deal with and lightly traced little circles on Maggie's stomach, watching her legs begin to get restless again.

"Can't think about you leaving right now, Mags. Enjoying the moment," I whispered against her neck.

She chuckled. "Sorry. We don't have to talk about it right now. I'm good, swear. Back to the kissing."

I put little openmouthed kisses down her neck. "This conversation isn't over though."

"But for now?"

"For now we can hit pause," I said as my mouth found her nipple. "As long as you understand one thing."

She gasped as I sucked on her breast. "What?"

"I'm not going anywhere, babe. Whether you are here or we're apart, I'm in this with you."

She was quiet as I'm sure that brain began swirling. Whatever, this baby, Maggie, me—we were connected. We just had to work out what those connections were. Later.

My tongue traced one nipple, then moved over to the other as her back rose up as she arched her breast to my lips. The first time we'd been together had been fast but amazing. Here, now, I was taking my time.

"More," she groaned.

I paused and looked up at her. "Not going fast enough for you, princess?"

She wrapped one leg around my ass, pressing my erection to her core. "I need you to touch me," she whispered.

My dick twitched. I tried to gain some control by taking a deep breath. "Your wish is my command, princess." I lowered my head and continued kissing my way down her body. I reached her center, running a hand down her inner thigh. More goose bumps followed my touch

"Cole," her voice trembled.

I felt that in my heart. And my cock, let's be real.

Maggie was restless, her body was reaching up to meet my mouth, and I didn't think she even realized it. I could smell her arousal and knew she was ready but wanted to prolong and treasure this moment. A glance at Mags showed her flushed cheeks and her eyes that were telling me she was ready for more. Damn, I wanted to worship her.

Opening her legs wider to accommodate my shoulders, I kept her eyes as I lowered my head and pressed a soft kiss to her core. Maggie's hips lifted to press herself against me even tighter. I groaned. This was how every fantasy of the past few years had played out over and over in my mind. I dragged my tongue through her folds, loving how wet she was. God, the taste of her. Better than I remembered. I committed it all to memory.

Maggie moaned again, "Cole." Her breath came in short bursts. I slid a finger into her core and felt her body flutter around me. Her legs tightened on my shoulders, pulling me closer and telling me she needed more.

I lightly circled her clit with my tongue once, then again when her pants increased. Watching her as her body told me what she needed next, I felt myself settle with a feeling of rightness, like I was supposed to be here.

Maggie rocked up to my mouth on a loud groan. It was rapidly becoming apparent that I needed to get her there, like yesterday. Not just for her, but for me too. As I sucked her clit with little pulses, Maggie continued to moan and arch off the bed.

Adding a second finger to my first one, I thrust them in as I moved to devour her. She arched and lost control as my fingers were squeezed as if in a vice. Her climax went on, and on, and on. I gentled my mouth, watching to see how sensitive she was. Finally as she began to come down, I slid back up her body and loved seeing the fire in her eyes when she opened them.

"How was that, princess? Worth the wait?"

She pulled me down for a deep kiss. Letting go, she smirked. "Don't be arrogant, Sullivan. Inside, now."

I pressed a kiss to her nose. "As you wish." As I shifted onto my forearms over her, my cock dragged across her inner thigh and nestled exactly where I wanted to be. Stopping right now was the last thing I wanted, but I had to be sure.

Her eyes met mine. "What?" she asked.

"I haven't had sex without a condom. Ever."

She laughed. "Well, a lot of good that did us."

"Babe," I growled.

"Sully, it's fine. I'm obviously already knocked up, and I was tested for STDs as part of my early screening. I'm clean."

I nodded, then looked back at her. "I got tested for everything too after the condom broke, just in case."

Her eyebrows drew together. "Why?"

"Well, I knew I was likely clean anyway, but in case I gave you anything, I wanted to be able to tell you as soon as possible."

Maggie arched a brow. "You thought you might have given me something?"

I locked eyes with her, "Do we really want to talk about previous partners right now?" I gently pressed into her, just a little. "I wasn't a virgin, Mags, but neither were you."

"Ugh, talk later." She rubbed her folds across me, and I nearly came right then. "Inside, Sully. Enough waiting."

She nodded, so I slid in. Damn if it didn't make me almost lose it at once. A wave of something hit me as my heart rate sped up as I slowly slid out, Maggie gasping and wrapping those legs even tighter to pull me back. Her body clenched around me, keeping me pressed to her. I tilted to adjust, working to hit that magical spot that should be about *there*.

Rocking up, she gasped, "More."

At the base of my spine, sensations began building. Maggie scraped her nails up my back and pulled me closer. I could feel the telltale signs of another orgasm as Maggie began to pulse around me. "Shit, Sully, I'm so close," she gasped.

Heaven.

My mouth found hers. "Me too, babe," I said as I thrust

my tongue in her mouth in time to our strokes. Resting on one elbow, I slid a hand between us and circled her clit with a finger. Faster, and faster, until she was there.

Her body clenched mine as she arched back, my name on her lips. I grunted, trying to race there with her as we crossed that line together, sensations swirling as my body melded to hers. I groaned into her neck as we shuddered together, riding out the end of our orgasms. Feeling completely wrung out, I collapsed and rolled us to our sides to keep my weight off her.

"No, I want you on top of me," she whispered, pulling me back up. "I love the feel of your weight on me," she said, wiggling below me.

"The baby." I started to move to the side.

"The baby is fine," she said into my neck. Kissing that spot I found irresistible, she went on. "Your weight makes me feel safe."

I pulled back, looking her in the eyes. My hands combed through her hair. "You're safe, Maggie. You're always safe with me." I leaned down, lightly kissing her lips before moving back up and watching her face. "You good?"

Maggie's eyes roamed over my face. "That was amazing. Of course I'm good." She looked to the side, then back to me. "I think it was good because it was you, but it had been a while too." Her cheeks heated. "I mean, there was the time with you, but no one for a while before."

I nodded, wondering how long and could I kill anyone who'd come before me? Not really, but maybe. That being said, this was Mags, and she was putting herself out there, which demanded equal vulnerability. "There's been no one else for me for quite a while either, Mags."

"Define a while, Cole." She watched me, and I could see the look of jealousy flashing over her face. I'd take that—

it showed she cared—but there was no need. There was no one for me but her.

My lips found her neck, and I pressed a kiss there before showing her my cards. "Almost a year."

Her eyes flew open, and she met my gaze. "A year?"

"Yep." I moved to bring my face over hers. I let my lips light over her nose, lightly kissed each eye, then finally came to her mouth. I kissed her softly, then pulled back. "As I said, I thought I wouldn't have given you anything, but I wanted to be sure."

We locked eyes, lost in the moment, before she pulled back from my gaze to kiss my neck. Maggie nipped my neck, then grinned at me. "Well, you did give me a little something."

"That I did," I whispered, dropping my head to her neck. I felt Maggie's hand slide down until it found mine, and she interlaced our fingers.

"What are you thinking?" I asked when I heard both our phones begin to vibrate at the same time. Looking over to the pile of our clothes, then back to Maggie. "Well, whoever that is at least didn't interrupt us until after," I grinned. "Do you want me to get your phone?"

"Not really. I really want to lie under you like this forever." She smiled at me while I rocked a bit on top of her. "However, if both our phones are vibrating at the same time, I need to know everyone is okay, so yeah, I guess." She wrapped her arms around me, not making it easy to get up to get the phones.

"I'm not going far, babe."

"Conceited much?" she asked as I rolled off the bed. I quickly moved across the room to my jeans where I pulled out both our phones. I looked down at mine and smiled before tossing Maggie hers.

"What?" she asked before looking down. I watched her face fill with worry.

"Read your text. I'm guessing you got what I did." When she didn't look down immediately, I added, "It's good news, don't worry."

She looked down and woke up the lock screen, opening the group text from my sister to the two of us. It consisted of a photo of her hand with a diamond ring on it that said, "I said yes!"

"Holy shit, holy shit, holy shit!" Maggie looked at me. "Max and Emma are engaged!"

"Looks that way." I grinned, settling back in the bed next to her.

She looked down at the picture again, and I realized she was blinking back tears but not fast enough as some spilled onto her cheeks.

"Hey, hey, Maggie, what's wrong?" I asked, wiping away her tears as I pulled her to straddle my lap in the bed.

"They're engaged," she said softly. "I mean, I gave Max ring suggestions weeks ago, but..." her voice trailed off, "they're getting married."

## 21

# SMALL TOWNS

***Maggie***

Glancing around the bookstore, I let the peace and quiet attempt to calm my jumbled thoughts. Sully got home from the brewery after I'd gone to bed last night. For the past two weeks I felt like we were doing some kind of dance around each other. The night we spent together was hot. Smoking. It just reinforced for me that the night back in April had not been exaggerated in my imagination. The things that man could do to me I'd thought only belonged in the world of my romance stories.

And so, the question begs, what the hell was I doing?

I'd woken up that next morning in a panic. Sully's arms around me and I wanted nothing more than to curl into them, feel his strength surround me. Then that damn inner voice chimed in, reminding me that the plan was to leave, not to get comfortable. That he was a good guy, but this wasn't his plan. That I wasn't his plan.

My inner voice is a bitch, I know. I'm thinking of naming her Hilda.

And yet I snuck out of that room like some kick-ass

ninja. I threw on some clothes and took off with absolutely nowhere I needed to be until I'd killed enough time and he'd be out of the house and off to work. Let's face it. I was a chicken.

Sully had been, as usual, amazing about it. When he came home the night of my great escape, he cooked. We watched TV. And then he brought it up. There is no other way around it, I panicked. Rational thought left the building. I was consumed with the notion that I was going to lose him, which was absolutely ridiculous but still overwhelming at the time, and my damn waterworks turned on.

Again.

Looking at Sully, I had told him I needed a friend right now, which was true, but what the hell was wrong with me? Being Sully, he of course agreed. And so fourteen days passed—*fourteen*—and nada. No horizontal action. Not one bit. Clearly I was an idiot.

And Sully? Still wonderful. He'd spent the past week cementing the notion that I would never find anyone else like him. *Never.* He'd been affectionate, rubbed my back often, hugged me when my hormones made me weepy, massaged my feet while we watched movies, made me tea in the morning, but nothing more. No kisses, apart from the occasional quick touch to my forehead. No more mentions of the night we spent in his bed.

He was completely respectful, and it was driving me crazy.

God, the man was perfect. He was doing exactly as I'd asked repeatedly, and I just wanted to jump him. What was wrong with me?

The bell over the door sounded, shaking me from my inner turmoil. Glancing up, I saw two guys in quiet conversation as they moved in and straight over to the fiction section of the store. I studied their faces, trying to figure out if they were former students or not. They had baseball hats pulled low, so it was hard to get a good read on who they were. Hazarding a guess, I'd put them at late high school or early college age.

"Let me know if I can help you," I called out.

One boy nodded, turning back to scan the spines in front of him. The other nodded in thanks and then gave me a second look. I saw the look of recognition on his face, meaning I had certainly taught him, and braced for a reaction.

"Ms. Jameson?" he said quietly. "I'm not sure if you remember me, but I had you for language arts in seventh grade six years ago. I think it was your first year? Taylor. Taylor Alman."

Warmth flooded my veins as I remembered that first class. They were beyond understanding and kind, two adjectives people often didn't associate with middle school kids. They had helped me find my way. I absolutely remembered Taylor. Sweet and shy, I had worried about him as he struggled to figure out where he fit in to the middle school hierarchy. Coming around the counter, I grinned at his boyish expression of happiness in this adult male body.

"Of course I remember you, Taylor. But thanks for saying your name. You wouldn't believe the amount of times people ask me if I remember them and my brain freezes up. It's horrible." I leaned against the counter, eager to catch up with Taylor and see where he'd ended up. Though Highland Falls was a small community, I couldn't keep track of all the paths of my former students. "So what are you up to?"

Taylor pulled off his baseball hat, running his hand through his blond hair. "I just finished up my first year at the University of Chicago where I'm studying business. I'm still not sold on my major, but so far it's been okay."

"I'm so glad to hear that," I said. "It can take a while to feel like you've found the right path for you. I wouldn't stress too much, just see what's out there." I glanced from Taylor to his friend who was still browsing, then back to Taylor. I didn't think I knew the other kid.

"John, come here for a sec," Taylor said to the other kid. He was Taylor's age, but I definitely didn't recognize him. John's dark skin would have, unfortunately, stood out in our small town. While our population was gradually becoming more diverse, we still had a long way to go. I hadn't taught John, but maybe he moved in after seventh grade.

"Ms. Jameson, this is John Sweeney. We both go to the University of Chicago, and he's down visiting my family this weekend," Taylor began.

"Pleasure to meet you," John said. After shaking my hand, he moved back by Taylor and stood close by. I glanced between the two of them, struck suddenly by the casual familiarity they shared, and realized this wasn't just a good friend but in all likelihood, a whole lot more. Thinking back, I didn't remember Taylor being out in middle school, but that wasn't shocking. A whole lot of kids are struggling to figure out who they are at that age, in many different ways.

"Pleasure to meet you too, John." I nodded toward Taylor. "I hope he's showing you all the great parts of Highland Falls."

"He sure is. I'm from Chicago, so it's a bit of a cultural shock in some ways, but I can see what Taylor loves about this place." John quickly glanced at his watch before speaking in a lower voice to Taylor. "We only have twenty minutes before we need to meet your mom at the deli. I'm going to finish looking for that book so we can head." Taylor nodded and ran a hand over John's lower back as he walked away before turning to me.

I smiled at him and nodded toward John, "Is that new?"

Taylor gave me an impish grin. "Being out or the relationship?"

I laughed, grateful he could talk about his sexuality with ease. "Either."

Taylor shook his head. "Actually, no on both counts. I came out to my family at the start of high school. To my friends and classmates shortly after that. And I met John at freshman orientation, and within weeks we began dating." His eyes looked a bit lost in thought for a moment before he continued. "Everything is good."

"I'm so glad."

"Actually, Ms. Jameson, I really am glad I ran into you here. I've always wanted to thank you," Taylor said softly.

Emotion welled up inside me. I had no idea what Taylor wanted to thank me for, but I could see he was overcome. "Taylor, I should thank you. I had you my first year, and God knows I was clueless on how to be a teacher."

He laughed. "That's not the way I remember it. What I remember is how you made me feel. I was struggling a lot at that time. In sixth grade I had finally admitted to myself that I wasn't attracted to girls the way my friends were. By the time I hit your class a year later, I was struggling with how I felt about myself. I hated that I couldn't just be like everyone else. I still remember a day that fall that you found me after school. My locker had been near your classroom, and I was crying. You came out of your room and asked me to come in and sit on a couch. You just waited there, without judgment, and gave me time to get myself together."

The scene Taylor mentioned sprang to the front of my memories. I wish it was the only time in the past few years I'd found a kid crying in the hall, but honestly, it wasn't. Middle school is such a unique time, filled with so many emotions. I would do anything to make it easier for my students.

"I do remember that, though I have to tell you that the reason I waited quietly was because I had no idea what to say," I said, smiling to myself. That was true for so much of my early years in teaching. Hell, it was still true now to some degree. There was no script to go by when trying to help students when they were struggling.

"That's okay. What I clearly remember was that you rubbed my back as you gave me Kleenex and told me that middle school can be a bitch and the most important thing to figure out before I headed to high school was who I wanted to be and who I wanted to surround myself with. You said one true friend was far more valuable than many friends who wouldn't respect who I was. And you told me that I was the person who got to decide what journey I wanted to take, no one else did." Taylor smiled down at me.

"Well, one, I'm sorry I said bitch to a seventh grader."

Laughing, he replied, "It did make an impact."

I went on. "I do remember that I didn't know what you were dealing with and didn't want to pry, so I just gave you advice based on what I struggled with in middle school. That wasn't my sexual identity, but horrible, backstabbing, so-called friends who spread rumors about me. People who looked down at me, who pitied me, who thought I was less than them because of the money, or lack thereof, that my family had. That was when I realized that as long as I had my friend Emma with me, all was well. I didn't need anyone else."

Taylor sat with that quietly for a moment. "I'm sorry you dealt with that. The reason I wanted to thank you was that I wasn't sure if you realized how impactful a conversation like that was with a kid. My aunt is a teacher, and she always says you hear about everything you do that's wrong but not often what you did that was right. Those words from you lifted me up over and over again until I was ready to own my identity. I felt like you saw me, you cared about me, and I can't thank you enough for that." His voice was overcome with emotion.

Instinctively, I leaned forward and wrapped him in a hug. I hated that any kid ever had to struggle, but I was beyond grateful to see this one standing here, owning his truth, and apparently doing very well. I wish that for all my students, for kids everywhere. Whispering in his ear, I said, "I'm so glad I could help. I wish I could have done more."

Pulling back, I saw John had joined us with a book in hand. I took it from him and circled back to the register, ringing him up as I saw him check in with Taylor, grazing his cheek with a kiss. I took John's credit card and then put the receipt in the bag and handed him everything back.

"I'm so glad you guys came in. If you're in town for long, stop by again. I'd love to catch up when you have more time," I said.

"You bet. Maybe we can get together for coffee?" Taylor said as he and John started to head toward the door.

"Anytime," I replied and watched them head out and down the block.

Looking down at my hands, I exhaled. Taylor's aunt was right. You often didn't hear about what you did that made an impact, though that was okay too. It was just nice to hear that something had. Hearing the bell again, I looked up and saw John walking back toward me.

I glanced around the counter. "Did you forget something?"

He smiled and shook his head. "Nah, Taylor's headed to the deli. I just wanted to come back and tell you thanks too."

I raised a brow. "Thanks, for what?"

John ran his hand over his short hair, then laid his hands on the counter across from mine. "My dad's a teacher too. I know the difference one good teacher can make in the life of a kid." He paused, seeming to get some thoughts together. "Taylor told me about growing up here, about coming out. It's not easy anywhere, but a small town like this can be tough."

I nodded. I didn't know what it was like to come out, but I certainly knew what it was like to have people talking about you.

John continued. "I just wanted to thank you for supporting your students, even when you don't realize you're doing it. That's huge, and you can have no idea of the impact you made. Or, actually, the impact you still make. It's like ripples."

I cleared my throat, looking up at John. "Thanks," I said softly, then smiled at him. "Are all nineteen-year-olds this wise now? They certainly weren't a decade ago."

He laughed. "Nope. I'm out here making a good name for us all. Catch me playing video games with Taylor, however, and you'd see a different side." He took a moment, looked me in the eye, nodded twice, then tapped my hand as he moved to go. "Keep being you, Ms. Jameson. Kids need that. Especially in a place like this." With that, he walked out the door.

I watched John walk out and head back down the block. His words washed over me, and like clockwork, the tears began. I grabbed some tissues and sank down to the floor, praying the store could be empty until I could get my shit together. Unfortunately, not much time passed before I heard the bell and my name being called.

"Maggie? Maggie?"

"She's got to be here somewhere. Maggie?"

I stood up from the floor area behind the counter, brining my used Kleenex as well as the box with me. Locking eyes on Ivy and Emma, I watched them take in what I was sure was my blotchy face, the pile of Kleenex, back up to my face, then they looked at each other and burst out laughing.

"Hey!" I cried, indignantly. Emma was bent over, trying to catch her breath, she was laughing so hard. "Some best friend," I muttered.

"It's just, I mean, I'm sorry, but you look...," Emma started.

"Pathetic." Ivy snorted.

I stood up straight and looked at the two of them with what I was certain was my best haughty expression. "I'm sure I do not know what you mean." I just got it out before the two traitors made it behind the bookstore counter and pulled me into their arms in a tight embrace. I held back a bit before Emma's fingers began to wiggle on my sides, exactly where I was ultra ticklish.

I twisted, trying to get away from her as my laughter bubbled up. "Damn you, Emma." I gasped. "Knock it off."

"Nope, not happening, Maggie May. You need to laugh more." Emma giggled as she got right under my ribs.

Finally I pulled back, avoiding Ivy where she leaned against the counter, watching the scene. I put a few steps between myself and Emma and raised up my hand to keep her at a distance. "Stay. What gives?"

Emma's hands immediately became animated as she waved them around and got serious. "You, Maggie. These tears. This isn't the you I know. You take life by the balls and squeeze out what you want—"

"Eww," Ivy muttered.

"Ivy, I'm making a point," Emma said.

"Just saying." Ivy grinned. "Balls..."

Emma's eyes rolled enough that my students would stand up and applaud. "As I was saying, Maggie, you seem lost. I'm not sure if it's the pregnancy, my bro—and if it's him, say the word and I'll kick his ass—or what, but you are not the fun-loving, kick-ass, take-no-prisoners Maggie that I know and love." Her eyes got suspiciously moist, and she almost whispered, "You seem lost."

And on that note, I did lose it. Tears. Rivers of them, flowing down my face. It was not a pretty cry. Not a dainty little sniff, but actual sobs.

Shit.

Emma and Ivy immediately wrapped around me again sans any notion of tickling as they could clearly see I had lost it. Emma began making hushing noises as she rubbed my back. Ivy just stood there, giving comfort in her solid presence.

Emma pulled my hair back, looking straight into my eyes, and whispered, "Mags, what is it?"

I looked around, taking in Ivy's bookstore, the soothing afternoon light from the street. Ivy left our embrace and grabbed some candles from below the counter, lighting them, and then she moved to the door, locking it, and flipped the sign to CLOSED.

"Hey," I protested, tears finally slowing. "We don't close for an hour or so."

Ivy grinned at me. "Babe, this is the benefit to owning

the store. We close whenever I want. And right now I think it is more important that we get some music on and dance. You, my beautiful girl, need to release some demons." She grabbed her phone. "Any requests?"

"Hold on, Ivy," Emma said, glancing back to me. "I want a minute with this one before we dance, though that sounds good too." Emma took both my hands in hers. "Spill, chickie. What's with the waterworks?"

My brain tried to make sense of all the emotions I was overwhelmed with, but it felt like swiss cheese. "Guys, I don't know. I think a lot of it is pregnancy related. Like you said, Emma, I'm not typically this emotional."

Ivy looked up from her phone. "Okay, I'll butt in. Clearly I don't know you as well as Emma. Maybe that is actually an advantage here. I have had a baby, and pregnancy hormones are no joke, true. But at least for me, they just heightened what was already there. Did something happen today that upset you?"

"Not really? I mean, I had a former student come in. I got to talk to him as well as his boyfriend for a bit." I thought about Taylor and John and smiled.

Emma tilted her head and considered me for a moment. "They didn't say anything to upset you?"

"Of course not! Taylor was always a sweet kid, still is. He even shared a memory from being in middle school where I helped him." I thought of John coming back in. "And his boyfriend actually came back in and told me how much of an impact I made on Taylor in a place like Highland." My eyes immediately welled up. Shit.

Emma and Ivy glanced at each other, then back at me. Ivy began gently, "Umm, Maggie, are you aware that you look like you're ready to cry again?"

I sucked in a huge stuttering breath, trying to regain

control. "Yes," I managed. "I have no idea why. What Taylor and John—that's his boyfriend—told me was sweet. I don't know what in the hell has happened to my eyes."

Ivy grinned, "Well, not to play armchair psychologist on you, but let's dive in, shall we?" Emma laughed, and I fought back a smile.

"Sure."

"Okay, so two former students—" Ivy began.

"Nope, one former student, Taylor, with his boyfriend from college," I corrected.

"Gotcha. Two guys came in and said nice things about you, went on their way, and you had a mini meltdown. Correct?" Ivy's expression could only be described as mischievous. She had a dimple pop out on her right cheek. Her blondish brown hair tumbled over her shoulders in waves, and her ice-blue-green eyes regarded me.

I looked from her to Emma, who was watching me with concern and amusement warring across her face. I smiled at her through my watery eyes, then looked at Ivy again.

She looked serious. "Okay, babe, let's talk this through. Were you insulted by what Taylor—that's his name, right?"

I nodded.

"Cool. So, were you insulted by what Taylor or his boyfriend told you?"

"Nope, it was nice."

Ivy thought about that. "So, are these tears of happiness?"

I thought about it for a minute. I did feel lighter, so maybe? "I'm not sure that's it. I mean, yeah, sure, their words were kind. Anyone likes to know they've made an impact, right?" John's face popped into my mind, and his voice reverberated through me. *Keep being you, Ms. Jameson. Kids need that. Especially in a place like this.*

"What is it?" Emma asked, moving closer to me. "You just thought about something big."

"It's nothing," I said. "I just remembered what Taylor's boyfriend, John, said." Glancing at Emma and Ivy, who were watching me expectantly, I repeated his words to them.

Ivy's face scrunched up in confusion. "So, are you insulted that he referred to Highland Falls as *a place like this*?"

"Nah, I know what he means. We're just not very diverse in any way you'd look at it: race, sexual orientation, religion, etc. He was just saying my presence makes a difference, which was nice to hear."

Ivy's expression moved to one of skepticism. "But you already know that, right?"

I drew my eyebrows together as I thought about Ivy's question. "Know what?"

Ivy looked over at Emma. "Is she screwing with me right now?"

Emma gave Ivy a look of solidarity. "Nope, she doesn't see it."

"Okay, you two nutcases. What the hell are you going on about?"

Ivy suddenly walked over to the huge chalkboard where I had written my list of *Ms. Jameson recommends* titles. She waved around the board. "Do you see this?"

I glanced over the board. "See what? The notes?" The board was covered with little messages from former students telling me what books they'd purchased or what ones they recommended to me. I had been reading them and writing back during my morning shifts each day I worked.

Ivy looked up to the sky. "Goddess, give me strength."

She took a breath, then moved back in front of me. "Maggie, I think it is the rare teen, or even young adult, that willingly writes public notes to their middle school teacher about what they're reading. And it isn't only that. I've only been here a few months, but kids talk about you all the time. They tell me about your class, how you care about them, how you give them advice, how you help them find books they can see themselves in. It makes them feel less alone. Hell, they've stood in here and recommended books to other customers from what they've learned from you."

"But—" I began.

"Nope, no disagreeing allowed here, Maggie. Emma, tell her. Am I right?" Ivy looked impatient, which was not a look I was used to on her face.

Emma nodded. "Sorry, babe. Ivy's right. Whether you want to admit it or not, you make a difference in the lives of the kids in this town."

I couldn't explain why, but their words were making my heart race. "It isn't anything anyone else doesn't do," I whispered.

Emma pulled me from my spot on the counter so that I was standing with her and Ivy. "Babe, there are some awesome teachers at your school, but whether it's due to the subject you teach, the way that you do it, or likely both, you are different. These kids need you and, I'd argue, you need them." Emma leaned forward to give me a loud smacking kiss on my cheek. Pulling back, she regarded me. "Whether you want to admit it or not, you've become an integral part of the fiber of this town, and *that*, my beautiful friend, is what I'm betting has you freaking with this waterworks display you've got going on."

My heart felt like it skipped a beat, maybe two. I couldn't be a huge part of this town. I needed to leave. This wasn't the plan. Closing my eyes, Taylor's teary face from years ago, standing at his locker, popped into my mind. I shook my head and opened them, seeing the messages scrawled all over the chalkboard. I took a deep breath in, held it, blew it out, and looked at my friends. "I can't think about this right now."

Ivy nodded, grabbing her phone. "So, what you're saying is that you need to dance?"

Yep, that's exactly what I needed. "Yes."

"Hey, you took a Sunday shift so I could get Addie to the birthday shindig of the summer. It's the least I can do." She scanned through her phone list. "Hmm, so how does Jeremy Loops sound?"

"Who is that?" I asked, looking at Emma who simply shrugged.

"He's from Cape Town, and he's amazing. Yep, this is it. I think 'Down South' is exactly what we need right now." Ivy hit a button on her phone and put it on the counter. Moving to dim the lights, her arms shot up as the song began. Her body swayed to the music, eyes closed. She seemed lost into the beat that flowed through the bookstore.

Looking at Emma, I held out my hand. She slid hers into mine, and I spun her a few times before we joined Ivy, the three of us swaying and dancing in her rapidly darkening store to the beat of a singer a half a world away. I closed my eyes, visualizing Cape Town, South Africa. Thinking of this man recording this beautiful song so far away, then months or years later the three of us dancing to it in the middle of Illinois, made me feel insignificant in the scheme of life. I thought of Taylor, of my students who left messages on the chalkboard, and part of my heart swelled. I was needed. I made a difference, beyond being a little girl the town looked after. I wasn't sure what that meant right now, but it didn't feel so bad.

One song changed to the next, the beat pumping through the store. I tipped my head back and smiled, letting the music fill me up as I spun around, laughter filling the space as we moved. God, or Goddess, as Ivy would say, I had needed this. Everything else could wait.

## 22

## TO CAN OR NOT TO CAN

***Sully***

The past two weeks had been the best and worst of my life. I felt like I was reading that damn book from high school... It *was the best of times, it was the worst of times.* Two weeks ago, Maggie had been under me. We'd connected in a way I hadn't ever before. Honestly, I wasn't sure how I could adequately describe what we were to someone else, because I couldn't make sense of it myself. It had been a while, as I told her, but that wasn't it. Maggie and I had hooked up back in April, and the same thing had happened. Connection. Sex was great—it always had been —but with Maggie it was something more. Deeper. What the literal fuck? She was all I could think about.

I'd realized I had feelings for Maggie a few years ago when she walked into the brewery, positively glowing with excitement over some gardening crap. Watching her face, lit up from within, it was like I woke up. I hadn't done anything about it then, just listened to her ramble on about plants and her need to have flowers for the monarch butterfly in her small garden. I'd nodded my head, not having a clue what she was going on about, but thinking she'd looked damn sexy doing it. That didn't stop me from going home and googling what the fuck she meant, then going out and planting a shit load of nectar plants for the damn butterflies. I'd known I wasn't in a place to be what she needed, yet, but I planned to get there one day. If I could plant some flowers to help these butterflies to make her happy, so be it.

However, last year at the start of summer, Maggie had come into the brewery on a date with some guy. Emma told me about it later, saying Maggie said he hadn't been anything to write home about. That didn't negate the shot to the gut I felt when I'd looked up from the bar and saw her sitting at a high-top with a guy who had his hand resting on her thigh.

The noise of the brewery had faded away, and my vision had tunneled so it was like the two of them were all I could see. I'd told Jake and Daryl that I forgot I needed to help my dad with something and had walked right out of the bar. I didn't think Maggie had seen me, but it didn't matter. Either I got out of there ASAP or I was going to drag Maggie out. I wasn't sure when the caveman persona had invaded my body, but that was the urge I'd felt standing there that night in my brewery. I'd been raised by a strong woman and truly believed women were equal to men in all ways or likely superior. That didn't stop the word that immediately popped into my brain that night while looking at Maggie with that dick.

*Mine.*

That night had changed me. I knew without a shadow of doubt where I wanted to end up and with whom. Any girl I tried to see after that might as well have had a neon sign over her head that flashed NOT MAGGIE because casual dating had lost any and all enjoyment. Those dates stood in the way of what I wanted.

No, what I needed. Or, to be more accurate, who I needed.

Now we'd been together twice. The first time things hadn't gone according to plan. Hell, I hadn't planned any of it. That night back in April I'd simply wanted to make sure she was safe. Well, that and to be sleeping next to her all night absolutely factored in. But I'd never thought we'd go there, not yet.

Waking up next to her had been like a dream come true. I'd started getting my hopes up, thinking that maybe it was time to see if she felt what I did. She'd joked with me for years about the two of us. I was just hoping that there was some truth behind those jokes. What followed that morning was the stuff of my fantasies but better.

And then the condom broke.

I still couldn't believe it. Doubly protected, just as my dad had preached to Max and me for years, and she still wound up pregnant. Not that I was complaining. Far from it.

I ran my hands through my hair and looked out at the quiet brewery. Jake was in the back, and lunch service would begin soon. We were meeting in a bit to talk about canning, a conversation I wasn't looking forward to, but all I could think about was Maggie.

I knew that everyone was surprised that I hadn't freaked at the news from Maggie, but honestly, my first thought when I'd found out weeks ago had been if she was okay. I remembered being worried about her finding out on her own. Being worried about her body, if she was struggling with this. I remembered wishing her mom was still around, wishing she'd talk to my mom.

Wanting to take care of her, to have someone take care of her.

I had the overwhelming feeling of needing to get my shit together, to be there for her and the baby as my dad had been for us. And I clearly remembered the feeling of everything being *right*. Maggie having my baby? *Our* baby? *Yep*, that was absolutely a plan I could get behind. Now just to get her to believe in it too.

I knew that she was skittish, and I didn't want to freak her out. Getting her to move in with me was huge. I was so damn grateful that she was there. Over the past few weeks, I'd gotten to be there for her, and it was everything I'd hoped for. I made her peppermint tea that helped combat her morning sickness. I pulled her hair into a ponytail and rubbed her back when it didn't work and she sat praying to the porcelain throne. I watched her throw the ball every night with Ranger before crashing on the couch. I carried her to her bed when she fell asleep trying to binge watch something on Netflix. In small ways, I'd become part of her routine. Not only did I not want that to end, I wanted more.

Two weeks ago, we'd fallen back into that bed together. God, nothing looked as good as Maggie's hair spread out over my pillow. My sheets still smelled like her perfume a week later. I'd put off washing them, but sleeping with her scent surrounding me relaxed me like nothing else could. Well, beyond having her in my bed. I'd hoped that night meant a new beginning for us. I should have known that nothing with Maggie would be that simple. Falling asleep with my arms surrounding her had been a dream, but I'd woken up to reality in the form of my empty bed.

That day I'd decided to take my direction from Maggie and hadn't brought anything up all day long, trying my damnedest to act normal. I'd gone to work, came home, cooked dinner, and acted like all was well. Finally that evening I decided I had to say something, had to try to address the giant elephant in the room.

It was a no go.

We'd sat in the living room, watching some show on TV about fixing up houses that she loved. I'd asked her what the previous night had meant to her, where she saw us. Two weeks later, I could still close my eyes and remember the pained look on her face, the words that had cut me to the quick. Maggie's face had swiveled to mine and her eyes filled up immediately with tears.

"Not now, Sully. I can't do this now," she'd whispered.

My mind had raced back over the previous night. Had I done something she didn't want? Surely not, or she wouldn't be sitting by my side right now. But I had to know, the thought made me ill.

"Did I hurt you? Did you not want that last night?" My throat had been full of emotion I didn't know what to do with. Even now, weeks later, it still got to me.

A tear had spilled over her lower lids, and she'd bit her bottom lip. "No," she whispered. "It's just, I mean, last night was beautiful, really. But I think I just really need a friend right now." She gestured between the two of us sitting on the couch. "I can't do this. Not now." She'd looked up at me, her eyes pleading. "Is that okay?" Maggie had looked down at her lap. "I'm so sorry," she whispered.

I'd looked at her curled up on the couch and realized she was lost and I could help. I wanted a hell of a lot more than friendship, but I knew Maggie. If you pushed her, she pushed back. And I wasn't the one carrying a baby who had absolutely not planned on that yet. If she needed a friend, that's what I'd be. I could wait, though my cock certainly disagreed. Grumpy bastard. It woke up every time she was around.

Trying to lighten the mood, I'd looked at her and said, "Mags, I've been your friend for years, and I'm not going anywhere." A look of relief had swept across her gorgeous face, so I continued, pushing my luck just a bit. "But with all those pregnancy hormones swirling around your bod, if you need to add 'with benefits' onto our friendship, just saying, I'm willing."

"Sully!" She'd sat straight up to slug my arm but then quickly nestled back against me.

"Bully," I'd growled as I grinned and kissed the top of her head, then nestled back into the couch.

I groaned. Two weeks. I'd thought that a few days would go by, and then she'd decide that she wanted more. No dice. My showers had gotten longer. Visions of Maggie in my bed, dancing around the kitchen, hanging out on the couch with her long legs propped up on the back would play through my mind as my fist would pump. But there was no relief.

"Sullivan!"

My thoughts came back to the present to see Jake making his way to the bar. I quickly gave my head a bit of a shake, attempting to get rid of any thoughts of Maggie. It was a losing battle.

"What's up? You look like shit, Sully."

Jesus. Jake had never been one to hold back on the truth. "Thanks, man. Appreciate the compliment."

"Just saying, you'd think you'd look a lot more relaxed for a guy who is living with his baby mama."

"Really? Baby mama? Who the hell are you?" I shook my head, wondering if Jake might be hanging around the college kids who were back for the summer and working at the brewery. People our age didn't use this term, did they? Or maybe we were just all getting old. Either way, it felt more like normal between us and I'd take it. We'd been working our way back to this for the past few weeks.

Jake laughed as he leaned against the bar where I'd been standing. "Screwing with you, man. Though I believe the term has been around longer than you think. At any rate, guessing you aren't getting any with your roomie?"

I felt a feeling of irritation rise up. "Jake, we are not talking about any sex that is or isn't happening between Maggie and me. Not happening. Told you a few weeks ago you and Harp are becoming a pair of gossips."

Jake slapped me on the back before moving behind the bar and grabbing a glass. "No need to say anything else. Your reply says it all anyway, man. I'll make sure to tell Max that we need to get our latest intel released onto the town's social media page by lunch."

He was full of shit. We all hated social media and attributed it to the downfall of the world. Upon reflection, that was a bit of a *get those kids off my lawn* type of reaction. I chuckled. Maybe my age was showing after all.

Jake scanned the taps. "What do you want?"

I looked them over. We had our beer on tap along with a few other beers from the area breweries. It had been a busy few weeks for us. We'd released two new beers this month. A Trip to Grandma's was doing well. Summer and fruity beers were a match for many folks. But today that sounded too sweet for my taste. "Evolution," I said. It was a triple IPA we'd just brewed, named after the album of one of my favorite bands. The citrus flavor with the hops sounded perfect for today.

Jake filled our beers and then nodded his head toward a

table in the corner where my laptop sat open. "That you?" he asked.

I nodded, grabbed my beer, and we headed over. Waking up the laptop, I looked over the spreadsheet I had open. It listed the costs for graphic design for the labels for the beer, cans, lids, four-pack or six-pack holders, equipment costs, et cetera. At the low end it would be around $150,000, and prices could go as high as a million, not that we'd need anything near that type of equipment. We weren't looking at nationwide distribution, just locally to begin. Even so, the numbers were overwhelming, to say the least. I was still nervous; my default was to be conservative with our funds. But Jake had been wearing me down over the past few weeks.

Jake sat across the table. "This conversation is long overdue."

"I know. It took me a while to go through all the information from the different brewers, suppliers, et cetera."

"Have you thought any more about that canning company that we met with yesterday?" Jake asked.

I paused, looking down at my notebook where I'd sketched out some ideas. There was a new company that was starting a canning business for small breweries in the Midwest. They had the equipment, and you paid them to do your canning for you. It was far less than doing it yourself, but if you planned on this long term, investing in the equipment was a better deal. Glancing at Jake, I nodded. "Yeah, I've been thinking about those numbers versus the ones we already had. What did you think?" I pushed my laptop to the middle of the table so we both could see it.

Jake looked over the spreadsheet and the notes. "I think it's the same premise as renting an apartment versus buying a house. Upfront costs are scary, but in the long run, it's worth it."

My stomach twisted. It meant another loan, which we could swing. I kicked myself once again for rejecting the loan last month. It was ridiculous, but now that we were operating in the black with all the start-up costs paid off, I hated to go back.

"Talk to me, Sullivan. This was your idea, your baby, and part of our ten-year plan. What's changed?"

I looked around the brewery and took in what we'd accomplished. I'd gone to school with no real direction, just the knowledge that I didn't want to sit in an office for my job. The brewery had been more than I dreamed. Yeah, the work, especially in the beginning, had been incredible. But now we had a manager. Our beer had won awards at several craft beer festivals in the Midwest. The restaurant business was fickle, but we had a loyal base. Our waitstaff worked well together. There was no desire for another location, or even to expand this one. The only part of our dream of expansion we had left was canning, and then just continuing to polish and improve over the years. Looking at Jake, I knew I owed him an explanation of where my mind was at. One of the reasons our partnership worked was our no bull-shit policy.

"Maggie."

Jake raised an eyebrow. "That's it? Maggie?"

"No man. Maggie and the baby. I mean, I've mentioned it, but it's just that with the baby coming, I can't decide if now is the time to invest more in this place when we're finally moving forward." I took a long sip of Evolution. "Damn, we make a kick-ass beer."

Jake leaned forward, tapping my pint glass with his own. "That we do. Actually, we make several." He took a swig of his beer, then focused on me. "Man, I get it. And while I've given you a ton of shit, I'm impressed at how easily you've adapted to the news that you're going to be a dad. But here's the thing. I think you're looking at this ass backward. This is an investment for your kid, an investment in the future. By putting up this money now, you are ensuring that our business will continue to expand. That's only going to help us stay afloat in the long run, not hurt us."

I rolled the glass from one hand to the other, mulling over Jake's words. In my gut I knew it was the right move for the business. I just couldn't wrap my brain around taking out a loan now. I felt like I needed to sock everything into savings yesterday. Maybe get an IRA or whatever parents did. "It's the loan, man. Last year we paid off the start-up loan from the bank, paid back our parents, and we were ahead of schedule. Just feels like getting another one seems like we're moving backward."

Jake looked out over the brewery for a moment, nodding his head, then looked back to me. "What about if we don't do a loan. What about asking for investors?"

I looked from my beer to Jake in confusion. "How is getting small loans from many people different than what we're talking about?"

"I mean, what if they aren't loans? What if we have a few people we're close with invest in this part of the busi-ness? We don't look at it as loan we have to pay back, but just a few people we split the profits with. I mean, if we wanted to buy them out in the future, we could, but maybe we wouldn't need to..." Jake's thoughts trailed off.

Investors in the canning side of the business. That wasn't an idea I'd thought of, but I didn't hate it. "I need to think more about that. Do you have anyone in mind?"

Jake cleared his throat. "Not really. It just came to me today when I was talking to my brother."

"How's Drew doing?"

"Exhausted. The dry conditions in the West aren't helping matters."

"Nowhere he'd rather be though, right?" I asked. Drew was a firefighter out in the Rockies. Wildfires were on the rise, and drought conditions were helping no one. I'd met him when he'd come to visit Jake during college and visited Jake here a few times, but mostly he'd stayed out West. He'd been to The Homestead, but since he'd finished college and joined the US Forestry Department's hotshot firefighter team, Jake didn't see him often. I knew Jake worried about him, but from all accounts, Drew loved it.

"It's hard to watch the news about those crazy fires in California and not wish he had a different job though."

I nodded. The thought of my sister being in danger on a regular basis was a punch to the gut. I didn't know how Jake dealt with it. Pulling me out of those thoughts, a hand crashed onto my shoulder in the form of one Maxwell Harp.

"Can I crash this cozy date?"

"What dragged you in here, Harp?" Jake said, smiling at our friend.

Max pulled up a stool and nodded over to the bar where Daryl was getting ready for lunch crowd. "Was up early working on the farm, and Emma left to go hang with Maggie. Figured I'd come up here and see you two."

I nodded, "And you wanted to try our new beer..."

"And I wanted to try your new beer."

I looked over to Daryl. "Evolution," I said, tipping my head to Max.

Daryl took care of the beer, and Max scanned my

laptop screen. Glancing from Jake to me, he asked, "You finally going ahead with the canning side? You'd make my life a fucking lot better if I could have just gone to my fridge to get a beer today instead of hauling my ass to town."

"But then you would have missed spending time with the two of us." I shook my head at him.

Jake let out a laugh, then said to Max, "I'm trying to convince this stubborn ass to go ahead with the investment. I just suggested we look to getting a few investors to help with the start-up costs. We can split the profits with them and not take the entire burden on by ourselves." Jake tipped his head at me, then turned his attention back to Max. "He's thinking about it, which is better than shooting me down immediately."

"I'd be interested," Max said quickly.

"Really?" I looked at Max in surprise. "You don't need to do that." I hated this feeling of asking for charity.

Max gave me a skeptical look. "Nope. Wipe that look off your face, man. You know how much I like your beer. This would be an investment and a damn good one at that. But I'd need to run it by Emma first—"

Jake interrupted. "Congrats on the engagement, man. Don't think I've seen you since I heard."

"Yep. Best decision I've ever made." The look of contentment on Max's face was not one I'd seen on him before.

I sat there, mulling over the thought of investors, the possibility of moving ahead with the canning. "Jake, I think investors could be a good way to go. Let me think some more about it tonight, and I'll get back to you."

"Planning on talking to Maggie about it?" Max grinned at me.

I glanced at Max, then Jake, who both were giving me

knowing looks. "Yeah, assholes, I do think I'll talk to Maggie."

Max and Jake both laughed before Max spoke. "Good choice, man. Women like communication, you know."

"Now you're a relationship expert?"

"Just saying we all know Maggie. And I know all about how pissed she was a few weeks back when she overheard you talking to me about pausing this investment. So maybe if you get your head out of your ass and stop shutting her out of conversations where you're considering what to do based on her, you'll get closer to where you need to be."

Fuck, Max was right. I was debating what to do next based on Maggie and the baby without even talking to Maggie about it. That smacked of some misguided old-school values and not just a little sexism. Not okay.

"Shit, thanks man. I do need to talk with her."

Max nodded. "Good. Now that we've got that settled, how about some food?"

## 23

## REDEFINING RELATIONSHIPS

***Maggie***

I pulled myself out of the tub, avoiding Ranger as I stepped down. I'd left the bookstore earlier with visions of this gorgeous tub in my head. Emma, Ivy, and I had danced away the past hour at the store. I'd laughed more than I had for weeks. Ivy shared her secret chocolate stash with the two of us, and we pledged to have margaritas together next summer when tequila and I were acquaintances once again.

I paused, grabbing the fluffy white towel, and looked down at Ranger. "I will be friends with tequila again next summer, right?" Thinking about Bridget, my principal, and her wife Sam, I knew that parents drank, of course. We'd had margarita night often over the years. But with a newborn? Toweling off, I realized I hadn't given a lot of thought to any changes to my life beyond the immediate ones.

God, I was an idiot. This baby was going to come out, and everything was going to change. *Everything*. A feeling of panic began to well up inside. My heartbeat thudded. I felt like there was pressure on my chest. My stomach rolled. *Breathe, Maggie, breathe.*

Standing there, staring in the mirror, I gazed at the woman looking back at me. I didn't remember my mom, bits and pieces, really. I knew I resembled her from pictures my dad had. Twenty-nine. I felt behind, like I should already have life figured out by now. When I was in my teens, I assumed I'd be living in a big city by now, far away from a place where everyone knew my life story before I'd even met them. A place where my actions determined what others thought about me, not my past. God, I felt like a failure.

Dropping the towel, I turned to grab my pajamas, and then I did a double take. Looking back in the mirror, I turned sideways. Whoa. I ran my hand over my stomach. It wasn't much, really, but it was there. It was just like I had eaten a huge meal and my lower stomach protruded a bit. No longer relatively flat, it was a visual reminder of what was to come.

My hand rested on my belly as I whispered, "Hey, little bean. Sorry for the waterworks today. Or maybe I'm not sorry. You're contributing to that too, aren't you? But none of those waterworks have to do with you." I rubbed my stomach, my damn eyes welling up again. "I cannot wait to meet you, cannot wait to hold you."

Looking up at the mirror, I caught my own gaze. What would my mother say if she was still here? I had a feeling she'd tell me I'd been far too hard on myself, but that was something I'd struggled with my whole life. I needed to be kinder to myself. I knew that. I felt like if everything could just pause for a few days, I could get my head together. That would be ideal but wasn't going to happen.

Shaking my head, I pulled on my pajama shorts and a

tank and headed to the kitchen. Today I'd begun the second trimester of this journey I was on. I hadn't had any morning sickness for a few days and actually felt ravenously hungry right now. Ranger bounded ahead of me down the stairs and skidded to a stop as he slid across the floors to the kitchen island. Standing there, in all his smoldering glory, was Sully.

"Hey, what are you doing here?" I asked. It was early evening, and I hadn't expected him to be home. Usually he worked on Sunday nights, so I had figured it was the pup and me for dinner tonight.

"Switched shifts with Jake today because he had shit going on," he answered. Leaning over, he gave Ranger a good rubdown and looked up at me. "When was he out last?"

"Right before my bath." I glanced at the large wooden wall clock across from the island. "Less than an hour ago. But I haven't fed him yet," I said in response to the excited thump of Ranger's tail on the floor. The dog knew what time it was and what he was waiting for.

Sully let out a low chuckle as he stood up. Mmmm. *Down, girl,* I told myself. His brewery T-shirt was worn and stretched across his shoulders. His jeans were faded, barely holding on in a few spots, and hung low on his hips. I licked my lips without thinking. Sully had starred in my fantasies since I became a teen, and living with him was making that even worse. I wondered what he'd say if I made a move, let my hand slide over his ass for a moment. He was holding back because I asked him too, right? Or maybe he was done with my ever-changing emotions. If I was in his place, I would be. *Get a grip, Maggie.*

"Is that it, boy? You want to eat?" he asked, pulling me out of my daydream.

Ranger spun around in a circle and let out a bark.

Sully smiled indulgently at the dog as he filled the bowl before looking over to me. "Were you getting ready to make something?"

I moved to the fridge, opening it and scanning the contents without really seeing anything. "Yeah, I was actually hungry today, so I figured I'd see what we have."

Sully moved behind me, resting his chin on my shoulder. "Do we have anything good in here?"

My heart thumped. Every part of my body came alive with him right behind me. I knew he didn't mean anything by it. Hell, how many times had he stood just like this as I looked in the Sullivans' fridge growing up? Sully and Emma's parents had always joked that all of us spent more hours staring in the fridge than actually cooking or eating. My mind knew that, but my body was screaming at the nearness of this man. When I was a kid, his casual way of touching me never failed to make my heart race. It seemed that adult Maggie had the same reaction.

The heat building in my belly and flowing downward was not helping matters. Holy hell. Taking a breath, I tried for cool and removed. "Back off, Sullivan. Get your own food."

Instead of moving back, he took a step closer. I could feel his breath on my neck. "Come on, Maggie. Play nice. Do you want me to cook for you? We need to feed this growing baby, right?" With that, his hands slid down to my belly. As they came to a rest, he stepped back and spun me toward him as he looked down. "Holy shit, Maggie."

Sully looked me up and down before putting his hand on my lower belly again. "Is it my imagination or did you finally pop?"

I wrinkled my nose, biting back my humor. "Um, that makes me sound like a balloon."

He pulled me in for a hug before standing back. "I hope you don't mind, but I'm going to get pretty excited here." I watched in fascination as he dropped to his knees in front of me, pushing Ranger out of the way. Looking up at me, his voice lowered as he tugged at the hem of my tank, "May I?"

I cleared my throat, trying to make sure I didn't clue him in on how arousing I thought it was to have this man kneeling before me. Glancing at my nipples, it seemed the entire body was not on board with the message. "Sure," I whispered.

Slowly he raised my shirt, tucking it right below my breasts, and slid my shorts down to right below my small protruding belly. He ran his hands over my stomach, over and over, staring like he was trying to process something. Still looking at my belly, he whispered, "Damn, Maggie." He sighed with a jagged breath. "I mean, clearly I know you're pregnant. I've watched you puke, cry, and deal with shit for the past few weeks."

My eyes were tearing up as I watched the reverent way he was staring at my stomach, like it was a miracle, which it was. Looking at me, I saw tears in his own as he wrapped his arms around my legs and pressed a kiss to my stomach. "For whatever reason, this just makes it seem all the more real." His forehead rested against me as I tried to pull myself together.

I let my hands drop to his head, combing back his hair, and I was lost. Shaking my head to rid myself of the trance-like feeling, I spoke. "Tell me about it," I said quirking my mouth. "I saw this when I got out of the bath and had a flash to what I'll look like in a few months."

"You mean gorgeous, of course."

"More like I swallowed a beach ball," I muttered. Tugging on his arm, I said, "Get up."

"Nope. I'm not done worshipping this belly," he said and pressed his lips gently to my belly button. Glancing back up, he asked, "We still calling the kid Bean, or have we moved up the food pyramid? He has to be the size of a prune by now, right?"

My heart thudded with what felt dangerously like love. "Yeah, I've been still calling him Bean, but no, that's not the right size." I paused, trying to remember the article I read. "A peach, I think."

"No shit? Wow." His fingers lightly trailed over my stomach as I tried, and failed, to hold back a moan. Looking down, I saw Sully's intense gaze lock onto mine. He continued to watch me as he ran a finger along my waistband of my pajama shorts. I had to say they were my shortest pair, and I *might* have worn them regularly because I knew they drove him a bit crazy. I mean, I said I wanted to be friends, but clearly my libido wanted more.

He traced up the inside of my leg before reaching the apex and paused. "Umm, Mags?"

I looked down, working to regain my breath. "Yeah."

His touch was light as his fingers traced the band around my underwear. "Trying to be a friend here, babe. What do you want?"

It felt like hours went by as we stared at each other. Then I gave in to everything my body was screaming for. "Sully, I need you."

He continued to watch me before he quietly asked, "You mean you need me for the next hour in a friends-with-benefits way, or something more? Not to say I wouldn't be there if it's the first, but I figured we might as well establish the nature of what this is."

I sucked in my lower lip as I debated how to be honest here. "Umm, I think something more?"

Sully's face broke out in a wide grin. "Really, babe?"

A tear flowed down my cheek, then another one. Fuck these hormones. Sully had, apparently, had enough and finally stood, pulling me against him. He kissed the tracks of the tears that had flowed down my cheeks as he waited for me to get my shit together.

"What are you thinking?" I murmured.

Sully's eyes searched mine. "I'm thinking that this feels right. You in my kitchen in your pajamas with a tiny belly popping out. I'm thinking I want you to get that. To understand that I'm not here only because your pregnant, that I'm here because I've wanted to be with you for some time. And I'm thinking that when I see a future, I cannot imagine you not in it." His eyes widened like he couldn't believe he had just said all that.

Hell, I couldn't believe he had. *This isn't real,* I told myself. Sully was in some fantasy world, and I was along for the ride. I needed to think, to really analyze all this, and in the safety of his embrace, I wasn't thinking clearly. My body and heart were melting into him, telling me to go with this. My brain was screaming that I needed to hop in my car and get the hell out of town.

"Babe?" Sully spun us from in front of the fridge to have my back to the island. He picked me up and settled me there so I could look into his eyes. "Say something."

Of course, *of course,* my eyes decided to well up again. "Damn it. This little bean, or peach, of ours is in danger of causing some dehydration here. I've never cried so much in my life."

"Want some water?" he asked with a smirk.

"Shut it. I need to get this out."

Sully lightly pushed my legs apart and settled between them. His hands found that narrow strip of skin on my back between the tank and shorts and began to trace light circles. God, that felt amazing.

Clearing his throat, he said, "Go ahead, princess."

I looked up at the ceiling, searching for courage. "I'm fucking scared, Sully." He started to interrupt, but I immediately looked at him and placed a hand on his mouth. "Nope. No talking until it is your turn." Sensing that he was going to remain quiet, I removed my hand and continued. "I don't know what I can promise you right now. I've always planned on leaving Highland. Coming back after college was just temporary."

His look was one of pain, but he stayed quiet and just nodded.

I squeezed his arms, then continued. "Some stuff that happened today is making me think more about that plan, but I don't want you to get your hopes up or make any decisions too quickly. I realized tonight that this," I gestured toward my stomach, "isn't a temporary change. I guess that should be obvious, but whatever." Taking a deep breath, I went on. "So I still need space to get my head on straight. I'm still a hot mess, but"—I felt my cheeks heat up—"I'm also saying I'd like to explore a bit more what we are as more than friends." I closed my eyes and gave my head a shake before opening back up and looking at him. "Okay, your turn."

He grinned as his fingers continued tracing my back. "So are you saying we're in a relationship?" He seemed to be holding his breath, waiting for my answer.

I smiled, grabbed one of his hands, and placed it squarely on my stomach. "Umm, Sully, I don't know if you're aware of this or not, but we're definitely in a relationship already."

He leaned forward and kissed my neck where it met my

shoulder. "Yeah, babe. I'm aware of that relationship." He ran his tongue up my neck and then snagged my ear. Kissing it, running his nose along my jaw, he looked up at me, and I worked not to shiver from arousal. "I mean a romantic relationship and"—leaning forward, his lips grazed mine, then pulled back—"a sexual relationship."

I watched him, my gaze warming as I thought of all that he was asking. My heart once again sang out, telling me to trust this, to jump, but my brain warned that it would be holding part of me back. I couldn't not give in to this, at least try it out, right? I'd always regret it if I didn't. I leaned forward, letting my lips caress his. "I'd be open to trying out those relationships too."

Sully pulled back and gave me a nod before he let his fingers run up my sides, under my breasts, as he pulled out my tank from where he'd tucked it. With our eyes locked together, he tugged off my tank. Dropping it on the counter, a wicked grin spread across his face.

"Does that mean," he began, his fingers running down from my shoulders to my breasts, circling one nipple, then the other. I squirmed, dying for him to put his mouth on me. He rained light kisses down before looking up and continuing. "If I carry you to my room right now, you will actually still be there in the morning and not try to sneak out on me?"

With that, he sucked in the nipple on my right breast, and I gasped. Arching into his mouth, I groaned. "I promise to not sneak out."

Moving to my other breast, his tongue flicked my nipple a few times, driving me mad. Letting go with a pop, he stood up and pulled me snugly against him so I could feel what I did to him. I ground against his erection, and he let out a moan.

Pulling back just a bit, Sully worked to control his breath, taking a deep inhale as he ran his fingers through my hair, then over my shoulders, to my back, over my breasts, to my thighs, to the waistband of my shorts, to my stomach. Reaching it, he rested them there as he whispered, "So, you're open to relationships. Does this mean I can call you my girlfriend?"

There was a hitch in my breath before I placed my hands over his on my stomach. "Why does that feel like a big step and also a small one all at the same time?" I asked.

His smile was wide as I quickly ran my hand over the scruff at his jaw before pulling him down for a quick kiss. Pulling back, he said, "Possibly because you're having our baby? But you are more than my baby mama, Maggie."

"God, I hate that term," I groaned, wrinkling my nose.

He leaned forward and kissed my nose as he whispered, "I love when you fucking do that."

I looked up at him, then down. "Sully?"

He sucked in a breath. "Yeah, Mags?"

My fingers moved to his jeans. "You are wearing far too many clothes," I said as I undid the button and slid down the zipper.

Laughing, he pulled me toward him, allowing my legs to wrap around his waist. "I bet we can fix that problem in my room."

My heart was thudding, but I was leaped. I ran my fingers into his soft hair and looked into his eyes. "Well, then, what are you waiting for?"

Sully picked me up and moved through the house before kicking the door shut behind us to keep Ranger out. He laid me down on his bed and then stood, his eyes scanning my body from head to toe and back again. Watching his eyes heat up, I grinned. "I'd like to point out that I'm still in far less clothing than you," I said as I dipped my thumb into my pajama shorts and ran it along the waistband. "Are you planning on changing that anytime soon?" I wondered how long I could tease him. Apparently, the answer was, not long.

"Fuck, Maggie," he growled while tugging his T-shirt over his head and throwing it behind him. Kicking off his shoes, he made quick work of his jeans and boxer briefs. "You undo me," he said as he lowered himself onto the bed and kissed his way up my legs to my belly.

My breath caught in my throat as my heart raced. I was doing this. We were doing this. I didn't want to analyze anything too closely for fear that my brain would override my heart. This was Sully. *My Sully*. I still wasn't sure if we'd be here without that broken condom, but I was letting that go for the moment. My future might be up in the air, but I was letting that go too. Right now I just wanted to feel. I wanted to give in to these feelings for this man that didn't seem to go away. And an orgasm or two wouldn't hurt either.

Sully gently kissed my lips, then pulled back and placed a hand on either side of my face. Lying on top of me with some of his weight distributed to his elbows and legs, he simply watched me. I felt treasured, priceless, locked in his gaze, but also like he was searching for something.

"What?" I asked.

"Trying to decide if you're here with me or in some other conversation in your head right now."

I smiled. "I'm here."

"Now you are," he replied with a smirk, leaning in to kiss the tip of my nose.

Holy hell, even that simple gesture made my body light

up. "Smartass." I raised my eyebrow at him, then nodded down my body. "Let's get the show on the road."

With a cocky grin, he kissed my jaw, dragging his stubbled chin across my skin. Goose bumps rose up across my body, and my breasts stood at attention. "You trying to tell me you want me to do anything specific, princess?"

My face heated while my core became increasingly aroused as he began to run his tongue down my neck, stopping every so often to nip and kiss his way down. "Screw off, Sully. You know exactly what I want." I fought back laughter as he hit an extremely ticklish spot.

Sully paused when he reached my breasts, looking up at me before pressing a kiss into their swells, pausing, and doing the same thing again and again as he worked his way across. "Sure do, Maggie, but I'd also like to hear it directly from you." He swirled his tongue around my nipple, sucking the peak into his mouth.

Gasping, I arched up, pushing more of myself into his mouth. There seemed to be a direct connection between my nipple and my clit, and a line of fire raced down. Damn, I'd never had anyone spend this kind of attention on me before Sully. "I, uh, right there." My breathing was coming in pants. "More of that."

Sully grinned as he continued to lavish attention on my breasts. Glancing up, he spoke between kisses. "Just this"—pause to tug on a nipple—"or should I keep going?"

I groaned. "Sully. Just keep kissing me." I swear if I wasn't so turned on by this man, I'd want to strangle him.

Sully's body was stretched out next to mine, his hands running up and down my body as he watched my restlessness as he moved from one breast to another. He seemed like he could spend forever here, and while that wouldn't be a bad way to spend my days, I'd also like to get to that big O anytime. My body was almost vibrating with arousal, but he kept backing off where I needed him. The sensations built in waves, but as the crest grew closer, he backed off. It was maddening.

He trailed one hand down my belly and paused with it right above my mound. "Here, princess?" His mouth dropped to my belly as he lightly kissed it, then looked up. "Shall I move here?"

My heart rate increased. His stubble across my belly was lighting me up inside as I arched in, seeking more contact with his mouth. "Yes," I gasped. Closer, just a bit more.

He slid his fingers into the waistband of my shorts and panties, pulling them down and tossing them to the side. I felt his eyes on me as he ran his hand up my inner thigh, putting some pressure on my legs to separate them. "And this?" he asked as he lightly ran his hand up but then pulled back before I could get where I needed to be.

Propping myself up on my elbows, I looked down my body at Sully, with his knowing grin on his gorgeous face. "Cole Sullivan!"

"What, baby?" he asked as he leaned forward and placed a light kiss below my belly button, then another a bit lower, and another. Then he pulled up and lay next to me as we locked eyes, and he gave me a grin.

"Seriously?" I asked him. "You keep getting me right to the verge of an orgasm, then you back off. What the hell?"

"Baby." He ran his hand over my thighs as he leaned on my side. "I'm sure I don't know what you're talking about." He tugged my nipple into his mouth as his hands roamed south, just getting to the good stuff before he pulled back and regarded me, his eyes glittering with amusement.

"Sully...," I warned.

Leaning down, his mouth right at my ear, his voice was gravelly as he whispered, "Babe, let me get you there. All the buildup will be worth it, I promise. Now, if you don't mind, I'm going to get to work."

His mouth dropped to my neck, with deep kisses as he worked his way down my body again before settling between my legs.

"Hmm, so wet, Maggie." I heard him say as he dragged his tongue from my entrance to slide around my clit and back. However, I was far more focused on the feelings his mouth was causing to wash over my body.

The sensations in my body began to race, radiating out from my clit, down my legs, and back up, before he leaned forward and took me in his mouth. Holy hell. It built and built to the point that I felt like I might shatter. My back arched off the bed, and the orgasm blasted through me in wave after wave like nothing I ever felt before. I briefly wondered if you could pass out from an orgasm. Yes? No?

The man was a magician.

## 24

# CARDS ON THE TABLE

**_Sully_**

We lay in bed, boneless after some of the hottest sex I'd ever had. Hell, every time with Maggie so far had been better than the last. I'd been with more than a few women over the years, but it had never been like this. It wasn't just because we were good in bed, but because this was Maggie. My mom had always gone on about how sex was different with someone you loved. And I knew deep down in my bones that I absolutely loved Maggie Jameson. I'd loved her since she was a kid, but this was a whole other level in regard to how I felt about her. I'd never had this depth of feeling for anyone.

As I lay by Maggie's side, my head was propped on my elbow to keep most of my weight off her. My other hand traced her breasts, and I palmed one, appreciating the weight and softness of it, then ran my fingers across the nipple.

"What are you doing," she asked, regarding me from heavy-lidded eyes.

"Your breasts have changed," I said quietly, leaning over

to kiss them, then looked up at her. Her beauty took my breath away.

Her smile was small, a bit tired. "They're sore, like before I get my period. But you can't see that. What do you mean when you say they've changed?"

I smiled, pushing her hair back from her face, and kissed her cheek. Sliding my arm under her neck, I stretched out a bit. I let my hand and run over her breasts again. "The nipples and here," I traced the areola, "have gotten just a bit darker."

Maggie pulled her head off my arm and the pillow, looking down her body. "They have?"

"Yeah, just a bit. They're more dusty pink now."

"Anything else?"

My left hand slid under her breast as I gently lifted it. "They're bigger."

Maggie laughed. "Yeah, they feel a bit bigger. That's not done yet, I'd guess."

"Works for me," I said as my hand moved and settled on top of her belly.

Maggie let out a laugh as she curled up next to me. The silence felt nice, comfortable. I wished for days on end where we could simply lay in bed, my hand on her belly, watching it grow.

"Maggie," I said as I ran a hand up and down her side, "should we talk about what comes next?"

"Mmmm?" she murmured with her eyes closed. "What do you mean?"

My heart sped up. Maybe I should just sit and enjoy where we were. And if that condom hadn't broken, if Maggie wasn't pregnant with my baby, I probably would. However, it felt like everything between us was more intense as a result of our circumstances. I really didn't want to rush her, but I needed her to get where I was at. This was more than friends with benefits. This was more than scratching some itch. This was *my* Maggie, and she said she was willing to try a relationship. I needed her to know I was all in, I'd been all in even before she gave me the news that rocked my world, and I'd continued to want this thing between us regardless of anything else that was happening.

"I want to talk about the future," I began. Maggie's eyes shot open as she looked up with what I could only assume was some apprehension. Shit. This could be a delicate situation. Could I just tag my mom in for this conversation? Probably not, but I felt like there should be a flashing neon sign above her head lighting up the word *caution*. *Okay*, I thought, *here goes.*

"Well, here's the thing. This little nugget," I put my hand back on her stomach, and a feeling of joy rocketed through me. That was our baby she was growing in there. Mind-blowing. Starting again. "This little nugget has given the relationship I wanted to start with you a different focus."

"What relationship you wanted to start with me?" Maggie's brows were pulled together, and she had this little line between them. Damn, she was adorable.

"Shit, babe, let me backtrack." I took a breath, going for broke here. She needed to know how I'd felt for a while. It was time to lay my cards on the table and see where she wanted to go from there. "I've loved you as a friend forever. I can barely remember my life without you in it."

"Not making my heart swell when I'm lying next to you, *friend*," Maggie growled.

"Easy, babe. My point is several years ago, I realized those feelings changed. I think they were moving gradually, but one day it hit me. You came into The Homestead dressed in cutoff jean shorts that made my dick jump to attention. You were going on about butterflies needing a place to land, and all I could think was that I wanted your legs wrapped around my waist."

"So, you're saying you were horny."

"For you, hell yes, but that wasn't the part that stopped me in my tracks. I realized I was thinking about you constantly. When I saw you with a guy, I felt like I was going to lose my shit. When you'd come to my place with Emma, or I to yours, I just wanted to be alone with you."

Maggie ran her fingers through my hair, letting her fingers travel down, and then placed a hand on my chest. Her brown eyes locked on mine, and I felt like I could lose myself staring at her. "So why didn't you make a move before?"

I rolled to my back, bringing Maggie with me so she was tucked against my side. I looked at the ceiling as I second-guessed every decision I'd made over the past few years. Then again, those decisions brought us to where we were, with a baby coming, and I wouldn't change that for the world. "I'm not sure I can put words to it. I wanted to get to a place where I wasn't in debt, where I felt like I could be a partner for you, before I made a move."

Maggie propped an elbow into the bed and looked down on me. "Let me see if I get this, Cole Sullivan. You didn't think I'd want you if you weren't successful?"

I rolled to my side and propped myself up on an elbow too, looking at Maggie and trying to figure out how to express my thoughts. Damn, this was hard. "Babe, it's not that. I just felt like you were it. Once I went in with you, if you wanted the same thing, that there would be no going back. I wanted to make sure my focus could be on you, not trying to get a business off the ground. It's only been in the past year that my work week wasn't like seventy hours a week. I didn't know what kind of boyfriend I'd make before."

"I'm giving you shit, Sully. I get it."

I leaned forward and captured her mouth in a kiss. God, just the fact that I could do that blew my mind.

"And Sully, for the record, I wanted the same thing."

"Really?"

Maggie laughed as she ran her hand up my chest and slid it behind my neck, pulling my head toward her. "Yeah, really. In fact, you could have asked me any time after about the age of thirteen, and I would have said yes to you."

I pulled back, feeling my eyes widen in surprise. "No shit?"

She pulled me back down. "No shit."

My lips caressed hers, but I made myself pull back one more time. "Maggie," I whispered, sliding my hand up her hip. Time to go big or go home. "I love you. I've loved you for so long I don't remember not loving you." My heart was hammering so loudly I wondered if she could hear it.

She let out a small sigh before brushing her lips across mine. "Cole Sullivan," she began.

"Yeah."

"I love the shit out of you." Her lips lowered to mine and parted. I slid my tongue into her mouth and drowned in the feeling that nothing could ever be as perfect as this moment. It wasn't everything—she hadn't committed to staying in town or letting me move with her—but small steps were important.

Speaking of small steps, I pulled back. "Can I run something by you about the brewery?"

Maggie's eyes lost the dreamy look she'd had and narrowed in focus. "Is this about canning?"

I nodded, looking down at her hand intertwined with mine.

She tugged her hand away and slid up, putting her back to the headboard. She pulled the top sheet up and tucked it around herself as she slid her hair behind her ears. "Okay, ready."

I burst out laughing. One, that was speedy. Two, she looked so serious. "What are you ready for?"

She shook her head at me, looking a tad exasperated. "Um, for you to finally *talk* to me about your business instead of just making decisions that seem to be impacted by me? Come on. I'm all ears, Sullivan."

I moved to sit up by the headboard next to her. Sliding a hand up her torso and tracing the lower half of her breasts, I felt myself get aroused again. "Well, not all ears..."

She slapped my hand away. "Sully!"

I laughed and then got serious, pulling the sheet up to my waist and sitting next to her. "I went to see Jake this afternoon. We talked about canning, what the initial investment is, when we'd see a payoff, et cetera."

Maggie held her hand up. "Back up. What was your plan originally?"

I leaned my head back against the headboard, thinking back to how much shit had changed in the past few months. "Well, our original idea was to do a low-volume canning operation. We have the space to set up in the building that we never converted over for the brewery. We were going to start with two beers and distribute locally."

"And," she prompted.

I swallowed. This was where the conversation could go south. "And you got pregnant, and I got nervous."

Instead of getting pissed, Maggie slid her hand into mine. "Why?"

I continued to look at the ceiling. "I don't know, honestly. I think it was a lot of things. I wanted to be here for you and our little bean. I wanted to focus my energy on what was happening between us. But"—my voice trailed off, debating how to say this—"part of it was fear about making a bad business decision, of failing."

Maggie sat there quietly. I couldn't look at her. I wasn't sure if she was disappointed in me, thought I was an idiot—whatever it was, I didn't want to see it.

Finally she spoke. "Let's tackle that in two parts. Part one, you thought the only way to be there for us was by not investing in your business?" The tone of her voice indicated she was confused.

I took a deep breath and tried to sort it out in my mind. "Looking back, I think I panicked. I mean, I knew canning would be an investment, but when I found out about the baby, I was worried about the comfortable place Jake and I had finally gotten the brewery to. We just paid off the loans from the bank and our parents in the past year. I guess I just worried that we were getting in over our head again and that wasn't responsible."

"I think I understand that," Maggie said gently. "So that leads into part two, the bad business decision?"

I looked over at her. She wasn't looking at me like I was making a fool or that she thought I was an idiot. She was looking at me with affection. I'd take it. "Yeah. I don't know if you'd remember it, but my parents had some pretty lean years. I think it would have been right before you moved to town, maybe a bit after." I shrugged, looking out the window. "I guess it impacted me more than I realized. I'm pretty conservative with our brewery, but it's paid off in the past."

I glanced over at Maggie, and she looked thoughtful.

Meeting my eyes, she whispered. "Seems like we have more in common than I thought." Giving me a quiet smile, she squeezed my hand again. "What are your options?"

I thought about it. "Well, really there are three. One, we continue like planned and take out loans. Two, we can use a third party to do the canning for us and pay them. And three, we can ask for investors in the canning."

She sat up and looked interested. "Investors?"

I nodded absentmindedly. I'd been thinking about it since Jake shared his idea this afternoon. "Jake brought up this idea today. We could have people we know put in small investments into the canning side of the business, split the profits with them. Potentially, if we wanted to, we could buy them out later or leave it."

Maggie looked out the windows mulling it over. "So, you wouldn't need to put up as much money..."

"Yeah, depending on how much money we got from investors, we'd likely be able to do it out of our reserves."

She tapped her finger on her chin. "So no loan, but not dealing with a third party. Seems like a win?"

I slid my arm behind her and tugged her over to lay on top of me. She laughed as her hair fell down in waves.

"I like talking business with you." I leaned up and kissed her nose.

Emma grew serious, "Sully?"

I tilted my head, considering her switch in moods. "Yeah?"

"Thanks for talking to me about this." She lowered until our lips met for a long, deep kiss. Pulling back, she ran her hand over the few days' growth I had on my jaw. "So you're going to go ahead?"

I watched her face for a few moments. Her eyes were shining with hope. I know she hated that our news had derailed my plans, but not as much as she hated that I'd made a decision because of her without talking to her. Lessons learned.

"I think we will. I'll talk to Jake tomorrow. Getting the investors lined up and not getting started a few weeks back from what we originally planned just means our first batch won't be ready until the end of summer, but that's fine."

Maggie smiled, and her beauty only seemed to intensify. I pulled her down and kissed her again. We still needed to talk—about the future of the brewery, about her desire to move and what that meant for us. But for now, for the next few hours, I was just going to enjoy this. Maggie, this little bean, my dog somewhere in the house likely eating something he shouldn't. Yep, life was pretty much better than I'd ever thought it would be.

## 25

## BEAUTY

*Maggie*

The bell over the door to the bookstore rang as Emma walked in, singing out a greeting. "Lunchtime, Maggie May. I'm *starving*." She came through the store and stopped in front of our counter, giving me some big eyes.

Laughing, I teased. "Are you sure you're not the one eating for two?"

She looked horrified. "Heck, no! Not yet, chickie. Having two pups is exhausting. I don't have it in me to deal with a child yet."

I slid the strap of my purse across my body as I came from behind the counter. "Hold on a sec. I need to tell Ivy I'm leaving." I moved to the small hall to the back and called out, "Ivy? I'm off."

Ivy's head poked out of the office in the back. "Cool! I'll be right up."

Turning back to Emma, I started to speak before she let loose with a big laugh. "Holy hell, Maggie. That shirt is glorious."

"Isn't it?" Ivy appeared from the back.

I shrugged, today I was sporting a pair of rolled-up boyfriend jeans that could still button because they hung below my slightly protruding belly. With them I had my black Converse and a white-and-black T-shirt with Sorry I'm Late proclaimed for the world to see. "Well, after some whispers at the grocery store last week from folks who I'm sure were just curious, I thought I'd just be a bit more in-your-face."

Ivy nodded, apparently approving of my plan. "I think if you let Lou take a profile shot and put it up on her social media, she could put any gossip to rest."

"Who says she hasn't done that already?" Emma laughed. Then she turned to Ivy. "What are you diffusing today? Smells amazing."

Ivy walked Emma over to show her the diffuser. I heard her talking about the citrus scents that she blended: orange, grapefruit, lime, lemon, and bergamot. No idea, but the smell was refreshing. The vibrations from my purse pulled me away from them. I tugged my phone out, and a warm sensation washed over me. Sully.

**Sully:** *Hey gorgeous. You need sustenance?*

**Me:** *Look who is whipping out some fancy words. But no, Emma and I are headed to the deli.*

**Sully:** *Cool. Dinner?*

**Me:** *Yep. After yoga. You talk to Drew yet?*

**Sully:** *After the lunch rush.*

**Me:** *Good luck.*

**Sully:** *Thanks, babe. Love you.*

I looked at my phone, at the two words that still felt like they took my breath away. It had been four days since Sully and I exchanged our first I love yous, and he put it out there multiple times a day since. I had too, but he seemed much more natural about it. Damn, he was a good boyfriend. Four days of agreeing to go ahead with this, and I hadn't regretted that decision yet.

"That's the sappiest expression I think I've ever seen from you, Mags," Emma called. I took my gaze from my phone up to my friends. Ivy and Emma were watching me from across the store with twin grins stretched across their faces. "Is that thanks to my bro?"

I rolled my eyes at her nosy questions. "Ignoring you, Em. Now, I thought you were starving."

Emma gave Ivy's arm a squeeze as she called out. "Order me the whole shebang, Ivy. And two diffusers, one for home, one for the library. Max won't know what hit him."

I laughed. Max would give zero fucks with whatever Emma filled up their house with. He would only care if it made her happy. It still made my brain whirl when I thought of how much had changed for my friends—or hell, for Sully and me—in the past three months. Max had only moved back to the area at the start of April. Since then, he and Emma had hooked up and now were cohabitating and engaged. Mind you they'd both harbored some major feelings for years, but it was still a bit of a race. Sully and I had not only ended up in the same house, but there was also the matter of our little bean growing away. Warp speed was our preferred speed, so it seemed.

Emma hooked her arm through mine as we sailed out of Pages with goodbyes to Ivy and headed across the square to the deli, Goodman's Deli. Opening the door, Emma gestured for me to go ahead of her. It was lunchtime during the week, so they were slammed as usual. The owner modeled this place on the New York delis of her youth, and it was an awesome spot for lunch. Emma and I stood in line to order from the counter as I waved to some of my former students who were working in the prep area. The smells were overwhelming in the very best of ways. Their bakery here was unreal, and the scent of fresh-baked cookies hit me first. However, the aroma of bacon also wafted my way, and my stomach positively growled. Maybe the bean was a fan of pork products? I knew I was.

"So...." Emma drew it out. "What did my big brother have to say that inspired that look back there?" Emma nodded back in the direction of the bookstore.

I shook my head at her. "Who knew you were such a gossip."

"You," she deadpanned. "This is not new."

"Yoo-hoo!" A voice carried across the crowd. Emma and I both turned to see Lou waving from a booth a bit ahead of where we were in line. She was sitting with two ladies that were likely in their eighties. I recognized them from the auction. Both women had fresh-set waves of silver hair. One wore some bright red glasses. The other one had a foot swinging from below the table, and I couldn't help but notice her black patent leather Birkenstocks. Their attention to detail made me smile, even while I felt their gazes rake over my belly.

"Hey Lou," I called back, figuring I might as well acknowledge her. God knows she'd just get louder if I didn't. The line moved up, and we were now closer to their table.

Lou raised an eyebrow as she took in my T-shirt. "Well, that statement is perfect, Maggie. Tongues are already wagging in town. Might as well throw it back at them."

I shrugged. "Figured you'd likely already done that for me, Lou."

"Got your back, girl. You know I do."

Her companions sat watching. I wondered if they wanted to get a notebook out to write this all down. Or hell, in this day and age, I was surprised someone wasn't livestreaming our conversation for social media. Whatever.

"You want to share genders? Names? Due date?" Lou asked. I noticed the two ladies leaned in at this.

"Sorry to disappoint, Lou. Nothing to share in terms of gender or names. The due date is right after the new year." I gave her a smile, even though part of me screamed that if I lived in Chicago, I likely wouldn't be explaining my personal life to people I saw while standing in line for lunch.

"That's enough, Lou." Emma said, squeezing my arm. "Hopefully that topped off your gossip tank for a week or two."

"Pshaw, you know me better than that, Emma." Lou shook her head in mock disgust, but then gave Emma a soft smile. "Missing you, neighbor. That Maxwell Harp better be taking good care of you."

"He is, Lou." Emma reached over to squeeze her hand. Then we moved up in line until we were at the counter.

My former student, Syd, stood behind the counter, waiting for our order. The giant chalkboard to the right announced the specials for the day. I looked it over and decided on a turkey and bacon sandwich with avocado. Emma got a large salad with chicken and poppy seed dressing. As Syd typed our order into the computer, I asked her how college was going. Taking my credit card from me, she gave me a shy look. "I finally declared a major."

"That's great!" I knew she'd been searching, trying to figure out a plan for some time. "What did you land on?"

"Education." She looked from Emma to me. "My

concentration is middle school with an endorsement in language arts."

Emma smiled at Syd, then bumped my shoulder. "And I bet you might have had some great teachers that influenced that decision."

"Absolutely," Syd exclaimed, glancing my way. "Ms. Jameson, I hope you knew how much you impacted me already."

My heart tugged. Syd was in my first class, same as Taylor who had been in to Pages last week. It was good to hear any positive feedback from that year. I'd certainly felt lost as I tried to figure out how the lessons from college worked with the reality of the classroom.

"Thanks, Syd. That's great to hear. And you will make an excellent teacher." I heard a throat clear behind me. I guessed the next customer was ready to place their order and didn't much care what Syd's major was. We waved our goodbyes and headed to a booth in the front of the restaurant.

Sliding across from Emma, I lost myself in memories of teaching here for the past six years. So far somewhere in the neighborhood of more than six hundred students had been through my classroom. I guess I hadn't given much thought to the lasting influence I might have on any of them as a middle school teacher. I mean, there were teachers before me, teachers after. What did one teacher matter in the long run?

"Earth to Maggie," Emma called. I met her eyes, and she nodded back to Syd. "I know you and Sully are hot and heavy. And please note I haven't asked what the plan is after next year, for which I feel like I should earn an award."

"Noted," I quipped.

"But are you thinking that wherever you land, you'll still teach?" she asked.

"Well, sure," I replied. "I mean, that's one of the best parts of my profession. Schools are all over the country, and there's a shortage of teachers in most places. I can likely get a job wherever I decide to move." I tried to picture myself teaching somewhere besides Highland Falls, but anytime I called up a classroom, it was my room just across town. Interesting.

Emma nodded. "Makes sense." Something over my shoulder caught her eye, and she started laughing. "So. Damn. Whipped."

I tilted my head in confusion at her. "What?" And as the words left my mouth, I felt a light touch move my hair off my neck. Looking up, Sully stood next to our booth.

"Scoot over, Mags," he said.

I shook my head. Surely I was hallucinating. Nope. He slid next to me in the booth, and I quickly moved over. "What are you doing here?" I whispered.

Sully looked up at the special board, then back to me. "Felt an urge for a BLT."

"You work at a place that could make that." I pointed out.

"Scenery is better here," he said with a raised brow.

"Do I need to give you two some privacy?" Emma crowed from her side of the booth.

I looked at her with an incredulous expression. The noise level in the crowded deli wasn't enough to cover the crying babies from the side room, the beep of a timer for something in the back. Looking to the right, I saw Lou waving at me as she jerked her head toward Sully. It appeared she mouthed *kiss him* while her friends nodded at me.

"Privacy?" I asked, while Sully wrapped his hand around my neck and squeezed. "What's that?"

Emma laughed out loud while Sully leaned over and pressed a kiss to my cheek. Even in the midst of the bedlam of lunch hour in the deli, this felt good. Safe. Solid.

~

### Sully

I jogged around Jake's house to his backyard. He had a great fenced-in space so that his dog, Chief, had plenty of room to run, even living in town. Jake had sent me a text that the crowd at the brewery was under control, so he was heading home to spend some time with his pup for a few hours before he headed back in. We could do a video call with his brother, Drew, from his backyard just as good as we could from the brewery, so I was in. And considering the day was a perfect June summer day, this was even better than the original plan in my book.

"Spencer?" I called, opening the gate and heading in his side yard. There wasn't a whole lot of plants back here, but it was a large expanse of grass for Chief, so it was likely perfect.

"Here," he called, coming out of the back door and down the steps to the yard, his chocolate lab following him briefly before taking off after a squirrel and barking up a storm. He handed me a can of beer. "Thought you might want to try this. It's a new batch from the place over in Savoy."

"Dirty Hippy?" I glanced down at the can and back to Jake.

"It's a lower-alcohol-content, English-inspired brown ale. Thought it would be good as an afternoon beverage for us since we both have shit to do tonight," he said, sinking down into one of the Adirondacks around his fire pit.

I sat on the chair next to him and heard my name. Glancing over at Jake, I noted the laptop he had opened on the arm of the chair he'd sat in. Apparently, he'd already started the video call as Drew's face was filling the screen.

"Hey, Drew," I said, acknowledging him. "How goes the life of a hotshot?"

"Smokey," he said as he raised up his own can in a pseudo toast with us. Jake and I did the same.

"Bro," I said to Jake, nodding at our cans. "Were you just in the mood for an English ale or did the name make you think of a certain bookstore owner in town?" I sat back in the chair with a shit-eating grin, waiting for Drew to grab on to that like a dog with a bone. However, he surprised me with his lack of surprise.

"Ahh, you mean Bookstore Ivy, Sully? Tell me more about her." Drew's grin matched mine.

"Fuck you all," Jake groused.

Hmm, Drew already knew about Ivy? I gave Jake another glance. He'd mentioned Ivy several times since they'd met about a month ago. His comments and interactions when the woman had come into the brewery a few times since had all been friendly, but with a hint of teasing. I had a feeling there was more there, but that was something to set aside for now.

"At any rate, we should get down to it," I said, pulling my chair closer to Jake's so Drew could clearly see us both. "Drew, talk to me about what you're looking for. I know you've already spoken to this big lug"—I tipped my head in Jake's direction—"but I want to hear directly from you."

"You're getting on my nerves, Sullivan." Jake said, but his body said the opposite as he stretched out with his feet hitting the bricks of his fire pit, the picture of ease. Jake grew up with two siblings, Drew and Steph. The three were extremely close and were happiest when giving each other hell. It was the way they showed that they cared. Since Jake and I had become friends a decade ago, I'd been able to hang with them all numerous times. The nights were marked with nonstop laughter. Whether it was in the stories they told or the jokes at each other's expense, I didn't know. But there was the undercurrent of love for each other always present. The Spencer siblings were as loyal as they came.

"Ignoring my big bro, I want to invest, Sully. Jake told me about how you all wanted to can and had that loan slip away," Drew said. My gut clenched, wondering if Jake told the real reason we hadn't got that loan. "I've been working for seven years out here. I live on base, and since I now work on equipment and training during much of the off season, my savings have piled up. That plus my job at the brewery down the mountain that I've had for many of the winters out here equals a pile of cash that I'd like to invest. Sinking some of it into your canning operation seems perfect."

The tightness that had been in my chest for the past month eased up. Jake passed me a spreadsheet. "Looking at the low end that we had originally wanted to start with, we needed to come up with a hundred fifty thousand. Drew has the capital to invest a bit over seventy thousand. Max already called. He wants to kick in ten. We easily have the rest, or if you don't want to take up most of our reserves, we could do a combo of reserves plus a small loan."

I glanced down at the paper spreadsheet. It was one I had detailing the costs of the start-up equipment. Jake had added the investors and remaining funds needed.

"Thoughts?" he asked.

I nodded, thinking. Looking up to Drew, I asked. "And this is what you want?"

"Yup. Sounds perfect," he said.

"Do you want to stay invested or do you want us to work out a repayment plan?" I asked. Better to be upfront and figure out where he was at. I noted that a grimace of some sort passed over Drew's face. Not sure what that was about.

"I think I'll stay an investor. Not sure how many years I have left out here. Might come your way at some point and hit you all up for a job," Drew said.

Jake had been looking down at his beer, but at this he looked up, intensely watching his brother. "Really? You thinking of getting out?"

Drew looked away from his computer as he spoke quietly. "Yep."

Well, that didn't answer much about his plans but told us that we didn't have to come up with funds to repay him anytime soon, if ever.

Jake cleared his throat, watching the screen. "Would love to have you back here, bro. Anytime."

Drew nodded, then said quickly, "Sounds good, guys. I'll arrange the transfer; just send me the details and the contract we need to sign. Gotta go." With that, he signed out.

Jake closed his laptop and leaned back into the chair. The summer sky was a cloudless bright blue. The day was perfection, that Goldilocks temperature of around seventy-five but little to nothing in the way of humidity. If only it could stay like this for the summer, but July was looming. With it would come the scorching summer days, so we'd enjoy this while we could.

I leaned back as well, watching Chief pace back and forth against the far fence, announcing his presence to anyone within earshot. "You know Drew was planning on returning?"

"Nope."

"But you think all is good?"

"Hoping so. The job has to be tough. Wouldn't blame anyone for being done after seven years or so."

I nodded, thinking of all that Drew had seen out there.

"So, you're okay to go ahead now?" Jake asked. I looked over and found him watching me.

My gut clenched once again. "Said it before and I'll say it again. I'm sorry as hell that I bailed on our original plan."

Jake watched me for a moment before speaking. He tapped his can to mine. "It's good, man. This is likely even a better scenario for us, and we wouldn't have had that without you bailing on the other loan." He looked away and leaned back again, but continued. "I know I was pissed at first, but it was because I wanted you to talk to me. We're a partnership, and you just went and had a solo gig for a while. But I get it, I do, and I'm glad this is where we ended up."

Lowering my head against the chair, I soaked that in. I don't know if I realized I needed Jake's forgiveness, but clearly I had.

"How are you and the baby mama?" he asked.

My eyes tracked a plane far from us making a path across the sky. I didn't spare him a glance as I spoke. "Fuck off, man. Told you not to call her that."

"Screwing with you, Sull. But you two good?"

I thought of Maggie at the deli today. The morning sickness, or all-day-sickness as she liked to call it, had vanished in the past week. Her face positively glowed, and I felt like something changed in her appearance every day. I'd sat with her and Emma and soaked in the rightness of our lunch, the beauty in being with this woman who I'd thought of as mine for so long. What was between me and Maggie was so much better than anything I'd dreamed that it scared me.

Once you found beauty, the idea of losing it was terrifying. And I was terrified and in love with my life in equal measure.

## 26

## HARD TRUTHS

***Maggie***

I sat on the chairs Sully had on his back porch, looking over the fields behind his place. The old farmer saying was that they expected a healthy corn yield if the corn plants were knee high by the fourth of July. Well, we were approaching the end of July, and the plants were closer to my height than hovering around my knees. I'd guess this was a good year.

A rare late July breeze waved away some of the humidity from my spot on the porch, allowing this time in the early evening to be blissful rather than stuffy and miserable. The fields of corn and soybeans rolled in waves, a sea of green stretching as far as the eye could see. I'd never lived in the country before moving in to Sully's place. If you had asked me before if I'd like it, I would've said it was far too isolated for me. I liked being able to walk places from my duplex. I loved the idea of living in a place like Chicago— the noise, hustle, and that you were one in a sea of people. On my visits to the city, I rarely had time to get into my own head, which I now realized was part of the appeal for me.

Here, on a farm, I was swimming in quiet. It was unnerving in a way, but also a peaceful feeling that was growing on me.

It had been over a month since Sully and I had committed to a relationship, and I was shocked to discover that the man gave good boyfriend. In all our years growing up, Sully had certainly had girlfriends, but none that were around for long. After the past five weeks, I wondered if those relationships had failed because the women were fools or, selfishly, if it was because he hadn't been with me. To be real, that was the preferred answer, but realistically, he likely hadn't been in the right place.

Either way, the man was the stuff romance books were written about. From taking care of me through the morning sickness stage to small gestures that showed me I was on his mind, he was straight out of my dreams. That wasn't to say he wasn't still the Sully of my youth. He teased Emma and me, just as he always did. He left his sweaty clothes in a pile on the floor of his closet. He hadn't yet met a hand towel that he would hang up instead of leaving it tossed on the sink. These annoyances didn't come close to outweighing the sweet moments though. The times that he made me dinner. The times that he brought me hot tea in bed when I woke up. The way he rubbed my shoulders as I stood at the counter preparing dinner. And I was leaving him.

I was a fool.

As summer had crept on, days passed into weeks, weeks became months. My belly ripe with the bean as he—or she —grew. Last week I'd crossed the sixteenth week mark. People now actively checked out my stomach. Strangers asked if they could touch my belly, and what was up with that? But as the pages on my planner turned, my heart sank as I grew nearer to my move-out date. Sully hadn't mentioned it, and I didn't want to bring it up. I had grown used to him, to Ranger, which was exactly why I needed to get out, to be on my own again. I couldn't get used to this. It would be too hard to leave next summer. We'd committed to a relationship here, now. But Sully's life was here and mine was not. My heart was destined to shatter in a million pieces when I left.

I dreaded it.

My phone rang from its spot on the arm of my chair. Glancing down, I smiled. Dad.

Tapping the screen to answer it, I put him on speaker and called out into the slowly darkening sky. "Hey, Dad. Where are you at?"

His gravelly voice flowed out of the speaker. "Hey, princess." He took a breath. "I'm in the Carolinas."

I smiled. My dad loved that route. He said driving into the Appalachians from the Midwest was such a scenic and peaceful drive. Then, coming out on the east, you flowed down to the coast toward the ocean. The entire journey met with his relaxed and chill nature. Nothing fazed him. He lived at peace with himself. Even when we'd struggled for money, he felt certain that everything would be okay. And we were, because so many people in town stepped up and made sure of it, from teachers who made sure I was fed at school and home when the times were lean to the Sullivans who asked me to stay over often to well-meaning church members who dropped off the clothes their kids grew out of. To my dad, it was the village taking care of us. We didn't have much, but he would certainly step up to help people anytime he could. To me, it was charity. I hated it, while realizing we absolutely needed it.

When Dad got his CDL license, however, things improved drastically. More than the fact that we were finally making ends meet, however, I was grateful he found a job that fit him. He loved the open road, and even though I didn't get to see him as often as I'd like, it was something I was grateful for.

"The Carolinas. That's awesome," I said watching Ranger tear after a rabbit in the yard, barking up a storm. "Do you have time to check out any of your favorite haunts before heading back this way next week?" Dad was scheduled to come through this way in a week or two before heading back to his base in Chicago. I hadn't told him about the baby yet. I really wanted to do that in person, and we were almost there.

Dad cleared his throat, which made me sit up and pay attention. "That's why I'm calling babe. I have some friends out here that asked if I'd want to stay for a few weeks. I have time off coming my way and thought I might use some days to head out fishing with them. Would you mind if we switched my time with you to after I get back to Chicago? So end of August versus the beginning?"

I closed my eyes, overcome with sadness. Of course I'd never begrudge his time with friends. He got to relax so rarely. And fishing was one of his favorite ways to pass the time. Sliding my hand onto my belly, I sent as much love to our baby as I could. I wanted to share this with him. I guessed the phone would have to do.

Opening my eyes, I glanced toward the drive as I heard Sully's truck pull in, gravel crunching under his tires. He pulled up to a stop at the garage and swung out of the truck to come my way. I raked my gaze over him. His dark hair curled up a little around his ears, disheveled on top. His jeans were worn with a hole by one knee, not because it was fashionable, but likely he'd torn it on something. He had a white brewery T-shirt on that was worn thin. And his work boots had clearly seen better days.

Sully's eyes were locked on mine as he hit the step to the porch as I cleared my throat, ready to tell my dad our news. "Sure, Dad. We can visit at the end of August instead." Sully's eyes narrowed. He knew how much I'd been looking forward to this. "But I need to—"

I heard a shout on the other end of the call and a huge laugh from my dad. "Babe, I gotta go. We're headed out, and several of the guys just got here. Call you soon?"

Tears welled up. I missed him, and it shot through me like an arrow. He was a nomad, and I wasn't the home base anymore. The more he traveled, the more he loved it. And as thrilled as I was for him, damn if I didn't want to have him here. "Yeah, Dad," I said in a scratchy voice. "Love you."

"Love you, baby. Talk soon." He clicked off.

My head dropped before I could even control it. A tear rolled down, then another.

"Hey, hey." Sully was in front of me, and before I knew it I was up, he slid below me, and I was pulled back to his lap as his arms went around me. "Babe, talk to me." His mouth pressed a kiss into my neck as he slid one hand up to my hair, tugging it out of the ponytail.

My absolutely grown-up reply was to rotate so that I could bury my face in his neck. I didn't dissolve into tears, I just breathed him in, soaking in his strength surrounding me. I needed him, needed this.

"I'm so glad you're here," I whispered.

~

**Sully**

Maggie burrowed in, as close as she could get. I ran my hands over her back, up to her hair, and back down. I'd come home jazzed. The canning operation was set up, and we'd be having the first batch ready to roll in a matter of weeks. Jake and I had toasted our future tonight, and I'd left him at the brewery to work the dinner crowd while I came home to Mags. We'd planned on grilling out tonight and enjoying the unusually enjoyable late July evening.

Overhearing just the end of her conversation with her dad, I knew why she was upset. She'd been looking forward to Tom's visit so she could finally tell him about the baby. Originally, she'd waited, wanting to be out of the first trimester. Though my parents knew, she hadn't wanted Tom stressing about her when he wasn't here. But when he announced a trip through in early August, she'd been excited to have a date when she knew she could share our news. And now that was put off a few more weeks. Not the end of the world, for certain, but a disappointment.

"Babe, how can I help?" I asked as I smoothed down her back again. She was in a worn T-shirt and yoga pants. The T-shirt likely fit normally, but now with her rounded belly, it stretched over her. I slid my hand onto her stomach. I wondered if he could sense his mom's sadness. Damn. Tom was a good guy, but right now I wanted to call him back and ream his ass, which wasn't fair.

Maggie took a breath, then another. I could tell she was fighting to get control. I wondered if there would ever be a day where she'd realize she could just fall apart and I'd catch her? I'd spend my life catching her, if she'd let me.

She pulled her head out of my neck, locking her eyes on mine. I saw her strength returning, along with the walls she surrounded herself with. Damn. "I'm good, Sull. Thanks." She sighed, looking out at the fields. "Guess you heard that Dad won't be coming until a month from now, huh?"

I tugged on her hair until she lowered her mouth to

mine. Brushing my lips over hers, I replied. "Yep. Sorry, babe. You ready for burgers?"

Her eyes warmed. I wasn't sure if it was the thought of food that brought her happiness or the fact that I wasn't going to make her delve into her feelings about this. I'd learned my lesson from Maggie, though. She faced things on her timetable. Rushing her to talk about it wasn't going to win anything for me.

"I could eat," she said with a small smile.

"Really?" I faked surprised. Nudging her up, she stood, and I rose up next to her. I whistled for Ranger, and he headed in our direction. We all hit the kitchen door at the same time. Opening it, I let the two of them in first before following them myself. Dropping my keys and wallet in the bowl by the door, I also shed my boots before looking over to see Maggie's head in the fridge.

"What are you and the bean in the mood for besides burgers?" I called as I headed in her direction.

"Hold on," Maggie said from the fridge. She glanced over her shoulder from her spot. "Beer?"

"Yeah." I looked past her, scanning cans and bottles at the lowest shelf. "Zombie Dust." She passed me a bottle before placing milk, cream, butter, syrup, and some leftover chipotles in adobo on the counter.

"What are you thinking?" I nodded at the counter.

"The bean is ready for a bit of heat, some spice. I put some sweet potatoes in over an hour ago. Thinking a sweet potato mash with a kick."

"Sounds good," I said, moving around her to gather the shit needed for our burgers.

Maggie fell in beside me, grabbing the bowls she needed. Within a few minutes, she connected her phone to my Bluetooth speaker and one of the albums from The

Killers filled up the space. Her earlier sadness seemed to be forgotten as she hummed, moving around me when needed, but always with a small touch or caress as she'd pass me. Over the past month I'd soaked in every moment with Maggie. Each day had been better than the one before.

My earlier dreams about her had been set on their head. Reality far surpassed anything I could have dreamed. Because my fantasies had never gone into the magic of the everyday. This, here in my kitchen, making dinner with a kick-ass album playing, my dog lounging off to the side, these were the dreams that I didn't know enough to have. This was the beauty of life, and I felt the primal urge to hold on to it with everything in me.

Hours later, Maggie was curled on her side in my bed with the sheet hanging low over her hips, the curve of her naked form before me. I ran a hand over her hip to the dip at her waist and up to her shoulder. Moving back to her waist, I slid my hand around to the front to check on the bean. She wasn't too uncomfortable yet, which was lucky. At this point in the pregnancy she was doing the sleep of the dead whenever she could. She slept a lot, and she slept hard. It was like her body was soaking in all the rest she could, knowing that one day in the future that would be a precious commodity.

Skating my hand across her belly, I whispered to our baby. It was an emotional hit every time I realized that she was growing a human, our child, in her body. How fucking miraculous was that? The notion that in a few months this kid would be in my arms was almost too much to get my mind around.

Sliding out from the bed, I stood and stretched. Ranger glanced up from his spot on the floor and moved to take my place in bed. He did this daily in the morning as Mags slept when I rose at my typical early time. Ranger had appointed himself her protector, and if I couldn't lie by her side, he would. He circled his large body on the bed and curled up against her back, looking at me as if to say, "I've got her." I had no idea what she'd do when school started. The early-morning hour was really going to be tough for her.

I headed through the darkened house to the kitchen. Grabbing a glass out of the cupboard, I stopped and looked out the window into the dark farmland. School. I didn't know the exact start date for the year, but it was barreling down on us.

What would the school year look like? She'd be having a baby halfway through. What then? And, most importantly, what would happen after? Did she still think about leaving Highland Falls? We hadn't talked about any of this, and I knew I was taking the coward's way out. I was avoiding answers I didn't want to hear. But I also knew the hand she'd been dealt absolutely fucked with the future she had planned. Hell, it did for me too, but the change was one I'd embraced.

This baby made me more excited about what we had in store, and I was damn grateful for the abrupt change in plans. I didn't know if Mags was there yet. I knew she was excited about the baby, but the idea of the baby potentially changing her plans for this summer? She'd accepted it, but I wasn't sure how she really felt about losing her summer of travel. And the future? I didn't know where she landed and had a feeling she wasn't ready for that conversation.

But the time was coming that we'd need to face some hard truths, and it was coming soon.

## 27

# AND THE WORLD STOPPED SPINNING

**_Maggie_**

It had been a long day, but Emma and Max had asked Sully and me to meet them for dinner at The Homestead. Honestly, right then I'd be happy with having a grilled cheese sandwich and curling up on the couch for dinner, but we needed to go. My hermit-like tendencies were becoming more pronounced as the end of the summer drew near. It also didn't help that my dad originally was coming to visit this week, but that had been pushed off until the end of the month. I'd worked to be happy for him. He'd had a great time in the Carolinas two weeks back and now was in Chicago getting ready for his next route, but I missed him.

Trying to get comfortable, I tilted my head to the side, stretching my neck and back as Sully's truck sailed over the country roads to town. I looked over at his handsome profile. He had come home to pick me up, even though I told him I'd be glad to meet him in town. And after the way he greeted me when he walked in the house, I was glad he did.

His hair was still damp from our shower with it curling up a bit at the ends. He had on one of his brewery shirts, though he wasn't working tonight. These had become some of my favorite of his shirts since they tended to be worn and stretched deliciously over his chest.

Sully glanced over at me and grinned before looking back at the road. His right hand slid over and found a home on my belly, caressing it in a way he always tended to when he was near. I let my legs stretch out in front of me and put a hand on top of his own. As my eyes drifted shut, I embraced the feeling of his hand on me. There was no question on my current state anymore. Since my belly first popped weeks ago, it had just continued to ripen, as Sully liked to say. My doctor assured me that everything was measuring just fine, but I worried about what the next twenty-two weeks would bring. I felt certain I would run out of room before the due date arrived.

"You good, babe?" Sully asked. "Would you rather stay home tonight?"

Prying an eye open, I looked over at him. "No, I just need to rest for a minute. I worked an extra shift for Ivy today and didn't nap. I'll be good. Promise." It was true, I didn't nap today. However, school started back up in three weeks, and how people worked full-time while pregnant was currently the fodder of my nightmares. I reassured myself I'd manage somehow.

Sully's hand slid down to squeeze my knee. "If you'd rather go home and have grilled cheese sandwiches on the couch, just say the word."

Damn, the man knew me well. I shook my head with a smile, and we continued toward the brewery.

This summer I'd been living in what seemed like a dream. Since that night where we talked about our future, Sully and I moved forward, exploring our relationship. At first, I waited for the other shoe to drop, certain he really didn't want this with me. But through his actions and his words, he'd shown me that this was exactly what he wanted. And as much as it scared the shit out of me, I felt myself trusting it while also worrying it was coming to an end.

I reached over, placing my hand behind his neck and running my fingers through his wet hair. "We're a bit late," I pointed out as I glanced at the clock.

Glancing over, he winked before looking back at the road. "Had to make sure someone was super relaxed before we could go."

Heat filled my cheeks. "Don't look at me like that. Emma and Max will know why we're late."

Sully chuckled. "Since they were hanging out at the brewery when I left to get you over an hour ago, I think they're going to know that already."

Oh holy hell. Letting that go, I moved on. "Are you and Jake ready to roll out the first batch of canned beer next week?"

Sully's grin spread wide on his face as he turned down the street the brewery was on. "Yep, right on schedule. Small runs at first, just to test the market and see what sells. Then we'll go from there."

Sully's willingness to talk to me about his business, to ask for my opinion, then weigh his information and make his own decisions, was a huge turn on for me. After he and Jake talked to Drew and Max back in June, they'd charged ahead, making their dream to get their small canning business set up and ready to roll a reality. I knew Sully still struggled with the risk involved—he'd shared more about how he worried about money as a kid on the farm—but he was feeling more confident about their investment the closer it got to putting their beers out in the world.

I twirled his hair around my fingers. "Do you think

Drew will ever come back and work at the brewery?" I'd met Jake's brother a few times. They were from the suburbs of Chicago. Sully hadn't met Jake until college. Drew was fighting fires out in Colorado, I wasn't sure if that would ever translate to a move to Highland.

"Not sure. He seems to like firefighting out West, but something he said tells me he might in the future." Sully parked, then looked at me. "Ready?"

I smiled as he slid out of the truck and came around to my side, leading me up to the brewery and into the restaurant.

The place was packed, even for a Tuesday evening. The weather was gorgeous, so it was nice to see so many people come to the brewery when they could be outside. We weaved through the tables until I saw Max and Emma at a low table over near the bar area.

"Maggie!" Emma hopped out of her chair to greet me, squeezing me to her before putting both her hands on my belly.

Laughing, I let her hands roam. "It's not that big, Emma."

Emma rolled her eyes and looked at me. "Sorry, babe. I'm going to be one of those crazy people who need to touch your belly. Prepare yourself now."

Well, she wasn't lying. She'd absolutely been a bit handsy over the past month. But it was Emma. Strangers trying to touch my belly creeped me out, but not her.

Sully pulled out a chair for me and then slid down next to me. "Usual?" he asked. I nodded, and he turned back to look over to Daryl and gave him a nod. I'm guessing that little communication meant our drink order would be over here shortly.

"You guys order yet?" he asked Max as he rested an arm

across the back of my chair. I leaned into him a little and thought longingly of yoga pants and the couch before bringing my attention back to the table.

Daryl swung by, dropping off some flavored seltzer water for me, a beer for Sully. I sighed, grateful Sully and Jake were now stocking some of my new favorite drink but well aware it would be quite a bit of time before I could have an alcoholic beverage. Oh well.

Max looked from Sully to me before breaking out in a wide smile. "Nope. We waited, though we could have ordered, eaten, and been home in the time it took you to pick up Maggie here." He stroked the beard at his chin. "I wonder why that is."

Emma slapped Max's biceps in laughter before looking at me. "Ignore him, babe. He's just jealous because he wasn't getting any."

"Emma!" I said, shocked at how bold my formerly shy friend had become.

"I do not want that visual, thanks," Sully said. Apparently, the best-friend-sleeping-with-my-sister topic was still tough for him. I found that rather amusing.

Max shrugged as he grabbed a menu. "You're just lucky she wouldn't go for it in your office like I suggested."

I coughed on the drink of seltzer I had just taken while at the same time I became intrigued. We hadn't messed around at the brewery before. That could be a possibility.

Sully didn't apparently share my interest, or just couldn't get past the visual, because he simply groaned.

Luckily, the waitress came up right as we were talking to take our order and got everyone refocused. Once she left, Max raised his glass and clinked his beer with Sully. "Thanks for meeting us, guys."

"Anytime," I said, smiling at the couple across from me.

Sometimes I still couldn't believe that Emma was with Max. She'd loved him for so long. Hell, I guess she could say the same for me, though she hadn't known how I felt about her brother over the years. Damn, a lot had really changed for us in the past four months.

Emma grinned. "Anytime? Don't pretend you wouldn't be happier on your couch right now Maggie. I know you."

"Sully's couch," I pointed out. "And yes, but I'm still happy to be with you all too."

Sully squeezed my leg under the table. "Babe, you live there. It's your couch too."

"Well, only for two more weeks. So, technically, it's better just to call it your couch," I replied.

Sully's head swiveled to mine. "Two more weeks? What are you talking about?"

I looked at him in confusion while hearing Emma's *uh-oh* and Max's muttered *well, shit.*

Looking from my friends to Sully, I tentatively began. "Umm, remember I moved in because I'd sublet my duplex for the summer and couldn't get into my new place until August? My lease begins mid-August, just a little under two weeks away." I racked my brain. Hadn't we talked about this? I knew we had when I moved in.

Sully looked pissed as he moved his body so that he was facing me. His arm stayed on the back of my chair while another one came to the table in front of me, effectively closing me in. "Why would you move out?"

What the ever-loving fuck? "Why wouldn't I?" I asked.

Oh boy. His face was not pleased. "I don't know, Maggie, maybe because we're in a relationship? Maybe because you're having my baby? Maybe because we're in my bed every night?"

Oh good Lord. Men are idiots. "Sully, slow your roll.

One, people do not need to live together just to have a relationship; to have a baby; or, newsflash here babe, to fuck. B, when did you ever talk to me about this? Am I supposed to be a damn mind reader? Because the last time I'm aware we had any conversation about any of this, I was living in your place until my new one was ready. And guess what? It's almost ready." I let out a giant huff of breath before sitting back and folding my arms across my chest, doing my damnedest to ignore the idiot male sitting to my right. It was only then that the sounds of the brewery hit my senses again. Oops. Maybe not the best place for this discussion.

Emma leaned forward. I noticed she had an amused expression on her face, but I was going to let that go. "Okay, kids. Good talk, good talk. But maybe we can table the yelling about sex or whatever for a bit? This place is rather busy tonight, and I don't think you necessarily want Lou to have any more gossip to share with her circle tomorrow than she already does."

Emma gestured over to a table about five feet away that her former neighbors, Lou and Verdell, were sitting at. Lou was clearly leaning forward, trying to catch the entire conversation at my table. When she caught my eye, she winked and said in a voice that carried, "Give 'em hell, Maggie. They like to work for it. Right, V?"

Verdell, ever patient with his wife, shook his head and patted her hand. I also noticed he gave a look of sympathy to Sully. Whatever.

I rolled my eyes as I looked back at Emma. "Your former neighbors are nuts. Do you miss that?" I asked, jerking my head.

Emma smirked. "I'm just surprised she wasn't taking pictures." She looked over, then back to us, laughing. "Never mind."

Our table looked over to see Lou with her phone raised, leaning out of her chair to snap some photos of us.

"Got what you need, Lou?" I asked, noting the peevish tone, but not having any desire to tamp it down.

Verdell chucked while Lou said, "Yep, thanks dear. Remember, girl power! And we'll have to catch up at the library soon."

Emma pulled out her phone. "Maybe I can text the girls and we can meet at the library for coffee tomorrow." She seemed engrossed in her phone while I tried hard to inch away from Sully, who seemed to have moved his seat even closer to my own.

Sully's arm suddenly stopped my movement as he gripped my chair back and slid the entire thing closer to him. When my side was pressed against his, his mouth dropped to my ear. "This isn't over, babe. We'll talk about it when we get home."

My back straightened, and I whipped my head to meet his eyes. "When did you become all alpha male on me? You can't just tell me what to do."

His eyes narrowed, but then I watched him take a breath and relax. It was like he was mentally making himself calm down. "Babe, I'm just saying you and I have some things to discuss that impact the three of us."

I closed my eyes and took a few deep breaths, calming my heart and giving myself time to think. If I wanted to be an adult here, we did need to talk. I think we had both used this summer as almost a departure from reality. While life did go on around us, we hadn't really talked a lot about the future and how things were changing for either of us. Considering that neither of us had a baby on the agenda for the new year, we probably needed to face reality. It had been nice to luxuriate in the newness of a relationship and not really think about the long term. If I was being honest with myself, a lot of the reason I hadn't looked ahead was I didn't know where I saw myself in a few years. I had a feeling that's why Sully avoided the discussion too.

Feeling calmer, I nodded slightly at him, then looked at Emma and changed the topic. "So, any special reason you all wanted to meet tonight, or did you just want me to finally leave the couch?"

Emma watched me carefully, and I knew she was deciding if I was okay. Apparently, she found that I was. Looking at Max, she said, "Actually, we have something to ask you guys."

Wrinkling my brow at Sully, he shrugged. Okay, he was as in the dark as I was.

"What do you need, Em?"

Max spoke up. "We set a date for the wedding and want to ask you guys to stand up with us." He glanced at Sully. "Best man?"

Sully grinned, "Of course, man. Honored."

Emma looked at me and grabbed my hand across the table. "Maid of honor?"

My eyes misted over as I whispered, "No one I'd rather stand up for."

Emma stood, tugging me up with her, and threw her arms around me. "I'm so thrilled for you, chickie," I whispered, rocking her back and forth.

"Love you, Maggie May."

"Love you too, Emmie."

I dropped back into the seat next to Sully, and he handed me a navy bandanna handkerchief to dry my eyes. "Thanks," I said. "Someday my hormones will be under control again."

"Happy tears are never something to apologize for," he said, taking the handkerchief I passed back.

I took a deep breath. "So, date?"

Emma smiled, intertwining her fingers with Max's. "Well, we really didn't have a specific date in mind. We're not in a hurry—"

Max interrupted, "Speak for yourself. I offered to go to the courthouse this weekend."

I laughed, taking a swig of my drink. "A bit impatient?" I asked, smiling at Max.

He shrugged. "I mean, she's already living with me. We own a dog—hell, we own two. I'm ready to be married."

Emma shook her head. "And I wanted a ceremony. I'm not going to go all bridezilla or anything, but I want my dad to walk me down the aisle. I want a first dance with Max to our song. That stuff."

Max nodded, and we all paused as our entrées were slid in front of us at the table. "So we decided we wanted to have the wedding outdoors at Highland Woods. That helped with the date a bit. We'd need to wait until at least May..."

"So we decided to go with the first weekend in June," Emma concluded. "That's a year after our engagement, plenty of time to organize a small wedding, for you guys to have a baby, and you should be out of school. What do you think?"

Smiling across the table, I felt happiness bubbling up inside me. Sully and I would have a six-month-old baby by then. Holy crap. I thought of Lee walking Emma down the aisle, of Anna dancing with Max at the wedding. They might be Emma and Sully's parents, but they'd also had a hand in raising Max and myself. "I think that sounds absolutely perfect. Let me know how I can help you plan."

We fell into an easy silence as we all dug into our dinners. Typically Emma and I had cheeseburgers when we came here after yoga, but tonight I'd been in the mood for comfort food. Risotto was a cold-weather dish for me, but tonight it hit the spot. I groaned as I took a bite. It was amazing.

"Babe," Sully said in my ear. "You're killing me."

I looked up from my steaming bowl to see that he was studying my mouth. I slowly licked my lips, which caused his eyes to narrow. "Sorry, but this is mushroom and bulgogi risotto. I cannot promise to control myself in its presence."

Sully watched me, then looked down at his own dinner, speaking under his breath. "I'm going to have to make a note to bring some of that home more often."

"Why?"

"So that I can do to you what I want to right now in the privacy of our home."

I heard Max choke back a laugh from across the table, but I was still focusing on the fact that Sully had said *our home*. I didn't think that was an accident.

After I finished up a dish that, to be honest, I could have eaten two servings of, I excused myself to the restroom. I took a moment while locked in the bathroom stall to center myself. Tonight's dinner had been great, and as much as I enjoyed the couch, I was glad we'd come. I needed to get out more. It was far too easy to stay home and hibernate. I missed out on experiences with my friends when I did that. While I was ready to head home, I also wasn't looking forward to the conversation Sully and I needed to have once we got there.

The door to the bathroom open, and a woman's voice entered my quiet space. "So do you think she got knocked up on purpose?"

I froze. I didn't know who that was, but surely they weren't talking about me.

Another voice, a bit slurred, responded. "I bet she did. I mean, who doesn't know how to prevent a pregnancy these days?"

Umm, birth control can fail, even if you think you're doubly protected, I wanted to shout. Who the hell were these judgmental Betties, and once again, were they talking about me?

"My sister was in school with her and her friend, Emma. She said Maggie always wanted to be in the Sullivan family, that they practically raised her, that she just leeched on to them." She let out a giggle. "I guess she found one way to become part of the family."

Bitch.

The other friend laughed. "Come on, Michelle. Admit it. You're just jealous because Cole Sullivan never picked up on what you're offering."

*Ahh, she wanted Sully, I thought. Well, fuck off, lady.*

"Whatever, Amy. He'll be available again soon, and I will be waiting. It's not like he's marrying her. He probably just feels bad that he knocked her up. That will pass."

The bathroom door opened again, and I sighed inwardly. Was there someone else coming to add on to what a manipulative person I was? God, this was the shit I didn't miss about living in small towns.

"Maggie," Emma called.

Great. Might as well face the music. I flushed the toilet and came out of the stall. Emma stood near the sink. The two girls I had heard were frozen, facing the mirror. From what I could see, looking over their shoulders at their reflections, there were in their early to midtwenties. Short, blond, and wore far too much makeup for either one to be Sully's type. I smirked as I caught their gaze. Their eyes widened, and they had the decency to look chagrined and hurry out, sliding by Emma as they went.

"What the hell was that about?" Emma asked.

"Small-town gossip." I waved them away. I didn't want to go into the many ways their words had cut into me. Box up those thoughts. I'd examine them later.

"Okay, Sully sent me back to check on you." Emma grinned. "Apparently he thinks you've been in here a while and wanted to be certain you were okay. Not sure he's ever noticed how long a date has been in the bathroom before..."

"Good grief. I haven't been gone that long." Drying my hands, I linked my arm with hers. "Let's go."

As we reached the table, my cell began vibrating. Sliding it out of my purse, I tapped it to answer the call before looking to see who it was. Sully slid my chair out as I sat down.

"Hello?"

"Maggie Jameson?" said a woman on the line.

"Yes." Damn, why hadn't I looked at the number. Now I was likely going to have to hang up on some poor telemarketer just trying to do their job.

"I'm calling on behalf of your father."

I sat up straight, my heartbeat pounding out a new beat. I felt Sully lean in, putting his hand on my arm.

"What about my father?" I saw Emma's gaze swing to mine, Max put down his beer.

I heard the words, "There has been an accident," and my world stopped spinning.

## 28

## HIS WHOLE WORLD

**Sully**

Glancing over at the sleeping passenger, I couldn't help but smile. Maggie had protested the notion of my inclusion in this trip, but there was no way in hell I was going to let her drive up to Chicago on her own. Fuck, my heart clenched when I thought of her face when she got the phone call about her dad. All color had drained from it, and I'd grabbed the phone and taken over without thinking. Not the way I'd usually play anything with Maggie. Typically taking over without asking would earn a harsh comment, if not a slug to my biceps while she lectured me about the capability of women everywhere.

The woman on the line had explained she worked with Maggie's dad, Tom. Maggie's dad was a long-haul trucker, and this week's route had taken him through Chicago. It seemed that earlier today there'd been an accident on the interstate, and he'd been taken to a hospital in the city. The woman, Irene, said he was in stable condition but would have to remain in the hospital at least for another day, if not two, and she thought Maggie should know. I'd quickly relayed that her dad was okay and was grateful to see color begin to return to her face. Giving Irene my number, I'd asked her to text the address to the hospital. Hanging up, I told Maggie we'd swing by the house, grab some stuff, then hit the road.

The overwhelmed state she'd been in had gotten us out of the brewery, home, and almost out the door again before she froze, looking over at me to ask what I was doing. When I'd replied she wasn't driving three hours north on her own in this emotional state, I saw her backbone straighten as she prepared to let fly whatever was on her mind. I'd quickly dropped my duffel on the island and moved toward her, putting my hand on her belly to remind her of the bigger issues at stake here.

With a light kiss, I'd pleaded the lateness of the hour and my desire to get her to a hotel for the night near the hospital so that she could see her dad as soon as visiting hours began tomorrow. I'd reassured her that I'd only had one beer, then switched to water with dinner, so I was perfectly fine to drive. I'd felt her entire body tense up before she took a deep breath and relented. I wasn't sure if it was the reminder of the baby she was carrying, her current state of exhaustion, or just the fact that she didn't want to be alone, but I wasn't going to question it.

Now it was a bit after eleven, and I was finally pulling into the parking lot of our hotel for the night. Irene had texted the address and let us know that Tom was looking good. He'd broken his left wrist and been knocked out but seemed to be doing well. If all went well overnight and with any tests tomorrow, the doctors hoped he'd be released tomorrow afternoon or early evening. We probably didn't have to come up, but I was certain Maggie wouldn't relax until she saw her dad with her own eyes.

Tom and Maggie had an interesting father-daughter relationship. Tom had been around when we were growing up, and my parents always included him in large family dinners with Maggie. Often Tom would be working, but Maggie would come. I figured it was one way they were sure she had a decent meal. My dad always said that Tom was one of the hardest-working men he knew. Unfortunately, the jobs he could get just didn't pay a lot, but that didn't change the effort the man put in.

Maggie had been crazy proud of her dad for getting his CDL as she neared the end of high school. Hell, we all were. She saw him a lot less often, but they talked on the phone quite a bit. I knew she'd looked forward to visiting with him at the end of this month, of telling him our news. Fuck, this wasn't the way I'd wanted that visit to go. But, I thought as I pulled in to park, at least he was going to be fine.

Glancing over at Maggie, my heart took a direct hit as I watched her sleep. The lights of the parking lot gave her a soft glow. The look of peace on her face reminded me of waking up next to her for the past few weeks. I'd felt we were moving forward together and that Maggie curled up next to me as we slept was something I could count on. Damn, her comment about moving out in two weeks had really rocked me tonight. That was certainly a conversation we'd need to come back to, but first to deal with her dad.

"Babe, babe." I lightly shook Maggie's shoulder, trying to wake her. "Princess, we're here."

Maggie stretched before sitting up and looking around with a bit of confusion. Meeting my eyes, she leaned toward me, grabbing my shirt and pulling my lips toward hers. I met them, softly, opening my mouth and letting her tongue find mine. Gently I sucked in her lower lip before pulling back, running my hand from her temple to her jaw.

"Not that I'm complaining, but what was that for?"

Maggie leaned forward again, lightly kissing me before pulling back. "Just saying thanks," she said, her voice thick with sleep. "It has been a shitty night in many respects, but I am glad you drove me. Hell, I don't even remember getting on the interstate outside Highland."

I chuckled. "I think you might have been out before we even left my drive. Our bean is clearly sucking you dry."

Maggie smiled, but then it faded. "Have you heard anymore from Irene?"

I glanced at my phone. "Not since I stopped to get gas. She just mentioned that he was doing well and would likely be released tomorrow afternoon before dinner as long as everything went well."

Maggie sighed in relief as she grabbed her bag. "That's good. Let's check in."

I watched her trudge away from my truck before I pulled myself out of a trance. Adjusting my jeans, I moved to follow her. Tonight was not about anything beyond making sure Maggie was okay, that she felt safe and secure. I just needed to remind my lower brain of what was, and wasn't, on the agenda.

The night passed in a flash, and all too soon Maggie and I were standing outside her dad's hospital room. I glanced inside and saw that it was a room for two, one bed currently empty. Tom's bed was near a window, but he was sleeping. I was grateful to see that beyond the cast on his wrist, Tom looked the same as ever.

I turned to face Maggie, resting my shoulder against the wall. Placing my hand on her hip and pulling her near, I trailed my fingers up and down her back. She was so tense.

"Why don't I head down to the coffee shop on the corner and get us some caffeine, maybe a breakfast sandwich or something. Give you and your dad some time. Sound okay?"

Maggie's eyes closed, and she nodded, letting her head fall against my chest, wrapping her arms around my waist.

I moved my hand up her neck and into her hair as I gently tipped her face back to look at me. "If you want me with you though, I'm here. What do you need?"

Maggie took a breath, her eyes sliding to look into the open door, then back to lock on mine. "No, coffee is good. It's just"—she took a deep breath—"he looks so small. I'm not sure what it is, but seeing him in there hit me. I mean, he's going to be fine. And I know I don't see him that often, but you know..." She bit the corner of her lip, looking unsure.

I leaned forward and ran my lips lightly across her forehead. Resting them there, I spoke. "Babe, he's your dad. I get it. It doesn't matter how much you see him. He's still your dad, and you love him. It's going to be okay."

Maggie's arms tightened around my waist before she stood up and took a step back. "You're right. And yes, coffee please." Her stomach then rumbled loud enough that I was surprised people in the hall didn't stop to appreciate. Her cheeks flushed, and she dropped a hand to her stomach. "And the bean is requesting food. The protein bar was apparently not enough."

Laughing, I kissed the tip of her nose. "My cell phone is on. If you need anything, text. Otherwise, I'll be back in less than thirty minutes. And"—I glanced at Tom, then back to Maggie—"if you need more time, just let me know."

Maggie pulled me flush with her and came up on her tiptoes to brush her lips to mine. "Thanks, Cole. Love you."

Damn if that didn't flood my body with heat. Even after

the past few weeks, I still got a thrill every time I heard her use those words. "You bet, babe. Love you too."

~

### *Maggie*

Sitting by my dad's hospital bed was not how I planned on spending my day. The chairs in his room had to have won some design contest somewhere for the most uncomfortable device disguised as a chair. I sat there, staring out the window, one hand holding on to my dad's, as I wondered when the last time I'd spent any amount of quality time with him was.

Looking over at his sleeping form, moments from the past twelve years passed by in a flash. Getting his CDL my senior year of high school had meant a more secure stream of income for our little family. My senior year had been a bit rough as I adjusted to him being gone more than he was home. I missed him like crazy. Since my mom had passed, it had been just the two of us against the world, getting kicked down more than we wanted. I knew he'd talked to Sully and Emma's parents about his new schedule, making sure they were looking out for me. I'd alternated between staying with them and staying on my own. Luckily, I wasn't the type of person to throw a kegger at my house. Honestly, I'd loved the time with the Sullivans that year. It was nice to not worry so much about groceries, bills, or even my dad.

When I graduated, my dad had talked to me about selling the house. He didn't need a home base. He had made friends across the country and would often stay with them if he had time off. Once he did that, I felt like we lost our touchstone. The more shifts he could get, the more money he could make.

All through college he'd send me money each month to put toward my expenses. At first, he tried to send more, but I nixed it. I knew that while he was certainly making more than he had before, it wasn't that big of a jump. I didn't want him putting himself in a bad place just to help me out. We ended up settling on him covering my books, and I asked him to put some aside for retirement. I knew he'd just started, but trucking was a hard business, and I wanted him to have options later.

He loved his job. Dad would say that they were the cowboys of the highway, that he was paid to travel. While I knew he didn't really do any sightseeing on his trips—you had to add the miles to get paid—I knew he loved being on the open road and where he could be outside, relatively speaking.

I looked him over as he rested. In the past twelve years we'd likely spent less than two months together in total, but just being in his presence brought a calmness to me. I ran my fingers over his hand. When had his hands begun to look old? His veins stood out in stark relief, surrounded by skin that had age spots. I wondered if I should lecture him about wearing sun screen when he drove again. Likely he wouldn't listen anyway.

Picking up his hand, I thought about all the jobs those hands had completed in his lifetime. He'd worked many jobs in fast food when I was a kid, managing the local burger place, being a substitute janitor at our schools, stocking the shelves at the grocery store. Honestly, I lost track of everything he'd done.

I thought back to Emma's words months ago, that maybe I'd been ashamed of my economic status growing up, maybe that was what was holding me back. All these years

I'd felt like the town was shaming me, but maybe I was shaming myself.

Tears sprang into my eyes as I watched my dad sleep. Heck, I was twenty-nine. When he was my age, he had already married his high school sweetheart, had a baby girl, and lost his soul mate. My heart ached for him. I spent all that time as a kid being ashamed of being the kid on free lunch, being embarrassed that my teachers often bought my gift for the gift exchanges, when I never stopped to be proud of everything he did provide for us. What the hell was wrong with me?

Dropping my head to the bed, I let the tears stream down into the rough blanket. This time I didn't even think I could blame the bean for my tears. Nope, I needed to shed these babies for the idiot I'd been. As I sat there, I felt my dad stir, and his hand dropped into my hair, smoothing it out.

His voice came out more gravely than usual. "There, there, Maggie May. What's with the waterworks, my girl?"

Raising my head up, I sucked in a breath as my eyes locked with his. "Dad," I paused, trying to pull myself together. In my best teacher voice, I got out, "Accidents are against our rules."

He smiled at me. "Sorry, peanut. There's some crazy-ass distracted drivers out there."

"Dad..."

"Baby, I'm going to be fine, promise." He smoothed the hair back from my face. "Now, are you okay?"

I bit my lip, hoping his ticker was in good working order here. "Umm, I've been waiting to see you in person to tell you about a bit of news."

His gaze sharpened on me as I listened to the sound of his heartbeat on the monitor. The noise level in the hallway was a gentle hum as we were cocooned in his room. "Good news?"

With a gentle nod, I moved to stand up, then turned to the side so he could see me in profile.

My eyes stayed locked on his face as I watched the shock hit him, then his expression softened. Whispering, he said, "May I?"

Tears slipped out as I moved closer to him, lifting his hand to place it flat on my belly.

"Oh, Maggie," he breathed out. "How far along are you?"

"Just over eighteen weeks. Again, sorry to spring this on you. I wanted to get out of the first trimester, and then our schedule wouldn't line up." I said, my heart rate finally relaxing now that I'd told him.

His hand stayed on my stomach as he looked at me with an expression filled with love. "And the dad?"

My face heated. I mean, if I was married, it wouldn't be so awkward, right? Here, it was like a neon light blinking and announcing I'd had sex and *oops!* Better just get on with it. "Cole Sullivan."

To my surprise, my dad snorted out a laugh. "So you two stopped dancing around each other finally?"

My head jerked back a bit. "What are you talking about?"

He shook his head slightly, like he couldn't believe I was this much of a fool. "Oh, baby. The whole town could see how you felt about him for some time. And the past few times I visited, I could see he felt the same for you."

I glanced over at his IV. "They must be giving you some good drugs here, Dad."

He rolled his eyes at me, his hand sliding over my belly. "A grandbaby..."

I looked at his bed, then at him. My dad was tall, over six foot, but on the thin side. "Scoot over," I said. He slid over, and I climbed up, mindful to be gentle with him, but needing to be closer than sitting in that horrible chair. As I stretched out next to him, my dad took his good hand and placed it on my stomach, wrapping his arm with the broken wrist gently around my body and pulling me close.

"How are you feeling about being a mom?" he asked, watching me with gentle eyes.

I closed my eyes, curling my head to rest it on his shoulder. "Nervous, excited, worried, hopeful," I murmured. I wondered where Sully was. The thought of coffee and breakfast sandwiches was much more appetizing than the current smell of antiseptic that pervaded the room. He should be back soon.

"Sounds about normal," he said. "And how is Mr. Cole Sullivan doing?"

"Beautiful, perfect, too good for me." I said as my eyes began to feel even heavier. "I keep waiting for him to realize that he doesn't need to be with me just because I'm having his baby."

My dad leaned over, kissing the top of my head. "Baby, I'm telling you that boy has been crazy about you for a long time. Did you ever think he might count this baby *and* you among his blessings?"

I chuckled as I let my body begin drifting off to sleep. "Daddy, you just say that because you love me."

"Do you love him?"

I burrowed my head down, relishing the feeling of being home. "Of course I do. I've loved him for years. But this wasn't his plan. I don't want to be a burden."

"Oh, Maggie. You could never be a burden." As I

drifted off, I heard my dad's quiet voice whisper, "And you are that boy's world, mark my words."

Oh, Dad.

~

### *Sully*

I pulled up outside Tom's room and looked inside to see Maggie curling up next to her dad. I stood there, holding our food, watching the two of them together. Maggie's eyes were closed as she rested her head against Tom's chest. Tom's eyes met mine, and he nodded as I moved into the room and closer to the bed, placing down our food on the rolling table. I heard Maggie's quiet voice, *I keep waiting for him to realize that he doesn't need to be with me just because I'm having his baby.*

I met Tom's eyes in alarm. What the literal fuck? I thought we were past this, but clearly Maggie still didn't get that even if she wasn't pregnant, I was exactly where I wanted to be. Tom lightly shook his head, keeping me in my spot.

I stood there, immobilized, listening to Maggie whisper to her dad about her love for me, but her fear about being a burden. Finally I heard Tom say to his daughter, *and you are that boy's world, mark my words.* I felt like my heart might break. Tom caught my eyes and nodded toward the chair by his bed with a jerk of his head. I lowered myself into the chair and pulled up next to Tom.

"She's out," Tom said. "She been exhausted a lot during the pregnancy?"

Well, I guess that conversation happened. Tom didn't look like he wanted to kill me, so there was that. I looked at her, my beautiful Maggie, and back to Tom. "Yep. More so at the beginning, but even now she has at least a nap a day."

Tom nodded, looking down at her. "My Ellen was the same way. Threw up a lot in the first few weeks. Slept a ton for the rest of the pregnancy."

I watched Maggie sleep before looking back to Tom. "Sounds like what Maggie has been dealing with." I cleared my throat, aware that talking about Ellen was not something I'd ever done with Tom or even much with Maggie. "Did Ellen cry a lot during the pregnancy?"

Tom's eyes sharpened as he appraised me. "You making my girl cry?"

Well, shit. I raised my hands up. "No, sir. It's just I've known Maggie since she was eight. She's one of the toughest people I know, male or female, and right now she can be moved to tears in a matter of seconds. Hell, she's cried more in the past eighteen weeks than I've seen her cry in the previous twenty-one years."

I was gratified as I saw Tom relax. "Sorry, Cole. Haven't had the protective father vibe flow out of me for a while. Yeah, Ellen did cry during pregnancy, but that didn't hold a candle to how easy the tears were to come on after the baby arrived. Be ready." Then Tom gave me an odd look. "Well, I mean I'm assuming you'll be around then too."

I felt my palms begin to sweat. Good Lord, it was like I was a middle school kid at a dance. Wiping them down my pants, I met Tom's gaze. "Tom, if she'll allow it, I plan on being around Maggie from now until the day I die."

"Are you saying you want to ask me for her hand, son?"

I chuckled. "Fuck no. I think if I asked anyone for permission to marry Maggie, she'd have my balls. She is clearly her own woman, and the only person who needs to be asked about her future is her." I leaned over, running my fingers through her hair. "She's just not ready for me to do it." Sitting back, I looked over at Tom, who was nodding.

"Yep, you know my girl. Better, it seems, than she knows herself right now."

"To be fair, she's had quite a bit going on," I said. "This pregnancy threw her for a loop." Looking at Maggie, I felt myself get choked up. Clearing my throat, I addressed Tom. "But I heard what you said to her. She's my world. And I'm willing to wait."

Tom kissed Maggie's head, then looked back at me. "I know you are, Cole. And you won't regret it."

I leaned back in the most uncomfortable chair I'd ever sat in and raised my coffee to Tom. Stretching my legs out in front of me, I said, "So, when can we spring you out of this place?"

Tom's full chuckle lightened the heaviness that had descended into my chest. Sitting in a hospital room in Chicago had not been on today's agenda. But looking at my girl stretched out in the bed next to her dad, my baby growing in her belly, I was right where I should be.

## 29

## WORTHY

**Maggie**

"Knock, knock."

I looked up from where I was sitting near my dad's hospital bed with Sully to see a woman standing in the door. Puzzling over who she was, since she clearly wasn't a nurse or doctor, I looked at my dad and saw that he was beaming. Interesting.

"Irene, come in," he said.

Ahh, Irene from work. Seems Dad had some news to share with the class. I glanced at Sully and saw that he was fighting a grin. Looks like we both were on the same page that this Irene was more than just a work colleague of Dad's.

I stood, leaning to the side to stretch my back. Then I moved to Irene and greeted her. She was about my height, with light brown hair pulled back in a long ponytail. She appeared to be somewhere in her fifties, and most importantly to me, she had kind eyes.

"Hi, I'm Maggie. Thanks so much for calling me yesterday."

Irene smiled. "Hi, Maggie. I'd recognize you anywhere from your dad's pictures. And I'm sorry I wasn't here when you all arrived this morning. I needed to check in with the company we drive for. I also figured you might want some time with Tom." She looked over at my dad, her eyes sparkling, then to Sully. "And you must be Cole." Looking back to me, she said, "Your dad messaged me a bit ago about your news. Congratulations!"

I smiled. "Thanks."

Sully stood, his hand reaching toward hers. "You can call me Sully. Most do." They shook, and he looked from her to Tom. "So, you're a long-haul trucker too?"

Irene nodded and gestured at our seats as she settled at the end of my dad's bed. "Yep. I've been driving for five years. I needed something to do after retiring from nursing and raising my kids. Met Tom through some friends and eventually joined the company he drives for."

Sully nodded. "I hope this doesn't come off the wrong way, but are there a lot of female truck drivers?"

Irene laughed. "Nope. I think the last study they did had female truck drivers making up around six percent of the truck-driving population. It can be a hard profession for a woman, but I do love it."

Dad smiled at her, leaning forward to grab her hand. "And it's going to be even better soon, right?"

"Absolutely," she said.

My dad settled back against the pillows he had propped behind him and looked at me. Clearing his throat, he appeared a bit embarrassed. "Sorry, Maggie. Maybe I should have started with introductions. Irene Smith, Maggie Jameson. Maggie, Irene is my girlfriend."

I snorted. "Figured that one out, Dad."

He let loose with a laugh. "You always were a smart

cookie. Irene and I are also going to start working in a lot closer quarters pretty soon, if this darn injury doesn't hold me up."

I quirked an eyebrow at him. "What does that mean?"

"We have decided to team up to drive routes," he said.

Irene glanced at my face and registered my confusion, so she explained. "Some people partner up to drive. Some folks love it, others don't. You are in a confined space, so you need to get along. You can sleep while the other person drives, then switch. We get paid for the distance we travel, so this allows us to get a bit farther in a shorter amount of time. We get paid by the mile and split the money down the middle. And as a female, it feels safer for a lot of reasons. Tom and I have been talking about it for a while, so we figured we'd give it a go."

I hadn't ever thought about the difficulties a female truck driver might face, but I knew the type of asshats that were out there. I liked the thought of my dad being less lonely too. "I think that sounds terrific." I looked from Irene to my dad. "So, how long have you two been a thing?"

Sully laughed outright while Dad and Irene just looked at each other. They looked so happy, I felt a lightness fill me up. Growing up, my dad had never dated anyone. It made me sad. I wanted him to be happy. However, I knew it would take a long time to get over the loss of my mom, as if that was even possible. Also, now that I was actually looking back with some clarity, I don't know when he would have had the time anyway.

My dad spoke. "It happened gradually. Irene lives here in the city and our company is based out of here. She's friends with a few people from work that I'd stay with when I was in town. I got to know her when she was still a nurse, took her on a few routes when she was considering getting her CDL, and then I realized we'd been in a relationship for a while and I hadn't even noticed."

Good grief. "Dad, one, you do not tell your girlfriend that you didn't realize you were in a relationship. And two, you've been dating for over five years and didn't tell me?" If I wasn't so amused at my clueless father, I might have been mad. As it was, I just wanted to give him a shit ton of grief.

Irene, luckily, was laughing too. She scored some points with me there. You need a sense of humor around us. "Maggie, don't be too hard on your dad. I made sure that this thing went slow and under the radar for him. He sure loved your mama, and I knew he was going to struggle moving on, even though I'd never ask him to leave her behind. Once I got him to see that I was okay with him caring about me while a part of him still loved Ellen, it all went much easier."

My dad interrupted. "Irene taught me that we don't let go of the people we've loved. We just make room for more people. I can love her and Ellen too." Then he looked at me with a sheepish grin. "And I'm sorry I didn't tell you about Irene. Our schedules are so insane. We'd go for months without seeing each other. It made it seem like we just started dating yesterday, when it hasn't been. That's one reason I was excited to switch over to team driving. And it will give us a taste of the future."

"Future?" I asked.

"Yep. We figure we have about three to five more years of driving in us, max. Then we're hanging up our trucker keys for the keys to an RV and hitting the road on our own schedules."

Watching my dad tell me about his dreams, I was struck by the relaxed look to him, one that I don't remember ever seeing before. I leaned forward and grasped his hand, then Irene's. "I think this is fabulous, and am thrilled for you both." Squeezing their hands, I released them and leaned back in my chair and into Sully, who had rested his arm across the back of mine.

"So, when you all coming down for a visit?" Sully asked, and the room relaxed into chatter about future visits and their favorite routes around the country. Watching my dad talk to Sully and Irene about his plans for recuperating, Irene fussing over him, and Sully and my dad joking about stories from our childhood, I felt a sense of peace descend as I realized just how blessed I was.

After being cooped up in the hospital all morning, Sully finally convinced me to take a walk around outside for a few hours. I was good-natured for a while—he clearly had a plan —but then I began to tire. "Are we almost to wherever you're taking me?" I'll admit it. I whined a bit.

"It's just here, right around the corner." Sully dragged me through a mass of people milling around on the side-walks in the August afternoon heat.

"Sully, it is an August day in Illinois. It is far too hot to be outside unless we're going swimming. What could you possibly have to share with me?" I grumbled. Being honest, I needed something to eat. I needed a breeze. And quite possibly, I needed another nap.

"Ahh, here it is. Little Bean, meet the Bean." Sully gestured from my stomach to the giant metal sculpture sitting in the open space in front of us. The metal acted as a mirror, reflecting back the people standing around it, taking pictures of themselves in the reflection.

Grinning at him, I moved forward and ran my hand over the stainless steel. "I believe this is actually called *Cloud Gate*, Sully. And I wouldn't have taken you for some-thing so touristy."

"Isn't that what dads do?" He asked, grinning. "I need a fanny pack and some tall socks with cargo shorts, right?" He kissed me on my nose before continuing. "Seriously, I felt like it would be fun to take our first family photo of us with our bean at the Bean." Pulling out his phone, he wrapped an arm around my waist and said, "Smile!" as he aimed his camera to take the picture of our reflection looking back at us.

Laughing at him, I dropped my head to rest against him and smiled up at the sculpture above us. Our first family picture. Wow, that hit me harder than I thought. Looking over at Sully, I intertwined my fingers with his. "Want to walk along the lake for a bit? There's likely a breeze over there."

Sully leaned over, kissed my temple. "You bet."

We headed over to Lakefront Trail and meandered along the path, staying out of the way for the serious folks squeezing in some exercise near the water. As we walked, Sully didn't try to pull me out of my thoughts, for which I was grateful. I needed some time to marinate in the realization that I was the one who needed to get over my humble beginnings and not be ashamed of them. Truly, my dad was someone to be celebrated. What was it about our society that led to me feeling bad for the fact that we struggled instead of being proud of the man he was and how hard he worked to provide for his family?

After a mile or so, Sully tugged my hand, pulling me off the path to come to the edge of the lake. Looking out over the water, I was struck by the beauty of Lake Michigan, just as I had been as a child.

"Do you remember coming here with my family when you were in junior high?" he asked, standing behind me and wrapping his arms around my waist. His hands, of course, rested on my belly.

I closed my eyes, lost in memories. "Yeah. I remember coming to the aquarium and standing outside it to look at the water with you."

Sully's head nodded behind me. "Yeah, my parents went in to get tickets, and Emma was practically dancing because she wanted to see a dolphin. Max went with her, and you asked me to come out here with you. I remember you standing still, looking at the lake, and whispering that it was just as beautiful as you imagined an ocean would be."

I laughed a little. "I hadn't seen much by that point in my life, certainly never an ocean. Looking at Lake Michigan, not being able to see the other side, it seemed immense."

Sully's lips trailed down the side of my face, settling into the crook of my neck. Propping his chin there, he looked out at the lake and spoke in a soft voice that enveloped me. "You told me that day that you'd never stay in Highland, that you wanted to travel around the world, that the world would be your home."

My heart tugged for that lost girl as tears welled up in memory. I had wanted so badly to flee a place that made me feel like I was trapped, on display, with no way to find any anonymity.

"Sully..."

"Let me finish, babe. Listening to your dad and Irene today, I realized he wants the same thing. He wants to travel. His home is currently his truck, but will be a RV one day. Maybe that's what you need? As he talked today, I realized we hadn't talked about that. Babe, I'm so sorry. I don't want you to have to give up your dreams, to settle, just to fit into my life. If you want to travel, we can find a way to do that—"

"But the brewery, your family," I started to say, feeling the moisture welling up.

"Maggie, you and this little bean are my family. If Highland Falls isn't your future, that's fine with me. Let's find a new future together." His kisses moved up my neck, reaching my ear. "You and this baby are my future. Whatever else it holds we can figure out together."

God, this man. I had so much emotion whirling inside me I felt like I might burst. I was tempted to retreat inward, to think about it for a bit. But Sully had been upfront with me, and I wanted to let him in. I needed to. "Sully, I'd love to explain where I'm coming from, but it's messy and I don't know if it makes sense to anyone but me. Fuck, it doesn't even make sense to me at times."

His lips left my neck, and I felt him move a bit back. I looked up, and he had looked over his shoulder. Tipping his head toward a park bench that overlooked the lake, he said, "Want to sit and talk? I feel like this is a sitting-down kind of conversation."

I nodded and we headed over. He sat and pulled me down next to him. He tugged both my legs up and rested them on his own. His arm wrapped around me while his hand played in my hair. He had positioned me so that I was nestled into him but still looking out to the water, which was perfect.

"Deep breaths, Maggie. I'm here for anything you want to talk about. It doesn't have to make sense. If you just need me to listen, I'm here for that too."

Okay, I had this. Maybe he was right. I really just needed to give voice to the emotions that were overwhelming me. I could do that.

"Well, this pregnancy has brought some old insecurities to mind that I hadn't really ever examined closely." I paused, looking at him.

"Do you want me to ask questions as you talk, or do you just want to get it all out and lay your thoughts down?"

Damn, who was this man? "I think I just want to get it all out. Then we'll see." He nodded at me, giving me an expression that indicated I should continue.

"Okay, so that girl who told you she needed to travel? That's always been my dream. But when I got pregnant and talked to your sister, she made me start to examine *why* it's been my dream. Through some stuff she said, some stuff I talked to my dad about, I realized a few things." Sully nodded, squeezing my shoulder.

"Well, I've always been ashamed by how little I had growing up. My dad worked hard, but we barely had enough to scrape by. Some kids at the school I went to before we moved to Highland used to make fun of me for being on the free-and reduced-lunch program at school. When we moved here, there were a few girls that would make fun of my clothes. My dad would buy them at the resell shop. Apparently, I was wearing the hand-me-downs of some of my classmates' siblings. I always felt like we were pitied and that everyone was talking about us."

I could tell that Sully wanted to say something, but he held strong.

"While you might want to tell me that no one felt bad for us like I was thinking, please know that just last night at the brewery two women were in the bathroom talking about me while I was in a stall." His eyes flared, but he let me continue. "They said I likely got pregnant on purpose to find a way to become part of your family."

Sully practically growled. "What the fuck? Who was it?"

"Shh." I put a finger over his lips. "Remember your promise." He stopped talking but looked none too happy about it. "It doesn't matter. What the girls proved to me that night was that I was right." Now he really looked pissed. "People will talk. It's the nature of small towns. Hell, maybe larger towns too. I have no idea. But what Emma and my dad helped me see, even inadvertently, was that I had another way I could look at the past. I could be embarrassed by what I didn't have, or I could be proud of what I did have. I had two parents who loved me and each other. Yes, I lost my mom early. That sucked. And yes, my dad worked long hours to keep us afloat, but through those actions he taught me a ton. He taught me about work ethic, perseverance, and love. I should be proud of my story, not embarrassed by it."

Sully had relaxed a bit, but I could tell he was still a bit tense. I looked away from the lake and smoothed my hand over his chest before picking up his other hand and placing it on my stomach, looking back to the water. "So now I'm trying to work out what the future looks like for me. I love my job. I love making a difference in the lives of kids."

Sully's lips came down to brush my cheek. "Is there anything else you love?"

"Hush, you," I said, leaning my head to the side to give him more room. Following directions well, he slid his mouth down my neck. "Yes," I whispered, "I do love you. But I'm still working out what that means though. I don't want you to leave Highland for me."

"But I would," he said into my neck.

"I know." I paused, watching the sunlight shining on the water. "I'm still struggling to feel worthy of this, of you."

Sully sat up quickly and looked down at me. "What the fuck, Maggie? You don't feel worthy of me?"

I closed my eyes and shook my head. "Cole, I know this doesn't make sense to you, and I'm sorry. You told me to lay it all out there, and that's what I'm doing. You are doing a shit job of staying quiet, I'll have you know."

"Sorry," he mumbled.

"This isn't for you to fix. I'm just working through some crap, and I need to do that before I can move forward." I took a deep breath. "I'm sorry."

Sully slid me over so I was now straddling him instead of looking at the lake. "Cole, this does not look appropriate."

He gave me a skeptical look. "Babe, one, we are completely dressed. Two, who do you know who is going to see us? And three, I don't give a fuck."

My eye roll was my only logical response.

He placed a hand on either side of my head and brought my lips to his in a deep kiss. A kiss that I felt into my core that made me question what would be so bad about having sex in a public place. *Down, Maggie,* I told myself.

Pulling away, he looked at me. "Okay, princess. I hear you. I don't know what it would be like to grow up in your shoes. I only know what it was like to grow up in mine. I feel like I should tell you that never, not for one minute, did my family ever pity you or look down on you, but I think you know that. Also, I feel like it's important to say there are assholes in the world that will talk about you, but I do think there is more good than bad in towns like Highland."

"I know, Sully."

"Nope, not done, babe. Finally beyond wanting to grab you and kiss you senseless in front of whoever those bitches were in the bathroom, I just want to say that you are worthy. You are worthy of all that is good in this world. But I also know I will never be able to convince you of that. Only you can. So, what I want you to know is that I'll be here. I'm here for you, waiting, and will gladly help you any way I can." His fingers ran through my hair, pulling some over my shoulders as he played with the ends.

I raised a brow to him. "Any way you can?"

"Any way, including loads of orgasms if you think that it would help," he said with a devilish grin.

"God knows it can't hurt," I replied.

"Well, let's go see if your dad is done with his evaluation and ready to head to Irene's. Then we can hit the road. We can be home in time for dinner, and I can get to work on that for you," he replied, sliding me off his lap and beginning to tug me away from the lake.

Laughing, I tugged his hand. "Sounds good, but I have one request."

Glancing over his shoulder, his smile blinded me. "What's that?"

"Food," I said simply.

"Italian beef? Cheese fries?" he asked, heading toward the road.

"Absolutely," I said. "Let's go."

## 30

## APPOINTMENT SURPRISES

**_Sully_**

The past few days had been crazy as hell. We'd returned from Chicago after Tom had been released. Maggie had told Tom that there was no reason for us to hurry back to Highland, but Tom had pointed out that Irene had everything under control. While I would have been fine staying, I'd also been anxious to check in with Jake, make sure that everything at the brewery had been moving along according to plan.

I looked out the windows into my backyard. The cornfields waved in the late summer breeze. I knew people loved their ocean views, but my ocean of corn and beans gave me a deep sense of relaxation like no other. Standing there, my hips propped against the counter, drinking coffee, I was filled with gratitude for all I'd been given.

The sound of Ranger's nails against the floor gave warning to his and Maggie's arrival. My girl was still half asleep when she showed up in the kitchen with my pup, her long hair tumbling over her shoulders. Her favorite sleep shorts and tank now didn't fit as they used to, the tank rode up a bit on her belly while the shorts were starting to slide below. I could just visualize what she'd look like in a few months, how gorgeous she'd be. Fuck, I didn't want to pressure her, but the thought of her waking somewhere I wasn't absolutely killed me.

Maggie came straight to me, sliding her arms around my waist and ducking her head into my chest. "Morning," she mumbled.

Leaning down, I lightly kissed the top of her head. "Morning, princess. Tea?"

I felt her head nod against me. "Peppermint," she murmured.

I leaned over and flipped the switch on the electric kettle that I'd already filled up with water when I was making my coffee earlier. Settling back with her in my arms, I continued to look out the window, mentally planning out our day.

"Oh." Maggie had a swift intake of breath.

Glancing down, I saw that her hand was on her belly.

"Everything okay?" I asked.

Maggie looked thoughtful for a moment, then she grinned as she looked up at me. "I've been feeling these weird sensations for about a week, but I thought it was indigestion."

I raised a brow, but my grin started to spread across my face as I realized what she was talking about. "But..."

Taking my hand, she settled it on her belly under hers. "But I think it's our bean moving."

Leaning down, I brushed a kiss across her cheek. "Not sure I'll be able to feel it yet, babe, but that's cool."

"There, right there." She looked up at me. "Did you feel that?"

Concentrating on Maggie's taut belly, I looked at her

earnest face. God, she was beautiful. For the first time, I wondered what our baby would look like. Looking down, I realized that I felt a little flutter under my hand, like someone was running a finger under my hand. "Whoa, was that the baby?"

"Yes," she whispered, eyes locked on mine.

Leaning down, I gently kissed her, keeping my hand firmly in place. Maggie opened her mouth to me, her tongue meeting mine immediately. She grasped my head, pulling me closer to her as she moved to wrap a leg around mine. I let go of her belly so that I could slide my hands under her ass to her thighs, picking her up and placing her on the counter. Maggie quickly parted her legs so that we were lined up in a way that made me want to scratch all our previous plans for the day.

After a few more moments, the whistle of the teakettle brought us back to the present. Leaning my forehead against hers, I worked to catch my breath. "Babe, we have to get to the doctor appointment."

Maggie laughed. "Yeah, yeah." She waited a beat or two, then looked up at me through her thick lashes. "Rain check."

I pressed a kiss to her cheek. "Absolutely."

Leaving her on the counter, I moved to the cabinet, nabbing the peppermint tea bags and a mug before filling it up with water from the kettle and setting it to her side. "So, agenda for the day?"

Glancing at the clock, Maggie tilted her head before proceeding. "We need to leave in the next half hour. Appointment is at ten. Then I told Ivy I'd work from eleven to three—"

I interrupted. "Want to swing by the brewery after that shift, then come to my parents' for dinner?"

Maggie stuck her leg out, hooking it around my hips and pulling me flush against her. I figured she could feel my reluctance to take a rain check pressed up against her.

Sure enough, Maggie looked at me with a wicked grin. "I don't think your entire body is on board with waiting." Her smirk relayed her amusement with my current predicament.

"You are not helping," I said, stepping back to adjust my jeans.

Taking my offered hand for help, Maggie grabbed it, slid off the counter, and picked up her tea. "So sorry, Mr. Sullivan," she said with laughter filling her voice.

I grabbed a kitchen towel and swatted her ass as she swung it, headed toward the bedroom to get ready. "Payback tonight for that, Maggie," I said, noting that my voice was far deeper than typical.

She glanced over her shoulder, brown eyes bright with amusement. "Counting on it, babe."

I dropped the towel and let my head drop as I braced myself again the counter. Groaning, I wondered what else I should be doing to help Maggie figure out her next steps. She'd asked for time, and I was glad to give it to her. But her move-in date for her apartment was a week from today. While she hadn't begun boxing up anything, I still had the countdown committed to memory. Staying had to be her choice. I didn't want to pressure her. But as I listened to her talk to my dog in our bedroom, I prayed once again that she would finally believe that I was in this for the long haul. Life without Maggie was not on my agenda. Not now, not ever.

An hour later we were sitting in the exam room, Maggie on the table as she squirmed while we waited. I glanced up at her from my phone. "Babe, why are you fidgeting so much? You okay?" I looked at her with a little concern.

"I'm fine," she said while, let it be known, she squirmed some more.

I thought back on the past hour. She'd had tea and a shit ton of water. Surely she had to pee, why not just go?

"Babe, do you want me to let them know you need to go to the bathroom?" Maybe she didn't want to parade out there to find a nurse in the ass-baring gowns they always put her in.

Maggie gave me a look that told me to mind my own business. Noted. I wasn't able to be at the last appointment due to some shit at the brewery. I wondered if we'd hear the heartbeat again today. I couldn't get enough of that.

Maggie moved again on the table, then crossed her legs.

"Princess," I said as I gave her a you're-full-of-shit look. The woman had to pee. Just as I was about to find a nurse myself, the door opened.

A tech walked in, and she said, "Are we ready to see this baby?"

Grinning, Maggie looked at me. "Surprise?"

I stood slowly, moving next to Maggie, "What's going on?"

She lay back as the tech moved next to her, pulling out some jelly. "We're going to see the baby today."

I slid my hand into hers. "Seriously?"

The tech put some jelly on her belly. She flinched. "Dang, that's cold." Looking back to me, she asked, "Good surprise?"

"The best," I said as I watched the tech slide the probe around her stomach.

Within moments, the screen filled with an image that I couldn't decipher beyond the beating that I knew was the heart. Pointing at it, I looked at the tech. "That's the heart-beat, right?"

The tech grinned. "Yep. Your kiddo's heart is pumping strong." She proceeded to point out various things on the screen, helping us to see the baby instead of the alien figure that appeared to fill the screen in front of us. As she swirled the probe on Maggie's belly again, she glanced at us both. "Do we want to know the gender?"

I looked at Maggie and smiled. "What do you think?"

She broke out in the widest grin I'd ever seen on her face. "I think that sounds amazing, but what do you want to do?"

I laughed, "Heck yeah, I want to know the gender if we can." Looking over to our ultrasound tech, I said, "Let's do this."

She grinned. "I'm pretty sure already, but let's just get another confirmation." Sliding the probe over Maggie's belly, she studied the screen. I had no idea how to tell anything, so I just sat back, enjoying the ability to watch our baby. What a miracle.

After a minute, the tech spoke. "I should say this isn't one hundred percent because babies can by shy. That being said, your baby is being cooperative, and I'd say with a great deal of certainty that you two are going to be taking a little girl home with you around the holidays."

"A girl?" I whispered, looking down at Maggie

Maggie beamed up at me. "We're having a girl? I was sure it was a boy!" Suddenly she looked concerned. "Is that okay with you?"

I leaned down and kissed her forehead. "Babe, I'm happy either way. Girl, boy, I just want a healthy baby." Pressing another kiss to her temple, I whispered, "And I hope that this baby will be joined by at least one or two more siblings in the years to come if that's okay with *you*."

Maggie closed her eyes, tears slipping out as she took some deep breaths. Opening her eyes, she looked up at me with shining eyes. "I love you, Cole Sullivan."

I smiled at her, leaning down to brush her lips with mine. Pulling back, I looked over to the tech who was watching us. "A girl," I said softly.

The tech nodded, smiling. "I'll print off some pictures for you all to take home."

Maggie moved a bit on the table. "Not to rush you or anything, but is there a way I can pee before the rest of the appointment continues? My bladder is seriously going to bust!"

The tech laughed. "Yes, I got all the images I needed. You don't need a full bladder for the rest of the appointment." She pointed to a door in the corner. "There's a bathroom in there."

"Thank God." Maggie shot up off the table and hurried to the bathroom, mooning us the whole way. I looked over to the tech and met her eyes as we both burst out laughing.

A girl.

## 31

## WHEN I KNEW

**Maggie**

After today's check-up, I was exhausted and seriously concerned about my stamina in two weeks when school was back in session. An ultrasound and a four-hour shift at the bookstore had me longing for my bed. Instead I had trekked from the bookstore to meet Sully, then we'd headed over to his parents' place for dinner.

Leaving the bathroom, I was wandering down the hallway and checking out pictures that Anna had hanging in frames along the wall. Anna had loved taking pictures as long as I'd known the Sullivan family. Their home had framed pictures everywhere. It was her form of decorating. I smiled as I watched Sully and Emma grow older from frame to frame. At some point Max, and then I, joined the pictures as we became part of their extended family.

As I moved into their family room, frames spilled over onto shelves and tables. I saw a picture of Jake and Sully, arms swung around each other in front of The Homestead back when they opened it. Grinning, I thought of Jake's conversation with me today when I got to the brewery. I told

Sully he had asked a lot of questions about my hippy-dippy employer at the bookstore. I made a mental note to see what Ivy thought of Jake. Could be something there.

"Penny for your thoughts?" Anna came up next to me, sliding her arm around my waist.

I leaned my head against her shoulder, finding comfort in this woman I'd known for the majority of my life. "Just looking back and remembering." I paused, thinking of how familiar standing here, in this house, after an amazing meal was. "Dinner was fabulous as usual. Thanks for having us."

"Anytime. We love having you kids here." Anna smiled and looked over at the shelves. "I love photographs," she said. She picked up a picture of Sally, a golden retriever they'd had when I met Emma. Sally had passed when we were in seventh grade, and I remember how devastated we all had been.

"What do you love about them?" I asked, my fingers sliding over a frame.

Anna glanced at me. "Pictures tend to be honest. You can't always hide the truth. Especially when they're candid, which, as you know, are my favorites." She gave me a soft smile.

*Hide the truth?* "What do you mean by that?" I asked, not sure where she was going with this conversation.

Anna picked up a small frame. "Well, for example, my Lee tries to keep his emotions in check. But in this photo with him leaning against the chain-link fence as he watched Cole play football, you can see his feelings plain on his face. Pride in his child, love too, nervousness that he would get hurt." She brushed her fingers over the face of her husband. "It's all there if you look close enough."

I nodded, seeing what she meant, but still not sure what the point was.

"Or this one." She pulled another frame down from the shelf. I glanced at it, seeing Sully standing next to me as we played a game of cornhole. Looking at my hair, it was during my last year of college. If I wasn't mistaken, Max and Emma were just out of the frame. It had been a cookout, one of the times Max had come back to visit after moving up north. Emma had been drooling over him, thinking she had no chance.

"What about that one?" I asked.

Anna smiled, touching Sully's face. "This is when I knew my son was gone for you."

I looked at her quickly. "What?"

"Oh yes," Anna said. "I remember Lou and I standing together at that cookout, watching the way he watched you. I knew it had changed, and I wondered when he would figure it out, when you would. When I printed out the pictures of that day, I saw it clear as a bell. He loved you." She held up a hand as I tried to interrupt her. "I know he loved you before, but this day"—she tapped the photo—"it changed."

Looking over the shelves, she gestured to several photos. "You can see it if you look at the pictures of you all before, then all the photos from then on. In the earlier ones, he clearly is looking at you like a friend, a little sister. But after?" She pointed out several framed shots, including one from this past spring. "He wants more, and the pictures don't hide those feelings. Nor"—she glanced slyly at me—"do they hide yours."

My heart was beating out like a steady drum. My eyes jumped from photo to photo, moving from ones from years ago to now. It couldn't be true, could it? I examined the photos, I looked at Sully's expression. It grew soft. Later photos showed his hand always on my arm, my back, my waist. My own body language was different too. I leaned into him. Even in a few when we were in the background, our gazes found each other.

I stepped back, taking a deep breath. *Holy shit.* Cole Sullivan loved me, I loved him, and he'd felt that for some time now, just like I had. He really wasn't just saying he wanted to be together because of the baby. I looked at Anna, my eyes swimming with tears. "Thanks for showing these to me." Taking a breath, I got out, "I have to talk to Sully."

Anna beamed at me. "Are you finally ready to move forward?"

Sliding my arms around her waist, I breathed in the smell of my childhood, of safety. Nodding against her shoulder, I whispered, "I've been an idiot."

Anna smoothed my hair back, her hands rubbing my back. "Maggie May, you are no idiot. You were protecting your heart." She gave me a small smile. "Your baby too." She pulled back. Her stare felt like it looked right to my core. "You're a mama now, and that's your job. But, my baby girl, my son is not one whom you need to protect yourself from. He will gladly take up that job for you. Or, more importantly to women like us, he'll fight right beside you while he hands you a sword."

I wiped away a stray tear or two. "Thank you, Anna," I whispered.

Letting go, Anna stood back. "He was heading outside with Ranger when I left the kitchen." She leaned forward, kissing my cheek. "Now, go."

～

**Sully**

Ranger and I left the kitchen and made our way across

the yard to a cooler. Leaning down, I grabbed a beer out and grinned. It was one of our first batches of cans. Jake had dropped a bunch off here for our family cookout before heading back to the brewery. He and I had played a game of cornhole while Maggie had taken a quick nap on the couch. Standing in the backyard of my parents' house, sharing one of our beers in our first batch for distribution, it had felt pretty damn good. Jake had called up Drew through a video call so we could toast our partnership before Jake had to head.

Cracking open the beer, I heard someone behind me and saw my dad making his way over.

"Is that one of yours?" he asked.

I nodded. "Black Hole Sun IPA."

"Got one for your old man?"

I passed him the one I opened and pulled another out of the cooler. It was ice cold, which was perfect on a hot August day like today. It was so muggy that my T-shirt was already clinging to me. I hoped the heat wouldn't be too much for Maggie. Maybe we should eat inside?

Ranger dropped a tennis ball at my dad's feet. He reached down and threw it, almost reaching the field of soybeans on the south side of their house. Ranger took off at a sprint. Dad nodded back at some lawn chairs. "Want to sit for a few?"

I moved back and lowered in the chair, stretching my legs out. This week had been nonstop since the call about Maggie's dad Tuesday, which was only four days ago. I hoped I could convince her to relax the rest of the weekend. With school starting back up soon, she needed to take any moments to relax that she could.

Tipping my head back, I looked at the sky. The sun hadn't set yet. At this point of the year we still had almost an hour until that happened. However, I knew my dad would fire up the grill soon. Everyone knew Maggie would be hungry in the next half an hour, and my parents were thrilled to make sure she was fed as soon as she wanted to be.

"Where's your sister and Max?" he asked.

I looked over to the back of the yard. Gesturing with my beer, I pointed to the path that took you down to the creek on the back of their property. "Headed down to the creek," I said. The creek was Emma's favorite spot. When she was stressed, she went there to think. All other times, she went there just to be near water.

Dad nodded. "No surprise there." He took a swig of the beer, then looked at me with a grin. "Just as good as in the brewery, son."

I smiled. "That's the idea," I said, holding out my can to cheers with him. He tapped my can with his own.

Leaning back in his own chair, I noticed he was watching me.

"What's up, Dad?"

Dad nodded, seeming to soak in whatever he was thinking about. Finally he decided to share. "Just thinking how proud I am of you."

I felt my heart speed up. Damn, I was thirty-two, but sometimes I felt like that fifteen-year-old kid on the football field, just wanting to make my dad proud. Swallowing a lump of emotion, I met his eyes. "Why?"

"Shit, son, there's so many reasons I'm proud of you I'd take the entire night if I was going to share them all." He smiled at me.

I looked at him, wondering what brought on the sharing of emotions. Not that Lee Sullivan wouldn't talk about the way he felt—he absolutely would—but it wasn't an everyday conversation. Dad sat there, relaxed, as I looked him over. My parents were in their late fifties but still looked a decade younger. My dad had been a high school football player too, and while he was years from that, he'd stayed in shape. Working on the farm had certainly helped him stay active. He had wrinkles around his eyes from being in the sun all the time but from laughing as well. He had a deep belly laugh that he let loose when he was entertained, which was often. Looking at him now, I had both a feeling of gratitude for growing up with such a role model, but also a pang of something like sorrow knowing none of us were getting any younger.

"So what's up with sharing the love today, Pops?" I asked with a touch of humor. "Getting emotional in your old age?"

Dad shook his head as he looked over to me. "Knock it off, Cole. Just sharing my pride. And since you asked earlier, I'll say that today I'm feeling grateful that you have a new life, a new branch of our family, coming at the end of this year. Also, I'm beyond thankful that you pulled your head out of your ass and got this canning business off the ground. What were you thinking?"

I looked over at him. "What the hell, Dad? You said I should talk to Maggie, but why didn't you tell me you thought I was making the wrong choice?" Hell, maybe getting his advice then would have helped me decide earlier.

He shook his head. "You're an adult now, Sully. I trust you to make the decision that's best for you. Can't say I don't worry at times, but your life is for you to shape, not me to manipulate." He gave me a narrow look, "And you're evading the question."

I smiled. It felt like a conversation from high school or

college. Dad was not one to lecture, but sometimes conversations with him began to feel like a tennis match. They kept you on your toes. That was for sure. This one, however, I wasn't sure how to dive into it. Leaning back, I looked into the early evening sky. A breeze had finally kicked up, bringing with it a needed relief. Ranger came back from wherever he'd been hunting around and collapsed in exhaustion at my feet.

"Well, Dad, Jake and I were ready to dive into canning this spring. But then with Maggie's announcement that we were having a baby, I got cold feet."

He nodded, gesturing for me to continue.

"It's like this. I was worried about making a big investment in the brewery, taking on more debt, when we had finally gotten to some financial stability. I was especially concerned about doing that when I needed to provide for my new family—however that family was defined." I rubbed my thumb over the label for the bear.

Dad cleared his throat. "Sometimes you have to dream big, take risks, to make your business grow, son. Your mom and I would have been happy to put our investment back into the canning part of the brewery."

I met his eyes. "I didn't want you to do that."

He studied my face. "Why?"

I looked away. "I felt a bit like a failure in asking for that. You were always so stable, such a perfect dad. I felt somewhat like I was already failing at parenting by not having a strong business set up when my child wasn't even in the world yet." I hung my head down, looking at the ground and Ranger's nose nudging a ball toward me even though he was so tired he couldn't lift his head out of the grass.

"Hey." My dad looked at me. "I'm not sure what

perception you have of me, but know that I'm not worried at all about the type of father you will be, Cole. You will be amazing. We all struggle. I had constant fears about the farm. Mother Nature, the costs of equipment, you name it, I worked a ton of hours because we couldn't afford to hire on help. I was constantly worried about not being home enough for you, Emma, or your mom."

I nodded, eyes locked on my beer can.

Dad sighed, leaning his head back. "You'll learn soon enough. Parenting is a crapshoot. You will never work as hard at anything else in your life while having absolutely no confidence that you're doing it right."

My palms began to sweat. "So how do I make sure to do it right?"

Dad's head turned toward me. "You love the shit out of your kids and their mom. Push them to be their best, and be their loudest cheerleader. Nothing else matters."

My voice was quiet. "Just love them?" I heard a noise and saw Maggie rushing my way. "I can do that," I whispered.

"I know you can, son."

I rose up and took a step toward the woman I loved with everything in me.

## Maggie

Rushing outside, I scanned the yard and saw Sully moving from a grouping of chairs where his dad and Ranger sat, and he was walking toward me. Looking past them, I could see the grain elevators of Highland in the distance. The trail for the creek was behind him to the left. I would bet Emma and Max could be found there. The creek was one of Emma's favorite places on earth, where she went to think. But Sully, he loved this yard. He and I had stood here so many times over the years. The sunset lighting the grain elevators was a sight to behold. I remember the first time he made me watch it. I had been in fourth grade. He had been in junior high.

Standing beside me back then, he'd whispered, "Watch, Maggie." As we stood, he'd said, "Sunrises and sunsets are two of my favorite things."

"Why?" I'd asked.

"Because my mom says they remind us to look for the beauty. There is always beauty," he'd said.

Coming back to the present, I reached him and Ranger, who'd run up to greet me and dropped a ball by our feet. "Hey, Sully."

Sully took the ball and threw it high and long as Ranger ate up the distance, running for it. "Hey, babe." He looked at me closely. "You okay?"

I moved toward him, wrapping my arms around his waist. "I'm good."

Sully's arms tightened around my body. "Maggie, what's up?"

I turned my head, resting it against his chest, and looked over the top of the tall corn as the sun had begun to disappear behind the elevators. "I love sunsets here."

Sully kissed the top of my head. "We certainly have seen our share from this spot."

Thinking of a Jason Isbell song, I whispered, "I hope we get to see forty years more."

Sully was silent, then he chuckled. "Are you talking about that song that Emma loves, 'If We Were Vampires'?"

"I introduced her to it," I retorted automatically. We all battled to be the first to find a good song, a good band. It was a bit competitive. Laughing at myself, I pulled back and looked up at him. The heat of the day was fading. There was a breeze moving through the corn that tousled his dark hair. The scent of the grill still pervaded the air but combined with the flowers from his mom's garden between us and the house. Sully's brown eyes crinkled at the corner as he gazed down at me with a questioning expression. I looked at the face that I knew so well, that person that would never hurt me, and finally opened my heart.

Taking a deep breath, I began. "I love that song too, and I'm realizing that forty years together is nowhere near enough with you." My voice cracked. "One day we'll be gone, and I'm going to hate myself for being an idiot and wasting even one moment with you."

Sully's thumb came up and swiped the tears that were flowing down my cheeks away. "Baby," he whispered.

The desire to bury my head and just hold him was strong, but I needed to get this out. I wanted no more secrets, no more holding back. "I'm so sorry, Cole. I'm so sorry that I didn't see it before. But I know now that you aren't only with me because of the baby. I know that I don't need to run away from Highland to be myself. I can stay right here with the people I love, with the job I love, with the town that I *do* love. This is my future. You are my future." I swallowed hard.

Sully's eyes twinkled with amusement. "Maggie, I'm damn glad to hear you say that." He began to lower down to a knee.

"Oh, no you don't," I said, quickly sinking to my knee myself. "I've been the pain in the ass here. I'm proposing to you."

Sully wasn't having it and joined me so that we were both kneeling, our bodies pressed together as our arms wound around each other, my belly preventing us from being completely against each other. "You are never boring, Maggie May. But there is no way I'm not proposing to you."

I reached up, pulling his face to my own. Kissing him hard, I pulled back. "What if we propose to each other? I'll go first."

Laughing, he nodded. "Of course you will."

I grinned at him. "Cole Sullivan, I'm sorry for being a horse's ass for the past few months. But I have my head on straight now, and I know what I want. I want my future to be with you. I love you to pieces. Will you marry me?" Even though I knew what his response would be, my heart threatened to burst out of my chest. Luckily Sully seemed to sense that, and he leaned forward to brush his lips against mine before he spoke.

"Maggie Jameson, I love the shit out of you. Kneeling here in this yard, with the sun going down, I know my mom was right. Beauty is in front of us all the time. Of course I'll marry you. I want forty years with you, and then forty more. I pray that one day, when we're old and gray, that I will go first because I don't want to spend one more day on this earth without you. You are my other half, and I'm so damn glad you realize that. I love you and this little girl you are carrying." He took my hand in his, and I gasped as I realized he was sliding a ring on it. Looking down, I broke. Every tear my body contained decided it was time to rain down. It was my mom's opal engagement ring that had sat in a special bowl on my dad's dresser as I grew up. Through watery eyes, I locked eyes with Sully.

He answered my unasked questions. "Irene brought this from her apartment when she came to the hospital. Your dad had stored his stuff at her place, and he called her to ask her to bring it when I asked." He paused, looking at my hand, then intertwining our fingers, he continued, "What do you say, Maggie May? Will you marry me?"

At that point I realized it was a lost cause and stopped trying to hold the tears back and embraced the ugly cry. Throwing my arms around Sully's neck, I got out, "Of course I'll marry you."

As his lips met mine, I heard cheering, and we broke apart to see Lee, Anna, Max, and Emma, as well as Ranger rushing us.

"Well, I guess that saves us time in getting the word out." Sully smiled at me. Leaning down, he brushed his lips against mine and whispered, "Welcome to the family, babe. I'm guessing this means you don't need to move out next week?" His twinkling eyes looked at mine in amusement.

Laughing, I shoved him away but then gladly accepted his help up from the ground. Looking from Sully to the people we loved surrounding us to our dog spinning in circles as he barked to the setting sun, I was filled to the brim. There is just so much beauty.

# EPILOGUE
## MERRY CHRISTMAS

***Twenty weeks later...***
***Sully***

Entering the house, the white lights from the tree bathed the living room in a warm glow. Glancing around, I noted the dishes on the counter. It appeared that Maggie's sweet tooth had required some cookies tonight. My stomach rumbled as I crossed my fingers that there were some leftovers.

Moving to the living room, Ranger popped his head up over the back of the couch, and I headed in that direction. All the lights were off except for our Christmas tree. Ranger's tail was wagging, but he wasn't moving to greet me, which led me to believe that Maggie was likely on the couch and Ranger wouldn't leave her. My dog, *our dog,* watched over those he loved.

As the couch came into view, my heart skipped a beat. Maggie lay there on her side, sound asleep. Gray leggings covered her long legs and settled low on her hips below the basketball-sized belly that protruded out. She'd apparently decided to skip the shirt and wore a red-and-black-checked bra and a Santa hat. Damn, she was like a present I wanted to unwrap. Maggie had been worried that I might not be attracted to her as her belly grew. Nothing could be further from the truth. As she grew larger, my desire intensified. Watching her nurture a life inside her, even when it drained all her energy, well, it was sexy as hell.

"Good pup," I said, giving Ranger some love as I pulled up an ottoman to sit next to Maggie. I assumed there was music flowing through the headphones she wore. Looking her over, I wondered if she'd been trying to wait up for me to get home from the brewery. My pants tightened. I wondered if there was a reason she wanted to wait up, but I quickly dismissed that notion. Since she got out for winter break from school a few days ago, she'd been so exhausted that she'd been asleep by nine p.m. every night.

Lifting her left hand, I ran my finger across the rings there. We'd gotten married days after we proposed to each other back in August. To the surprise of no one, Maggie had zero desire for a large wedding. She'd wanted to get married in my parents' yard, with our family and closest friends in attendance. My mom had organized the entire thing the night of our engagement. Tom and Irene had immediately come down from Chicago. Friends and family were invited and told to bring a dish to share. Lou had been ordained years ago online and performed the wedding. As the sun set behind the grain elevators, Tom had walked Maggie down a small aisle to me. She was absolutely gorgeous with her baby bump and a simple dress. It had long sleeves and lace but was short so I could see her miles of legs that ended at her favorite cowboy boots.

I'd glanced at Max, who grinned standing next to me as he muttered, "No, you two can't disappear right now."

Looking over to Emma, she'd winked at me. I'd tried to

school my face into a look that wasn't filled with lust but failed. When Tom and Maggie had reached me, she burst out laughing, leaning forward to kiss me while she said, "Soon, I promise." Oh well.

Lou had grinned at me from her spot in front of the fields with a comment about keeping it in my pants, and our brief ceremony had begun. I didn't remember much. I'd been far too captivated by staring at Maggie's face. The sunset had lit her up with this warm glow. With my woman in front of me, our good friends standing up with us, and the small gathering of family and friends watching with mason jars filled with their beer of choice from the brewery, I couldn't imagine a more perfect way to get married. As we became husband and wife, the sun set and the lightning bugs came out. Exactly as she'd hoped, people stayed late and danced under the stars. It was magical.

Coming back to the present, I sat and watched her stomach. The lights from the Christmas tree in the corner of the living room bathed her in a low light. I grinned as I saw my daughter shifting to find room inside. Maggie was due in the next two weeks, but her doctor had said she was likely going to go early. That was fine with me. I couldn't wait to meet this little girl and begin our next journey as this new family of three.

Maggie stirred from her spot on the couch, her eyes shooting open to look at me.

"Hey, babe," I whispered. "Loving the hat and bra."

She gave me a sleepy grin. "I wanted to surprise you, but I was so tired. And I'd been having these pains all day, so I thought I should sleep."

Excitement immediately began to flow through me with not a little amount of trepidation. "Um, pains as in contractions?"

She gave me what I referred to as her teacher look. "Um, yeah." Gesturing to her body, she looked back at me. "I'm thirty-eight weeks pregnant. Of course I'm having some contractions. It only matters when they get close together." She paused, placing her hand on her stomach. "Hmm, like they seem to be now."

My heartbeat sped up. "Are you sure? You don't seem to be in a lot of pain."

The look she gave me clearly said that men do not know anything about pain or labor. "Cole Sullivan, of course it hurts. But it's supposed to." Swinging her legs to the floor, she began to struggle to stand as I quickly got with the program and helped her up. "Okay. Ranger needs to go out. I need a shirt. Grab my bag and text the group chat to tell them we're headed in."

I stood there for a moment, in awe of this woman, of women everywhere. If men had to have the babies, clearly the human race would have died out.

"Cole," she snapped. "What are you doing?"

I felt my face soften as I moved forward, pulling her to me as I kissed her gently. "We're having a baby, Maggie."

She kissed me back, then looked in my eyes, "Yes, we are, and unless you feel like learning how to deliver one, I'd say we should get to a hospital. You on board with that?"

Laughing, I said, "Dog, bag, text, drive. I'm on it. Ranger!" Ranger froze from where he was prancing around Maggie and looked back to me. "Let's go."

I raced us to the hospital while Maggie laughed through her contractions, reminding me that first-time moms generally had no need to hurry. I was ignoring that entire line of thinking. Just her comment about delivering a baby was enough to send me into a bit of a panic. No, thank you.

Maggie was right, of course. We had several hours to

spare. It didn't matter. Watching her, I was in complete awe. We got to a room, and she put on the gown they gave her. She'd decided she wanted it just to be the two of us in the room, so I had texted the crew to let them know we were there, but they could wait to hear from us before coming. Of course that meant that I was certain they were all in the waiting room. Maggie's dad and Irene had texted that they were headed our way.

Several hours later, when I was sure that men were by far the weaker sex, I looked up to see Maggie's dad Tom walking into the room. We had decided that he could come in first to meet our newest family member. I sat beside Maggie in the hospital bed, holding my heart wrapped up in a blanket, otherwise known as our baby.

"Maggie was amazing, Tom," I whispered as he came closer.

"Wouldn't have doubted that for a minute," he said, leaning down to kiss her forehead. Looking at her, he put his finger under her chin. "So glad Irene and I got here in time. You look beautiful."

"Exhausted," she whispered.

"Of course, but beautiful," he whispered back. Looking over to the gorgeous dark-haired baby I had wrapped up in my arms, Tom said, "Now who do we have here?"

I moved to stand, then lower our baby into Tom's waiting arms. Maggie cleared her throat. "Dad, meet your granddaughter, Ellen."

I watched his eyes widen and then immediately fill with moisture. Tom scooped her up and pressed his lips to her forehead.

"Ellen," he said, his rough fingers brushing over her little face. "God, how I wish your grandmother could see her namesake."

I lowered back down by Maggie, curving my arm around her as I watched her watch her dad. "She can, Tom. She can."

Maggie continued watching Tom, who was now singing what sounded like Van Morrison's "Brown Eyed Girl" to Ellen and swaying in front of the hospital windows. She looked up and whispered, "Thanks, Mom."

So much beauty.

# ACKNOWLEDGMENTS

Holy moly, two books out into the world. Who would have guessed it.

I have to say, much like my second child, my second book was a bit easier to wrap my brain around. At least I knew what lay before me.

Thanks, as always to my people:

My Marco Polo team that cheer me on when I'm editing. Again.

My Voxer team of Karen and Cindy who read as I write and give me loads of feedback.

My #Quarantine Book Club that has encouraged me along the way.

My writing group, Heart and Scroll that have given me guidance when I was lost.

My school. Writing romance while teaching seventh grade is interesting. But amazing colleagues and administrators that support you? That makes it all worthwhile. And if they dress up as your characters for release day? Well, they are just awesome.

Authors that have replied each and every time I ask for

help. I'm looking at you, Sara Whitney, Jamie Schlosser, Skye Malone, and Kate Canterbary. And Kate, one day I'll make you a t-shirt that declares you the best hype gal around because that's what you are. All my love.

My family. My parents for the encouragement. My sister-in-law and brother for celebrating my first book with style. My husband and sons for understanding that my time is now completely divided.

My community. I love my tiny town. While I'd like it to be a bit more like Highland Falls - can we get a brewery again - there's a reason I based my fictional town on the one I live in. It's the best.

And Teri, we lost you while my first book was heading to publication. You're missed, but still in the hearts of all teachers who knew your work. I'll recommend a few books to kids today and #SpeakLoudly on your behalf. Give them hell up there in heaven. I'm certain you have a lot to say.

# ABOUT THE AUTHOR

Kat Ryan is a middle school teacher by day and a budding romance author in the free time she steals for herself. She loves to write about small towns, found families, strong women, and cinnamon roll heroes that love them. She's a sucker for a HEA and more than a bit of steam in the stories she writes.

Kat lives in the Midwest with her husband and her two teenage sons where she consumes a steady diet of coffee, chocolate, and romance books. And while her students and sons plan to never read the books she writes, her husband has and continues to cheer her on.

Want more from Sully and Maggie? Subscribe to Kat's newsletter on her website, https://katryanwrites.com. All "extras" for each of Kat's book are linked in the newsletter that comes out every month.